DOLL MANOR

Chantal Noordeloos

Published by Horrific Tales Publishing 2019

http://www.horrifictales.co.uk
Copyright © 2019 Chantal Noordeloos

A CIP catalogue record for this book is available from the British Library

ISBN:

To Daan, my soulmate and the man who has to live with me when I write horror and scare the bejeezus out of myself. Thank you for your unending understanding and support.

To my Japie, who shares my love for horror and torments me with his evil jokes. Thank you for taking this wacky life journey with me.

To all who helped make this book possible. You all rock.

And a special extra big dedication to my editor Lisa Lane. I love working with you more than anything. You're amazing.

Chantal Noordeloos

Doll Manor

BY

Chantal Noordeloos

PROLOGUE

"Shh," he whispered as he pushed the needle through the soft skin of the girl's lips. To her credit, she didn't even whimper. The others had, despite the drugs he had given them. Whether it was strength or utter terror on this girl's part, he didn't know, but he admired it either way.

A thick crimson bead of blood welled up in her cupid's bow, holding there for just a second, swelling, until it burst into two individual streams that ran down her chin. He made to dab at it with a tissue, but the sight of the blood mesmerised him. There was power in this blood. Well, there was power in all blood, but some was more vigorous than others. How funny it was that such strength was hidden in such an innocent package. Children made the best sacrifices; they weren't tainted by an overabundance of knowledge or choice. They were... pure.

The long lashes, so much like a doll's, fluttered as he pulled at the needle, letting the black thread glide through the bloody flesh. She couldn't feel the pain. He had given her too many drugs for that. And the thread was no ordinary thread; it was part of the spell. Still, she could feel something. He knew that from the others. A hint of pressure, or perhaps a tingling.

"There's a good girl." He spoke in a low voice while he stroked his fingertips across her forehead.

Her skin was so soft and fair. It looked like porcelain yet felt like velvet, smooth and supple to his touch. The girl couldn't have been more than nine or ten years old. She was perfect.

Pale skin wasn't a prerequisite. He loved all skin tones on his dolls equally. As long as they were beautiful in that symmetric way, and had big eyes, he longed to have them for his collection. Most important, however, was the power of the blood. The man had a talent for sensing that special energy. He could feel it from simply looking at a person.

He dabbed at the running drops that tinted the girl's skin like red rain. Crimson flowers blotted on the white of the tissue, releasing an energy that thrummed in his hands. It already affected him, and he was stronger for it. The man allowed himself a satisfied sigh as he absorbed it; he was getting better at his craft with each girl he transformed. Even as a student, he had picked it up with incredible speed. Far exceeding expectations. He was special.

Tears escaped the girl's large, blue eyes, and her lips showed just a hint of a tremble. He held the needle away from her face and grabbed a cotton handkerchief instead of the paper tissues. There was an uncharacteristic gentleness in his touch as he wiped her tears away. The eyes never stopped following his face.

"I know you think I'm going to kill you." The man let out a light chuckle. "I see how you could think that. My methods must seem so strange to you." He shot a glance over his shoulder at the operating room, looking at a metal container filled with the glistening entrails of the girls he had changed earlier that morning. "I really *do* need to keep this place clean and tidy," he said in a sing-song voice. Flashes of the other children ran across his mind.

The girl blinked, movement of the long lashes drawing him out of his thoughts. He focused on her again, his frustrations melting at the sight of her loveliness. Her body was so rigid. He'd never had one that remained so still before, and he couldn't believe his luck. Ready to become one of his beloved dolls.

He leaned over and whispered in her ear, "I'm not going to kill you, my precious." His lips brushed her temple. "I'm going to let you live forever."

Humming a soft tune, he took her lips between his thumb and forefinger and pushed the needle through again.

This time the girl let out a little sound—the tiniest of moans —which disappointed him deeply. He preferred the silence. That way he could see their acceptance, which made turning them so much easier. It was better if they understood.

When he finished the final stitch, he made a tiny knot and snipped the end. The string emitted a faint luminescence, indicating that his spell was working. The man leaned back and admired his work. Perfect, even stitches held her lips closed with just a hint of a pout. Using a clean rag, he wiped the few remaining drops of blood from her mouth. He would turn her into a doll before crusts could appear. If it had been possible, he would have prepared the dolls after he had stolen their breath—they didn't bleed anymore once deceased—but it simply wasn't an option. If he did that, he could not restore the sliver of life to them and they'd just be dead. They needed to be conscious for the process; that's how blood magic worked. It wasn't always convenient—especially when you wanted them to look as good as possible—but at the same time, he liked having them see what he did to them. That was definitely a bonus.

They were frightened, of course, but the honor he was bestowing on them was a great one. He was sure that during the whole process they would come to see that, and they would understand he wasn't just killing them, he was reinventing them. His task was not unlike that of a god, creating new life out of something old.

The girl was strapped to a chair, but it was time to take her to the table. He untied her bonds with care. Most of them tried to run despite the mind-clouding drugs, but not this one... this one was different. She would be the loveliest of all. Besides, he had bonded with her blood already. He could feel it, and he was sure she could, too.

"Shh," he said again as he lifted her. Her body trembled, and her big eyes remained fixed on his. He held her like he would a princess, and his lips curled into a gentle smile that shone from the depths of his soul.

"You're so special," he whispered. Gently, he lay her down on the table, though it was no ordinary table, this one. It curved up at the top, so she would be able to watch the transformation process. He took off the pajamas the girl was wearing. The top was a long sleeveless pink shirt with an image of Snoopy kissing the sky on it. The bottoms were just a pair of black shorts with pink lips all over. Not appropriate at all. She would look much better in the white lace dress with the blue satin ribbons he had for her. They would really bring out the color of her eyes.

After the pyjamas, he removed her underwear. Out of a sense of modesty, he placed a towel on her exposed lower body. She wasn't a doll yet, and he had no interest in little girls. Not in that way. There were no breasts, not even budding ones, he noticed to his delight—he'd had unpleasant surprises before in the past, much to his regret. Those girls he'd killed; they were no use to him.

The girl's body began to shake violently.

"Are you cold?" he asked. The basement was always a bit chilly. She didn't respond. All she did was stare at him.

He caressed her cheek. It was so pale, and cool to the touch. Her lips were turning blue.

"Never mind," he said, giving her his most encouraging smile. "Soon, you won't feel the cold anymore." He took her arms and bound her to the table. He readjusted the towel, making sure the girl could keep her modesty, then pulled on his operating scrubs over his clothes. He tied on the cap and placed the surgical mask over his nose and mouth before pulling on a set of latex gloves.

Only then did he open the operating kit and lift out the knife.

He held it up so she could see the obsidian blade and silver markings on the handle.

"This is a very special knife," he said. "It's magic. With it, I can turn you into an eternal doll. You'll live forever... how would you like that?"

The girl's blue eyes focused on the knife. If it was possible, they grew even wider. They froze for a brief second and then rolled back, exposing their whites, and the girl's head fell to the side. Her body spasmed once and then was still.

The man smiled. It didn't matter that the girl had lost consciousness. He would wake her when he started working on her. He ran his finger against the flat end of the obsidian blade, touching the silver writing. The language was ancient, but he had always known it, just as the magic had always been a part of him.

The girl still hadn't woken. He would have to work fast before the anaesthetic wore off. There was no need for her to feel any pain. She would only scream and rip open the stitches on her mouth. He didn't want that.

A little dose of smelling salts brought her awake and she blinked at him, as if confused about where she was. Or perhaps it was the scrubs, he thought.

"I'm going to start now," he said. "You don't want to miss this." The eyelashes fluttered when he put the point of the knife against her skin, pressing down just enough to tear the outer layer. The blade lit up, absorbing the blood before it could spill. He pressed harder, cutting through the tissue and the baby fat underneath. He tore through muscles and tendons, opening the girl up enough to reach her glistening inner core. She still didn't make a noise, the brave little thing. Her eyes were impossibly wide and her whole body was rigid. The way the table positioned her body, she had a good view of what was happening to her from her torso down. She stared at her own flesh as if she couldn't believe what she was seeing. He felt proud that she wasn't looking away. Her eyes shifted to his again. There was a question in them that he could read, or at least he thought he could.

"How are you still alive?" he asked in her stead. He grinned behind his mask, his own breath hot and moist. It smelled a little sour. "That's the magic, my child. I told you I wasn't going to kill you. I didn't kill your friends either. I just made them... better. I will take everything out of you, except that which makes you who you are. I shall leave you your mind; it will belong to me."

Tears flowed across her cheeks, and she let out the softest of sobs.

"No crying, my precious," he shushed. "Your life will be so much better. You won't grow up or grow old. Instead, you'll stay pure forever. Imagine what a wonderful life it will be. You'll never need for anything anymore. No food, no sleep... nothing. All you'll need is *my* love, and I have plenty of it to give. Especially for you, because you are the most extraordinary."

With delicate fingers—his mother used to tell him he had the hands of an artist—he peeled away the white flesh, exposing the ribs and all the ugly organs underneath. First, the intestines came out in great, sloppy handfuls. He knew that it wasn't natural for this to be as easy as it was. He had tried this before without the enchanted knife. That was years ago, and the girl had been much younger than this one. What a mess he had made then, and the doll had been nothing more than a butchered corpse. It had been too difficult to empty the body without damaging it. But now that he had the knife, the thread, and the spells, everything was different. The inside of the dolls came away so easily. There was little challenge in taking them apart and putting them back together. Very little indeed...

Next came the stomach and liver, meaty and almost gelatinous to the touch, clearing a path. He pushed his hand in the warm, slick cavity of her chest and reached for her heart. It was still beating when he took it out—the spell would keep the organ pulsating—and he had to be very gentle. The other organs didn't matter, but damage either heart or brain and his doll would turn into a corpse. That's not what he wanted. Corpses rotted and were filthy. Not at all doll-like. The heart kept them alive, so he took it to keep it safe. The brain had to remain in the body. It would give them individuality and the means for him to control them. Both organs were irreplaceable.

He held the heart in two hands, showing the girl. She stared at it. She could only move her eyes now, at least until he said otherwise. The wideness had gone from them, convincing him she had come to accept her fate. They all did in the end.

The heart pulsed in his palms, tickling his skin. He held it up with the same reverence as a priest offering the Eucharist and walked toward his desk, where an ornate copper box waited. Symbols that pre-dated hieroglyphics decorated the outside. The interior was lined with purple velvet. When he placed the heart inside, the fabric lit up with the same faint blue-white light as the knife had. The velvet absorbed all the blood leaking from the heart. It, too, was part of the blood magic.

The man closed the box and secured it with the tiny brass key in the iron lock. With a gentle motion, he removed it, attaching it to a key-chain holding more than two dozen others, all forged from the same metal. They jangled as he moved them to a heavy oak cabinet and placed them in a drawer.

"There you go. It'll be safe." He turned to the girl. "Safer than it was in your body. Your heart belongs to me now." With an abrupt movement, he closed the drawer, tapping the wood with his fingers.

"We need to put you back together again. This is the fun bit." He picked up a large burlap sack that stood on the floor next to the desk. A purple ribbon held it closed, but a faint scent of lavender drifted up from it.

"This is so much more appropriate than all those icky guts, don't you think? You'll smell of lavender forever." He opened the sack and pulled out a handful of cloth purple flowers. Their scent was a little overwhelming, and he pushed them inside the gaping opening of the girl's torso. "See? Much better." He stuffed handful after handful. The girl's eyes never moved, just stared into a distance only she could see.

After he filled her, he took the needle he'd used to stitch her lips together. His needlework was exceptional, and with the white thread, he could barely see where the skin was put together. Very different from the mouth, where he had used thick black thread. The very fibres were doused in the blood of a black cockerel, which did not turn the thread red, but a deep black, and it was spun during the winter solstice.

He cleaned her up. The knife only drained the blood from the body, but not that which had dripped from the organs as he'd taken them out. There were red splatters everywhere. He unbound the girl and lifted her from the table.

"I'm going to bathe you now, and then I'll put on your pretty dress," he said to her as if he were talking to a baby.

With gentle strokes, he used the soap to cleanse the body, scrubbing away all the filth. The wounds were already starting to heal. Every mark his blade had made would eventually fade, but only if he did everything according to the procedure. There were dolls he'd made in the beginning that hadn't turned out as fine as this one. He had learned, and he'd become more delicate with each new one he made.

When she was clean, he picked her up. Her body was slippery, and he held her tight so as not to let her fall. Using a plush towel, he dried off all the moisture. Then he dressed her in the clothes he had put aside for her. He hoisted her into frilly drawers and a chemise, which were the perfect underclothing. Gently, he pulled a white lace dress over her head and arms, and he fastened its light blue ribbons at the back. He curled her hair, adding more ribbons. With paint, he gave her soft, pink lips, and he airbrushed a blush on her pale cheeks.

"There... you're perfect." He stood back to admire his work. "A real angel." He smiled and tapped his lips with a forefinger. "That's what I will call you: Angel. That name is so much more appropriate for you. Perhaps I should make you a set of wings. Would you like that?"

The girl was already cooling when he picked her up again. He carried her into the *special* room. With his elbow, he pushed down on the large brass door handle, opening the ornate wooden door. Inside was a large, nineteenth-century nursery. White wallpaper covered in pink rosebuds lined each wall. A large wooden rocking horse stood off to one side. The whole place smelled strongly of lavender. Everywhere the eye could see, there was doll furniture. Beds, tables with doily tablecloths, chairs—both the rocking kind and the normal kind—toy chests, dressing tables. All placed in neat order. From every part of the room, dolls stared at him with their blank eyes. Some of them were made of porcelain, but twenty-seven were made of flesh.

Twenty-eight now, he thought, with pride swelling in his heart. He found Angel a nice place on a rocking chair. She was surrounded by her two friends, whom he called Betty and Pearl. She would be at home here, and she would never be lonely. He kissed her on the forehead and turned before he could see the single tear that fell from her large, blue eye.

CHAPTER ONE

An angel lying on a little cloud.

That was the thought in Freya's head as she regarded the baby, doing her best not to cry. The hormones still raged through her body, causing her to feel constantly overwhelmed.

The baby slept so peacefully in her little crib. White fabric decorated the sides. A mobile with the dangling characters of Winnie the Pooh still moved gently in a slow circle, even though it had stopped playing the soft tune long ago.

She watched her baby girl sleep. The sight was such a contrast to how Freya looked right now, dressed in disposable overalls, her gloved hands covered with the blood of her latest victim. It made her want to jump straight into the black gaping hole in the bottom of Lucifer Falls.

Freya's fifth, and latest, victim had been heartbreaking. Not as terrible as her first, who had been her own lover, but definitely one of the saddest she had killed so far. A young girl, barely seventeen years old, her past filled with abuse and neglect. Freya had discovered her on the streets of Edinburgh, where she found most of her victims. It was far enough from home to not raise suspicion, and close enough for her to travel up and down in a weekend.

The homeless were the most anonymous people she could find, and also the most tragic. The promise of hot food and a roof over their head was usually all it took to get them to go with her. She would offer them a job in a hotel that was still in the making. Some were sceptical, hardened by a life on the street, but there was always that one person who was desperate enough to come along with the pretty and kind lady. Especially the younger ones, who were so lost and afraid. Holly had been such a girl. She was eager to work, and just wanted a place to be safe. She had survived begging—occasionally stealing—and wanted some stability in her life. It was exactly what Freya needed. She had taken to Holly, and because of it, she experienced the loss of this girl's life very deeply. The guilt over her murder was soul crushing, which was exactly what Freya had intended it to be. She thought of the girl with her homely face and sad brown eyes. Reality had done its best to beat this girl down, yet she'd endured and survived those hardships in the hope of a better tomorrow. Thanks to Freya, the girl would never get the chance to turn her life around, to find happiness. The thought of it made Freya sick to her stomach.

When she closed her eyes, she could still see every blow she had dealt with the hatchet. Each sickening, meaty thud that sounded when the blade connected with the flesh, drawing blood that spattered everywhere, still rang in her ears. The girl hadn't even tried to defend herself—like her last victim—the shock of Freya turning on her having left her stunned. Instead, she had curled up in a little ball, holding up her hands, and cried for a mommy that would never come for her. Freya had kept apologising as the large blade sliced through the young flesh, cutting skin and muscle. After several chops, the girl had lost half her hand. The blood had squirted from the wound like something out of a Hammer horror movie, covering most of Freya's safety goggles and blurring her vision with a haze of red. The girl's cries had destroyed a part of her, and she had shed tears herself, but she would not stop.

She had imagined it was Emily who cried out for her, and that made each blow of the hatchet feel as if she cut into her own flesh. If only she could have killed her quickly and not so messily, but she couldn't take the chance. The sacrifice had to be a real one, not an easy one. Magic was never easy, and there was plenty of magic in the deaths she provided. This had to be as much her sacrifice as it was her victim's. The girl could only offer her life, but Freya had to offer her soul, her mind, and her pain. Time and again. It was she who had to live on, who had to endure the nightmares and the terrible knowledge that she would have to take another life within three months. And she would have to care for them again, relive the same agony. As much as she wished for this to become easier with time, she knew it couldn't.

That was the whole point.

Her eyes remained fixed on her hands. The blood wasn't the issue—Freya had seen more blood spilled than the average war hero, and nothing could outdo the trauma of that first equinox a year ago—but the tears of her victims always got to her.

The room temperature dropped several degrees, signalling the arrival of a spectral presence. Freya wrapped her arms around herself, doing her best to keep her bloody hands away from her chest—as if it were possible to make her overalls dirtier than they were. Bam—her best friend, whose life had been taken by Angel Manor a little over a year ago—moved toward the crib.

"Isn't she, like, the most gorgeous thing you've ever seen?" Bam's ghostly voice crooned. She waved her hand slowly above the sleeping baby, as if trying to touch the little girl. "I wish I could hold her."

"You *can* hold her," Freya reminded her friend. "You're getting so much better at your skills."

"No, I can pick her up. That's different than holding her. I want to feel her warmth, smell her baby smell... feel her heartbeat." There was a sadness in the hollow eyes that was very unlike her; even in death, Bam usually seemed to be full of life.

Freya sighed. "I wish I could pick her up and run away from this house—so far that we would never have to return."

"You could." Bam raised her eyebrows and smiled. "The spell is lifted. You're not stuck here anymore."

"You know what would happen."

Bam shrugged and floated to the other side of the cot. "The whole world would die." She let out something that sounded like a puff of air. "Death isn't so bad. You'd be with me." She shrugged, but Freya could see by the wry smile on Bam's face that she didn't mean it. Not really.

Freya shook her head and stood up, holding her bloody hands in front of her, careful not to touch anything. "I'm with you now, Bam. That's good enough for me." She sighed and took one last look at her baby. "Let's leave. I don't want Emily to wake up." She ran her tear-stained cheek across her shoulder, which was one of the few places of her overalls not covered in blood. With a heavy heart, she left the small yellow and white bedroom. The corridor was dark, but she wasn't afraid of the dark anymore, not like she used to be. Part of her felt like she was the darkness now, like she was a part of this house. With long strides, she made her way to the newly renovated bathroom.

"I wish I could, like, leave," Bam muttered wistfully. "I may not have died here, but this is, I don't know... my resting place?"

"I'm not even dead, and I'm bound to this house even more than you are." Freya spoke with some bitterness in her tone. "You could say this is my place of unrest."

"You were, like, bound to this house before you ever set foot in it. Such is the way of the world. For a while, you seemed to accept that, but now..." Bam cocked her head as she floated along. "You've been so freaking glum lately. What's the matter? You've totally not been yourself."

"Nothing." Freya opened the door with her elbow. She didn't want to get smudges on the door. "It's just, it's been a year..." *The anniversary of Logan's death*. If only that sacrifice had been enough to keep this house protected. It had been goddamn big enough. It should have given her a free pass out of murdering other people. But it didn't. She wanted to tell Bam how much she missed Logan, and how greatly she still suffered from the sacrifice she made, but she couldn't talk about her grief to anyone. Not even the dead. So, she swallowed hard and continued, "I've been doing this for almost a year. This... killing."

Bam stopped at the bathroom door. As always, she'd come no further because of the tub. Bam had drowned in one, though miles away, but Freya knew her friend still feared the mere sight of a bathtub.

Freya pulled her gloves off above the sink, and a few drops that hadn't quite dried yet splattered on the white porcelain. She grabbed the soap and scrubbed her hands frantically, harder than she needed to, washing the little bit of blood that tinted her fingers. "I still haven't found a solution to this yet. I don't have anyone to help me."

Bam frowned. "You haven't exactly looked."

"I've been busy. This motherhood thing is taking a lot out of me." Freya's eyes found the deep-set eyes of her dead friend. "I need help, Bam. I can't keep doing this. Sooner or later, someone will catch on."

"You have me," Bam said in a quiet voice.

"And I love having you." Freya bit her lip and struggled to find the words. "But you can't help me with killing anyone, or disposing of the bodies. And besides, you've been a bit absentminded lately. Should I worry?"

"It's, like, not easy being a ghost, you know," Bam said. "You can't blame me for being a little forgetful at times. Just like I can't blame you for being all emo and frazzled now that you're a mom. We both have our problems."

It wasn't just Bam being forgetful. She looked different... more translucent somehow. Freya shook the thoughts from her head, pushing away her fear that Bam was slowly fading away. She was probably making a mountain out of a molehill. Bam seemed fine now.

"I'm sorry, I didn't mean to put you on the spot." Freya splashed cold water on her face, ignoring her friend's sad expression. "I feel like I'm losing it. The last thing I want is to go psycho and end up like the Angels."

Both shuddered at the memory of the nuns who had once roamed the halls of Angel Manor. The thought of them still woke Freya screaming almost every night. She had locked up the cellar where they'd been trapped and put a few protective runes around it—the latter was to make sure the spirit of Bam's brother Chuck would never again come out, at least not in her lifetime—but she avoided it like the plague. It was stupid, she knew. The nuns were gone. They had moved on to some other place—probably Hell. And yet despite her fear, her loathing, she wished she had never released them. They had existed to sacrifice to the sleeping Horseman beneath the house without actually having to spill new blood.

If only her aunt had told her about their existence, and their purpose, in time. It had been so incredibly stupid for her aunt not to have contacted her before, when her kids died, when surely she must have known Freya would be her heir. Freya had agonised about that fact a lot over the past year.

Had her aunt hoped she could give her legacy to someone else? Or had she attempted to get in contact, but Freya's mother had prevented it? She had tried to talk to her parents about her aunt and about the house itself, but Mom still refused to discuss anything about Angel Manor. Freya had decided not to push the matter any further after the last heated argument. She considered talking to her father in private about it, but she never got up the nerve. How would she explain what had happened in that house? Would he even believe her?

And if he did, what good would that do? He would probably try to convince her to get out of the house, that it wasn't her responsibility. Whatever his stance would be, the chances that she would find out what she needed were slim. If it led to an argument, it would be enough to push her over the edge. She couldn't deal with that now. She had enough drama of her own without having to deal with her parents. Angel Manor had torn her further apart from them than she believed it would. It alienated her. It was as if she were in an abusive relationship with the brick and mortar around her. This house was a reality on its own, and reaching out beyond it seemed unthinkable.

Perhaps if her aunt had tried to reach out, she had given up, too. Whatever the case, the old woman took her secrets to the grave with her. The way things had gone had been so stupid and careless. The weight of the world had rested on the whims of one insane old woman. And now that burden sat on Freya's shoulders.

If she had the chance, she wouldn't have kept the secret to herself; she would have shared her knowledge with Bam and Oliver, and they would have been her guardians with her. *Living* guardians. Oliver might not have gone insane the way he did, and Bam certainly wouldn't have died. So many ifs, buts and whens... there was no point lingering on them. She had to keep looking forward and make sure she learned from past mistakes. Ignorance came with a terrible price.

She had pulled the plug on construction about two months before Emily was born. The hotel was almost finished. She'd made sure the living area was done, plus a little panic room that served as a Plan B, which soothed her paranoia. With Bam's help, she'd installed magical wards to deter evil and supernatural creatures. There were some old tomes on the attic—also not a place Freya enjoyed spending time—that contained spells. Freya used Emily's nap-time to read and study, but most of the words made little sense. If only she had someone to teach her...

Luckily, she was able to understand the basics of the protective wards. The rituals were reasonably straightforward, as were the incantations, and as far as they could tell, the wards were active. Bam had functioned as her spiritual guinea pig, and the panic room was one of the few places she couldn't venture.

Sometimes, she would sit on the narrow bed inside the cramped room, Emily in her arms, fighting the urge to close the door and be safe forever. She was so tired, and she dreaded the thought of running a hotel that was built on top of death itself. The whole idea just felt stupid now. It wasn't entirely dumb; the plan had some merit on paper. Drawing people in would also mean drawing victims to her. But tourists would be missed, so that made it riskier. And what if people got curious? What if someone found Chuck?

Running a hotel would also generate an income, which was something she would desperately need in her near future. The real world had decided not to stop and give her a break just so she could keep it safe. It demanded she support herself and her child. The last of Bam's money would get the place up and running for at least two years, and hopefully after that it would make a profit.

But for fuck's sake, where was she going to find the energy to be involved with anything aside from her baby and the damn sacrifices? Running a hotel was a job bigger than she could handle; running a hotel built on top of a sleeping Horseman with a psychotic ghost trapped in the basement, that was more than she bargained for. There were times she could barely get out of bed in the morning. If Logan had been here, things would've been different. But Logan was dead, his body decomposing down below where the Horseman slept. She hadn't even given him a proper funeral, and no one in that entire year had ever come to ask about him. Not even Terrence. He had disappeared from her radar just like everyone else had after Logan's death. The lack of interest over his disappearance had messed her up almost as much as the fact that she was his murderer.

Almost.

Sometimes she wondered if there was someone or

something secretly looking out for her, since she'd literally gotten away with murder five times, and she wasn't exactly a criminal mastermind. Even the investigation into the deaths at Angel Manor had been a laugh. They hadn't even searched the house. Oliver had taken the blame for the deaths, but there had been something really wrong with the way the police handled it all. She hadn't noticed at first —the shock of that night had taken all the focus away from reality—but as time went on, she often thought about how oddly events had unfolded. Even the papers had been almost silent about the incident. There had been some vague little article in the *Skye Times*, but nothing worthy of the number of deaths that had occurred that faithful equinox. The whole incident had been swept under the rug.

Bam hovered near her and put two cold arms around her shoulders. They weren't really touching, but the chill emanating from her friend created the illusion that they were.

"You're going to be fine, Frey," Bam whispered, her breath frigid against Freya's cheek. "You were, like, chosen for this because you can handle it. Me, I would have totally gone nut-balls. I think I kinda did go insane when I was alive. But you, my beautiful Viking princess, you will prevail, because you were, like, made for this."

Freya took a step back. "I'm not sure that's a compliment." She grabbed a washcloth and cleaned the taps with it. "Made for murder..." She shuddered. "Not loving it."

"Lighten up," Bam said. "You know what I meant."

Freya clenched her fist around the fabric and scrubbed harder. "I really should be more careful with cleaning. If the police ever come to check out the house, I'd be screwed. Luminol would light this place up like a Christmas tree."

Bam did a little pirouette. "If it ever comes to that, I will, like, appear and scare them all to death."

Freya opened the tap again, letting the water stream out with a hiss. She rinsed the blood from the rag as best she could. "Sounds like a plan. Maybe wear a nun's habit... I hear nuns are scary."

"I think I can create a nun's outfit," Bam moved her hand across one arm, and a long black sleeve appeared. She had been practicing her transmogrification and was getting better at adapting her clothing to her will. The sleeve disappeared, and Bam wrinkled her nose.

"As long as you don't make me go naked." Bam held her head high. "I may be dead, but I still have dignity." Her pink, translucent hair was teased by an unfelt wind, and her deep eyes sparkled. Freya snorted.

"I think it's *you* who keeps *me* sane, my friend. I don't know what I would have done without you."

"I have my uses."

"Speaking of your uses, would you mind functioning as baby monitor for a few hours?" Freya placed the wet rag over the tap and started to unbutton her plastic overalls.

"Do I ever mind?"

Freya stepped out of the suit and tossed it onto the plastic tarp she had laid out. "No, but I still want to ask. Politely and all."

"Anything else I can do for you, milady?" Bam asked with a mock British accent.

Freya shook her head. "Right now, I need a moment alone to grieve, okay? I just took a life, and I need to wash my hands of the proverbial blood as well as the physical blood."

Bam pouted. "The living are so sensitive about death."

"Just watch Emily for me, please." Freya peeled off her t-shirt and put it aside from the disposable overalls.

"I'll gladly watch your little one," Bam said. She curtseyed and disappeared through the bathroom wall. When she was gone, Freya allowed her tears to flow. Now was the time to mourn the life she'd taken.

She stepped into the water. The bath was a little too hot, so she sat down carefully. The heat stung her skin, but the gentle pain had a delicious tingle. It made her feel alive. Her arms were crossed in front of her chest, and she sat forward, leaning against her knees in the warm water. She sobbed so hard that her lungs and throat ached with the tension.

By the time her tears were spent, the bath water was cold and her swollen breasts reminded her she needed to feed her child. She stepped from the bath. The water had made her skin soft and slick, and she wrapped a towel around her. Shivering, she made her way to her bedroom, where she slipped into her pyjamas before returning to Emily's room. Bam was hovering over the baby, singing soft lullabies. Anyone else would have been afraid, seeing a spirit so near their child, but Freya felt safer for Bam's presence.

They were still looking for the spell that had trapped the dead in Angel Manor until a year ago, but Freya knew that even if they found it, they would still need to acquire enough victims to recreate that horrible scenario. Blood would have to flow, and people would have to die. Perhaps more people than she would kill in the next ten years, and that made it even harder.

She had tried to reach out to others for help. Several times, she attempted to contact Madam Florifera, but if the old woman was still alive and had gotten the letters Freya sent, she wasn't responding to them. Freya really couldn't blame her. If she'd had an opportunity to get far away from Angel Manor, she would have taken it, too. She walked toward the window and looked out over the dark terrain. A full moon illuminated the grounds. The place would have been beautiful if it weren't so cursed. The house was stunning, especially now that it was mostly renovated, and the surrounding land was breathtaking in every season. Freya had never learned to appreciate it, not even the first time she had come with Oliver and Bam. She sighed when she thought about Oliver. The house would have been more merciful if it had taken his life along with everyone else's. But it let Oliver live... sort of. One of the few survivors of the bloody events the previous year, he had belonged to Angel Manor in a way that none of the others ever had. In a way, he belonged to it still.

She had visited him a few times, hoping to see the old Oliver in his eyes again, but there had been nothing more than a vacant madness. It was another reason to hate this house.

A chill betrayed Bam's nearby presence. She pointed at the sky with her pale finger. "Look, a falling star. Make a wish, Frey."

Freya watched the short dash of light disappear in the sky and bit her lip as she thought. "I wish... I wish I would get some help."

CHAPTER TWO

Had she been asleep? Freya wasn't sure. Perhaps she had dozed briefly, but an unfamiliar sound in the house made sure she was wide awake now. Sweat made her palms clammy, and with wobbly knees, she slid from between the cool sheets of her bed.

Her bare feet soundless except for the smallest hint of a meaty thud on the stone floor, she made her way to Emily's room. Not because the sound had come from the child's nursery, but because she needed to make sure her baby was safe.

Through a crack in the door, she could see the familiar sight of Bam hovering over the sleeping child. Her pink hair looked strangely iridescent in the light of the moon, and it moved as if it had a will of its own. There was a tenderness in the spirit's expression, a sense of peace. Freya was about to push the door further open, to be a part of this harmonious scene, when she heard the sound again. It was strange, like nothing she'd ever heard before. A puff and a clunk at the same time, but... different. Something was calling her without words.

Curiosity pulled her away from the nursery and deeper into the corridor. Her muscles clenched with the apprehension of what she would find, but her nerves were remarkably steady. The floor's cool marble sent shivers down her spine, yet she couldn't force herself to stop to get her slippers. Instead she moved on, guided by a sense of purpose. *Something* drove her forward.

The house was silent now, and somehow Freya still knew exactly where she was going. Her senses were in tune with every inch of Angel Manor—a familiar sensation, like it had been in the past, before the house was made dormant. This night, the house seemed very much alive again, though it lacked the dominance she had once experienced. There were no spells binding Freya to it; there was something different... a deeper connection. They were equals now.

Slowly, she ascended the wooden stairs. Flashes of memory plagued her, reminding her of when the stairs were built—and by whom—tugging at her emotions. She shrugged them off.

Her hand trembled slightly when she opened the door to one of the partially finished rooms. Inside, the moon illuminated the bedroom with a pale glow. Between the furniture, covered in off-white sheets, stood three figures. Freya needed no light to see them – the images were as clear as if the sun were shining overhead.

She froze.

"Hello, my pet," said the middle figure with a deep, warm voice. She was a portly lady of middle age, with a friendly face and copper red hair done up in a messy bun. The hair was graying on the sides, while her rosy cheeks and bright green eyes showed only a few wrinkles.

"We've been waiting for you," said the lithe figure on the left, with a voice high and clear like glass bells. The speaker was a young woman, whose hair had the same shade of copper as the older woman's but hung loose around her bare shoulders.

"We have little time," said the third and oldest figure. Her white hair, which still had the slightest hint of red to it, was done up tightly, pulling her wrinkled face into a stern expression. Her thin body resembled that of the young woman's slender form, only after the years had wreaked havoc on it, turning it from lithe to gaunt.

"Erm, would you mind telling me who the hell you are, and what you are doing in my house?"

"That's two questions, duck," said the portly woman.

"We go by many names," said the young woman. She smelled like daffodils and crocuses. "It is difficult to define who we really are."

Freya shook her head. "Seriously, just tell me what you want."

"Hush, girl. We still have questions to answer," the old woman said. "We are here to restore the much-needed balance."

"What balance?" Freya asked, not even bothering to hide the irritation in her tone. "You come here unannounced, in the middle of the bloody night, break into my house, won't even tell me who the hell you are, and you come to restore the balance? Jesus, what the fuck?"

"That's your third and final question, dear heart," said the portly woman.

"My what?" Freya grimaced. "I don't understand what's going on."

"We have come to wake the house from its slumber, child," the old woman said haughtily. "It has been dormant for too long, and you will need its aid more than ever."

Freya took a step forward, her teeth clenched as she spoke. "Like hell you are. Do you know what this house does when it's awake? It's bloodthirsty."

"How simple the world is when you perceive everything to be black and white," the old woman said. The light of the moon touched her white hair, and a mysterious smile played around her lined lips. There was wisdom in the old eyes, but a sparkle of mischief gave her an almost youthful expression.

"Listen, lady, it's late, and you're making precious little sense." Freya rubbed the bridge of her nose. "I'm a little sick of games. If you're here to help me, then please, help. But enough of these riddles. I've been through too much for this shit lately."

"We are here to help. But only you can accept our help," said the youngest woman. "Being dismissive won't be in anyone's best interest, and it wastes our time."

"Why do you want to wake the house?"

"This house is important, my darling," said the portly woman. She stroked one of the wayward locks from her forehead and tugged it behind her ear. "There are only few places like it, because it takes its power from the nearby gateway—and Lucifer Falls is arguably the most powerful place in this mortal domain. You must take it as a blessing... as an ally."

An image of John Phillips's torso, cut in half by Angel Manor's attic floor, swam in front of her eyes. "A blessing?" she said hoarsely. "Lady, you must not have met this house."

The three women laughed as one. Their voices were melodious, but there was a cruelty to the laughter.

"We have met *your* house, child," said the crone.

"But you really haven't yet, dove," said the mother.

"And we think it is about time you do," said the maiden.

Freya took several steps back, until she hit the wall behind her. "What do you want from me?"

The women smiled like hungry wolves. They were spinning... no, it wasn't them, Freya realised It was the room. It was swirling, and they were standing perfectly still. The sound of wind raced all around her, as if she were caught in a storm. Hot acid rose from her stomach to her throat, and Freya closed her eyes. She slid down the wall and curled into a little ball. When the noises stopped, Freya opened her eyes, and to her horror, she saw she was in the basement.

Her blood ran cold, and she sprang to her feet, regaining a sense of orientation and searching for the nearest exit. When she turned, an image startled her, and she froze. She saw herself.

"Who put this damn mirror here?" she whispered.

"There is no mirror," the image of herself said in a voice that was soft and high, and Freya muffled a scream with her own hand. "There is only you and I."

"Oh, Jesus," she muttered into her palm.

"I am not Jesus," the image of her said.

"I know that," Freya retorted testily. "I... I think I know who you are. You're the house."

"That is who I am." The expression of the house was solemn, but it didn't seem quite genuine. The face was similar to the wax statues at Madame Tussaud's. It didn't seem quite real.

"They woke you up? Those women? Who were they, anyway?"

"They are known by many names. The Fates would sound most familiar to you." The house caressed her own cheek as she spoke, rubbing the palm of her right hand across the side of her face.

"Greek mythology," Freya muttered as she tried to remember who the Fates were, but it had been too long.

"Yes. They woke me." The house stared at her with the strange, dead eyes.

"Right." Freya looked at the floor and sought the right words.

"You hate me," the house said.

Freya's head jerked up. "I..." She nodded. "I hate you. You are a punishment to me I don't feel I deserve. The things that happened here... I shouldn't have witnessed those things."

"You cannot hold me solely responsible for the tragedies that befall within my walls. Perhaps I derive some pleasure out of them, but even that is not my choice. In a way, I am as much of a victim of all this as you are."

"I don't even know what you mean by that. How are you a victim? You're a house, a murder house..."

"I was born to this."

"Well, *I* wasn't born for this, and *I* had a normal life before I came here."

The house stared straight past her. The rubbing stopped, and the young woman raked one sharp fingernail across the skin. Blood welled out of the wound, but not enough to drip down the cheek.

"You are wrong, guardian. You don't even know who you are, because it's not time for certain answers yet. One day you will find them, when the time is right. And you will know that you *were* born for this. *Your* bloodline is what made me what I am today." She raked the nail against her cheek a second time, creating a mirrored line of red. With dainty fingers, she stripped a thin line of skin from her cheek. She held the skin in front of her open mouth and curled her tongue around it before letting it disappear. Freya shuddered when the replica of herself chewed. A slight smudge of crimson surrounded the glistening wound.

"What do you mean?" The skin on the back of Freya's arms rose into tingly goosebumps.

"I will show you, if you will allow me." The spirit of the house looked at her with her dark eyes. They were a different shade from Freya's own, and yet they were so familiar.

"Yes," she said.

"I will take you to a place that is here, and simultaneously is not." The spirit opened her mouth, releasing a plume of dark smoke that dissipated, casting a dense mist around her. The house trembled and sighed, as if it were a living being. The floorboards creaked under Freya's feet, and she looked down to see them splitting open with a loud crack. Before she had time to be afraid, the wood morphed and curled around her ankles. At least it looked that way, because Freya couldn't feel the wood. She felt... something, but it was an odd sensation, like wind, not the solid touch of wood.

"Can I get hurt here?" Freya asked, watching the wood snake upward toward her torso, enveloping every inch of her.

"Only if I allow it."

"Oh." The comment didn't ease her fear. With an unsettling speed, the wood curled around her neck and face, blotting out the light. Freya tried to feel if there was anything around her. As she stretched out her hand, she saw there was nothing. In a daze, she looked down to where her body used to be, but it, too, was gone. She consisted of nothing more than thoughts and sound.

"You are a part of me now," said the disembodied voice of the house. "You will see what I see, and you will feel what I feel. First, I shall show you the beginning."

"It's very cold here," Freya said to the darkness. Even without a body, she could feel a chill that touched the very core of her being. She tried to make sense of her surroundings. At first, she thought it was just empty, but then she sensed something in the murkiness. There was a thumping sound, faint, like a pulse, below her. *The Horseman*, she thought. *I can feel him.*

There was something else she picked up on, an entity that wasn't quite defined yet, like a seed planted, but not yet fed, and not quite ready to grow. Freya concentrated on it, trying to understand what she was dealing with. There was a power in whatever lay dormant, which struck her as familiar. *It's linked to Lucifer Falls.*

"This is the beginning?" Freya asked.

"It is," the house said. "Can you feel the guardians overhead?"

Freya concentrated. There were voices above her. More than voices, there were emotions, and she could feel the odd mixture of them.

"I can hear children laughing," she said. A heavy weight pressed down on her heart when the laughter turned to screams. She tried to shift, but was again reminded she had no form, belonging instead to her surroundings. The disembodiment terrified her.

"They're dying up there..." she whispered. The blood of the children seeped through the earth, like molasses, down to its hungry recipient. Freya imagined the fluids running down her face as if it were crimson rain, but in truth it went straight through her. Beneath, the sleeping Horseman fed on the young deaths. A great sense of satisfaction that didn't belong to her washed over Freya. It only increased the sadness she already struggled with.

"A sacrifice is made and accepted," the house said.

"And you feel the pleasure of it."

"I do not quite exist yet, but yes, the part of me that has developed feels the hunger and the saturation of the sleeping captive."

"This is not just the beginning you're showing me, is it?" Freya asked. "It's the beginning of you."

"Watch," said the voice, which now sounded far away.

Freya wondered what she had to watch, since she couldn't see a thing, but before she finished the thought, someone stepped on the land that belonged to Angel Manor, and in the dark a spark of light grew. First small, like an electric worm, but then it expanded and blossomed, and it reminded Freya of one of those water and light shows she used to love as a child. A plethora of colours shot around in jagged lines, blending and dancing together as if they were alive. *They* are *alive*, Freya thought. *They're creating the soul to the house.*

The colours settled, shaping a form that looked like a young girl.

"All this happened because someone entered this terrain?" Freya asked. "Who has that much power?"

The young girl turned around to face her, and Freya saw the answer in the child's features.

She had seen an old faded picture of this girl last year, when she had looked up information about Angel Manor. It was a face she wouldn't forget easily. It was the girl who built the house.

"Beth."

"I do not know why or how she made me who I am," the young girl said, watching her with the same dark eyes that had looked at Freya from her own face. "There are many answers I do not have. What she brought me is what links me to you."

"This is why you don't want me to hate you? Because we're somehow linked?"

The girl shrugged and raised her head to the noises from upstairs. "I did not grow until Beth built me the house, and I became a physical personification."

"Did Beth know about you? That you exist?"

"Yes, though I do believe she was in denial for most of her life. Only in death did she fully accept my presence."

"Where is she now?" Freya asked. "I've never seen her or any of my relatives in this house. Why aren't they tied to it?"

The child cocked her head slightly and narrowed her

eyes. Her silence lasted only a few seconds, but passed slowly like long minutes. "I grant the kin of Beth freedom after death. Another will come and take their place."

"So, when I die, I get to go free?" Freya's heart skipped a beat.

"I cannot answer that question yet. Times are changing, and it makes the rules fluctuate. We find ourselves in a situation where we have to look to the future rather than the past." The girl's little hand, still chubby with baby fat, lifted and pointed behind Freya. She didn't turn—there was no body to turn—but she shifted her gaze. From the darkness, two figures became distinguishable. Both were male, one tall and broad, the other thin. Desire emanated from both the figures, but in different forms. There was lust and caring, which clashed with the hunger for power and death. It was unclear which male wanted what, but they were both ravenous.

"Salvation and Doom," the house said.

"Are they my future?" Freya asked, annoyed with how meek her voice sounded.

"They are both your, and my, future. I can sense them coming, and you will need to prepare."

Freya turned back to the girl, who now looked like her mirror image again. "Prepare for what?"

"I wish I knew," the girl said. "I will stand by you as much as I can, but remember that I am fickle, and susceptible to magic. I am not a reliable ally."

"Gee, thanks for nothing," Freya said. She became aware that she had a shape again, and she lifted her hand to look at it. "What was the point of us meeting if you can't tell me what I'm supposed to do?"

"The point was so that you could figure it out for yourself, knowing that you have more resources than you were aware of. The point was that you know we are linked, you and I."

"Fat lot of good that does me. I don't even know how to use our link to my benefit."

"Then learn, guardian. Because the world is changing, and you will need to adapt."

Freya rolled her eyes. "Could you be any vaguer?"

As if in answer, the figure became evanescent, fading before her eyes.

"I didn't mean..." Freya said, reaching forward.

"I will try to guide you to the best of my capabilities, but it is up to you to listen." The figure melted into the darkness, leaving Freya behind. The house was watching her, and Freya had no idea what to do next.

CHAPTER THREE

"Your horoscope predicts good things for this week," Bam said as Freya entered the kitchen, holding Emily to her chest.

"Love your outfit." Freya inclined her head toward the fluffy pink footsie pajamas Bam was wearing. "Very morning appropriate."

"I thought I would try to be as normal as I could be," Bam said. "I think this is very *me*." She pulled the pajama hood over her head, and to Freya's amusement, two long ears drooped down.

"Very you," Freya agreed. She yawned, put Emily in her bouncer, and grabbed the coffee pot with its fresh brew. The timed coffee maker had been a blessing. She hadn't cared for coffee much before, but motherhood had made it essential to her diet.

"It says here that you will get an unexpected financial bonus." Bam looked up from the newspaper, which was hovering in front of her.

"You're getting crazy good at holding stuff," Freya observed, pouring the coffee into a white mug with black kittens. "I'm impressed. Though for the life of me, I don't understand why you would waste time on reading that garbage." She pointed at the horoscope section.

"You don't know that this is garbage."

"I know." Freya sipped her coffee, letting the hot liquid kiss her upper lip. "You should know, too. Aren't the dead connected to a greater something?"

Bam raised her eyebrows. "A greater something? Like,

38

what? A spiritual kumbaya?"

Freya snorted, holding her hand before her mouth to prevent the coffee from spraying out.

"Honestly, Frey," Bam rolled her eyes. "You, like, think horoscopes are crap, but you believe in some pretty shady crap yourself."

"Touché," Freya said, wiping Emily's cheek. There was still a sheen of breast milk on the baby's skin, and she was starting to doze, the way she always did after a feeding. "So, tell me about the fortunes I will get."

"It wouldn't hurt to get some money," Bam said. "Especially since you don't seem to be too keen to open the hotel."

"I'm not," Freya muttered, and she sat down at the kitchen table, pulling the bouncer toward her. "I just couldn't handle the responsibility right now. Not on my own, anyway."

"You are going to have to do something eventually," Bam said. "I could see if there is some way we can get more money from my parents..."

Freya looked up, perturbed. "How, Bam? Were you planning on contacting them?" She raised her hands in a questioning gesture. "They buried you."

"No, but maybe a wayward letter in my handwriting got lost and—"

Freya shook her head. "Not unless we're desperate. We put your parents through enough shit."

"There are other ways to make money than running a hotel, you know?" Bam offered.

"Yeah, I thought about that too. I think when Emily goes on solid foods, I should go and find a job. I could wean her off the breast milk, and then I can find her a good daycare center. I just hope I can find a job that will make me more than daycare will cost me." Freya sighed. The thought of getting a job made her want to crawl in bed and pull the covers over her head, but she knew Bam was right. She had to do something.

"Or we could, like, pretend you're a psychic, and I will be your pet ghost, and we'll do a con act together," Bam said cheerily. "I could wear weird oldie worldie outfits."

"Let's call that Plan B," Freya snorted, and she took another sip of coffee. Emily snored softly. The idea was oddly appealing.

Ding-dong!

Emily let out a sudden cry and Freya jumped, almost dropping her coffee. She shared a startled look with Bam as the doorbell sounded again.

"Who the fuck would that be?" Freya wondered out loud as she gathered the perturbed child into her arms.

"Are you expecting someone?" Bam asked.

"Obviously not."

Emily whined, and Freya bobbed her up and down as she made her way to the front door. She pulled the door open and looked into the pock-marked face of Nigel, her postman. Nigel was a funny-looking man with a square chest, pot belly, and thin, crooked legs. He raised his bushy salt and pepper eyebrows at her—his eyes darting between her and Emily—while his mouth twisted in a surly grimace.

"I've got a letter here for you to sign, lass," he barked in a heavy Scottish accent. Freya blinked, needing a moment to decipher what he said, but she spotted the white letter right before he thrust a clipboard in her direction. She accepted the blue ballpoint pen he pushed into her hand. With a meaty finger, he tapped the paper on the board, indicating where she had to sign, and held the clipboard up high enough for her to place her signature. He muttered something she couldn't understand, but his annoyance was made clear from his tone. Freya, wrestling with a distraught Emily, scribbled her name at the appointed place, and before she was done, Nigel pulled the pen out of her hand and shoved the letter at her. He didn't make eye contact with her as he did, and he hobbled off as soon as she took the letter. It was obvious that Nigel didn't like coming to Angel Manor. The people of Skye were still deeply suspicious of it, and Freya couldn't blame them. She closed the door as she tried to calm the screaming baby.

Bam floated toward her, leaning in to make eye contact with Emily, and the baby instantly stopped crying as she saw the friendly ghost's face.

"Thanks," Freya said, exhaling with relief.

"Was that Nigel?"

"Yes, and he was his usual sunny self," Freya answered with a wink.

"Oh, be still my heart," Bam mocked. "That man's smile can, like, light up a room. He's so dreamy."

They both laughed, and Freya held up the envelope. "I wonder what it is. I had to sign for it and everything."

"Open it." Bam leaned close.

Freya peeled open a corner of the envelope, slid her finger in it, and pulled open the rest. The paper tore with a satisfying sound. Freya pulled out the contents, accidentally dropping the envelope to the ground. She folded open the piece of paper and gasped.

"What is it?" Bam asked.

"A note, with a bank statement to a savings account." Freya held up the check with trembling hands. "It has fifty thousand pounds in it. And the account is in my name." She looked up at Bam. "Can someone even do that? Open an account in someone else's name? I don't remember signing for anything."

"I don't know. I don't think so." Bam bent down to see the check. "What does the note say?"

Freya focused on the piece of paper in her hand. "Never heard of this bank, either... the Deligati? Remind me to Google that later." She shrugged and read the note out loud: "Every year, an appropriate amount will be deposited to this bank account. It is meant for you to live on, so that you can focus your attention on the tasks you need to perform for Angel Manor. This will not answer your many questions, and it will only raise more. Please believe that the money is real, and it will sustain you. Our apologies that this aid came so late, and that we have not done more for you over the past year."

"We?" Bam asked. "Who is we?"

Freya shot her friend an incredulous look. "You're asking me? How would I know? It's obviously not the mailman doing this."

Bam shrugged, and added in a conspiratorial tone, "Or maybe it is. I mean, like, we don't know who Nigel is. Perhaps he is a millionaire philanthropist." She snorted, and Freya rolled her eyes.

"Very funny."

"Could it be from your parents?" Bam asked, her attention pulled toward Emily again. She made a face at the baby, who stared at her with big, murky blue eyes. "You can open bank accounts in your kid's name, I think."

Freya looked at the note and shook her head. "Of course not. They wouldn't write about my duties to Angel Manor, would they?" Emily pulled the note from her hand and licked it.

Bam nodded. "Yeah, that was silly of me. I wonder what this means?"

Freya folded the bank statement and put it in the pocket of her jeans. Then she pulled the note away from Emily, who was wrapping her lips around it. "It means that I was right. There are people out there who know about Angel Manor. I just wish I knew who they were." She crumpled the note in her hands. Her heart pounded in her chest. "I don't understand why they won't just contact me. They could tell me so much, and help me with this fucking house, or something. Why the mystery?"

"Maybe they're in trouble," Bam said. "I know you don't like to talk about it, but think about it, that thing in the basement... that has got to be part of something bigger, right?"

Freya held Emily tighter to her chest. "He is," she said, her voice unintentionally hushed. "He's a Horseman, right?"

Bam wrinkled her nose. "Well, obviously. He, like, rides a big-ass horse."

Freya shook her head. "No, that's not what I mean. He's one of the Four Horsemen."

"Of the Apocalypse?" Bam whispered.

"Yeah. I have a theory about him, too."

"About the master who sleeps?"

"I... I think that's Death in our basement." Freya pointed with her free hand, and she mouthed out the word "death" rather than saying it out loud.

Bam's eyes were wide, and she looked more translucent, as if she were fading.

Freya's heart skipped a beat. "Bam, are you okay?"

Her friend shook her head, a blank expression on her semi-transparent face.

"Bam!" Freya barked, and she snapped her thumb and middle finger in front of the staring eyes.

The eyelashes fluttered and Bam closed her eyes. When she opened them, she looked at Freya as if she had awoken from a deep sleep. "We... we were talking about something," Bam said with a groggy tone in her voice. "I zoned out for a second or something."

"Jesus, Bam, we were talking about the sleeping thing in the basement, and you just went completely blank on me." Freya moved Emily, who was tugging on her shirt, from one arm to the other. "Is this something I need to worry about? Can't you talk about what it really is or something?"

Bam raised her eyebrows in surprise. "We've, like, talked about it a million times before."

"But I never said it was Death before." Freya narrowed her eyes, looking for signs of Bam blacking out again, but her friend maintained eye contact.

"You think it's Death?" Bam looked skeptical. "Like, the Grim Reaper? Coz if that's a thing, I haven't met him."

Emily's little nails raked across her skin, leaving thin, white marks as Freya pulled the small hand away from the collar of her t-shirt. She thought for a second.

"No, if there was a Grim Reaper, it wouldn't be asleep. I think... I don't know how things like that work, but it doesn't sound logical." A faint whiff of feces tickled her nose. Freya lifted Emily up, sniffed, and pulled a face. "Oh boy, someone needs a clean diaper." She held the baby at arm's length and smiled at her, but her heart was still pounding.

"What were the Four Horsemen again?" Freya asked, as she made her way through the halls, holding Emily in front of her. The baby looked at her with big eyes, her tiny forehead wrinkled. "War, Famine, erm, the other one, and Death." Freya looked at Bam, who was floating next to her. There was no sign of fading anymore, but Freya wasn't reassured quite yet.

"And you think that the sleeping master is the Horseman

44

of Death?"

"Yeah," Freya opened the door to the nursery. "Makes sense, right?"

"Yes, it does. And if there's one Horseman under Angel Manor, there must be three others in, like, different places. At least, I assume they won't all be buried together... Oh, god, Frey, what if they're all buried together? Like, maybe they are buried on top of each other, or all in one tomb or something..."

Freya shook her head. "No. Remember I told you about the dream I had?"

"Where you met the house?"

"Yeah, that one. Well, I sensed the sleeping thing under the floor. There was definitely just one of them."

"Which means..."

Freya put the baby on the changing table and pulled at the snaps of the pink onesie. "Which means there are probably more people somewhere who are making these sacrifices. So, we're not the only ones who know about this. Maybe the reason why the people who gave us the money haven't done more is because they are busy with one of those other Horsemen?"

Bam nodded, and Freya pulled Emily's chubby little legs out of the onesie, moving the fabric far away from the diaper zone. She unfastened the diaper, jerking her head back at the overwhelming stench that emanated from the exposed green-brown mass.

"Pfft, for such a little girl, you sure make a big stink," Freya said in a sing-song voice. She smiled at the baby, making faces as she carefully pulled the loaded diaper away from Emily's bottom. The baby mimicked some of her facial expressions, and Bam laughed.

"I'm glad I don't really have a sense of smell anymore,"

the ghost said as Freya folded the diaper. Bam took it from her and disposed of it. There was something hypnotizing about watching Bam do any mundane activity. Her touch was more a sheer force of will than actual touching. Her hands never really made contact with anything she lifted or moved, so sometimes they would go straight through the object. It was more as if she floated things, but she was becoming so proficient in her new skill, she was almost as useful as she had been in life. Yet it cost her a lot of energy, Freya knew.

"What bothers me, though," Freya said, "is if they were aware of my existence, and they knew I was new to this, why didn't they call me or something? I get that you can't come over, but why no contact at all? Even now, they're not revealing themselves to me. They're just giving me a note, and I'm supposed to figure out what it means by myself."

"It is odd," Bam said, as she opened the diaper genie with a wave of her hand rather than using her foot. "But there could be lots of reasons for it. Maybe this is not the last you'll hear from them, like, whoever they are. Maybe they'll contact you soon, or something? Then you can ask them."

"Well, if they don't contact me, I'm going to find out who they are." Freya pulled the bank statement from her pocket. "No way they didn't leave a paper trail with this."

"You go, Nancy Drew," Bam giggled.

Freya burst out laughing. "I have no idea where to start with this. Maybe call the bank or something?" She wiped the last remains of poo from Emily's bottom. "But I feel I have to do something, you know? Or I would go mad. And I really do need help. Not just financial help; I need people."

"What are you going to do with the money?" Bam asked.

"Are you kidding?" Freya said. "I'm keeping it. It will simplify my life significantly. Not looking a gift horse in the mouth here, no matter how dodgy the horse-gifter is."

"Good for you," Bam said, then she gasped. "Oh my God, Frey..."

"What?"

"Your wish totally came true." Bam punched her shoulder. She couldn't feel more than just a wave of cold. "You wished for help, remember? Well, you got it."

CHAPTER FOUR

The radiator ticked softly as it fought the chill that had spread throughout the mansion. The kitchen was warm, especially after Freya had used the oven to make herself a beef and stilton pie. She rarely cooked elaborate meals since she was always cooking for one. Emily still only drank breast milk—and the occasional bottle, if Freya was too tired to feed her at night. Bam needed no food, but she did enjoy spending time with her during dinner. Meal times were Freya's favorite part of the day. She almost felt normal then... almost.

"I've been thinking," Bam said. She was making two stuffed bunnies float through the air as Emily tried to reach for them. It was a skill her daughter hadn't quite mastered yet, but she was clearly getting better at grabbing.

"You've been thinking," Freya said as she took a bite out of a roast potato. It was a little too well done—she wasn't a great cook—but it tasted nice enough. "Why does that make my spider sense tingle?"

Bam frowned and focused her attention on Emily again. "The other night, after, well, you know... we talked about you needing people."

"About needing help, you mean?" Freya asked.

"I think you need more than just help." Bam's large eyes met hers.

Freya frowned. "I don't follow."

"You were right, Frey," Bam said. "You need more than just me. You need to be among the living."

"What brought this on?" Freya asked.

"Don't you think I know about your crying?" Bam's lip quivered a little. "Your sadness... even the house feels it."

"I..." The blood drained from Freya's cheeks, and she held the fork so tightly in her hand that the metal bit into her skin.

"I know you're lonely, and you're worried." The two bunnies gently floated to Emily's lap and rested there. Bam stood from her place and moved toward Freya. "You worry about turning into those nuns, and I think you may have a right to worry. The only people you interact with that aren't dead already are the people you plan to kill. You need more human connection than that."

"No," Freya said. Tears were threatening to well up in her eyes, but she fought it. "If I care for people, they die. Aside from Emily, I don't want to get close to anyone ever again."

"Wow," Bam said, as she settled down right next to Freya. "That's, like, the biggest load of bullshit I have ever heard in my death." She rolled her eyes and shook her head. "So, you're just going to be this crazy hermit lady who spends her time with a baby and a ghost? How do you think that will affect your daughter?"

Freya jerked her head back and glanced at Emily, who had managed to wrap her hands around the ear of one of the bunnies, and was staring at it in wide-eyed wonder.

"I don't..."

"You are her role model. Do you expect her to live a life with no friends, no human connections aside from yourself?"

Freya squirmed uncomfortably in her seat. "That's not fair. You know I don't."

Bam was unrelenting. "How about, like, having your daughter deal with a crazy mom? Because if you stop having normal human interaction, that's what you will be."

"Jesus, Bam!" Freya exclaimed. "Take it easy on me, will ya? Don't you think I have enough on my plate right now to have to worry about that, too? I barely have my shit together as it is."

"That's my point. You have too much on your plate. There is no relief. You're, like, either taking care of a child, or taking care of the world. When are you taking care of, like, yourself?" Bam reached out for her, the cold hand touching her cheek like an icy breeze.

"This is bullshit," Freya said. "What do you want me to do? Go clubbing?"

"Maybe," Bam said. "You're a young woman. Clubbing may be, like, a bit much, but go have dinner with someone. Or go have a drink in a pub." Bam raised a finger as if she'd just had a great idea. "You could go see a movie with someone."

"Who am I going to do those things with, Bam?" Freya said. "I don't know anyone here. To the locals, I'm just the lady who lives in the haunted house. People aren't exactly dying to come over. And I don't want them here..."

"They don't have to come here. You could meet in town."

Freya shook her head so hard her braid slapped her shoulder. "I'm a mom. What am I going to do, hire a babysitter? I don't want strangers in this house. It's bad enough having to find someone every three months to watch Emily when I go hunting for a sacrifice."

"I can babysit. I could watch her when you hunt, too."

"You're a ghost. I can't let a ghost babysit my kid."

Bam crossed her arms. "I babysit every single night."

"While I'm *in* the house," Freya argued. "I'm always nearby."

"I babysit when you sleep." There was an indignant tone in Bam's voice that made her seem more alive than ever. "I

50

can handle a couple of hours while you are in the pub."

"I..."

Bam leaned forward, her hair moving as if she were under water. "Come on, Frey, you know I wouldn't suggest this if I didn't think I could do it. I love Emily more than... than, like, anything. I wouldn't put her in danger. And who could take care of her better than I could? I'm already dead, so nothing can kill me." It was a joke, but Freya understood the earnestness of her friend's intentions.

"I..."

"When is the last time a human being touched you? I'm not even talking, like, sexy touching. Just held your hand or gave you a hug."

"You mean, someone I didn't then brutally murder?" Freya said. She wanted it to sound like a joke, too, but it just came out flat.

"You're still alive, baby," Bam said. "Better start acting like it."

Freya started to object again, but stopped. Why couldn't Bam stay with Emily for a couple of hours? And it would be nice to see real people, talk to them.

"Maybe you're right. Not dinner, but just to get out of this house without having to kill someone would be a pleasure," Freya admitted.

"See, there you go," Bam said, perking up. "I'm glad you agree."

"Okay, tell you what," Freya said, spearing a pea with her fork and holding it up. "When Emily goes on solid foods, I'll—"

"Tomorrow night," Bam interrupted.

Freya lowered her fork. "What's tomorrow night?"

"Your date."

"My what?" She dropped the fork on her plate.

Bam smiled in impish triumph. "I made you a date."

Freya's mouth fell open. "You what?"

"I made you a date," Bam repeated the words slowly, as if she were talking to a small child.

"What? How? With who?" Freya asked, still gawking.

"Online, on that eHarmony site."

"You went online?" Freya tried to collect her thoughts, but they were too scattered.

"You make it sound like I possessed the web, or something," Bam pouted. "It's not that hard, you know. I didn't forget how to do the normal human things. They just take a different kind of effort for me now, but I can press a few buttons."

"You didn't just press a few buttons... you made a dating profile for me." Freya leaned back. "Fucking hell, a ghost created my dating profile. That's just bonkers."

"Hey," Bam said, sounding genuinely annoyed. Her physical appearance changed slightly, like the sky does before a storm. She was darker somehow. "Stop your bitching. I, like, got you a total hottie to go out with. He's only on Skye for a few months. Some sort of researcher or something, I don't remember." She cocked her head. "He will be a perfect practice distraction for you until you're ready to do some serious dating."

"A moment ago, we were just talking about meeting people, and I'm suddenly going on a date." Freya rubbed her temple. "I don't know if I'm ready for this."

Bam sighed. It didn't sound like exhaling a breath, not the way the living sounded – it was more like the noise of gravel being pushed around. "You're not ready because you're still hung up on Logan?"

"I..." Tears pricked behind her eyes. "I killed him, Bam."

"If you hadn't killed him, he'd be dead now anyway," Bam retorted. "You killing him was probably more merciful than what would have happened to him otherwise. You need to stop this line of thinking, Frey. You can't never date again because of Logan."

Freya pinched the bridge of her nose. "It's only been a year."

"Only a year?" Bam said, and her eyes held Freya's. "That's, like, forever. You don't have to marry this guy. Just a date. A drink, in a pub. Just an hour, maybe two or three if he's fun. Nothing more."

"It does sound like fun," Freya said. "Besides, I don't think I could stand your whining if I didn't go."

Bam laughed. Her body language became friendlier, and she looked lighter again, as if the sun peeked through the clouds. "You'll have fun, and if you don't, you will never have to see this guy again."

"Good point."

"Besides," Bam said, wiggling her eyebrows, "if he turns out to be a real jerk, you can always feed him to Angel Manor."

CHAPTER FIVE

"I just realized how long it's been since I've been on an actual date," Freya said. "I don't even know what to wear." She stared at the different outfits she had thrown on her bed. "I could just wear jeans and a jumper."

"That's not very sexy," Bam said, wrinkling her nose. "You should wear your little red dress. You look really hot in that."

"No way," Freya said. "It's too cold for that dress, and I don't feel sexy with the little mom-pouch I haven't managed to get rid of." She grabbed the lower part of her stomach to demonstrate that there was some fat stored under the skin.

"Well, wear something that does make you feel sexy," Bam said.

"I don't know if I want to look sexy for this guy yet."

"Did you see his picture?" Bam pointed at the screen of the computer that held the profile picture to a man called Wulf Frigg. A handsome man with a mysterious half-smile stared at them from the screen. He had curly blond hair and deep green eyes.

"We don't know if he really looks like that, though," Freya retorted. "That picture looks suspiciously like one of those stock photos. I won't be surprised if my real date is with a five-foot ginger man."

"Or with Nigel," Bam laughed.

"Crazier things have happened to me," Freya muttered.

"Okay, so not too sexy. But maybe at least something that makes you feel good about yourself? How about your black skirt, with the black tights and that cute purple top you have?"

Freya nodded. "That would work. I could put a cardigan over it, for the cold, but I can take it off in the pub, and—"

The doorbell cut her off mid-sentence. The two women stared at each other. Emily let out an uncharacteristically loud wail.

"You didn't give him my address, did you?" Freya asked Bam as she picked up the screaming baby.

"No," Bam shook her head vigorously.

"Then that can't be him."

"Go open the door," Bam urged. "I'll take Emily."

"But she's so upset..." Freya looked at her crying baby.

"I got this. I'm, like, the baby whisperer." Bam opened her translucent arms to take Emily. She was still sobbing as she floated in the ghostly grip.

Freya ran out the bedroom and through the corridor. By the time she reached the door, her heart was pounding, and her breathing was heavier than normal. To her surprise, she saw an unfamiliar postal worker carrying a large package.

"Emily Masters?" the man asked in a thick Scottish accent.

"Emily is my daughter," Freya said, clinging to the door.

"I have a package for her. If you're the mum, you can sign for it." He pressed some buttons on a black machine the size of a large calculator and handed it to her with a little plastic stick.

"Where's Nigel?" she asked.

"Nigel?" The postman furrowed his brow.

"Our regular postman?"

"I don't know, ma'am, I only deal with international post," the postman said as he moved the machine. "I'll need your signature, please. I can't give you the parcel without it."

"I wonder who it's from," Freya muttered as she signed her name.

"Don't know that, ma'am. It's from America, if that helps any?"

"I would have guessed the Netherlands, since that's where my parents are from," Freya said, handing him back his machine, "but America?"

He shook his head as he clipped it onto his back pocket and lifted the box. "That's what it says."

Freya looked at the parcel. "I don't think I know anyone..." Then her voice died away. She did know people in the States.

Bam's parents.

With a soft "thank you," she took the parcel from the man's hands and turned to go inside. She wondered if she should ask Bam to be present when she opened it. *If* it was a parcel from her parents. Maybe it would be for everyone's best interest if she looked at what was inside first.

She took the parcel to the kitchen, where she cut the thick tape with a knife. The cardboard groaned as she ripped the box open, and bright green Styrofoam nuggets spilled out over the top. Freya carefully pushed her hands inside the sea of neon until her fingers touched something solid. Whatever it was, it was packed in a thick layer of bubble wrap. Carefully, Freya pulled the object from its protective prison and inspected the almost oval shape. The bubble wrap was see-through, but it had so many layers it was impossible to tell what it held in its core, and the outside was held shut with long strips of tape.

With a sharp fingernail, she went to work on the strip. She worked meticulously until the first layer of bubble wrap opened up like a flower, revealing another layer underneath. It took her several minutes to peel away each sheet, and the object underneath became clearer with the unravelling.

It was a doll. A large porcelain doll, which was only a few inches smaller than Emily. The toy had a heart-shaped face with large blue eyes and long, dark lashes. The chestnut hair was done up in two long pigtails, and she wore a burgundy dress with a matching bow on her head. The doll looked old, but well cared for. It smelled like a nursing home, musty but clean.

Freya put the toy on the kitchen counter and took a step back to look at it. She had never been a fan of dolls—not even when she had been a child—and they creeped her out a little. This one wasn't an exception.

The stone blue eyes stared at her, and she fought the urge to throw the whole thing in the bin. She scolded herself for being so silly. She felt a pang of guilt for not liking the doll. Whoever sent it had been very kind, and it wasn't meant for her; it was sent to her daughter. She could imagine Emily liking this when she was bigger. Though why any kid would want to play with a porcelain doll was beyond her. Aside from being creepy, they were fragile and didn't make very good toys. Not that she was an impartial judge on this; she didn't like plastic dolls either. Freya had been more of a Lego kind of girl. She had only barely tolerated Barbies.

"Emily is awake," a voice behind her said. Bam hovered near her, a dreamy expression on her face. "What's that?"

"A doll."

"Duh, I can see that, you muppet." She rolled her eyes. "Where did it come from?" Bam reached out a hand to touch the doll, but something made her change her mind and she pulled away as if afraid to be stung.

"The States. I thought maybe your parents sent it?" Freya said, watching Bam's reaction. "I haven't looked for a note yet."

"Doesn't look like something my folks would send." Bam shook her head. "It's not one of my old dolls. Besides, why would they send you a doll?"

"Whoever sent it didn't send it to me. They sent it to Emily."

Freya put her hand back in the box and groped around. It took a few moments of digging until she found the corner of a red card. She pulled it out and held it up triumphantly. It was one of those corny cards with embossed roses on the front. She turned it around, and the only thing written on the back, with elegant old-fashioned penmanship, was: "Her name is Sofia. Take good care of her."

There was no name signed.

"How odd," Freya said. "Who would send that?"

"Not a clue."

"It has to be someone we know, because they know Emily's name. But who do we know that lives in the US?"

"I know plenty of people," Bam said, "but I doubt any of them sent it. Check the return address."

"It's a P.O. Box."

"Helpful."

"Maybe it's the same people who opened the bank account?" Freya rubbed her temples. "I don't know if I can take any more surprises."

"Getting free money and pretty dolls?" Bam said. "I can, like, think of worse things that could happen to you." She gave Freya a scornful look. "What are you complaining about? It looks like your luck might be turning around."

"Fair point – though if people are going to spoil me, I would rather they send me the spell so that I can reinstall murdering ghosts in my house," Freya said, holding up the doll, "instead of sending me creepy toys."

"It's not creepy," Bam protested. "It's cute." The ghost frowned and thought for a second before she added, "I think…" She cocked her head at it. "Okay, maybe it's a little bit creepy."

"I just don't know how I feel giving a stranger's dolls to my child," Freya said. "Not sure what it is, but I'm feeling a bit paranoid about it."

"Don't put it in her room yet until you know where it came from," Bam shrugged.

"Yeah." Freya put the doll back on the counter, readjusting her dress. "Emily is too little anyway. I'll wait till she's older to give it to her."

From the baby's room came a disgruntled cry that tore her from her thoughts. "Speaking of which, I need to feed Emily."

"Go, I'll watch the creepy doll."

"It'll watch you," Freya retorted, and she quickly made her way to the crying child.

CHAPTER SIX

The pub, despite being quiet on a Tuesday night, was a sensory overload. Freya sipped her cheap white wine while her heart beat to the tune that only the extremely anxious know. She had changed her mind at least five times since she had gotten into the taxi, but each time she had convinced herself that Bam was right, she needed a break. It wasn't as if she were committing to a serious relationship; she was having a drink with a guy. There would be conversation, and maybe some mild flirting, and she might actually feel like a human being again, instead of a murderous milk machine.

Besides, Bam would never let her live it down if she stood this guy up. She would just have a drink, and if he was boring, or some sort of jerk, she would get up and leave. It wasn't as if she owed anyone anything. Yet, no matter how reasonably her inner voice explained the situation to her, her heart kept racing and her hands wouldn't stop shaking. *Poor guy is going to think he's on a date with a mental patient*, she thought.

"Freya?" a smooth, deep voice asked, and Freya looked up into the most handsome face she had ever seen. Her stomach exploded in a storm of proverbial butterflies. Wulf Frigg had looked good in his picture, but the photograph could not have prepared her for meeting him in real life. She bolted to her feet, knocking her wine glass over. Gasping, she hurried to pick up the glass, managing only to spill the remaining contents all over her hands.

"Oh erm, sorry, I..." Freya stammered.

"Here, let me help." Wulf grabbed a napkin with one hand and dabbed at the table, while with his free hand he waved the bar woman over.

"I'm so sorry about this." Freya stepped back to avoid the wine waterfall dripping along the side of the table. "I'm a little clumsy."

He looked up at her, his green eyes piercing straight through any defences she had intended to put up. "I like clumsy women." His smile was bright and genuine, and Freya's heart fluttered.

"Your picture really doesn't do you justice," she said spontaneously, and when she realized what she had just said, a deep blush blossomed from her neck to her cheeks. She could feel the heat spreading across her face. "Oh dear, I said that out loud, didn't I?" she muttered.

Wulf laughed, and stepped aside to let the thin bar woman with dyed red hair and muscular arms clean the table with a grey rag. When she was done, the woman shot Wulf an appreciative glance before she moved back to her place behind the bar. The handsome man didn't even seem to notice.

Freya ran her hand through her hair. "Can we please start over?"

"Freya?" Wulf said, winking at her, causing another wave of stomach butterflies to flutter. He held out his hand. "I'm Wulf."

"Nice to meet you," she said with a relieved smile. They sat down at opposite ends of the table, and Freya found it difficult to look straight at her date.

"I... I can't get over the fact a guy like you would be on a dating site," she said. "What's wrong with you?" She meant it to be funny, but as she said it, Freya wasn't sure if he would get the joke.

Wulf laughed. "I could ask you the same thing. You're a very beautiful woman."

"I'm also a mother of a young child, with no social life," Freya said. She pushed a lock of hair behind her ear and stared at her empty glass. "So, now you know what's wrong with me."

"I have a terrible track record with women who dazzle me and then break my heart," Wulf said, and Freya found the courage to look at him. "That's what's wrong with me."

"Why a dating site?"

"Well, after my last girlfriend, I vowed to never be in a relationship again, but that didn't work out for me." Wulf scratched behind his ear. "A friend of mine uses these dating sites, and he convinced me to give it a try. I was reluctant at first, but—and I realize this might make me sound like a total creep—it was actually your profile that convinced me to sign up. He showed it to me as one of the potential women he thought would be good for me. There were a few women in his selection that I wasn't so impressed with, but there was something about your profile. You mentioned that you had a tough time with your last relationship, too, and that you weren't the type to jump into a hot and heavy affair right away."

Freya raised her eyebrows. "I mentioned all that?"

It was Wulf's turn to look surprised.

"Sorry," Freya giggled. "I didn't actually create my profile. My friend... she thought I should date again. I should have looked at what she had written about me."

"That would explain it." He smiled. "Well, here we are. How about I get us a couple of drinks?"

"Thank you, that would be nice."

"White wine?" he asked, nodding at the empty glass.

"Yes, sweet white wine please," Freya said. He walked to the bar, attracting the eye of most of the patrons. Freya was dying to tell Bam about her date, and it hadn't even really started yet.

Wulf came back holding a glass of white wine and what

looked like a Coke. He placed the white wine in front of her and sat down again.

"Tell me about yourself," Freya said, taking a nervous sip. "Your profile said you were a researcher, but it wasn't specific on what you do."

He drank from his Coke, an uncomfortable smile on his sensual lips. "I'm afraid you might think less of me if I tell you."

Freya blinked. "Now I'm really intrigued. What do you research?"

"I study paranormal phenomena." He cocked his head a little, his eyes observing her reaction.

"Oh, right," Freya said.

"A lot of people don't believe in it. I don't blame you," he said, shaking his head.

"Oh, I believe in paranormal phenomena... trust me, I believe." She took a deep gulp of her own drink, cautioning herself not to say too much. *Does he know where I live?* she wondered. *Is that why he sought me out? For my house? Why else would a guy like that want to—*

"You sound pretty convinced. Did something happen to you? Maybe in your childhood?" He looked interested, but his questions weren't pressing. "Most people who believe have had some form of spiritual encounter."

"Have you heard of Angel Manor?"

He sat back and seemed to think. "No, that name doesn't ring a bell."

"You are an investigator of paranormal phenomena on the Isle of Skye, and yet you haven't heard of Angel Manor?" She raised her eyebrows. "Are you kidding me?"

"Eh..." he shrugged. "I'm assuming there is a haunted house story there somewhere? I tend to ignore those, because ninety percent of haunted houses are just owners looking for attention. Most of the time, they want to write books about their house, and want to boost sales or something. I don't want to be an enabler to scam artists." His face was deadly serious now, and Freya felt as if a weight had been lifted from her shoulders. *He's not here for Angel Manor, he's here for me.*

"I didn't know that. It's a pretty infamous house here," she said, looking into her glass. It was almost empty again, and the wine was making her head feel like it was filled with cotton balls. "What are you here to investigate?"

"Have you heard of a place they call Lucifer Falls?" The serious expression on his face now revealed a hint of eagerness. She laughed, not out of mirth but bitterly.

"Have I ever..."

"You've been there?" he asked.

"I can see it from my house," she said, regretting her words instantly, but she just couldn't stop herself.

Wulf's eyebrows shot up in surprise. "Really?"

"Yes, it's a big, gaping hole at the bottom of the cliff outside Angel Manor, where I live." She wasn't sure why she was so honest with him; she hadn't meant to tell him where she lived or about Angel Manor, but for some reason it just felt so good talking to another person. Her guard wasn't as functional as she thought it would be. Maybe it was the wine.

He looked embarrassed. "You live in Angel Manor? I... I didn't mean to imply..."

She held up her hand. "No, honest, you didn't offend me. I'm not looking for publicity. I just thought that maybe you were on this date because you had heard of my house."

He shook his head. "I'm on this date because I liked the look of your profile. Can't recall if anyone mentioned it to me."

She snorted, her head spinning a little.

"I'm not here about your house, and we won't talk about it... unless you want to."

Freya smiled. "Well, maybe if this is a good date, I may invite you over sometime so you can see its view of Lucifer Falls for yourself." A rush of heat across her face announced another deep blush. "I can't believe I just said that, about ten minutes into our first date," she muttered apologetically. "I think I've officially had enough wine for this evening." She pushed the glass with its remaining sip away from her and looked at him. He had an amused smile on his face.

"Trust me, if you would invite me to your house, the last thing I would be interested in is Lucifer Falls."

***

"Tell me everything," Bam screamed as Freya closed the door behind her. "I want to know all the sordid details. How was he? Did you kiss?"

"No kiss," Freya said. "We agreed we wouldn't kiss, though there might be kissing in the future, because he wants to take me out again. If you're willing to babysit, that is." She gave Bam her best puppy eyes.

Her friend twirled, her ghostly form looking more solid than ever. "Am I ever!" she cried. "Freya, this is wonderful. What is he like?"

Freya took off her coat and hung it on the cast iron rack near the door. "This guy is amazing. He was so handsome it almost made me uncomfortable. That picture did not do him justice."

"He looks *better* than his picture?" Bam said, gawking, "You have to bring him to the house. I need to see him."

"I don't know if that's such a great idea..."

"Oh, come on. It's not like I'd come out and be all ghosty. I'll just spy on him from a distance." An impish grin played across Bam's lips.

"That's not what I meant. I don't know if it's a good idea to have him over at the house," Freya said. "Though I may have half invited him already... I was a bit tipsy. Drank my wine too fast, and the year of alcohol abstinence has made me a bit of a lightweight." Freya gasped and covered her mouth. "I shouldn't have been drinking anyway, I'm supposed to breast feed." She slapped herself in the forehead. "I'm so stupid. I'll have to look up now how long that stays in your system."

"Relax, Emily will live being bottle-fed for a day or so, and you can just use that breast pump to get rid of the boozy milk." Bam made a dismissive gesture with her hand. "How much did you drink anyway?"

"A little bit more than one glass. I spilled most of my first drink."

"Oh, you were clumsy."

"Oh yes, I also knocked over the candle twice and made a napkin smolder, until we decided I shouldn't be near an open fire ever again." Freya bit her lip.

"Aww, you must, like, really like this guy," Bam cooed. "You get extra clumsy when you like someone."

"Yay me," Freya said sarcastically.

"But he liked you enough to ask you on a second date."

"Yeah, apparently he likes 'em clumsy."

They both laughed.

"Oh, and guess what?" Freya said. "He's a paranormal investigator."

Bam raised an eyebrow. "Did he ask you about the house?"

"No, in fact, he hasn't heard of it. He's here for Lucifer Falls, though."

Bam pursed her lips. "Perhaps he can, like, tell you a bit more about it? Since we still have a bazillion questions."

"Yeah, maybe," Freya said. "How is Emily?"

"Slept the whole time like a baby," Bam assured her. "Didn't wake up once."

"Would you mind preparing her a bottle and bringing it to me upstairs?" Freya asked. "I'm going to feed her before I go to bed."

"No problem," Bam said as she floated through the wall.

Freya almost ran to the nursery. Emily was awake when she entered the small room. The baby kicked her legs excitedly as Freya bent over her crib. She pulled the baby from her white cloud and held her close.

"Your Aunty Bam was right, Emily. We need people around us if we're going to stay sane," she whispered against the baby's head. "We'll need each other, but we will need others too." She kissed the baby's warm skin and sighed. "I feel more human already. Just from having one drink with a nice guy. And he *was* nice, Emily. He was so nice…"

A solid hand rested on her shoulder, and Freya turned around in surprise. Her eyes met the dark eyes of the house. It looked at her solemnly from the face of a young girl with black ringlets.

"Why are you here?" Freya asked, her heart suddenly pounding in her throat.

"Something is coming…" the house whispered. "You need to protect me."

"I have to protect you?"

The house nodded. "I'm afraid…"

CHAPTER SEVEN

"Do not enter, for you can easily get lost," Koji Akagi translated in his flawless American accent. He pulled on the yellow-and-black-striped rope that barred the path. He adjusted his glasses. Two signs, one small and yellow with black letters, the other a larger white one with a red slash through it, dangled on the end. The rope was tied on each side to some low hanging branches, and it swung lightly when he let go.

"Looks like we're on the right path, dude," George Hamish, a tall, chubby guy with curly hair and little black-rimmed glasses—which looked similar to Koji's own—grinned. "Enter we shall." He stepped over the rope and held it up.

"We're already fucking lost," Tara Creed said with a wink at Koji. "Lost causes." Her accent betrayed she was a New Yorker, born and bred. She was a hardened soul with a tragic past, but somehow she managed to be the one who kept all of them together. Koji admired her strength, though she frightened him a little at times.

Tara pulled her brown locks in a ponytail before she slipped under the rope, then stepped aside to let the rest of the group through. There were seven of them in all: some students of the film academy, some actors, all of them American except Koji. They were close, all bonded by their fascination for film and the macabre. When Koji had mentioned his grandparents lived close to the borders of Aokigahara, they had been enchanted with the myths and legends surrounding the suicide forest. The plans developed quickly for making their own horror documentary with live footage in the woods. The first two weeks, they would just go exploring, and film whatever they could find. After that, their movie would become more scripted. Parts of the footage would be uploaded to YouTube as a teaser for the film, in the hopes it would fool people into thinking this was a straight up documentary rather than a work leading up to fiction.

Tara was the brains behind this master plan, and they had all followed her lead. Japan had been the perfect setting for their film. Aokigahara was filled with so many myths for them to work with, and the forest itself was visually stunning. According to Amy, the only great horror movies that were ever created all came from Japan. Not everyone agreed with this, and many nights were spent discussing the merits of different cultures within the horror industry.

Now that they were actually here, in the middle of the forest, some of the bravado they had shown during the planning turned to a more timid feeling of awe. The denseness of the local flora was overwhelming to anyone who saw it for the first time. The underlying myths and the morbid truths about this place seemed be absorbed by nature itself.

"Where are we going to set up our tents?" Lucas Johnston asked, removing his Green Bay Packers ball cap and wiping his forehead. "This place isn't exactly level, ya know? It's going to be difficult to pitch them."

"How are we going to put the pegs in this hard ground anyway?" William Smith asked, digging his toes in the thin layer of soil. "There's volcanic rock under here."

Tara put her fists on her hips and cocked her head. "Don't you think I've thought of all that?" She looked from William to Lucas. "I did some fucking research before we came. Stop tripping about the tents. I have an idea. If we can't find a good spot, we'll pitch them on the path, and we'll set them up the way rock climbers do. Easy peasy."

Amy Steward put her arm around Tara's shoulders, as she stared at the two boys. "I suggest we make setting up camp our main priority. I would like to have a base that we can work from. You know, set up the batteries, get some of the stuff hooked up, that sort of thing."

Lucas raised his eyebrows so far his cap moved. "God forbid you'd be unplugged from the modern world for more than three minutes," he said in his thick Wisconsin accent.

She pulled back and pointed at him. "Oh, I'm never unplugged for more than one, Lucalicious." She gave him a wicked grin. "I'm connected 24/7." She held up her phone, which was showing nothing more than a blank screen, while she mouthed "connected." Then she turned around with a twirl and made her way to Koji, who was uncomfortable with her propensity for close physical contact. Lucas pulled his cap back over his forehead and muttered, "Let's see how long your phone will stay connected in this place." He made eye contact with Koji and asked, "Why did we bring her again?"

"Because she's the best camerawoman we have," Tara said, trying to hide her laugh. "We can't help it that you banged her."

Lucas cringed. "One night... I was drunk."

They all laughed at him, and William patted him on the shoulder. "Come on, Lucalicious," he said in a mock falsetto, "we got some tents to pitch."

Lucas punched him on the arm, but there was a smile on his lips.

They walked deeper into the woods. The path became narrower as they moved forward, becoming less path-like with each step, and the overgrowth had taken over like crawling intruders.

"It's so quiet here," Summer Beauregard said. She pulled her white knitted cardigan over her slender, tanned shoulders. Summer was the perfect name for the slight girl with the light blonde hair and pale blue eyes, who always had a warmth about her. "It wasn't this quiet when we went in." She wore a shy grin.

They all stopped to listen for a moment. It *was* very quiet. Not unnaturally so; the wind could still be heard rustling the leaves, and here and there the snaps of twigs betrayed that there was more life than met the eye. But the overall stillness was unsettling.

"There's not even birds singing, or anything." Summer let out a nervous giggle.

Tara nodded, her eyes still peeled on the green canopy of trees. "This place is really perfect. I hope we can get this fucking creepy atmosphere caught on tape."

The corners of Summer's lips twitched. "Right," she said, taking a deep breath.

CHAPTER EIGHT

"Wow, I take it all back. Dolls aren't cute at all. At least not those ones. They're, like, really creepy." Bam pulled her knees to her face, the way she had done when she was alive. She sat huddled in one of the grand chairs in the living area and stared at the row of dolls that Freya had put out, nine of them in total now, gradually sent over the past few weeks. They were beautifully made and probably antique. Each had come with a note that read their name, though she couldn't remember any of them. Freya glanced at her friend, who looked so real. She had barely been translucent for the longest time, and she hadn't had any of her weird spells. For a moment, it seemed nothing had ever happened, as if Bam had never died, as if she were solid. Having a dead person in her life was conflicting.

The dolls sat and stared at her with their blank eyes. Whoever had sent them had taken good care of them. Aside from the colour of the clothes being faded, they looked good as new. They even smelled nice, as if someone had washed them with lavender perfumed soap.

"I don't know what to do with them," Freya said. "These must be worth a fortune. And they're not sent to me, but to Emily. I can't just get rid of them." She picked up one of the smaller dolls and moved its arms so that it clapped its hands. "And at the same time, I still don't feel comfortable accepting gifts from a total stranger."

"You didn't have any problems accepting money."

"That's different. I see the money as payment for a job I'm doing." Freya stretched her arms. "I'm keeping the world safe, and it's only right that I'm compensated. But these dolls... I just don't know if they come from the same person. It feels different. Who would send a bunch of expensive porcelain dolls to a baby? I never liked it, but it just gets weirder with each one I get, and now I'm second guessing if I should have accepted them at all."

Bam cocked her head and narrowed her eyes at the dolls. "You got a letter with this doll, right?"

"Yeah, well, another card, but it was an anonymous one again. No explanation, just an instruction. It said that I should put the dolls in the nursery, because they would protect Emily. Which in itself was odd enough." Freya sighed and leaned back her head. "The thing is, they actually might. Remember those gold shields that we sold? Those were magical, too. Maybe these dolls are the same thing?"

"Maybe," Bam said, her face still serious.

"I'm really sick of all this mystery." Freya put the doll down and wrapped her grey cardigan tighter around her shoulders. The chill of the evening had set into the house, and the fire hadn't managed to heat up the large room yet.

There was no sympathy in Bam's face. "Sorry to say it, Frey, but suck it up, buttercup." Bam's voice was not cold, but firm. "Your life has been pretty sweet lately, I would say."

"It has, which is exactly why I'm so stressed right now."

"You're stressed because you're feeling happy?" Bam shook her head. "You really are a sucker for punishment, aren't you? You got this hot guy totally doting over you and you're mewling about everything."

"I'm not mewling," Freya said, slightly indignant. "I'm stressed because I have only a few weeks left before the winter solstice and I haven't even made progress on finding a victim yet. Wulf has been too much of a distraction. I..." Her blood ran cold at a thought she didn't dare to say out loud.

"Oh, for fuck's sake, Frey," Bam said, erecting herself to

her full height. "There is still enough time, and no, you won't have to kill another guy you like just to make a sacrifice. Stop freaking out over that. It's, like, getting on my nerves."

"I'm sorry, I didn't mean to be such a baby about it all, but..."

Bam stood over her, and suddenly she looked so tall and so ancient despite her pink hair and young face. "I get it. Killing Logan left a scar. But in a couple of weeks, you are going into Edinburgh and you are going to find a homeless person. It never takes you a long time to care for these people. Hell, you'd suffer for killing them even if you took some random victim, because that's the kind of person you are. But you, like, always need to go that extra mile of suffering, just to be sure, or something. Whatever. It'll be fine. And then you'll mourn for a few days, and you'll pick yourself up again, and maybe you will finally get hot and heavy with that dreamy guy of yours. Which would be about time. It's been almost three weeks."

"What if I'm not allowed to be happy?" Freya asked in a small voice.

"Get over yourself. Seriously. You can be happy and miserable all at the same time, just like the rest of us. Wulf is not a distraction, he's an anchor. And you need to stop coming up with excuses not to let him close. He's been the dutiful friend to you for the past three weeks, taking you out to dinner and movies, but you and I know you both want more."

"He told me he wouldn't do anything until I was ready," Freya said. "I told him I might never be ready."

"What did he say?"

"That as much as he would like this to be more than a friendship, if friendship was all I could offer him, he would gladly take it." She smiled at the memory. "He said my friendship was by no means a pity prize."

"I would have so humped his bones if he had said that to me," Bam said wistfully.

"You know, maybe I should invite him here sometime... let him meet Emily. And you, though not directly. Or maybe I should let you meet, since he's interested in supernatural phenomena. You can't get much more supernatural than you."

"I put the super in supernatural," Bam said. She spread her arms out and struck a pose.

Freya grinned at her, but her face fell flat.

"What?" Bam asked.

"After all the bad stuff that has been happening, it's weird to accept that sometimes good stuff can happen too," she admitted.

"Look at it this way, hon. Sometimes life totally gives us something in return for all the shit we, like, have to put up with. There are times life gives us gifts in the form of hunky men, and there are times that that gift comes in the shape of creepy dolls. If that happens, then so fucking be it." She took a floating step toward the dolls and reached out to one of them. A blue spark flew from the porcelain with the sound of a hiss and a pop, knocking Bam back several feet. Bam disappeared as she hit the ground, and Freya screamed. She ran toward the place where her friend had disappeared and touched the floor. Her hands ran across the wooden floorboards, trying to find any sign of Bam, even though she realized that it was madness.

"Bam," she cried out. "Bam, where are you? You can't leave me alone. You can't leave me." Tears were flowing again, and the raw panic was blanking out her thoughts. She couldn't think straight, and she just didn't know what to do.

"Bam," she sobbed.

"Now we know what the dolls do," a voice behind her

said. Freya turned, and relief washed over her as she saw the spirit of her friend hovering near. Bam's eyes were round—she looked frazzled—and she stared at the porcelain army. "They ward off ghosts."

Bam turned to her with that wide-eyed look, and for a moment there was perfect silence, until they both started laughing again, this time in a combination of nerves and relief.

"Oh god, I was so scared I had lost you," Freya said.

"That thing knocked me straight through the ground. I think I actually disappeared for a second." Bam moved closer to Freya and the laughter died from their lips. "Holy cow." She shuddered. "Don't put them in Emily's room. Not unless you need to. They make me uncomfortable, and they'd hurt me if I were to accidentally touch them."

Freya got to her feet and looked at her friend. "I won't. I'm not about to ward off my number-one babysitter."

"If Chuck ever gets out, though..." Bam looked at her, and Freya averted her eyes. "Not that I think he can get around the protective spells we have up already, but still..."

"If Chuck gets out, I'm getting an exorcist. If it wasn't for me being afraid of losing you in the progress, I'd have him exorcised in the blink of an eye. I don't like having that bastard in my house, where my child sleeps."

"It's going to be fine," Bam said. "Just find a nice place to put those... like, far away from me." She sneered at the porcelain figures. "Now that I know what they do, I suddenly feel really uncomfortable around them. Even at a safe distance."

"Well, at least we know whoever sent them means well. It's nice to have someone looking out for us," Freya said. She gathered four of the nine dolls in her arms. Their porcelain bodies were cold to her chest, as if they had been outside for a long time.

"That's a good thing," Bam said.

"I'll put these in the storage room. There's nothing but crap in there anyway; I don't think you'll want to go there."

"How about you put them in your panic room?" Bam offered. "I can't go in there anyway, and if something happens, you and Emily will just have some extra security."

"Good idea," Freya nodded, though the idea of being stuck in that tiny room with these dolls didn't ease her thoughts. "I just hope whoever is sending these creepy things, they'll stop. I think nine of them is enough."

CHAPTER NINE

They had set up camp in a small clearing that wasn't too far from the path. All of them agreed this was the best course of action, seeing as they didn't want to get lost. The forest was not only very large, but the density of the flora made it difficult to navigate. Koji knew a little, but not enough to be a confident guide. Besides, they still needed to go into town for their provisions, so they couldn't go too deep into the Jukai.

They had been rather careful these past few weeks, sticking together and going out in teams instead of alone. Walkie-talkies served as the main way to communicate with each other, since their cell phones didn't work this far into the woods. They'd all chipped in for a satellite phone, because "you never knew what could happen" and Koji was the burdened bearer of the damn thing. He was fluent, and no one else spoke more than a few words of Japanese. Tara had tried to learn some basics before they left, but she wouldn't be able to have more than a very superficial conversation with anyone.

They had encountered quite a bit of bad luck with equipment that refused to work, and the tension had been mounting. Living together in the close quarters of an uncomfortable camp did not help the mood. Aside from the faulty equipment, the lighting was poor in the woods, and they only had a few hours a day to utilise if they wanted to get the right shots. As much as they thought they had prepared, it became obvious that this project was bigger than they had expected. Tara didn't like how far behind they were with filming as a result, and there was a general disappointment that they hadn't found anything beyond a very old tent and some discarded possessions so far.

The others had decided to go and explore again while

the light was still good—going a bit deeper into the woods this time, and leaving Koji at the camp on his own. He'd busied himself with tidying up the campsite, but the group stayed away longer than expected and he decided to lie down on his air mattress and read for a while. Somewhere in his backpack, he also had a copy of *Kuroi Jukai*, a romanticised story of two lovers taking their own lives in these very woods, which was the book that had truly transformed the Aokigahara into the suicide forest. *Jukai*— loosely translated as sea of trees—was the name the locals gave these woods, and *Kuroi Jukai* meant black sea of trees. He had picked the book up on a whim while they were travelling, in a little bookshop. Yet, somehow, he couldn't bring himself to read it, when he was alone in the actual woods, so instead he grabbed his kindle and opened *Harry Potter and the Goblet of Fire*.

He had expected the Aokigahara to be creepy, so when they first entered the woods, he had been relieved that it wasn't as bad as he thought. But the deeper they went into the forest, the more oppressive it became. The nature didn't change that much, nor did anything that was visibly apparent. But there was something menacing that Koji simply couldn't describe, and the longer they stayed the more nervous he became. He understood what drew people to this place, and why they chose to take their lives. It tickled a deeply rooted inner darkness in him. There was something strangely liberating about the Jukai, as if it offered a morbid freedom from the daily oppression. Koji had lived most of his life in the US, but he knew from his upbringing there was a lot of pressure on his people to live by certain "codes." This thick forest broke all the rules and saw you for what you really were... a being of raw, chaotic emotions. It was appealing and appalling all at once.

"*Kon'nichiwa?*" *Hello*? A high-pitched Japanese male voice startled Koji, and he dropped the book. Embarrassed, he turned over and stuck his head out the yellow tent.

"Hello," he replied in Japanese, as he looked up at the man who sat squatted outside. The stranger was short, with a long forehead and receding hairline. Koji guessed him to be around fifty. The man wore thick, black-rimmed glasses, a dark blue rain-resistant coat, and a black backpack on his shoulders. The most startling thing about him were the snow-white gloves on his hands, which were a bright contrast to his dark clothes.

"Are you okay?" the man asked in his hoarse, high voice, the polite smile showing a hint of concern.

"Eh... yeah?" Koji wasn't sure if he should come out of his tent or stay. He was sort of frozen to the spot, sitting in an uncomfortable squatted position.

"I'm the nature guard," the man said. "I'm on suicide watch."

"Oh," Koji said, barely able to hide his relief. "Right."

"How long are you staying?" The man sat perfectly still and balanced, as if he were sitting on a little stool, his elbows resting on his knees, his hands in front of him.

"A week or two. Not too long," Koji answered, feeling the way he used to when he would be called into the principal's office. "I... I'm here with friends. We've been here for a while now."

The man's face brightened with relief. "Ah, you come here to see the forest."

"Yes. We... we're doing a documentary on it." Koji crawled forward, out of the tent, and got to his feet. The man was shorter than he was, and Koji wasn't tall himself. He scratched his head and gave the man a crooked smile.

"That's good," the man said, his voice even higher now. "I was just worried."

"Yeah, no, of course." Koji thought he would be worried too, if he found a guy in a tent in these woods. "You're on suicide watch." He felt sheepish as he said it.

"Yes. I come here once a month and do what I can to

help."

"That's really good. Do... do you find a lot of, erm...?" Koji grimaced, pushing his glasses to the very top of his nose.

"I have found over a hundred dead bodies, if that's what you're asking." There was sadness in the man's face. "I report them to the authorities when I do find them."

"Right." Koji was struck by a sudden idea. "Listen, my friends are doing a documentary."

"You mentioned that," the man said.

"Perhaps you would let us interview you? Since you know this place so well?" The idea excited him. They had talked about interviewing locals, but they had been a little divided on the matter. This guy would be perfect, if he wasn't camera shy.

"I wouldn't mind helping you. My name is Hayashi Toshiro," the man said, using his last name first, as was custom, "but please call me Toshiro. What is yours?"

"I'm Tsukino Koji. Please call me Koji. I'm here with a group of American friends."

"I thought I heard something in your accent," Toshiro said with a friendly smile. "I suspected you weren't raised here."

Koji nodded. He was about to mention his grandmother used to say the same thing, when he heard the voices of his friends approaching. William's deep voice was audible above all the others.

"Perfect timing," Koji said. "Come and meet my friends."

"Koji, you should see what we found..." Summer was the first to reach them, holding out something that looked like a dirt-covered white booklet. She stopped in her tracks and raised her eyebrows when she saw the man.

"Summer," Koji said, then he glanced at the others behind her. "Guys, meet Toshiro. He's a nature guard and knows a lot about this place. He's here on suicide watch." Koji shot Tara a meaningful glance. "And he doesn't mind being interviewed."

Excitement lit up their faces and they crowded around Koji and Toshiro, muttering a mixture of English and Japanese greetings. The newcomer smiled and nodded at everyone. It was Tara who shushed the muttering.

"Give me a second to prepare some questions," she said. "Koji, you're going to have to interview him. It's best if you just let him talk as much as possible. We'll translate later and put subtitles under him, or dub him, whatever works. Maybe we can even do something a bit more dynamic, like follow him around while he shows us some of the forest?" She looked from Koji to Toshiro.

Koji translated her words, and the stranger nodded: he wouldn't mind showing them the route he was taking.

"We need to move fast, while we still have the light." Tara pointed at George. "I'll need you and Amy for camera and sound. Koji will do the interview, and I'll direct. The rest of you can stay here. We need to hustle before we run out of daylight. I'd say we have two hours max."

Amy ran to fetch her camera while George strapped on his portable audio recorder and armed himself with a boom mike.

While Tara scribbled some questions, Koji turned to Toshiro. "You can tell us what you're doing as we walk. Perhaps you know an interesting place to guide us to."

"I can think of many interesting places. There was a place I just passed. You might have some findings there."

Koji's blood ran cold. "Did... did you find a body?"

Toshiro shook his head. "No, just remnants of someone who passed through. There are many paths that lead to such places. I can show you them."

Amy moved her way around them, her camera ready, and George still fiddled with his sound.

"Ask him about this," Summer said softly as she pushed the white booklet into Koji's hands. "I think it's something interesting."

Koji looked at it, and a cold chill ran down his spine. It read: "The Complete Guide to Suicide," by Wataru Tsurumi. "It's a suicide manual," he muttered and saw Summer cringe.

"We're ready," Tara stated, signaling to Koji. He cleared his throat, and at the word "action," he made a nervous introduction of his guest. The camera wasn't pointed at him, only at Toshiro, whom he asked to tell them something about the forest.

It was obvious the man had been on camera before. Koji knew they weren't the only tourists interested in the morbid tale behind the woods. Toshiro spoke naturally, with the air of someone who had a great passion for Aokigahara. He told the camera he had lived here for over thirty years, that he was a geologist, and that his job was mainly environmental protection. As he walked, he told how he studied volcanic eruptions, and the plantation at the foot of Mount Fuji. His job had started out being just that, but on his journeys, he had found so many poor souls in the woods that they had affected his life in a way. Other than his studies, he made regular hikes which he called "suicide prevention patrols." He would try to find the living who were still in doubt, and he would talk to them.

"Often," he said, directly into the camera, "a kind word, or a little company, can prevent someone from doing a terrible thing. This is a bit of a calling of mine."

"Are there many people who aren't sure?" Koji asked. He pushed his glasses further up his nose. It had become a habit over the years.

The man sped up his step and beckoned for them to follow. "Let me show you something," he said. They made their way past thick bushes and down a slippery slope, to a clearing where they saw at least a dozen different ribbons. It looked like a combination of a crime scene and a children's party. There were many different colours, but most of them were blue, green or yellow.

"What is this?" Koji asked.

"Aokigahara is notoriously big, and people are afraid to get lost. It's those who aren't sure that need a way back. They bring this tape, which they use to mark their path. That way, they can leave should they want to."

"Like Theseus and the labyrinth," Koji said, deep in thought. "They face their own minotaur in a way." The man nodded, but Koji wasn't sure he understood the reference, judging by the blank expression.

"I believe it's not just those who are in doubt who spin these colorful paths. A lot of people wish to be found... after. There is a belief that if the bodies are not found, the Jukai claims the souls. They spend eternity lost and screaming while their bodies shuffle around searching for company."

"I've heard these myths about suicide, too. I always thought they were to discourage people from killing themselves."

"Jukai has always appealed to those who sought death. Even before it became famous as the suicide forest, it was a place where people brought their elders if they couldn't take care of them anymore. They would abandon them here. *Ubasute*, it's called."

Ubasute. Koji knew this darker side of his birth land well; it was still very much present in many of the Japanese poems and myths.

"At first, it was only the locals who came here to die," Toshiro said, adjusting his glasses. "But in 1960,

Matsumoto Seicho wrote *Kuroi Jukai*, and that gave the Aokigahara a new voice. Suddenly, people from all over Japan came to this place as a final stop in life." He shook his head and ran a hand through his hair. "I have even found the bodies of foreigners. It always surprises me that there are those who are willing to die in a strange place, where the spirits are so different from their own."

A soft breeze played with the leaves and the plastic ribbons swayed gently back and forth. Toshiro looked at them and touched a blue one. "I often follow these," he said. "There's always something at the end. Not always death; most of the time, it's a sign of life that has passed through, but sometimes I find a body." He beckoned them, and he walked off, taking the path of the blue ribbon. Koji stared at the black backpack, then followed, staying out of the way of Amy and George, who were capturing every movement.

They trailed the tape, which weaved its way through the open areas of the forest like a plastic path. Koji was aware of the heavy pounding of his heart, and from the silent way they all walked, he suspected he wasn't the only one who was nervous about where the blue ribbon led.

"You are leading us to the place you went to before?" Koji asked.

"No, I've not followed this ribbon yet." The man never looked around. The blood drained from Koji's face. He wasn't sure if he was prepared to find anything quite yet. Not this late in the day... maybe not ever, even though he knew this was what they had come for.

The blue ribbon moved away from the cluster, off on its own tangent. The woods were getting darker and denser, and it became a struggle to walk without getting snagged on some of the more prickly plants. Amy almost fell once, nearly dropping her camera. They had to ask Toshiro to slow down his pace, as the little man was too fast. He nodded, but there was a determined look in his face. Koji wondered if the man was preparing himself for finding a potential body, too. It couldn't scare Toshiro as much as it did him; after all, he had seen over a hundred corpses. Yet, it couldn't be easy either. Could it ever become easy to find those who had taken their own lives?

The blue tape stopped. The last part was tied to a low-hanging tree branch. At first sight, there was nothing around.

"Normally, we find signs of humanity," Toshiro said. "We find a tent, or some personal possessions. Things that have been discarded." He looked around.

"There's something over there," Koji pointed at a green plastic construction that stood a distance farther between some bushes. "It looks like a tent."

"Guys, I just spotted something over *there*." It was Amy who spoke. They followed her voice and found her staring at a porcelain doll nailed upside down to a tree. The sight of it made Koji uneasy. There was something extremely unsettling about the image.

"It's not Japanese." Toshiro examined the doll. "It's a Western thing. One of the tourists must have left it."

"Are you getting this?" Tara urged Amy closer to the tree. She took a long shot of the doll, getting it from all angles.

"This looks staged somehow," Amy said. "You can't 'nail' a porcelain doll to a tree. It'd break."

"Maybe there were other movie makers," Tara said. "This could be a prop that people forgot to take with them. It reminds me of something out of a horror flick." She turned to them. "We'll edit that out. Let's use it as some scary symbolism instead. Our audience will love it." She shrugged. "We should check out that tent."

They approached the green plastic shelter with solemn care. There was a heavy scent of gasoline in the air, which made Koji wonder. Why would anyone bring gas to a forest?

"Let Toshiro open the tent, but Amy stay on him." Tara motioned for everyone to stay out of the shot. "We want to get the suspense as he looks inside."

Koji translated to the older man, who looked troubled. "I think I should look in first. If there's nothing there, the camera can look too."

"That would make the tension less interesting for the viewers," Tara explained, while Koji translated. "We'll blank out the faces if there are any people inside."

The geologist frowned again, but reluctantly agreed to let Amy get close. He called out, asking if anyone was there, but there was no response. When he opened the flap, shock registered on his face, and nausea made Koji's stomach turn.

"Oh my god," whispered Amy. "There's someone in there." She didn't move, her camera pointed to the inside of the tent.

"Are they dead?" Koji asked, afraid to look.

"He's covered in blood. It's fucking everywhere. He has to be dead, he's just lying there with his eyes open."

Koji looked at Tara, who had her hand raised to her mouth.

"What do we do now?" he asked in Japanese.

"I make a note of where I found him and tell the authorities." Toshiro looked crestfallen. He took a step back. "It's a Western boy."

Koji couldn't resist. He leaned in, and as soon as he peered inside the tent, he regretted it instantly. The whole interior was covered in blood. Not just a splatter; it looked like someone had thrown buckets of red paint around. The corpse of a man no older than twenty lay on top of a soaked sleeping bag. His eyes were wide open, but rolled back all the way—white circles in a sea of red, staring at nothing.

Blood-stained hands were bent into claws, stretched out in front of him. His blond hair stuck up in red spikes. It was the single worst thing Koji had ever seen in his life. Bile rose up in his throat and soured his tongue. For a moment, he thought he would vomit, but he managed to swallow the acidic taste.

"What the hell happened here?" Koji said in English. "This doesn't look like an ordinary suicide. How did he die?" He leaned even closer. "Jesus, this blood is still wet. This didn't happen that long ago."

There was a silence around him, and his stomach dropped. *Could we have prevented this?*

Suddenly, the corpse moved. It was so fast that Koji barely had time to register what was going on. His heart almost stopped, and he screamed. The corpse shot toward him. Fingernails raked painfully across the skin of his cheeks. Koji's screams were joined by those of the others. Amy was still hiding behind her camera, but she moved away. They all tried to move away from the tent. Koji was on his back, crawling backward like a spider as the thing in the tent moved forward.

"Laney," it moaned. "Laney..."

The eyes were so wide, stark blue against the red of the blood, rolling around in his head, and his mouth was wide open in a horrified gape. The man stopped crawling. Instead, he curled into a little ball and started to cry.

"Holy shit," George said. "Is he hurt?"

Toshiro bent down and began examining the man for wounds. The man on the floor looked emaciated. His skin seemed to hang loose over his bones.

"Are you okay?" Tara's voice sounded shaky. "What the fuck happened to you?"

The man didn't respond; all he said was "Laney" between sobs. His shoulders shook, and he made a strange wheezy noise as he cried.

"Who's Laney?" George asked. "Is *she* okay?"

"The blood can't be his," Toshiro said in Japanese. "I can't find any wounds on him. The blood must belong to someone else."

Tara squatted next to Koji, who was still sitting on the ground. "What did he say?" she asked.

"He said the blood doesn't belong to the guy. It's someone else's."

Tara grimaced and leaned back. "That's a little disconcerting. I hope he's not a fucking killer or anything."

"Come on Tara, would he be lying in a tent, wigged out as fuck, if he was a killer?" George asked.

"Maybe. You'd have to be pretty fucked up to kill people and splatter their blood all over a fucking tent." Tara looked angry. "Koji, do you have that satellite phone?"

Koji nodded, then changed his mind and shook his head. "It's back at the camp."

"I'll go get it," Tara said. "You guys stay here." She gave Amy a meaningful glance, and Koji felt a moment of disgust that she'd given the signal to keep filming.

"Laney," the guy called again. "I need to find her."

"Can you tell us what happened? Whose blood that is?" Amy asked, still pointing her camera at the man on the ground. George seemed indecisive as to what to do. He held the boom microphone near, but he looked ready to drop it. His face was pale, his grey eyes were wide, and his mouth was slightly open. He kept looking around, as if he were searching for something.

"The blood..." The man looked at his hands now. Whatever shock he was in, he seemed to be brought back to the here and now by their presence. "I... I wasn't sure if it was real, or if I was just going crazy. I feel like I'm going crazy. I've lost so much time. I can't remember, my mind, it... it's playing tricks on me."

Toshiro asked Koji to translate, and he did as well as he could.

"What happened to you?" Amy asked.

"I lost my sister. We saw the doll and then she was gone. So, I went looking. Only... I didn't find her. I... I was so lost and all alone." A sob escaped his lips, and he hid his face behind his bloodied hands. "I don't even know how long I've been here. It feels like I've been here for years, but it could be just days or weeks... Everything is such a blur. I made a fire, and I ate things I could find, if... if I could think straight. But I can't remember most of it. I just remember... Frogs, I ate frogs..." He sobbed again. "Please help me. Surviving, that's what I was doing. Surviving until... until I found that thing..."

"What thing?" Amy asked, her face pale.

"I touched it," he said and then he repeated that same phrase. "I touched it. The man saw me and he... oh god, I touched it. I shouldn't have touched it."

"You touched what?" George asked. "What man? What did he touch?"

"Calm down, guys. Tara's getting the phone, and we'll call someone," Koji said. Toshiro had placed his hand on the sobbing man's arm, and Koji knelt next to him.

"What did you see?" he asked the man, who looked up at him from behind his red fingers.

"I... I'm not sure. There was this thing in the ground. Like a plaque, only... different." He pointed north, staring silently for a few seconds. "I touched it and I heard screaming. There was this guy watching me, and I called for him, but he didn't respond. And then... and then..." His eyes rolled from side to side with the memory, and his voice sounded strangled. "Blood came up from the ground. It was everywhere. Like a red swamp. I ran, but it followed me, welling up from the earth wherever I went. And the screaming, it followed me, too. It was horrible." The man let out a trembling whimper. "I... I found the tent, and just wanted to be safe. When I was inside, something came in with me. It was... it... like a... a... she..." He shuddered. "When it caught me, I thought I died, but then I heard your voices. And I... woke."

Koji swallowed hard. "What came in with you?"

"I think it was a woman, only it wasn't any ordinary woman. She... there was darkness."

Koji turned to Toshiro. "Are there any legends about a woman in this place?"

Toshiro shook his head. "Only about a monk who is supposed to live here. I have yet to meet him, so I don't know if the stories are true."

A gust of wind blew through the trees, making the leaves rustle like soft voices whispering in the night. For a moment, Koji almost thought he could hear words, but he knew it was madness. He looked at Amy, who seemed to be listening to the wind as well. He didn't like the expression on her face.

"I'm going to go look for this plaque he was talking about," Amy said. "We need to catch this on film."

"Are you nuts? There's a blood-covered guy here," Koji snapped. Her coldness bothered him. "Let's just stay together, okay?"

Amy turned to the trees again, as if she could hear them speak to her.

"Come on, I can't pass that up. Do you really believe blood came from the ground? This guy is clearly nuts. Besides, it can't be that far, and if we don't go now, we might not find it again." The dreamy eagerness in her face made his stomach tighten.

"You're going to leave me here with this guy?"

Amy made a face. "You have Toshiro with you. That guy over there weighs like a buck and a half. You two can take him. And Tara will be back at any minute. Don't be a wuss."

"Amy, you always do this. Take unnecessary risks. What's wrong with you?"

"I won't go very far, just take a peek. It'll either confirm his story, or we'll know that we're dealing with a maniac. I'll take George. If it'll make you feel better, I won't get too close, okay? If I find it, I'll make sure we come get you guys."

Koji and George shared a look. He could see the discomfort in the big guy's face. "You don't have to go," Koji said, but George shrugged.

The wind played with the trees, and George turned his head. "There's no danger," he echoed, unconvinced. He shrugged again, his shoulders hanging like a rag doll.

"The blood seems real enough," Koji pleaded. "There could be danger."

"If there's any danger, it's that guy," George muttered. He looked tired. "Keep an eye on him. Tara should be back soon."

"Whatever happened to 'don't split up'?"

"Dude, this isn't a horror film. It'll be fine," George said. "Just focus on that weirdo, and Amy and I will be back before you know it. Besides, she's right. We might not find it again."

Amy called George over. Armed with her camera, she made her way to where the man on the ground had pointed. Koji watched them disappear into the undergrowth with a heavy stomach. He looked at Toshiro, and suddenly felt very abandoned. It wasn't just Amy's choice to leave;

she took risks, but she would have never gone off with a blood-covered guy in their midst. It just wasn't logical, even for Amy. He couldn't figure out why George wasn't seeing it either.

The leaves rustled again, as if they were laughing at him. Jukai was pulling at them. He could feel it. It was driving them apart.

Toshiro looked at him from behind his large glasses.

"I'm afraid," Koji said. The man nodded, but didn't respond. Something was happening, they both sensed it, but Koji wasn't sure what.

CHAPTER TEN

Your life is a precious gift from your parents. Think about them and the rest of your family. You don't have to suffer alone. Call us 0555-22-0110.

She didn't have to see the sign that stood on the main path of the Aokigahara forest to know what it said. The letters, magic in their own way, shone bright in Marie-Claire Florifera's mind's eye. There was power in these words, because they were filled with love and compassion. Unbeknown to the author of them, they had saved many lives. Some even called the number, while other lost souls just had their inner void filled with every syllable carved on that sign. Words could do so much, the old medium knew: they could harm and they could heal.

But not all lost souls were nourished by the magic of compassionate words. Some were drawn into such a darkness that a mere spark of light wasn't enough to guide their way out. This place, Marie-Claire had to admit, was a perfect place to die. It was so still; she had never heard such silence before. It was unnerving to a woman who relied on her ears in a way she couldn't on her eyes, or at least it would have been, had she not been able to see the forest through her third eye. Her corporeal eyes saw nothing of the mortal world, yet they were very sensitive to the world beyond the veil, and she could see both magic and spirits even when those blessed with normal sight couldn't. After last year's incident, when she'd tried to help those young people with their haunted house on the Isle of Skye, her vision had grown even stronger. Aokigahara was molded part by mundane and part by magic, the latter being the parts Marie-Claire could see as clear as day.

Her gift—or curse, depending on which way one chose to look at it—drew her toward the supernatural areas in the world. She had almost died at Angel Manor and had witnessed the brutal deaths of those she cared for. The worst loss had been Ruben... she hadn't even been there for him when he died. After his death, Marie-Claire Florifera wanted to turn her back on the other world. The grief she still felt, and the emptiness his passing had left in her life, was enough to make her want to give in. She had shied away from everything for several months, but the spirits hadn't turned away from her.

Now, more than ever, she had become a beacon for those who had crossed beyond the veil but couldn't move further to truly break away from the mortal world. They spoke to her with greater desperation than before, yet no more coherent. They needed something from her, and they tried to warn her, but she just didn't know what for. Their visits were overwhelming. Something had changed, perhaps in her, or perhaps it had changed on a larger scale, but Marie-Claire couldn't deny it—her experience in Angel Manor had triggered something. If she didn't go to it, it came to her. There was no ignoring it.

In the end, she had made peace with her lot in life and given in. It was a spirit in the shape of a young girl that finally broke her determination. Marie-Claire had struggled to see the child back in her little apartment in Quebec. The child had been nothing more than a shadow, an echo of the past, running through her house. But it had been the need of the spirit that had alerted Marie-Claire. There was such a raw urgency to it that she wasn't able to think about anything else. The child, without words, had touched her heart, as if she were somehow linked to it, and the old medium had known where to go. This place of death and desperation.

Aokigahara.

In her mind's eye, the forest looked different than it did to those who could only see the physical plane. The trees were made of shadows, their leaves formed from dull light. Marie-Claire had seen inanimate objects before—some things were just touched by magic—but she had never seen a whole forest. It was nothing short of a miracle.

There were souls everywhere, just out of reach, peering from between the branches and bushes at her, but never coming closer. She could feel them, but not see them; they were hiding. The only spirit that had revealed itself to her—and so strongly—was that of the young girl who had led her to this place.

Here, in this sea of trees, she could see the girl in her full glory. She was young, only four or five years old. Most of her hair was sleek black, and it hung straight in front of her pale face, with a hint of curls in the back. There was something a little bit off about the girl, as if someone couldn't decide what she should look like. *She's unfinished*. It was just a fleeting thought, but it bothered the old medium. The girl had to have died here—why else would the child lead her to this forest?—though Marie-Clare doubted if it was suicide that would have taken a girl at such a young age.

Perhaps she had just been a local child. With her black hair and pale skin, she looked like she was of mixed race. Though pale, she wasn't quite white, but not quite anything else either. The girl peeked out between the dark locks of hair. The eyes were almond shaped, and as indeterminable as the skin colour Japanese blood, maybe, but mixed with what else?

Marie-Claire took a deep breath, inhaling the scents of Aokigahara. The woods consisted of mostly young evergreen trees, which had a distinct waxy smell to them. The vegetation was thick enough for this forest to gain the nickname "Sea of Trees," amongst other, more sinister monikers. Aokigahara had been a regeneration out of the woods that were destroyed by the lava of Mount Fuji, centuries ago, which made it a relatively young woodland. It was ironic that youth and regeneration would be such a temptation for those who sought to end their lives, Marie-Claire noted. Another inhalation. She could smell something else in the air aside from the evergreen... the scent of death.

The spirit turned and motioned with a hand. *Come with me*. It frightened the old woman to follow the girl deeper into the dark woods, and not for the first time, she missed having people around her. She'd made a promise to herself after Angel Manor that she'd always work alone so no one else would get hurt. But deep in her heart, she knew it was a lie. She needed people in her life.

The girl moved away from her. Not quite walking, not quite floating, but gliding in a way that was unique to the dead. Marie-Claire followed. Her physical disability made the going difficult. The trees were filled with magic, and she could see them. But the undergrowth, the small burrows, and dead branches remained hidden from her sight. Tangles of roots grabbed at her feet, and she fell more than once, cutting open her skin and tearing her clothes.

The obstacles weren't just physical. The desperation of Aokigahara pressed heavy on her heart, whispering to her in the deafening silence, through the leaves. *Life is senseless*, it seemed to say. *There is a better place than this world, a place you will be accepted, and where you will meet those you've loved and lost again.*

"*Je suis une vieille femme folle*," she muttered, grabbing on to the trunk of a tree. *I'm a foolish old woman.* Something snagged at her coat, and she tried to pull herself loose, only to get tangled even further. *What was I thinking, coming here alone?* she thought. Tears ran down her face, and grief tore at her soul. If only she still had Ruben to look after her.

Perhaps there was a reason that she'd been led to this forest. This was a perfect place to die. Hadn't she thought just that a little while ago? The whispering trees could be right. Maybe the only way to stop the pain was to take matters into her own hands. She would finally be at peace. Perhaps she *would* see Ruben again.

Marie-Claire leaned against the trunk of the tree, her eyes closed and her head resting against the rough bark. A small hand touched her face, cold fingers caressing her flesh. She opened her useless eyes. The girl hovered a few feet in the air, staring right at her, but didn't speak, only shook her head. She had never come this close before, and the sight of her snapped the old woman from her crushing sense of despair.

"This forest, it's doing something to me," she whispered. "It's trying to seduce me to be a part of it... but why?"

The girl answered by pointing deeper into the green darkness.

"There's something out there?"

The girl nodded. She held out her tiny hand, and Marie-Claire placed her own wrinkled hand in it. To her surprise, the girl was as solid as any living being. She had experienced this only once before. A year ago... in Angel Manor.

Marie-Claire shuddered, but she followed the child deeper into Aokigahara.

CHAPTER ELEVEN

"Does it live up to its haunted house reputation?" Freya asked as she opened the door to Wulf. The cold had turned his cheeks a deep pink color, and his green eyes sparkled.

"Maybe before you renovated it," Wulf said. "You still haven't told me anything about your experiences with this house, so to be honest, I don't really know what reputation it's trying to live up to."

Freya gently slapped him on the shoulder. "Don't tell me you haven't asked the locals about the stories. Some researcher you are." She shook her head.

"I told you, until you brought it up, I had no interest in this house." Wulf stepped inside. He looked around the entrance hall with a moderate expression of awe. "I decided I would rather hear the stories from you. If I find them interesting enough, then I'll talk to the locals. It's been tough enough getting those people to talk about Lucifer Falls."

"Did you see it coming up?" Freya asked.

"It's kinda hard to miss." Wulf said with an impish smile on his face. "I have seen it several times before, though. I just haven't gotten close to it yet, which is something I plan to do during the solstice. Apparently, that's when I have the highest chance to read some of its EMF."

The blood drained from Freya's face, and she took a deep breath to steady herself. "Yeah, both the equinoxes and the solstices have a strong effect on the spiritual world," she said softly.

Wulf gave her a curious look. "You've hinted that you've had experiences, but you've never elaborated." He ran his fingers across the side of her face, pushing a lock of hair behind her ear. His touch made her knees tremble.

"I don't know if I'm ready to talk about it yet," Freya admitted. "Stuff has happened to me, and it's all very complicated. We've only known each other three weeks, and though I really do feel I can trust you, I..."

He leaned in, his eyes holding hers, and his hand rested on her cheek. "No rush. This is your thing, and if you want to tell me, I'm here. I just don't want you to feel that I'm putting pressure on you. If you never want to tell me, I'm okay with that."

She touched his hand and smiled. "Thank you. But I promise I will show you something out of the ordinary tonight, if you think you're ready for it."

"I was born ready."

Freya shook her head. "Trust me, you weren't." She looked past his shoulder and saw her reflection in the mirror, except... it wasn't her. The dark eyes staring back at her were not her own. *The house is watching*, she thought. A wave of nausea churned through her stomach. The house moved in the mirror's reflection, touching Wulf, running her hands through his hair and kissing his ear. Freya blushed and her heart raced.

"I need you to make me a promise," she said with a hint of urgency, holding up her index finger. "I am dead serious about this."

"Okay," he said, the smile fading from his lips. "Shoot."

"This house is dangerous. Or, at least, it was. I don't know for sure if it still is, but there are definitely dangers. I can't have you wandering around here. You need to stay in the places where I tell you to go, which is the part of the house I live in."

"You do make it sound tempting to wander," he said with a wink, but when she shot him an angry glare, he looked like a scolded schoolboy. "I won't go off on my own, I promise. If there are parts of the house you wish to show me, I will obviously not object, but I won't go roaming around on my own." He crossed his heart with two fingers. "I swear."

"Good," she said, "because people have died in this house, and I don't want you to join them."

***

"I need to rest, *ma petite*," Marie-Claire said, and she let go of the cold, soft hand. She turned her blind eyes to the child. "I'm an old woman, *tu sais*." *You know.*

The spirit nodded, standing very still. Marie-Claire sat down on the uncomfortable ground. She sensed an unusual number of rocks under her hands. She clenched her fingers around one of them and lifted it. There was no magic in them, so she had to see with her touch rather than her mind. The rock was the size of her hand, mostly smooth with rough edges. It made her wonder what these woods looked like to those who could see, if it would look very different from any normal forest. It certainly looked different to her.

Whatever was in the trees, it came from the earth, and it had a voice. The dead girl's touch had muted the whispers, but now that she was sitting down, Marie-Claire could hear them again. Thousands of faint voices that spoke quietly of sacrifice.

"It's no coincidence that people die here, is it? The ones who battle darkness are drawn to this place for a reason." She looked at the girl. It was amazing how bright she looked, how real. Marie-Claire had learned that spirits with a physical form were far more dangerous than any other, but that didn't worry her. There was a reason why she was here, and if it was to die, then so be it. The woods made death sound so appealing. Darkness was spreading in her heart again, tugging at her, telling her it would be okay to rest. She wanted to give in, but instead she got to her feet.

"I think I need you to help me, petite," she said. "This forest is very intent on having my soul, and you seem to be the only thing that stills the whispers."

The spirit offered her a cold hand, and once again they made their way through the forest.

***

His eyes were in the house now, though he couldn't see clearly. There were too many forces that blurred his vision. The guardian—what a lovely creature she was—had locked his dolls up in a place where magic was contained. Not that it mattered; he would send someone to release his precious children soon enough. What bothered him was the guardian's reaction to his present. What woman did not like beautiful porcelain dolls for her baby girl? Why would she not display them? She had just thrown them in a pile on the floor, and her actions had enraged him.

There were others in the house, which was an inconvenience to him; he had wanted the guardian and her child alone, isolated. One was of the world beyond, and she would potentially be the biggest threat to him. She was strong too, the pink-haired spirit girl. When she touched his doll, he could feel her power. It was still so strong, even after his many efforts of weakening her, but his magic simply couldn't touch her in the way he wanted it to. Spirits had no blood, and that made his magic less effective. Especially with this girl, who was protected by something—but by what?

It was important he get rid of her first. Her presence could mess with his plans, and the last thing he wanted was for the guardian to have allies. Especially not strong ones. He knew how to do it. Before the guardian had locked his dolls away, the doll maker had let them roam around the house. It was only a matter of time before he would set things in motion. Angel Manor would be his, and he would claim it with blood.

CHAPTER TWELVE

"What are you trying to show me, *enfant*?" Marie-Claire's back and feet ached from all the unaccustomed walking. "We've been in the woods for hours now. I'm getting cold and sore, and I feel terribly lost."

The spirit looked at her. It didn't speak to her exactly, not like some of them did, but somehow Marie-Claire knew she was telling her that it would be a little while longer. There was something Marie-Claire had to witness.

"That doesn't answer my question. You dragged me out here, to this place of suffering... what are you trying to show me?"

An image appeared in her mind. It wasn't clear, but there was a feeling that accompanied it: a feeling of dread. Even if she couldn't quite make out what it was, the image made sense.

"There's something in this forest that's drawing these poor souls to it," Marie-Claire whispered. "It is turning them into... martyrs..." As she said the last word, she felt an overwhelming surge of the emotion coming from the spirit.

Marie-Claire straightened herself, despite the pain in her feet and back. "Lead on," she said with a calm voice. "Show me what it is and what I can do."

The spirit took her hand again and led her forward.

***

She spotted the thing the spirit meant for her to see from a distance. The magic she could see in her mind's eye became stronger, the colour a more defined purple, as they moved deeper into the woods. The trees were fed by a source of power, which lay in the middle of a brightly lit area. Whatever was in the centre, a faint palpitation vibrated from it, as if it had a heartbeat.

Marie-Claire's legs were weak as she walked the purple path toward the object. The spirit let go of her hand, allowing her to move forward herself. The world around her looked so marvellous, and it was a delight to see everything in such detail, even if it did lack natural colour. Every branch, every leaf, every plant, they were all part of this magical place, all infused by some sort of power. There was no good or evil behind it, just a strange necessity. It called out for sacrifice, and Marie-Claire fought hard not to let it drag her too far.

She inched closer to the thing on the ground, struggling to keep her balance. It looked like a large circle. What it was made of, she couldn't tell, but there were symbols carved into it, which shone even brighter than the plaque itself. The words were not in any language she understood. She spotted something else as she observed it more closely. It was subtle, but it was there... a hairline crack.

Marie-Claire struggled to breathe, as if the thing at her feet were stealing the very breath from her lungs. The light pulsation made the earth around it tremble, and it coursed through her own body, as if she were standing on the chest of a giant.

"Spirit, what is this?" Her voice was hoarse. "What am I looking at?"

"The beginning and the end," a voice in her head told her. Marie-Claire bent forward to touch the glowing material, feeling it against her bare skin. An electric sensation forced her to withdraw her hand with a jerk. She straightened herself and looked at the child with a gasp. The innocent face of the girl spirit had changed into something demonic. The eyes retreated in the skull, deep and dark pinpricks, while the mouth opened into a gaping dark maw, filled with needle-sharp teeth. It flung itself at her, screaming without sound, pouncing against her chest. It was heavier than expected, not enough to push Marie-Claire over, but the force made her stumble. Frightened, the medium took a few steps back, unsure what to do. The ghost came at her again, exposing fangs and clawing at her with its tiny hands. Their touch stung, and Marie-Claire warded off the angry spirit with her arms.

"*Je t'en prie*," she begged. *Please*. "I know you don't want to hurt me. If you wanted to really hurt me, you would have done so by now." She thought about how solid the hand had been when she had held it earlier, in contrast to the more wraith-like form the child now took. There was something amiss, but Marie-Claire couldn't figure it out. Instead, she let the child spirit drive her further back.

Suddenly, the girl stopped moving and returned to her former state. She hovered for a second, then pointed at Marie-Claire's feet. Slowly, the medium looked down, her heart pounding. There was a small clearing in the undergrowth, and something underneath shone with a faint blue light. It was pale in comparison to all the purple magic there, but strong enough to come through. It was a spell she recognised; she had cast it before.

"This is a circle of protection?" Marie-Claire met the spirit's gaze again. "You wanted me to stand inside it, to protect me?"

The spirit didn't exactly say anything, but Marie-Claire knew the answer was yes. She pointed at the strange plaque at a distance.

"Something has happened to that, and you want me to witness what will happen next."

No answer. Marie-Claire nodded with a heavy heart. She wasn't going to like what would happen next, she was sure of that.

The crude circle was barely large enough for her to sit down in, but she was grateful to whoever had created it, whether it was the ghost or someone who'd taken the precaution long before. Somehow, she managed to find a position that allowed her to rest her aching feet and still see the plaque, while also remaining out of sight. With solemn resignation, she closed her eyes, which allowed her to see her surroundings even better.

She spread out her mind's eye, chasing the fading magic along the ground and through the trees. Her thoughts didn't have to travel far before she found life. Someone was approaching. Marie-Claire couldn't see them—they weren't magical—but she could feel them. The magic of the plaque responded to them; it called for them, just as it had called to her. This was a powerful place, and it had little love for humanity.

***

She had once been a little girl, but now she was a pretty dolly. Somewhere in the back of her mind, she remembered the name she bore in life. *Imogen*. He had taken that name from her, the man who was now her father and her master, and he had given her the name "Beatrice." He had taken so much from her, and though he had left her mind, it was only shattered fragments of memories that remained. She was his to control now, and she knew she had to bring a message to the one who was trapped in the big house.

It was easy to get in. The master was with her always, and he had magic, which would open doors that didn't really exist. He told her she was his eyes and ears now, and she had to see, observe, and she did. This place was dark, and she could feel the magic around her. If her master weren't holding it at bay, she knew it would crush her, tear her limb from limb. His presence urged her forward, toward a large stone slab. She knew what it was. Or rather, he knew what it was, and she could hear his thoughts. It was the seal, the very thing he had been looking for. There were cracks in the marble. The enchantment of the seal might have been healed, but the stone was beyond repair.

Her mind warned her she was frightened, but the

master's voice lulled the fear away. Nothing could harm her now. Not if she obeyed him.

"What the fuck are you supposed to be?" a raspy voice, bitter and filled with death, asked. She could feel the pure unadulterated hatred emanating from it.

The girl couldn't answer, but the man inside her did. Not through her lips; they were stitched shut with the strong magic thread.

"So, you are the one they're hiding down here?" The man's voice was hollow in the stone cavern.

"I asked you something, you little monster. Who are you?" the stranger asked. "Or more to the point, what are you? Why do you sound like a fucking man?"

"It doesn't matter who or what I am," the master said. "It merely matters why I'm here."

"You're here for the house," the spirit said. "I can smell it on you."

The doll looked up to face the boy. He was shifting into different physical personifications. It was easy to identify that the spirit was trying to frighten her, and the master inside her laughed at the idea. The boy chose to present himself in an array of decaying entities. Maggots crawled around under his flesh, eating their way out of his soft rotting eyeballs and dropping from his mouth as he spoke. Paper-thin skin was pulled tight across his form, tearing just enough to show a hint of glistening muscles.

"I'm here for the house," the master agreed. "It's rather a special place."

"Because of that thing," the boy pointed at the seal.

"Among other things. Chuck, is it?" the doll cocked her head.

"Yes," the word was barely above a whisper.

"There are more things that make this house so remarkable, Chuck." The doll took a step in his direction. "Not everyone is aware of that. This particular part of land has always been a central point, even before they trapped the Horseman. There was a reason why the most powerful of all the seals was buried here. And why it's so close to such an unstable point like Lucifer Falls. You must feel something too, being a spirit."

"I... I feel something, all right," Chuck said, picking a long centipede from his black tongue.

"But you don't quite know what it is?"

"Yeah." Chuck leaned over the doll. "There's something I don't quite know about you, too."

"You would be correct about that."

"What do you want with the house?" Chuck asked.

"That is none of your concern," the master answered.

"Are you going to destroy the house?" There was a hint of worry in the spirit's ethereal voice.

"Destroy, no... I'm a creator, not a force of destruction. I forge new things out of the old." The doll folded her arms, and she glanced at the seal.

"You don't want that seal to open, then?" Chuck asked slyly.

"Oh, I do, but not yet." The doll lowered herself, hunching on her knees. She reached out one hand and touched the marble slab. "Not until I'm ready." She rubbed her hand across the cool stone. "This will be the last one that we shall open."

"Who the fuck is 'we'?" Chuck held his decomposing face at an angle.

"My order, the Blood Magi."

Chuck let out a sound that was somewhere between a scoff and a laugh. "Sounds fucking retarded."

"It is of little concern to me how it sounds to you, dead boy." The master's voice was cold. "The seal is not your affair, and you would do well to stay out of it."

"*She* won't let you, you know." Chuck glared at the ceiling. The doll could feel the hatred of the spirit wash over her. If she had been an ordinary girl, this spirit boy would have murdered her by now. It was in his nature. He had been a bad soul before he died, and death only made him worse.

"She?" the master asked.

"That bitch who lives here. She trapped me in here. Keeping me away from my sister."

"Oh, she'll *let* me. When the time comes, not only will she allow me to do whatever I want, but she will be mine, as will this house."

Chuck made the odd sound again. "Are you going to kill her?" There was blood lust in his voice.

"Not yet. She's the guardian of the seal, and she plays a part in this ritual. There is a connection between her and the house that is useful to me." The doll got back to her feet and faced Chuck. "There is, however, one thing. I can't have any spirits tied to Freya, or this house. You... interfere, shall we say? You are a liability, so I'm going to have to show you to the light."

Chuck took a step back, his disintegrating eyes wide with terror. "I ain't the only one here."

"I know... there's the girl." The master inhaled deeply, inflating the doll's hard chest with air. "You will have to take her with you, when it's time. It's most important that she leaves."

Something changed about the spirit, and the doll could

feel the hot excitement.

"You're going to let me have Bambi?" the boy changed his physical appearance. He looked more alive now, more solid.

"That's all you've ever wanted, isn't it?" the master said.

"She is my only desire," the boy whispered. His cheeks were rosy, and there was a possessive glint in his eyes.

"Then you will have her." The doll straightened herself and held the boy's eyes. "She is yours, when I tell you it's time. You must take her away from this house. Lead her to the gate of light that I will open for you. Do you understand?"

"Sure," said Chuck. His tongue, now pink without a hint of larvae, ran across his lips.

"You will only get the girl if you obey." The doll held the boy's glance. "When the time comes, I will let you go. You will get the girl, and you will leave this place. Do I make myself clear?"

Chuck puffed up his chest, and he squinted at her. "Now I see what you are..."

"Then you know I'm not to be trifled with."

CHAPTER THIRTEEN

Freya held Wulf's hand as they entered the nursery. She placed her finger on her lips, silently indicating him to be as quiet as he could. There was a gentle smile on his face when he looked down at the sleeping baby.

"I'll let you meet her when she's awake, too," Freya whispered.

He nodded in return and slid his arm around her waist, pulling her close to him. They stared at Emily for a few seconds, their sides pressed against each other, until Freya broke the silent moment. She stepped away, grabbing his hand, and led him out of the room.

"Emily is the most important person in my life, but I want you to meet someone else who is very dear to me." Nervous sweat began to form on her palms. She wasn't sure about this meeting, but something in her gut urged her that this was the right time.

"Okay," Wulf said cautiously.

"This person... it's not an ordinary individual." Freya bit her thumbnail. "Maybe I should have told you about her first, but I think it might be better if you just see for yourself."

"I'm very curious now," Wulf said.

Freya pulled him closer to her, still holding his hand. "I need you to not freak out, okay? You're in no danger."

"Why would I think—"

"Bam, you can come out now," Freya said, pushing a finger to Wulf's lips to silence him. Her friend came through the door, uncharacteristically shy, and slowly

111

floated toward them. Freya watched Wulf's facial expressions like a hawk, searching for any signs of fear, but there were none. He was exceptionally calm; she couldn't even spot any surprise in his face.

"I see why she would keep you a secret," Wulf said, his eyes fixed on Bam, who was more translucent than usual. Her slender body was clad in a very ghostly white dress, and her pink hair was longer and paler somehow, as if she were trying to look the part. Freya raised her eyebrows, but swallowed any critique she wanted to express. This was Bam's moment. Just as she had been lonely, she couldn't imagine what Bam had to go through. Freya was the only person she ever spoke to.

Bam floated closer. Normally, her floating looked more like walking, but this time she floated as if she were flying, the white dress billowing behind her. Her face was solemn —a perfect mask of a tormented soul.

"Eh..." Freya was taken off guard a bit by Bam's strange behavior. "Wulf, this is my best friend, Bam."

"Nice to meet you," Wulf said. "Were you friends before you... crossed over, or did you meet when Freya moved in?" He directed his questions at Bam, who was still playing the demure ghost part. Freya looked from her to Wulf and back again, and when she was about to answer the question herself, Bam spoke in a low mournful tone.

"This house," she said in a terrible English accent, "plucked me from a young and promising life." She let out a sigh, which didn't sound quite right—her sighs were always a bit off.

Freya had had enough of the theatrics. "Seriously?" she asked. "What are you doing?"

Bam shot her a warning look, and she hissed from the corner of her mouth, "He wanted to see a ghost. I'm giving him a ghost."

"You are a ghost," Freya said, raising her hands.

"Yeah, but I'm not a typical ghost." Bam put her hands on her hips, lowering to the floor now. She became more solid as she spoke.

Wulf laughed. "Please, Bam, just be yourself."

"I wanted you to, like, have a special experience, meeting your first ghost," Bam said.

"Meeting you is special enough," Wulf assured her. "And besides, you're not my first ghost."

Bam gasped as if he just announced he had been cheating on her, and Freya raised her eyebrows.

Wulf winked at her, then his attention went back to Bam. "I don't think I have ever seen such a strong projection as yourself before," he said. "I have met quite a few different spirits—ranging from the recently deceased to those who had been long dead—but you seem almost alive."

"We think it's this house," Freya answered. "The spirits here are always... stronger." She shivered involuntarily.

"Yeah," Bam chimed in. "Which, like, hasn't always been a good thing."

"Let's save that story for another day," Freya said. "I think one ghost is enough for tonight."

**

Freya woke to the gentle stroking of Wulf's fingers on her cheek.

"I should go," he whispered. "It's getting late."

"Where's Bam?" she asked groggily, her eyes still half-closed.

"She went upstairs to watch Emily. The baby was crying, and she didn't want to wake you."

She opened her eyes and stretched. "I fell asleep." Her eyes darted toward the television. "I missed most of the movie."

"It was pretty boring," Wulf said.

"I'm sorry I fell asleep. I must have been terrible company."

He placed his hand under her chin and lifted her face toward him. "You're never terrible company. You're adorable when you sleep." His face was close to hers, and she could feel the heat of his breath.

"Do you feel better now that I know about Bam?" he asked, still close to her.

"I do. One less secret," Freya said, leaning in a little further. She imagined she could hear his heart pounding. Maybe it was her own, because it was beating so loudly, she was sure they could hear it all the way to Edinburgh.

"That's good," he said, "because I want you to feel better. I really like you, Freya. I hope you know that."

"I do," she said, "and I really like you."

He came a little closer, his lips almost on hers. "Would it be too forward of me if I kissed you now?"

"Probably," she said, her lips curling in a smile, "but do it anyway."

When his lips touched hers, the world seemed to explode in invisible fireworks. Her stomach released the hordes of butterflies that had been fluttering around in one fell swoop, and Freya was glad she was sitting down, or her knees would have buckled under her.

"I really do have to go, though," Wulf said, his voice filled with regret, pulling away from their kiss. "It's dark, and I have a long way to travel. I don't think we're ready to go further than kissing quite yet." He smirked. "At least, not tonight. Not with your friend and your baby so close by."

"Right," Freya said. She longed to kiss him again, but she knew if she did, she wouldn't stop at that. "Let me walk you out."

He kissed her again at the door, hungrily and filled with passion. She almost begged him to stay, but something in her stayed strong. When he closed the door, she leaned against it, her hand on her chest and her head against the wood.

Oh, God help me, she thought, *I think I'm in love with this guy... and I barely know him.*

CHAPTER FOURTEEN

From her hiding place in the woods, Marie-Claire could see the strange magical centre of the clearing. The pulsating had grown louder. Something was happening, Marie-Claire could feel it, but she couldn't see. Someone was there—she could hear their footsteps, and a muffled sound of what she believed to be crying. The ruffling noises sounded like perhaps there was a struggle.

"Spirit," Marie-Claire whispered, looking at the little girl who was sitting next to her in the circle, her knees pulled up to her chin. "I can't see what's going on. Can you tell me what is happening?"

The girl looked at her with a cocked face, as if she were trying to read something in Marie-Claire's expression. Then the small hands shot out, the thumbs—now once again as solid as those of a living child—pressing against her eyelids. Marie-Claire almost cried out in surprise, but she calmed down when she realised the spirit wasn't trying to harm her. Her body twisted in shock as her essence combined with that of the girl, travelling through the mind of the dead child. She could feel the despair, the hurt, the betrayal, then suddenly a strong light blinded her. Marie-Claire realised she was looking through the eyes of the girl, seeing what she saw. She had done this before, look through the eyes of another, but only with the living. The last time she had attempted this was with the girl named Freya, who lived in that awful house. Seeing through the eyes of a spirit was different. There was no mind in the way; it was as if she were seeing with her own eyes but had no control of her movements. The child turned her head, so that Marie-Claire had a better view of what was going on. She saw a man—at least, she assumed it was a man—dressed in a long, black robe. The hood was pulled all the way over his head, hiding his features. He was holding on to a slender person with a bald head wearing the Kasaya robes of a Buddhist monk.

The monk was putting up a weak struggle, half-walking and half being dragged toward the area of the plaque. His soft sniffling echoed through the woods. He looked broken, resigned to his fate, whatever that was to be.

They stopped before the plaque, and the man in the robes pushed the monk to his knees.

"Aokigahara," he said loudly and in English. "I have found your last guardian. There is nothing you can do to protect yourself anymore. You must submit to my will and to the will of my order."

Marie-Claire wasn't sure, but it looked as if the man were growing... or perhaps the monk was shrinking. The bald man looked to be no more than a child now. The hooded figure pulled him up by his clothes, forcing him to remain erect while still on his knees. His hand—slender and elegant—covered the bald scalp. The man pushed a dark metal blade against the monk's neck.

"I will sacrifice your guardian as a boon to the ancients, and break the second of the seven seals." He pressed the blade deeper, cutting the monk's flesh. Now the monk tried to fight back, but the cloaked figure held him in place with ease. "In the name of the blood..." The blade sank into the coarse skin, sawing at the muscles and fat of the struggling monk. Blood gushed forth, tainting the victim's clothes with a deep, dark color. If the monk ever intended on crying out, he was too late. The dagger cut through vocal chords as if they were made of butter. Either the hooded figure had inhuman strength, or the dagger had powers to make this possible. The man pulled the almost severed head back, revealing just a peek of bone under the mutilated and bloodied flesh.

Marie-Claire's hand shot up to her neck involuntarily. She had seen many ghosts in ghastly states, and after last year she was no stranger to murder, but seeing it so clear, through the eyes of the spirit girl, made her feel as if she were a part of this macabre ritual.

It took all the willpower she had not to cry out. Everything in her told her to stop what was happening, but she was nailed to the spot. And what could she do? Throw herself at this monster? She was just an old woman who could see things that others couldn't, and she had no power to stop this much evil.

One more hack severed the top from the shoulders, and the man held up the fragile decapitated head of the monk as the body slumped forward. His voice was loud now, booming throughout the area. "I command the second of the seven seals to yield to me. Let the souls of the martyrs cry out for vengeance."

The earth trembled and something in the distance... *cracked*. Overwhelming power seeped into the soil around her.

"*Mon Dieu*. The second seal," she whispered to the spirit girl, quiet enough to not be overheard. "That's what you're showing me. The seven seals, they're not a myth?"

The girl didn't answer, but Marie-Claire saw the truth reflect back at her from those dead eyes.

"Someone is trying to trigger the Apocalypse..."

The girl turned toward where she had seen the man, but he wasn't there. There was still some residue of his presence, but he had disappeared, leaving her with a heavy heart. The girl took her thumbs away from Marie-Claire's eyes.

How does one stop an Apocalypse?

The ghost curled into a ball and threw herself against Marie-Claire, hitting her so hard it created the illusion she was a girl of flesh and bone. From everywhere, Marie-Claire could see the spirits approach. They were walking slowly, determined, as if hypnotised by something. There were so many of them, all those whom the Jukai had claimed. When they reached the seal, they threw back their heads and screamed. Their voices were filled with pain and rage, making Marie-Claire's skin crawl. There was so much anger filling the air, and the spirits' screams spoke of vengeance.

She wrapped her arms around the child, who, she realised, was also protected by the magic circle. Somehow, Marie-Claire knew, the world would never again be the same.

CHAPTER FIFTEEN

The house cried out. It was a scream that was part-terror and part-pain, and it woke Freya from a fitful nap. The warmth and the safety she had felt last night had dissipated in a cold, dark void. Her body ached, as if she had woken up from a recent beating. Every inch of her throbbed with a dull soreness, and it hurt to sit up. Something was happening, but Freya didn't understand what it was. Under the ground, she could feel the Horseman stir, but the sensation was fleeting, and in the next moment, the pain left her body like a sigh. Freya looked at Emily—who lay sleeping next to her on the big bed—and pulled the baby close. Emily opened her eyes and smiled. She wished Wulf was there to make her feel protected, but all she had was this precious child she needed to care for. Freya curled up, holding her daughter to her chest, and sobbed until sleep took her once more.

***

Bam felt the tremor through her whole being. The house moaned softly, like a woman mourning the loss of a loved one. The overwhelming anger and sadness of it tugged at her. Bam wasn't connected in the same way as Freya was, not now, not since the spell was broken, but she was still linked to this place, and she was sensitive to its temperaments—which, in return, affected her own mood. Her heart was heavy, and a seed of fear blossomed in her core.

Something was happening, and she could feel it, but she wasn't sure what, or how it was connected to Angel Manor. It had nothing to do with her, and yet it had everything to do with her. The house seemed to respond to a call from another thing in another place. Something that was familiar.

Within the walls of the mansion, the atmosphere mutated into something even darker, more ominous. The stone angels that stood outside in the courtyard shifted ever so slightly. Bam could sense their restlessness, and it worried her.

She moved through the corridor, unsettled and unsure how to respond to this intangible change. Her first thoughts were with Freya and the baby. Had they felt it, too? Was this tremor a physical manifestation, or something only the spirits could sense?

Her questions were instantly answered when she reached the main hallway. The side tables were knocked over and the paintings all hung askew. The tremor had cut the lights in the lower part of the house—Freya always left some lights burning in case there would be a need for her to flee—yet a dim illumination glowed in the distance. She pulled back into the west corridor. Footsteps of someone coming down the stairs reverberated through the first floor. From her hiding place, Bam watched something small—was it a child?—make its way across the hall. She hadn't realised there was something in the house until now, which surprised her. She didn't think anything could get past her, not in this place. And yet there it was...

It was a child—three, maybe four years old—only it wasn't alive. And at the same time... it wasn't dead either. This was no spirit. Bam felt a natural revulsion that froze her to the spot. The girl—it was clearly a girl—reminded her of something. It took her a moment, but then she knew what it was that looked so familiar. The child was dressed in a similar fashion to the dolls that had been gifted to Emily. Even her hair was curled in the same manner. She was a little bigger, and her mouth was stitched shut, but the resemblance to those toys was uncanny.

Jesus, that's even creepier than those fucking nuns, Bam thought. *I'm going to have to warn Freya about this... after I figure out what this thing is up to.*

The doll stopped in the middle of the entrance hall, then

crouched. She drew something on the ground with her chubby finger, and to Bam's surprise, she actually saw a faint pattern. It faded almost as soon as it appeared, but she had seen it. The pattern had let out a shrill hum, what Bam imagined a dog whistle to sound like. It went through her very core. The doll got to her feet, moving quickly now, the heels of her hard shoes clicking on the marble floor as she went out through a door in the wall—one that Bam had never noticed before—like a thief in the night.

She floated toward where the door had been, but there was no sign of it now. Even when she made her way through the wall, studying the inside, she couldn't detect anything out of the ordinary. Whatever had opened that door, it had successfully closed it again as well. Bam didn't like the idea of someone or something being able to access Angel Manor without her and Freya's knowledge. She wondered if the house was aware of it, but nothing she could see or feel indicated that this was the case.

The first thing she had to do was warn Freya, and she was about to make her way upstairs when a sense of foreboding hit her. Something was amiss. Somewhere in the depths of the house, something... clicked. She stayed very still, concentrating on her surroundings. After a few seconds of silence, she heard something that she would liken to a *whoosh*.

It had been a while since real dread—the tangible kind that was fresh, rather than borne of memory—had dominated her mind, but Bam remembered the emotion well. The strongest association she had with terror was Chuck, though her fear of him in death had been different than she had sensed for him in life. He couldn't kill her anymore, but he still tapped into something primal within her being. This, whatever it was, did the same thing. Carefully, she moved toward where she had heard the sound. Anxiety coursed through her essence, and Bam realised she hadn't felt this alive since her death. It wasn't a good feeling.

"What the hell am I afraid of?" Bam whispered to herself, trying to stimulate her own courage. "I'm the damn ghost here. Nothing should scare me." She turned a corner, staring into the darkness. "Not even creepy, not-quite-dead girls." She froze. "Oh fuck..." Ahead of her sat one of the dolls. This was definitely a doll, not a little girl. It looked so innocent, just sitting there, but Bam could feel there was something wrong with it. "Didn't we lock those up? Or is it a new one?"

Behind her, she heard light footsteps, as if a child were running. She turned to see, but nothing was there. When she turned back to the first doll, it was gone, too.

"Shit," she cursed. "Okay, that's totally creepy. I can't believe I, like, thought those things were cute." The sound of footsteps came from the south wing, and there was faint laughter.

Bam blinked. "Damn it, I'm the scary thing here," she muttered, but she didn't feel as tough as she acted; one of the dolls had given her a nasty shock before. And even if it hadn't hurt her, nothing would make her want to go into the south wing. That's where the door was that led to the darkness sleeping below, but worst of all, that kept Chuck locked up.

She glided to the door that led to the south wing, but she stayed there, refusing to go on.

"I should go wake Freya," Bam whispered. "Not because I'm scared, but she needs to know—"

There was more laughter, and the sound of metal hitting metal. The noise ran through her whole spirit, and Bam whimpered. All her will to run to Freya had left her. She had to stop whatever was happening, but she was paralysed by fear. Whatever that doll-like girl had done, she had awoken something in Angel Manor. Bam could feel it. It wasn't the house itself—she would have known if it was— but it was something different. A thing that didn't belong, and it was going to ruin everything. There was that hollow sound again, of an object banging against metal. It had a strange hypnotic rhythm to it. Bam dug deep for her courage, thrusting her fear aside, and made her way into the hall.

Nothing can hurt me; I'm already dead, she repeated over and over in her head. *There is nothing to fear but fear itself.*

To her horror, she saw that the door leading to the basement was open. The chain was pulled in such a way that the heavy door couldn't close, and the metal was clanking against the door.

"Oh no," Bam said, all her courage melting like snow before the sun. Behind her something moved, and she turned around to see a terrifyingly familiar rotting face.

"Chuck..."

"Hello, sister, did you miss me?"

CHAPTER SIXTEEN

They all felt it. Every single living soul in the Aokigahara, and even those who lived on the border of it. The shock went through all of them, touching the deepest darkest crevasses of their being, running along their immediate bloodline and touching those linked. A burst of magic, long forgotten to the human minds, coursed through that tiny part of the world like an earthquake.

The souls cried out, all those who had laid their lives down to serve the forest, and their screams could be heard for miles. The living responded in two ways. They were either afraid or compelled, drawn by the raw emotions that were an ethereal representation of human suffering, to scream along. There was something appealing in that unnatural howl of rage and torment. As if they had hidden the misery from the world for too long, and now all it needed was to be released. Generations worth of wrongdoing, of people who died out of love, out of perverted joy, out of cruelty, out of sickness, out of nature's whims, and the people who died too soon and too painfully... all of it reeled within this scream.

Some who heard it believed the end of the world had arrived. Others knew it was only the beginning of the end. There was so much more to come, and it would be even more terrifying.

***

Koji exhaled, aware that he had been holding his breath long enough for it to sting his lungs. His surroundings seemed to be brought to life from a frozen scene. The scream—or whatever it had been—had stopped time for just a second. Had he imagined it?

A sudden and staggering sadness made him ache for his home in the US. *It feels so far away now*, Koji thought numbly. *What time is it there? I don't even know what time it is* here *anymore*. It was near dark. *I feel so lost*.

He looked down at the bloodied man, still visible in the dimming light, who lay on his back staring at tree branches high above. The grey eyes appeared almost white, making him seem dead, but the rapid movement of his chest betrayed signs of life. He was panting heavily, like someone on the verge of hyperventilating. Koji crawled away from the man and got to his feet. Toshiro was still frozen in his position, his face down and his hand outstretched, while three fingers touched the shoulders of the man on the ground. They were both perfectly still, except for the breathing. It was as if he were looking at a lifelike statue.

Koji took a few random steps, eager to get away from this place, yet not sure where he wanted to go. He didn't want to wait here, alone, with these two strangers. Toshiro could look after the weird guy covered in blood; it wasn't *his* responsibility. He just wanted to go home... because he knew something bad was going to happen, and if it was, he wanted to be where he was safe and loved. He turned around, trying to find his bearings. The trees all looked the same to him, and he needed a moment to collect himself, to remember which way led back.

When he completed his circle, the bloody man stood behind him, the grey eyes still vacant. Toshiro was nowhere to be found.

"It was that plaque," the man said in a hollow voice. "That's the cause of all this. There was something bad inside, and now it's out."

"I don't know," Koji said, feeling utterly lost, his eyes still searching for Toshiro. "Whatever that was..." The presence of the man put him on edge. There was nothing about him—aside from the blood—that could be perceived as a threat. His demeanor seemed friendly enough, but still...

Koji's nose reminded him of an earlier observation. There was a strong smell of gasoline. "Do you smell that?" he asked the bloodied man.

"The gasoline?" the man nodded. "I think it's coming from there." He pointed at the tent. Koji saw the tent flap move, and he wondered if Toshiro had gone inside for some insane reason. The stress made him struggle to think straight.

He pulled aside the flaps of the tent and looked inside. The sight of the blood welcomed him again, but there was no Toshiro.

Obviously, Koji thought. *Why would he go in here? What was I thinking?*

Something bothered him about the blood. Actually, two things. First of all, it hadn't congealed yet. It looked completely fresh, which was impossible, since it usually didn't take much longer than fifteen minutes for blood to congeal, and they had been there longer than that. The second thing that bugged him was that it only covered the inside of the tent; there was no indication of it on the outside, aside from the fresh traces the guy left when he came out of the tent. When they first arrived, they hadn't seen any blood, nor had they smelled it. *Come to think of it...* that was a third thing that bothered him, he couldn't smell it.

"How did you get the blood on you?" Koji asked, turning to the man. "You can't have had it on you when you entered. It would have been everywhere. So, it can't have been the blood that came from the ground."

"I told you, it followed me inside."

There was something fragile in the man's grey eyes that made Koji's stomach sink. It was as if he wasn't there anymore, like something had broken his spirit. *This guy isn't right in the head*, he thought.

The man sank to the ground again, sobbing. "Laney," he

cried. "Laney, I'm so sorry. I don't want to do this... I don't. I just want to go home."

Koji took the moment to step away, accidentally pulling over some of the tent's construction. The structure of the shelter lay sprawled across the ground, covering the few meagre belongings that were inside. The man tilted his head back and looked at Koji.

"Please don't leave me here. I'm not a bad man, they're just in my head."

"Who the hell are *they*?" Koji asked, cursing himself for even talking to this insane guy. *God only knows what he did*.

"The voices of the wood. It... it started with that fucking doll."

"Doll... like the one on the tree?"

"Yes. It... it opened its mouth..."

"Jesus." Koji wanted to run, far away from this crazy guy. "You stay here. I'll get someone." He turned, only to be stopped by the figure of Toshiro.

"We need to find help," Koji said, relieved to see another person. "This guy is messed up." Toshiro nodded. The friendly eyes looked vacant now, and a horrible sense of dread came over Koji. The short man was holding a red canister in his hands, which had that same gasoline scent he had smelled before. Koji had a dozen questions on his lips, but all he could do was hold Toshiro's eyes, feeling a strange emptiness as he watched the man take the cap off the canister. He was afraid he would be doused by gasoline, and Koji was ready to turn and run, but instead he watched Toshiro empty the canister over his own head. The clear, brownish liquid poured down the man's hair, face, and shoulders, knocking the black glasses askew. It drenched his shirt and his trousers.

"I feel their pain and share it," the kind-hearted man

said softly, his inexpressive eyes staring past Koji. "The world is dying, and we are the voices of the martyrs. Our scream must be heard."

When the canister was empty, he put it aside in a gentle manner, as if it were made out of porcelain and needed to be treated with care.

"Toshiro." Koji sought for words of wisdom, or some inner strength that would will him into action; anything to stop the geologist, but nothing came to him. He was frozen in fear and comprehension—he knew what was about to happen, and that somehow rendered him immobile.

Toshiro patted his pockets and pulled out a lighter. He looked at it with a strange fondness.

"The time for humanity has passed. We tried to rule the earth, but she was not for our taking. We never loved her like we should." His thumb ran across the striker wheel, his gaze now holding Koji's.

"You don't have to do this." Tears ran down Koji's cheeks. The sight of the man, drenched in gasoline, was so incredibly tragic that it broke his heart.

"Do you not see it? I do." Toshiro ran his thumb across the wheel again, but nothing happened. "These people, they did the right thing. Their sacrifice, it was to keep the world turning. They offered themselves to the seal. Their deaths were not in vain. But now that the seal is broken... there's no more hope. We should all sacrifice ourselves to Mother Nature for what she has done for us. There is no life for us, not in the new world."

Koji took a step back. "You're not making any sense..."

Toshiro smiled a distant and hollow smile. "Yes, I am." He struck the wheel again, and this time a light ignited. The small man pulled the fire to himself, and with the sound of a wind gust, a bright flame burst into life. It spread in an instant across the figure, who still stood smiling. Paralysed by fear and horror, Koji watched the man in front of him. First his hair melted—which gave off a noxious scent—and seconds later his skin turned red, then slowly black. The fat began to bubble, popping in white boils. The aroma of cooked meat overwhelmed the smell of melting hair and gasoline—it sickened Koji that the smell was actually oddly pleasant. Toshiro's skin dripped slowly down his skull like candle wax. His glasses, twisted by the intense heat, slid from his face, and his clothing melted into his broiling skin.

It wasn't until his eyeballs burst, sending sizzling droplets of liquid into the air, that Toshiro seemed to realise he was on fire. That exact moment was the worst of all, that moment of understanding. A scream escaped from the blackened lips, and the man flailed his arms as the flames devoured him, stumbling around until he tripped over his own feet and fell to his knees. The terrible tantalising smell of cooked pork filled Koji's nostrils, making him feel morbidly hungry. Toshiro still wailed as he moved in a strangely elegant death dance, his torso twirling, while his arms swung back and forth like flaming banners. Finally, he stopped and slumped to the ground. After a few weak spasms, his body went still, transformed from a living person into a hunk of cooked meat.

Koji stared in shock. It was his fault Toshiro was dead; it wasn't as if the man had threatened to harm him. He had plenty of time before he got the lighter to work... he could have stopped it. Instead, he had been so hypnotised that he had done nothing. The thoughts spurred him to action, as he took off his coat and beat at the flames still smouldering on the body. A fear that the fire would spread was only vaguely in the back of his mind.

Grief and shame burst from him in heaving sobs as he fought the dying flames, until a noise made him look to the side. Right into the cold grey eyes and mad smile of the bloodied man. By the time Koji noticed the rock in the man's hand, it was already swinging toward him.

The last thing Koji heard was the sickening crack of his

own skull, and then he sank into darkness, his nose still filled with the meaty scent of cooked flesh.

CHAPTER SEVENTEEN

"You don't look pleased to see me, Bambi." Chuck ran the back of his fingers down his neck and across his chest. His head was cocked, a mocking pout played around his lips, and he looked exactly like he had when she last saw him alive.

"Fuck you, brother," Bam said, trying to sound strong.

"Oh yes," Chuck said in a low voice, "that's exactly what I intend to do, for the rest of eternity." A cruel smile played on his lips.

"You come near me, and I'll..."

Chuck's eyebrows rose, and his smile changed from cruel to amused. "You'll what? Call for Mommy?" He laughed, and his eyes darkened. "Kill me?"

Bam shook her head and took a step back.

"I'm already dead, Bambi, and so are you." Chuck stepped forward. He moved like a panther stalking its prey, the expression on his face deadly. Bam tried to remind herself that she was dead, there was nothing he could do to hurt her. And yet... her brother had a hold on her, an unspoken power. He always had. When he was near, no matter what she had learned in life, she was that young girl again.

"How did you get out of your prison?" her voice trembled.

He paused and looked at her. "That little girl who speaks like a man." Chuck took on an expression of contemplation. "She's an odd duck, isn't she? Not one of us, but not one of them either."

Bam nodded. She had felt it, too, a girl who walked the world between the living and the dead. "Why did she let you out?"

"We, you and I—" Chuck pointed a finger from her to himself "—need to leave this place. We're in the way. Disruptors, shall we say."

"Disruptors to what?" Bam was genuinely intrigued now.

"The energy of the house?" Chuck shrugged. "The magic spells? Who knows? But we need to leave."

Bam folded her arms. "And you're just going to let yourself be sent away? That doesn't sound like you."

"I didn't get sent, Bambi," he said sharply. "I was bribed."

"You're a spirit. What could anyone possibly bribe you with?"

"You." Chuck grinned maniacally. "All I ever wanted was you."

"You can't have me, Chuck." Bam made fists, but she couldn't feel her own skin as she touched it. "I belong to no one but myself."

"Yes, I can, Bambi," he spoke in a soothing voice. "I can have you as often as I want. No limitations. I don't have to hide my desires anymore. You will be mine, and I will take you and hurt you as often as I please."

Bam stood frozen, her mind searching for an escape. She wanted to react, but before she could open her mouth and retort, something happened to the house. Bam had felt it before—though the last time was stronger—over a year ago. The light... it was here again, beckoning her to come through and take her leave of the mortal world. Last time she sensed it, Chuck had stopped her, but this time... this time he wanted her to go through.

The light called to her, promising her peace and rest.

How could anyone hurt her when she was beyond that place? Chuck's threats were hollow, they...

Chuck took her hand. She felt it. Not as flesh against flesh, but as essence meeting essence. He was rotten to the core. His darkness touched her in ways she didn't want to be touched, and Bam panicked again. What if he was right? What if her eternity would be spent with him?

Bam pulled away from her brother and ran, anxiety ruling her mind. The light was not just affecting her, it was affecting him, too, and Angel Manor around them. It stirred, reaching out to her. It was different now, different from when it stole her soul. The house was... friendlier. It, too, urged her to the mystical luminescence, pushing her toward safety rather than holding on to her with its cold clutches.

She ran toward where she could sense the brightness, in the depths of the manor. Chuck was behind her, and Bam didn't know what to do. Perhaps she could draw him into the light, but stay behind herself for Freya and Emily. They needed her. She half-ran, half-floated down the basement steps.

And for the first time, she saw it.

The portal of death. Right above the seal, in the place where the nuns were once held.

It was beautiful.

Chuck had caught up with her, and he stopped.

"I've never seen anything like it." His voice was childlike now. "Bambi, it's like the end of the rainbow."

"Yes," Bam said. She tried to understand the different colors, which were unlike any she had ever seen. More vibrant and powerful. She imagined she could actually hear the colors, as if they were soft humming notes.

Chuck stepped forward, his eyes round and mesmerised,

tears glistening in the corners.

"Oh, Bambi," he sighed as he reached out his hand.

Bam concentrated and used all the power she had to shove him. When she connected, she could feel her light pushing at Chuck's darkness. He looked back at her, his face changing from a mask of confusion and fear to pure rage. Bam refused to let it shake her and she pushed harder, shoving Chuck into the light. Something grabbed her brother, shadows shaped like claws wrapped all around his essence, snatching him away. His screams echoed in her ears.

The luminous particles caressed her, doing their best to seduce her into joining them. Bam pulled her hand back and stepped away from the light.

"Not today," she said. "I'm not ready to go yet."

"Aren't you?" a male voice asked. She turned around, but there was nothing there, just a voice. It sounded sweet and tempting.

"Why would you stay, Bambi?" the unseen stranger asked.

"It's *Bam*," she shouted. "I will stay because my friend is here, and she, like, needs help."

"How will you help? You are not meant to be here. Your soul has been loose on this mortal world for a long time. It makes you weak."

"I'm not weak, I'm getting stronger. I can, like, feel it. I can do more things, I learn new things every day."

"Just go into the light, child. You will be a danger to your friend if you stay here," the voice said, soothing. "Who knows what you will become if you remain? Spirits never maintain their original essence. They change, become something loathsome. Why would you have that happen to you?"

"Who are you?" Bam asked. "Why should I, like, believe you?"

"Because," the man said in an amused drawl, "I'm the man who is trying to protect your friend. And you can help her, too, but in order to do that you will have to step into the light."

Bam turned around to walk away, to get far from the seductive colours, away from the lulling tones of the man's voice. Something caressed her hand and she paused. There was love in that light, and salvation. Tears running down her face, Bam turned and almost leapt into the luminescence, but a thought stopped her.

"The dolls, they're yours, aren't they?"

"They are," the man said.

"They're not here to protect Freya at all," Bam said. "You would have, like, introduced yourself or something if you wanted to help Freya. Something isn't right here, and I'm not going to fucking listen to you." Bam turned her back to the tempting lights, but she couldn't move. Nine dolls stood before her, emanating a menacing power. Their porcelain arms were stretched out toward her, the chubby baby fingers bent into stone claws. She had touched one of them before, and it had sent her flying, so Bam worried what would happen if all nine were to touch her. They surrounded her, and the only way out Bam could see was up. She willed her essence to float toward the ceiling, but something pulled her back down. To her horror, Bam saw that the dolls were inhaling—as if they were trying to suck in her essence.

"You may not have any blood for me to control," the man's voice said sharply, "but I do have a few magical aces up my sleeve. I have had some time to prepare how to deal with you. And deal with you I shall, before you have the chance to become a threat to me. If you won't go to the light, I will tear you apart and trap you in a different way."

Bam struggled, but the dolls were so strong. There was pain—almost as real as when she had been alive—as the fabric of her being unravelled She screamed, but no sound came out. Near her, the light pulsated, offering her a release from the agony, and Bam, in a last desperate effort, pulled free and ran toward the portal, spreading her arms as a bird in flight as she jumped into the light.

She was free.

CHAPTER EIGHTEEN

"This isn't funny anymore, Bam." Freya hated that she was so near tears. This house had made her cry more often in the past year or so than she had her whole life before it. "You need to come out, because I don't know what happened to you."

Freya sat on the stairs, her head in her hands.

"Bam, please." She knew her friend wasn't in the house; she couldn't feel her presence anymore. Still, despite knowing what she knew, Freya had looked everywhere.

Except the basement, and Bam would never go to the basement. Neither of them would. In general, they stayed clear of the entire south wing, if they could avoid it. It was easier pretending that was the only really bad place in the house. There were memories everywhere, but the south wing still felt like it was filled with ghosts. And not the good kind.

Freya was wandering around the main lobby when she heard the sound of a car driving up. She ran to the window, curious, and peered through the dirty glass. *I need to get someone to wash these windows for me*, she thought, as she rubbed away some of the grime with her sleeves.

It was Wulf. He slammed the door shut and walked at a brisk pace in the direction of the row of stone angels. Freya was relieved to see him and sped toward the main door.

"Freya," he called out before even reaching her. "Your message... you said it was urgent?"

"Bam," Freya called back. "I can't find Bam. I looked everywhere, and she's just gone..."

He stared at her, his face worried. "I'll help you look."

"The only place I haven't looked was in the basement, but she can't be there."

"Do you want me to go check?" he asked.

"No, I don't want you to go there. No one should go there, it's dangerous." A heaviness weighed on her chest that made her struggle to breathe normally, as if some unseen hand were trying to strangle her.

He pulled her close to him, lifting up her chin so that she was forced to look at him.

"I won't," he said. "If you don't want me to go there, I won't." His thumb brushed her bottom lip, and he gave her a reassuring smile.

"I'm so freaked out," Freya said, fighting a new wave of tears. "I don't know what to do without Bam."

"I'm here," he said, wrapping his arms around her and pushing her head to his chest. "If Bam's in this house, we'll find her."

***

"Anything?" Freya held out a mug with tea. Wulf put down his EMF meter and took the mug from her.

"Nothing," he said, taking a sip, "but I'm really not equipped for this. If you give me some time to set something up properly... I will need help, too."

"No," Freya said. "It's useless, she's gone. I can feel it."

"You don't know that," Wulf said.

"The sad thing is—" Freya stared at her mug "—I *do* know. I have known since I woke up. I just didn't want to believe it. She's gone." Something in her voice cracked, and Wulf took a step toward her, but she lifted her hand to stop him.

"I don't know how to get her back, but I need her. I can't do this alone."

"You're not alone." He hunched, trying to meet her eyes. "I'm here."

Freya smiled, though she wondered if it masked her sadness. "We've only just met, and you have no idea what burden rests on my shoulders. I don't even know if I could tell you. Bam... she was my ally. She was my rock when I needed her."

"I can't take her place, but I can offer you a shoulder to lean on if you want it." He patted his muscular shoulder, and a familiar flutter twirled through Freya's stomach. "I know we've only just met, but we click. You know?"

"We do," she admitted. "Having you here... it's... nice."

"I could be here more often," he offered. "Help you out with Emily when you need it. I'm a great cook..." A crooked smile curled around his lips. "It won't replace Bam, and I am deeply sorry that she's gone."

Freya's bottom lip trembled. "I just want to know what happened to her."

"Spirits are often tied to a place. As far as I know, only a few things can make them leave. One is if they are tied to a new place. This is extremely rare, but it can happen if they're deeply connected to another person. They can sometimes shift places of existence. The only other thing I can think of is if Bam somehow managed to go through the light and cross over to the world of the dead."

"How, though?"

"Someone could have performed an exorcism, or maybe it was just time for her to go."

"No one knew she was here but me, so I doubt someone performed an exorcism. Besides, I'm pretty sure I would know about it. It's my house, after all." She didn't want to say that she was connected to the house, and that she knew what it knew. It was a theory that gave her doubt of late anyway, since either the house had been oblivious of how Bam departed, or it was withholding information from her.

"Then, maybe, it was her time to go."

"Maybe it had something to do with what happened when I was sleeping," Freya said. "I took a nap with Emily, and something happened..."

"What?" Wulf put his mug down on the kitchen table.

"I... I don't exactly know. It was like some sort of earthquake. Didn't you feel it?" She pointed at the slanted pictures on her wall. "Even knocked over some furniture in the hall. I cleared most of it up."

"That's odd. I didn't feel any earthquake."

"Oh," Freya said.

"I believe you, though," Wulf amended. "Today was weird. It was just off somehow, you know?"

"Yes. Maybe that's why Bam left... maybe all this is just the beginning of something much worse."

CHAPTER NINETEEN

"It's a fucking satellite phone," Tara said in a raised voice. She was still stressed from earlier, having almost gotten lost in these damn woods by herself. "It can't fucking *not* work." She snatched the phone from Lucas's fingers and tried to get it to pick up some sort of signal. But no matter how she pressed the buttons or how she held it up to the sky, it didn't respond. She swung back the phone as if ready to throw it, but held on tight. There was a temptation to try her own phone—which was resting safely in the back pocket of her jeans—but if it didn't work an hour ago, it wouldn't work now. The boys were responding so slowly, and she wanted to slap the vacant expressions from their faces. She had no idea what the fuck was going on, but she wanted to call the police and get the hell out of Dodge.

Filming in the suicide forest didn't seem like such a wonderful plan anymore. She wasn't sure what changed, exactly, but something had. And now she was stuck in this forest, with some blood-covered crazy person and a bunch of nimrods that walked around as if they were on drugs. Not to mention the idiots that just seemed to have wandered off somewhere and were now nowhere to be found, like Summer. She could really use a bit of sanity right around this time.

"What do we do now?" Lucas asked. His voice sounded distant, as if his thoughts were somewhere else. He appeared distracted, his eyes glancing toward a certain spot.

"We go get everyone, and we're leaving this place," Tara said.

"What about the film?" Lucas said. His voice had an

agonizingly slow lull to it, which made Tara want to shake him violently. At least he was responding. William was just standing there, staring at one spot. The same one Lucas kept looking at.

"Fuck the film," Tara snapped. "William, what the hell are you looking at?" She stood by him and peered along his broad shoulder. There was nothing there except darkness. Some parts of this forest were so black they looked like night during the day, but the shadows had started to spread even throughout the areas that were still semi-lit.

"Where did Summer go?"

Both guys pointed at the spot where they were looking, and for some inexplicable reason, Tara's courage sank to her stomach. She was the only one who walked toward the place they were pointing at, her feet heavy as lead. Everything inside her screamed to turn around, pick up her shit and just get out of this forest, but her legs kept driving her forward, as if she were hypnotised She had to see what the boys obviously knew. She just *had* to see it.

Tara pushed a few branches aside and moved forward. She knew she was on the right path. What made her so sure was a mystery, but she just knew. Just as she knew that the weird shock wave she had experienced had been a bad thing. Something was happening, and she was in the middle of it.

A soft sobbing grabbed her attention, and Tara pushed her way through a thorny bush. It snagged on her shirt and trousers, nicking the skin of her face, neck and hands, but she kept walking. In a small clearing, she found Summer. The girl was holding a pair of scissors, and was cutting her own hair while crying.

"Summer?" Tara asked, incapable of keeping the shaky nerves out of her voice. "What are you doing?"

"I'm paying for my sins," Summer said. "I'm too vain. My hair... it is a symbol of my vanity, and I must give it up."

143

"Have you lost your fucking mind?" Tara's heart pounded in her chest like an angry fist. "Put down the scissors."

"I'm not done yet," the blonde girl said. Her hair was in disarray. Some parts were still long, while others were short. She must have cut into her clothing as well, because they were a mess, too. Her shirt hung around her body in ribbons, and there was not much left of her leggings. The skin that was exposed was covered in deep scratches. Summer sobbed and pulled open the scissors, holding them like a barber's blade. She ran the blade across her scalp, cutting skin and hair alike. Tara cried out, hiding her mouth behind her hand, as the girl pulled off a small piece of flesh.

"Stop that, you fucking asshole," Tara screamed, and she stepped forward to physically stop the girl, but Summer shot her a hateful glare that stopped her in her tracks.

"You should take my example," she said, in a low voice that made Tara deeply afraid. "You have been plenty sinful too."

"William, Lucas," Tara screamed, without taking her eyes off Summer. "I could really use your help here, guys."

"They're not coming." Summer actually giggled. "They understand. They accept that they are sinners too, and that the sin must be cleansed."

She cut another piece of her scalp, hacking away at it, and Tara's stomach turned. She wanted to help her friend, but something in her nagged and prevented her from getting close. *This bitch is going to stab me*. Tara still bore the scars of the last woman who had attacked her with a sharp object, and she had learned her lesson.

"Please stop this." Tara couldn't control the tremble in her voice. "Your hair can't be the source of your vanity anymore. It looks fucking awful. You can just quit, now. No need to go cutting yourself."

"It's not just my hair," Summer said, looking very sad all of a sudden. "Or my clothes." She tugged at the cut ribbons of her shirt. "I'm also very proud of my big blue eyes."

"No," Tara cried and rushed forward, her fears forgotten. She grabbed for Summer's arm, but it was too late. The point slid in with a wet pop. Further and further, until she hit some resistance. Somehow, with an unnatural strength, the girl still pushed on, driving in the scissors all the way to the handle. Red and yellow liquids ran down the blades. Summer's body jerked and then toppled backward. Tara caught her and held on as Summer twitched once more and then went still.

"No!" The body slipped from Tara's hands. The scissors stuck up from the girl's ruined face like an alien tree, and rivers of blood ran down her cheek. The other eye, blue and beautiful, accused Tara with its cold, dead stare.

Your fault. You let me do this.

"I tried," Tara whispered through her tears. She wanted to believe it, but she couldn't. She'd had her chance, could have stolen the scissors away before it was too late. But she'd let her fear—fear for her own safety—stop her.

And now Summer was dead.

"William! Lucas!" she screamed. With heavy arms, she cradled the dead body against her and rocked it back and forth, as if shushing a baby.

"Why?" she asked, but she knew the answer. She had felt it in the air, that need for destruction, for self-sacrifice. Summer must have listened to that voiceless call, while Tara just wanted to get away from it. Who else would listen to it? Her blood ran cold as she thought of the two dazed men who were only a few feet away. Gently, she put Summer's corpse down. Her shirt was covered in blood and clumps of hair, but she barely noticed it.

Her mind was racing as she walked through the bushes, back to their small camp. She was filled with questions.

They couldn't just leave Summer out here, but the idea of having to carry the corpse out of the woods was nothing short of horrifying.

She emerged from the bushes, the news of Summer's death wilting on her lips as her eyes caught sight of William. He was looking up, and Tara followed his gaze with a rapid growing sense of dread. To her horror, she saw what had captured her friend's attention.

It was Lucas.

He was dangling from a tree, his body swaying softly, almost peacefully. Below his feet lay the Green Bay Packers cap he had been wearing. Around his neck was one of the ropes they had brought for the tent. One of the ropes *she* had brought, so that it would be easier to set the tents up on shallow soil. He must have hung himself soon after she went into the bushes, because there was no life in him as far as she could see. Tara bit her lip as tears threatened to burst free. She wanted to scream at William and curse him for just standing there, but hadn't she done the same with Summer? Just stood there?

"We should cut him down," Tara said in a weird daze. While her emotions ran rampant under the surface, she couldn't express them. It was all just too much. She turned to William, hoping she would find something in his face that she could relate too. Maybe a similar shock to the one she felt, or a sense of disgust... anything. Instead, she found a smile.

"Fucking hell, William. Lucas is dead. Summer is dead," she yelled at him. "I don't even know what the fuck is going on. Fuck." Her fist shot out and caught him in the chest. Suddenly, everything that was bottled up came out. The weird numbness turned into a bitter pain, and she desperately wanted him to feel it, too. It was all so mental. She punched him again, but he didn't even flinch. Only after the third strike did she notice that he was holding a screwdriver in his hand. Tara automatically took a few steps back out of self-preservation. He smiled at her vacantly, and she realized the screwdriver was not for her.

"Oh no, you fucking don't, you cunt." Tara ran toward him and slammed her body weight fully into him. She wasn't going to stand by and watch another one of her friends die. Not on her watch. Whatever this fucking thing was, maybe she could knock some sense into William. She grabbed the arm with the screwdriver and struggled with it. When she couldn't outmatch the large man's strength, she bit his hand until the metallic taste of his blood made her gag. But instead of screaming out in pain, William just had that weird, placid smile on his face.

"Let go, William," she screamed. "Put the fucking thing down."

He pushed her away, hard, and she almost fell. William was much stronger than she was, but Tara was tenacious. She pulled at him, trying to make him focus on fighting her rather than on the screwdriver. For a while, she thought she was winning, until he reared back and smashed his fist into her face. Bright stars exploded in her eyesight, and she stumbled back. A heavy blow struck her in the stomach, doubling her over and crushing the breath from her lungs. She gasped, and the stars grew brighter. Her legs went weak and she fell to her knees, fighting to breathe.

When her vision finally cleared, it was just in time to see William lying down on his side, the screwdriver held to his ear. He lifted his head and brought it down onto the point of the tool. It slid in with a soft crunch, no louder than someone crumpling paper.

He died still wearing the same creepy smile.

Tara closed her eyes and sank to her knees. She wanted to stop what was happening, but she didn't know how. The unseen force was pulling at her, telling her to give up. But whatever it was, it didn't know Tara very well. She was not going to let it beat her down, and if there was anyone still out there to save, she would find them, and she would save them. For Summer. For Lucas and for William. Her body aching from the beating she'd endured, Tara got up and stuck out both her middle fingers to the trees above her.

"Fuck you, Aokigahara!"

She wouldn't leave them behind, but she was going to find some help first. She grabbed the satellite phone that lay in the grass and ran toward the path. Perhaps she could get some reception out of the damn thing if she moved away from this spot.

There was no way Tara would go back in that forest alone.

CHAPTER TWENTY

Marie-Claire lay curled in the protective circle, her hands covering her ears, overwhelmed by the grief and the anger emanating from the spiritual world around her. They were so loud, the dead. They had awoken to the wrongs visited on them, and on the world. The martyrs were no longer that; they had twisted somehow. They were new spirits born of wrath, and there were so many of them. Too many. There were those that should have passed over, and yet...

There was a moment when Marie-Claire believed the sheer power of their anger would kill her. That she was doomed somehow. Until the child put a hand on her arm and a soothing calm washed over her. The girl looked at her with her black eyes, and the world disappeared for a moment. Mesmerised by those dark orbs, Marie-Claire reached out for the child's face.

"*Ma bichette*, who are you that you have known to show this to me?" she asked. "You're special, *n'es pas*? You're not just one of the spirits of this forest who committed suicide here." Even now, Marie-Claire still had no idea of the girl's heritage; she seemed to have a little bit of everything in her. Certainly, she wasn't local.

For the first time, the girl spoke, using Marie-Claire's own voice, without ever moving her lips. "We are the guide. We are the enabler and the preventer."

Marie-Claire sat up and frowned, her eyes scanning the ground, searching for thoughts. They were tangled in her head, but she knew she missed something.

"The enablers? Are you somehow claiming responsibility for what is happening right now?"

"It was we who started it all, as was demanded of us. But as we have aided one side, we must now aid the other. There must always be balance. We are of the bloodline, and must serve the world."

"And you want *me* to stop all this?"

"We want to give you the opportunity. Whether you stop it or not, is up to you. Our tears will be spilled for humanity, and we will suffer with them, but we are only allowed to offer equal opportunity. We may not be involved beyond that."

Marie-Claire shook her head. She wasn't asking the right questions, but what were the right questions? She rubbed her temples and tried to think rationally. Then she looked up. "What do they call you?"

"They call us the Lamb."

The Lamb.

"We have shown you," the spirit said. "This burden rests on your shoulders. You will not be alone. There will be others like you."

A soft wind blew through the still woods, rustling the leaves. Fatigue made her thoughts heavy and slow. "How will I find these others?" she asked.

"They will find you, Marie-Claire Florifera. You are the beacon to which they will drift. If you make the right choices."

Marie-Claire rubbed her wrinkled hand across her lips. "I never wanted any of this."

"No one wants the terrible responsibility that life throws at them. Yet, you get the obligation that befalls to you. No more and no less."

"I... I want to get out of these woods. Will you lead me out?" She struggled to get to her feet. Her back hurt, as did her legs, but the weight on her mind was so much greater than any pain.

"I shall lead you to your way out." The girl took her hand and guided her through the shaded forest.

***

Tara stumbled through the darkening woods, her flashlight doing little to illuminate her way, which made the forest even creepier. She'd thought she'd been on the path back, but somewhere along the way it stopped looking like an actual path. Perhaps she had made a wrong turn somewhere, she didn't know. Her sense of direction was usually pretty solid, but this place... it messed with her head somehow. The beating she had taken didn't help either, and her cheek throbbed with pain.

Occasionally, she had called out for the others, hoping maybe someone else had the right idea and would try to make their way home. It would be a lot less scary not to be alone right now. But there had been no response other than the soft rustle of the leaves. Nothing around her looked familiar, but she refused to let her growing desperation control her.

Roots and stones did their best to trip her, and branches slapped at her face. Each time she paused to catch her breath, she tried the satellite phone, but it stayed dead. She cursed the company they'd bought it from and vowed that if—*no*, when, *can't think like that*—she got out of this damn forest, she would not only demand her money back, but punch the clerk in the face.

Something rustled nearby, making her heart jump in her throat. She shone her flashlight in the direction and the edge of the beam caught something that reflected the light back. It was moving, but only slightly. The blood ran to Tara's cheeks as she struggled with a mixture of hope and fear.

"Hello?" she said, her tone a little hushed by the frightful anticipation of what she would encounter.

"George? Koji? Amy?"

There was no answer, and Tara weighed the decision between walking away and investigating. She decided to go with the latter, though she was on her guard. Something in the direction of her flashlight creaked, and she nearly lost all courage to move on. With trembling legs, she made her way through the undergrowth and stopped after a few feet. It wasn't difficult to see what had made the noise and the movement; it was another body. The sight of the chubby figure and the familiar orange and black sweater, with the reflective stripes around the cuffs, made her heart sink.

"Oh, George," Tara whispered, "not you too..." She knew it was him, everything about the big man being familiar, and yet, for some masochistic reason, she needed to see his face. With lead in her shoes she walked forward, illuminating the swaying corpse, determined to cut her friend down. When she shone the light on his head, she regretted it instantly. The soft features were swollen and had a blueish tint. His eyes bulged, as if they were grapes that were ripe to pop out of his skull, but the most disturbing thing was the thick black tongue that hung between his swollen lips. Tara turned away, her mind numb with shock. She looked at the knots that held the rope up. There were so many, she didn't know where to begin. Tara let out a single dry sob.

"I'm sorry, George," she said, not looking at the corpse. "I can't fucking do this right now. I'll send someone for you later, buddy. There's nothing I can do for you." She pushed her way back through the undergrowth and toward the path she had been on, speeding up her pace to a fast walk. The urge to run and scream was fierce, but Tara forced herself to keep focused.

A noise made her stop. Something moved her way. Not fast, but it was coming in her direction. Tara hoped it was someone, anyone, who would help her. But a second thought hit her. *What if it's another crazy person?* She pushed herself against one of the trees, taking advantage of the growing darkness. Part of her wanted to cry out, but she couldn't help remembering the look on Summer's face, that glance of pure malice and contempt. Whoever was out there... they could be dangerous, either to themselves or to her. Tara wasn't sure if she could handle witnessing another suicide, and she didn't have a clue what she would do if she were to get attacked. Yet, at the same time, whoever was out there was still alive. They could also be lost, just like her. The indecision made her legs weak.

Someone cursed, softly, in a foreign language. Definitely a person. It wasn't Japanese; it was French. With a deep breath, Tara mustered all her courage.

"Hello?" she said, not too loud. "Is anyone there?"

"Yes," a voice answered. "My name is Marie-Claire Florifera, and I do believe, *ma cherie*, you are my way out of these woods."

Tara shone her light forward, and it captured an old woman with light brown skin and long white hair. Something bothered her about the lady, and she couldn't quite decide what, but it made her wary. Then she realised what she found disturbing: The woman didn't react to her flashlight. Tara shone it straight in her face, and she didn't even flinch. The eyes were just dead and white.

A ghost! Tara took a step back, prepared to run.

"You'll need to help me, girl," the woman said. "I'm blind."

"What? What the fuck are you doing in these woods?" Tara remained poised and tense, still unsure if she was seeing a person or some sort of apparition.

"It's a long story, child, and one I must save for another day." The old woman's voice was calm, but resolute, easing Tara's fear. She leaned against one of the trees, catching her breath. "Right now, we need to find our way out of here before we join the spirits of the dead."

"That's what I've been trying to do, but I think I'm totally fucking lost."

The old woman smiled, and something about it eased the fear in Tara's chest.

"Don't worry, *cherie*. Together, we shall find our way to where we need to be."

***

Koji woke up to near complete darkness, and for a moment, he wasn't sure if he had his eyes open or closed. His arms were tied over his head, and they ached as if red-hot pins and needles had been stabbed into them. Then someone shone a light in his face, blinding him. He pulled away, squeezing his eyes shut against the stinging light. It took him a moment to remember why he was here in the first place, and the pain quickly turned to fear. He tried to glance in the direction of the person bearing the light.

"Why are you doing this?" Koji asked.

The person in front of him cried softly. "I don't know," he said with a soft voice. Koji recognised it. The bloody man they'd found. The one who'd hit him. "Something is making me do this. Someone... I touched that thing on the ground, and now I'm no longer alone in my head. That guy, he had dolls... I think he's in here with me. It's not just him, either." He moved like a caged tiger, ramming his palm against his temple.

Koji tugged at the ropes binding his arms. They didn't budge. He could barely feel his hands, except for a painful tingle.

"You don't have to do this," Koji said, wondering with a rising sense of dread what "this" exactly was. The whole thing seemed very surreal.

"I do. You have no idea, but I really do..." The man's voice cracked. "You see, when I do what they say, they let me sleep. And when I sleep, I don't feel this pain. I... I think

I slept for days when you found me. Your light, it triggered me to wake up."

"My... my light?" Koji asked. "I don't have a light."

"Yeah, the people like you, they have a light. Inside of them, I mean. There's more of you, and now... now you're just bait."

Koji shifted in an attempt to get more comfortable.

"Please, I don't have a light. Please just let me go! This is so crazy... really crazy. Please."

"The end of the world is coming," the man said. Koji opened his eyes again. "And we must all pick sides. There are those who understand how foul humanity really is, and if we help them then maybe we will get a place in the new world. But the ones who would try to stop us. The ones with the light... We must destroy them."

"Was your sister one of those?"

"She was." The man sniffed back tears and then continued. "I... I didn't know at first. She went missing. I followed and was led to the place where it all began. When I saw the plaque on the ground, I knew it needed to be opened, and so I tried. I even managed to crack it, but Laney, she... she tried to stop me. She had the light, too. I was told to destroy her..."

"Maybe you didn't kill her. It could be that you don't have it in you," Koji said, trying to keep his voice soft and soothing—he knew he was grasping at straws, but perhaps the unhinged mind was open to manipulation. "Perhaps your sister isn't even dead. We could go find her, see if she's okay."

"I do have it in me. I know I do..."

"I don't even know your name." If he could just keep the man talking, maybe he could get him to see reason.

"Mark," the man said. "My name is Mark."

"My name is Koji." He remembered a TV show, or maybe it was a movie, where someone explained that you need to get a killer to see you as a person rather than a target. It could help. How, he didn't know, but he was willing to try anything at this point. *This guy killed his sister*, the evil voice of doubt whispered in the back of his head. *Can't get much more personal than that...*

"Hi, Koji," Mark said. "It saddens me. I don't want to kill, but they demand it."

Any hope Koji had died with those words. He felt sick to his stomach.

"You don't even know who *they* are," Koji said, desperation causing his voice to rise again. "You don't have to do this. No one is making you do anything. I don't understand what's happening, but it sounds like you don't either. Instead of this, why don't you untie me, and we'll go look for your sister together, okay?"

The man moaned again, doubling over. Koji wondered if he could kick far enough to hit his head. But even if he did, what good would it do him? He'd still be tied up, though it could potentially buy him time. He kicked forward, but didn't even come close.

"You don't know what I have done," Mark groaned. "To my sister, to other people... I don't even know how long I have been here. Days? Weeks? Months? Everything is such a blur, but they... the voices, they help me survive. I only survive if I listen to them, and they want me to kill. I need to take the lives of the special people, the light ones, those like you..."

"You don't have to do that at all," Koji said. "We can leave this place together, and I can get you some help."

"I... I think I ate someone, Koji," Mark said, on his knees now, the light faintly illuminating him. "I think I ate another human being."

"Jesus," Koji said, struggling to find the words.

"I had to eat and drink to survive. Eat, drink, and sleep... that's all I did. Didn't feel the cold or the pain anymore. They wouldn't let me feel. They let me sleep."

"Yeah, okay," Koji said. He watched the man squirm, then suddenly he stopped. For a moment he seemed frozen, then Mark straightened up and shined the light on Koji's face. When he spoke, there was a cruel hardness to his voice that hadn't been there before.

"Make sure you scream nice and loud." The flashlight illuminated a large hunting knife and Koji's guts clenched. "I need you to lure the others."

"No, please—" The point of the blade stabbed into Koji's ribs, slowly, with enough pressure to hurt but not pierce his clothing. Koji's fear erupted in a scream.

"Stop!"

"I'm just going to hurt you a little." Mark's voice dripped with evil. "Get you warmed up before I really carve into you. I changed my mind. I *do* want to kill."

He pressed harder this time, the blade slicing through the fabric to nick his flesh.

Koji started to cry. Hot tears ran across his cold face. He was going to die here, his body added to those that disappeared forever. The forest whispered to him, laughing. Perhaps his soul would wander here for eternity, crying in the darkness...

"When it's time, I'm going to cut open your stomach and let all your intestines fall out. I want you to see what you look like from the inside before you die."

"Please." The words came out fast; he was blubbering like a baby, but he didn't care. "Please don't do this. I don't want to die."

"Everybody dies, Koji," Mark said. "At least now you'll die for a cause. You die for..." his words stopped abruptly at the sound of a hollow *thwack*. The light fell to the ground, and a moment later, Mark's body followed, hitting the earth with a heavy thud.

"Koji?" A familiar voice at the verge of panic, whispering. "Is that you?"

"Tara?" Koji's fear intensified. Something told him there was more danger, that she'd brought it with her.

"Holy shit, Koji, was that guy torturing you?" Tara shone a light on his bonds.

"Untie the boy," said a strange voice with a hint of a French accent. "*Dépêchez-vous!* Hurry up. You hit this one hard, but not hard enough to keep him knocked out forever. Unless you are willing to kill him. His spirit stirs even now."

Tara fiddled with Koji's bonds. "They're really tight. I need a knife."

"He had one," Koji nodded toward where Mark had fallen. Tara shined the light on the figure on the ground and grabbed his knife.

She put the blade to the bonds and sawed at the rope. "Hold still, I don't want to cut you." Her breath was warm on his cheek, and her body felt like a welcoming part of reality. He rested his face in her neck and cried as she untied him. When the final bit of rope fell apart, gravity pulled him down. Tara grabbed at him but couldn't hold him, and they landed hard on the rocks and sticks. He tried moving his wrists, but they were so numb he couldn't feel them, as if they were ghost limbs. With throbbing fingers, he rubbed his flesh back to life.

"Help me tie this fucker up." Tara shined her light around the ground. She held up the pieces of rope. "It's a bit short, but I think this might do."

He moved forward, feeling like Pinocchio with his wooden limbs, and helped her lift Mark. The dead-weight of the man was hard to pick up, but the thought of him waking up frightened Koji so much he found strength he never knew he had. They positioned him against one of the smaller trees.

"No need to make him stand," she said. "Sitting is better."

Koji held Mark's torso upright, while Tara pulled his arms around the tree. She fiddled with the rope.

"That should do it." She stepped away from the unconscious man.

"Are we just going to leave him here?" Koji frowned. "He could die if no one finds him."

"We'll send someone," Tara said. "It's more than that motherfucker deserves, but we're the good guys here. We're going to call the police anyway, and an ambulance, to pick up... That guy you met..."

"Toshiro?" Koji asked. "He's dead. You must have found his remains."

"Shit, Koji, it's not just Toshiro..."

"Who else?"

"Did Toshiro commit suicide?" she asked. "Or did this guy kill him?"

"No, he set himself on fire," Koji said. "Right in front of my eyes. I didn't even do anything. I just froze."

"Yeah, so did I when Summer killed herself."

Koji gasped. He thought of the beautiful blonde with the warm smile. Her laughter rang in his ears. "Summer?

"Yeah. William and Lucas, too." Tara shook her head. "I'm sorry to be the one to tell you this, but they're all dead."

"I don't understand what's happening," Koji said.

"Me either," Tara muttered. "Some fucked up shit, that's for sure."

"What about Amy and George?" Koji asked. "Where are they? Are they dead, too?"

"I found George," she said, her face stern. "He hanged himself. I haven't seen any trace of Amy, though. Not since I left to get that fucking useless phone. It's still not working."

"I'm not surprised. There is something really wrong about this place," Koji muttered. "Here's hoping Amy is still alive."

"Yeah," she said. "We should really get out." Tara stood up and pointed at the old woman, who was seated nearby, her head down. "We can't risk looking for people that might be dead. I'll grab the blind lady, and we'll start finding a way out. Maybe it's a good thing I got lost before, or I wouldn't have found you." She squeezed his arm. "I'm glad I did."

"I'm glad, too," Koji said. "And grateful. Thank you for saving my life."

"I couldn't have done it if it wasn't for her."

"Who is she?"

"Her name is Marie-Claire Florifera. She says she's a medium."

The answer surprised him. "Wow," he said. "Does she know what's going on?"

"I'm not sure. She's told me some shit on the way over, but it's pretty crazy. I don't know what to believe." Tara pulled on his arm, and he followed.

"Yeah, that Mark guy said some crazy stuff, too." He looked back at the tree one more time. How quickly the tables had turned, he thought, but he knew they could turn again, and he feared the idea. He wasn't religious, but he prayed to whatever gods or ancestors might be listening that they would find their way out of the forest.

"Don't expect things to get better once we're out, young man." The old lady lifted her head, the milky-white eyes visible in the sparse light, as if she were reading his thoughts. "I fear our trials have only just begun."

CHAPTER TWENTY ONE

Freya leaned back, feeding Emily from her breast, while Wulf was doing the dishes. She breathed deep, savouring the lingering scents of the spaghetti bolognese that Wulf had cooked for dinner.

"He cooks *and* he cleans," she said with a smile. "You must be the perfect man."

Wulf laughed. He rinsed one of the plates under the tap and put it in the dishwasher.

"How are you feeling?" he asked.

"Empty," Freya said. "I feel like all my tears have been spent today. Sorry I cried so much."

"You just lost a friend," Wulf said. "No need to apologize. I would probably cry, too."

Freya looked at the nursing baby and ran a finger across the soft skin of her cheek. "I lost her before... when she died." She sighed. "When she came back, I thought I would never lose her again."

"Loss is unfortunately a big part of life," Wulf said as he put a cup in the machine.

"What makes me so sad is how much she loved Emily, and now my daughter will grow up without remembering what Bam was like." Her eyes went moist again. "Damn, I guess my tears aren't spent, after all," she muttered.

"It's up to you to remind Emily. Share your memories of Bam with her."

"It's not the same," Freya said, wiping the tears from her eyes.

"It isn't. It never is."

"Have you lost loved ones?" she asked

He turned to her, but didn't look at her face. Instead, he stared at his shoes. "More than I felt I could deal with. I know loss."

"I'm sorry," she said, and she detached Emily. With a fluid motion, she pulled her nursing bra back over her exposed breast and readjusted her shirt. She held Emily over her shoulder and patted the baby to burp.

"You know what helped me through it?" Wulf said, now holding her eyes with his own.

"No?"

"People." He grabbed a dishcloth and wiped his hands as he walked over to her. He slid into the seat next to her and took Emily from her arms. "Me and Emily, we'll get you through this."

A warm feeling came over her, and for a moment everything just seemed as it should be. *This is what it would have been like if Logan were still alive*, she thought. *I never believed it possible for me to feel like this again.*

She leaned in and kissed him. His lips were soft and warm, and they chased away the emptiness she felt.

"I think we should put Emily to bed, don't you?" he said, his voice low and husky. There was a hunger in his eyes, and she shared his desire. She longed for him to fill her, both emotionally and physically.

"I think you're right."

***

His hands were on her waist when she closed the door to the nursery. Gently, he tugged at her, turning her around. She let him guide her, clearing her mind of all thoughts, except for those of his touch. With a gentle pressure he pushed her against the wall, pressing his lips against hers. There was more passion in his kiss than there had been before, more urgency. He wasn't holding back now, and her body responded to him. Wulf was different from Logan in so many ways. The coy way Logan had touched her was a contrast to the confident fingers that explored her midriff.

He pulled her away from the wall, leading her—backward—to her bedroom. His lips never left hers as he pushed open the door, guiding her through the darkness. The movement of his tongue against hers was hypnotic, the rhythm speeding up in time with their beating hearts. His warm hands moved across the front of her shirt, resting on her top button. He pulled back, his face visible in the light of the moon shining through the bedroom windows. There was a question in his eyes, and though he never uttered it, she understood. *Are you sure about this*? She nodded, and he undid the first button, his eyes on hers, a hungry smile on his face. A second button loosened sent an electric surge through her body, and she took a deep breath before pressing her lips against his again.

The cool air hit her skin as Wulf removed her top, and she, in turn, tugged at his shirt, pulling it over his head. She gasped at the sight of his chiselled chest, which could have put the statue of David to shame. Gently, she ran the tip of her tongue along his collarbone and up his neck. He moved his head to catch her lips again, and his hands had found a new target: her jeans.

Less than a minute later, Freya was down to her underwear. With a gentle, but still forceful nudge, he pushed her onto the bed. His face was intense when he rid himself of his own jeans. The deep green eyes never left hers as he lowered himself onto the bed, crawling over her like a panther. He paused for a moment, drinking in the sight of her body, before he kissed her again. His movements forced her to half sit up, and he took the opportunity to free her from her bra. He admired her naked breasts, then kissed them, letting his tongue and teeth play with the nipples. Freya threw her head back, the pleasure of his touch making her body ache for him. A familiar pang throbbed between her legs that yearned to be caressed.

He read her body and let his fingers stroke over the fabric of her underwear. Somewhere in the back of her mind, Freya lamented that she wasn't wearing a nicer set, or that she hadn't shaved more recently than a few days ago, but his touch made her forget her worries. The fingers explored, pulling away the fabric, where flesh found naked flesh. His thumb rubbed the exact right spot to make her cry out in pleasure, while his middle finger found its way inside of her. He kissed her again; she felt his smile against her lips when she moaned in delight.

His hardened member pressed against her thigh, and she longed for nothing more than having him inside her.

"Do you have protection?" she whispered, hoping that she would be strong enough to refuse him if he said no.

"Yes," he said, his voice little more than a deep breath. The fingers left her, and she heard something rip, then the sound of a condom being unfolded. Seconds later, he was against her, pressing against the lips of her vagina, while his mouth found hers again. He kissed her for a long time, holding himself outside her, until she wrapped her legs around him, and he pushed. There was a slight delicious sense of pain when he entered her, which quickly melted to pleasure. She opened up to him, as he pressed deep within her. His thumb found her clitoris again, and he rubbed it in rough circular motions as he found a pounding rhythm with his pelvis. She squirmed, finding her own cadence. He brought her to pleasure, letting her scream out in ecstasy, only to build up her climax again. Over and over, relentlessly, he brought her to new heights, until he himself was spent and they fell back onto the pillows in exhausted bliss.

Freya curled herself around him, resting her head on his chest.

"I feel safe," she said softly, looking up at his face.

"Despite everything that happened, I really do."

He didn't respond. To her horror, Freya detected a grim look on his face. She closed her eyes and tried to rid herself of the image. *I know too little happiness to let anything ruin this moment*, she thought. But she was wrong...

CHAPTER TWENTY TWO

"We're lost." Tara stood still, aiming her flashlight at the ground around her. "We're so fucking lost. I can't see where we're going, and I just don't have a clue anymore."

Koji shined his own light and tried to make sense of his surroundings. If the woods were ominous by daylight, they were downright scary by night. The strangely curled roots were dangerous in the dark, tripping them up at each turn. There was something about the forest he hadn't noticed before. It was as if the surroundings were alive.

"We will find the way out, *ma cherie*," the old woman said in a calm voice. "Don't let this forest deceive you. It wants us to feel hopeless and helpless, because it recognizes that we are a force to be reckoned with." The woman looked like a ghost with her white hair and her light-colored dress.

"Do you seriously believe that shit?" Tara swore. Pressure made her testy; Koji had known her long enough to not want to push her buttons at this moment. "We're just fucking lost. The forest isn't plotting against you."

"I found you for a reason. I was led to you."

Tara shined the light in the woman's face. "By whom?"

"A spirit who called herself 'the Lamb.'"

Koji frowned, and Tara threw up her hands. "For fuck's sake... the Lamb? I don't have time for this bullshit. We just need to find a way out of here."

"The Lamb..." Koji mused out loud. "Sounds like a cartoon," he snorted softly, "or a sock puppet." He scratched his head, feeling a little grumpy himself. The fear was still strong, but the exhaustion was even stronger. They had been wandering for hours, and he just wanted to get out and rest.

Tara sighed audibly.

"Actually," Koji muttered, "it sounds like something biblical."

"Biblical..." The old woman raised a hand to her mouth. "It has to be, that would make the most sense." She thought for a moment. "I come from an atheist family myself. My mother was a very modern French woman for her time, but I have read the Bible, a long time ago, when I tried to make sense of my visions. Wasn't Jesus called the Lamb of God?"

"How the fuck is this relevant to our current situation?" Tara said. "We are trying to find a way out. Unless that Lamb spirit is willing to guide us from here, I think we need to focus on what's going on right now."

"Because whatever happened here didn't stay here. I can sense it all around me, and I fear it."

The old lady's words made Koji's blood run cold. He linked his arm in hers again and held her close. She was so thin her bones felt as though they could break if he used too much strength.

"Okay, so maybe we can figure out what's going on, once we get out of these woods, though," Koji said. "I think this discussion will be much more effective when we're not so tired and cold." He shot Tara a nervous smile. "And scared."

"We will need to do more than just talk about it, my boy. We will need to find kindred spirits."

"Or kindred livestock," Tara said, her voice filled with sarcasm. It was only to mask her fear. He shared her sentiment and understood the need to ridicule.

"This is no joke, my dear," the woman said. "The Lamb

spoke about the seven seals. This was the second one to be broken..." There was some strength in the older woman's grip, and the thin, bony arm squeezed Koji's so tight that it hurt.

"The seal was broken?" Koji scanned his memory of the strange conversation he had with his captor. "I..."

"Whatever is happening in this forest, I fear we are about to see worse things outside of it." Marie-Claire ignored Koji's stammering.

"That's a comforting thought," Tara said, her expression glum.

Koji pushed his glasses up his nose, still trying to remember what Mark had said about the seal. At the time, it had just sounded like ramblings from a crazy person, but now...

"Do you know what's going on?" Tara asked.

"I know what's happening," the old woman said to Koji. *"Allez savoir pourquoi...* for whatever reason, someone is opening the seals. But I don't understand what our role is in this yet."

"The seven seals?" Koji said.

"Yes... and if they're broken, they will bring the Apocalypse down upon us. The Lamb said that someone was triggering the Apocalypse on purpose."

"Who would want the fucking world to end?" Tara snapped. "We'll all die if that happens."

"I think whoever is doing this doesn't believe that it will end the world."

"They believe they might be resetting it," Koji said. "That guy, Mark, he said some weird stuff like this too. He was going on about cleansing the world. And something about angels and demons and a war.... There were two other parties, or something, but I don't know who they were. I wish I'd listened better to him. His words... they didn't make a lot of sense, and I was so scared..."

"What the fuck?" Tara said. "Now you tell us?"

"I must urge you to hold your temper, Tara," the old woman said. "Koji hasn't had a lot of opportunity to tell us what has happened to him, *n'est pas*? And sometimes we don't remember what we have heard or seen until it is important for us to remember."

"Whatever," Tara shrugged. "So, we think it's the seven seals... because that's not disturbing as hell."

"I was there when the second one opened. These things harbor a kind of power that is beyond compare. I have rarely felt anything quite like it, and I have been around some darkness that is not of this world. It would not surprise me if we are directly linked to what is happening right now in some way."

Koji patted the old woman's hand. His heart was pounding, and he tried to remember what the exact words of that crazy man had been when he was about to plunge a knife in his gut. He couldn't remember; all he recalled was how frightened he was. It was something about pestilence...

"We *are* dealing with the Apocalypse."

Tara made a scoffing noise. "Don't worry. We've survived at least five Apocalypses so far. Maybe even more, let's see..." She held up her hand in the light and counted them down. "There was that Nostradamus one in 1999, the year 2000 January Apocalypse, and another one in the same year in May. I think there was one in 2008, and then there was the one in 2012."

"Laugh, *ma cherie*, but this is real. There is so much to this world that you couldn't even imagine." Marie-Claire sighed. "I fear for us all."

"I think it's okay to be afraid. Though the concept of this

being a magical thing sounds a little far-fetched. Especially since we haven't explored the other options at this point. This could possibly be explained with really mundane evidence," Koji said. "Perhaps there's some toxic gas, or plant or whatever, that's messing with our minds. It can cause people to do strange things. It would explain the suicides. It would be a good reason why you had the visions you had, or why Mark said the things he said."

"It would also explain why they killed themselves the way they did." Tara was leaning against a tree to rest, eyeing them from beneath a fringe of brown hair. Her ponytail had come mostly undone. "You don't just scalp yourself with a straight face. That would have to hurt, and yet it looked as if Summer didn't feel a thing."

Koji cringed. He pictured Summer's smiling face again and tried to ward off the horrible image of her peeling off a bloody scalp.

"Toshiro didn't feel anything until he was almost dead," he added, pushing away the memory.

The old woman shook her head. "It's a good theory, but I don't think so, *mon chere*. Not after what I saw. And remember, I had visions before I ever came to Aokigahara; I've been a medium for many decades." Florifera ran her slender hand across her nut-brown forehead. "The seal was deliberately opened with an offer. I saw a man sacrifice a man who was dressed as a monk."

"You saw?" Tara's voice was sharp. "I thought you were blind."

"My eyes cannot see what you can, *ma cherie*, but I am far from blind. I can see a world that you can't. And sometimes that world will lend me its eyes to look into yours."

Tara looked at the woman with quiet resolve, but the expression of her face softened.

"This is some fucked up shit, right there. If I had any

idea something like this would happen, I never would have come to fucking Japan in the first place." Tara shook her head. "I was just trying to turn my fucking life around."

"*Cherie*, I don't think you could have escaped this. Like I mentioned before, whatever happened here had a ripple effect to the outer world."

Tara sighed. "I don't even want to think of that. It would make it so much easier if it was some sort of local hallucinogenic..."

"Life doesn't always offer us the easy way out," the medium said. "I agree with your need to get away from these woods. Even if it's just to ensure our physical safety."

"And then what are we going to do?" Tara asked. "If you're right, if this doesn't stop here, what will we do?"

"I don't have a plan yet. Information is our strongest weapon at this point, and we must gather as much as we can find."

"Where do you find information about something like this?" Koji asked.

"In history, in books, in people," Florifera said. "Something this big leaves a trail. We already know parts of it. If it's biblical, then there will be texts on it containing the hints we need. Perhaps theologians can help us find out more about the other seals. There must be experts on the matter who have written papers or books. It's our job to find them and gain their help."

"I guess that makes sense," Koji said.

"Sense, yes," the old woman muttered, "but what keeps bothering me is that the girl called herself 'the Lamb.' I just can't get that word out of my mind. When I first met her, I believed her to be an ordinary spirit of a victim. I just don't think it was Jesus, but I can't explain why."

"Well, first of all, Jesus was a grown man," Koji

ventured.

"That doesn't matter to the spirit world. The really powerful ones can appear to me in different forms. The girl could have simply chosen her form to be less threatening. But still, I'm so convinced it wasn't Jesus. I feel like the girl is a piece of a puzzle, somehow. She also spoke about herself as 'we.'"

"So, what do you think it was?" Koji asked. "Any guesses? Could it be an angel? Or maybe a demon?"

"I wish I had answers, *mon chere*," the old woman said. "But I simply can't make sense of the girl yet." She half-turned to Tara. "Tara, the Bible, you know it better than I... is it specific that Jesus was the Lamb?"

Tara shrugged. "The Bible is rarely very specific. I think it mentions that the Lamb opens the seals, but I don't think it specifically said *Jesus*. It's not like I can quote the Bible exactly or anything. Go look it up." She turned and strode off. Koji studied the face of the blind woman, who seemed deep in thought. He gently pulled her along, not wanting to lose sight of Tara.

"*Allez*, we need to catch up with your friend," the old woman said. Koji nodded and led her on. He stumbled over a root, and it was the strong hands of the fragile woman who caught him. She surprised him, but he managed to compose himself enough.

"It's a scary thought that someone is willing to break the seals," Koji said, fiddling with his glasses. "Even if they don't trigger the actual end of the world, a 'cleansing' sounds pretty devastating."

"I think you are absolutely right, *mon chere*," the old medium said. "But some people don't care to devastate. The world is filled with people who would gladly sacrifice others for such trivialities as 'opinions.' Imagine what a zealot could do if they believed the sacrifice is a noble one."

Koji shuddered, and his mind wandered to the suicide

bombers he had read about. *Imagine if people like that were to find out that there was a way to trigger the Apocalypse. Wouldn't they believe their god would keep them safe?* The thought made his blood run cold.

CHAPTER TWENTY THREE

"Holy shit, Freya, are you watching this?"

She didn't respond. Her thoughts drifted to Bam while she was breastfeeding Emily. She missed her friend, and hoped that wherever she was, she would be safe.

"Freya," Wulf's urgent voice snapped her out of her thoughts. "The news..."

She glanced up and saw the frazzled face of a reporter.

"Thousands of suicides in New York..."

Freya didn't hear the rest of the words. She stared mutely at the distant shots of broken bodies lying on the streets.

"It was like it was raining, only it wasn't water falling." The woman's dark skin was slick with tears and ruined makeup. "I've never seen anything like it. This one guy, he just fell right in front of me. There was blood everywhere. I saw things..." Her words ended in a sob.

"Jesus, they show that on the news?" Freya turned her head away. "What the fuck is going on? This is happening in New York?"

"It's happening everywhere around the world," Wulf said, and he zapped through several channels. More and more grim images of crying people and ambulance personnel clearing away bodies flickered across the screen. Freya could barely take in the visuals.

Emily cried and squirmed, snapping Freya out of her reverie, and she realised how tightly she was holding her daughter. "This has something to do with Angel Manor," she said softly. "I don't exactly know how, but there's something familiar about this."

"Right," Wulf said. He stared at the TV screen, his face filled with tension.

"Right?" Freya shifted her weight, holding Emily up for burping. "What do you mean by that?"

"Nothing, you're probably right."

"Right about what?"

Wulf didn't meet her eyes. "The Angel Manor thing. If you think it's connected, then it probably is." He looked at his hands, a pained expression on his face.

"You are acting really weird." Freya patted the baby on her back. "What's going on?" She narrowed her eyes at him. "You show me people are committing suicide all over the world, and I say it could have something to do with the very house we're sitting in, and your response is, 'You're probably right.' That doesn't add up."

"Freya," he turned to her, but couldn't look her in the eye for more than a second.

"You're hiding something from me," she said. "And I want to know what it is."

"I... I haven't been honest with you." Wulf buried his face in his hands. "And I have a confession to make." He cleared his throat. "When I said I never heard of Angel Manor, I was lying."

Freya nodded, her mouth a thin line and her soul filled with fire. "I always wondered why you weren't curious about this house," she said softly. "You tried to make me believe that was because you liked me, and you weren't interested in my secrets. But that's never been true, has it? The reason why you didn't want to know, is because you already knew."

"Not everything, but I found out soon enough."

"You sought me out because of the house."

"Yes." He had the decency to look ashamed. "I wasn't quite prepared for meeting you, though. What I feel for you... that's real."

"Don't," she said, her voice breaking. "Don't try to charm me, not now. Not after..." Emily bounced in her grip, and she smiled at the baby, though her heart was filled with sadness. "Is Wulf even your real name?"

"No, but it's the name I go by now." He sighed. "I can't share my real name with you, because that would put you in danger."

"Put me in danger..." she laughed, but the sound was bitter. "You know what this place is, right?"

"Yes, I know what this is, and I know who you are."

"So, you are more than just an investigator of psychic phenomenon?" She sniffed.

"I am," he admitted.

Freya frowned. Her heart pounded with a dull beat. "Then why are you here?"

"I'm here to keep an eye on things." He took a deep breath. "Because of what is happening surrounding the seals, and you're the guardian to the seventh seal," Wulf said.

She blinked. "Seventh?"

It was his turn to look surprised. "Surely the Praestes have told you about the other seals?"

"The who?"

He grabbed her arm. "Freya, don't kid with me here... the Praestes, the organisation that watches over the seven seals. The ones who instruct you? Who provide you with the necessary sacrifices that need to be made to preserve the seals?"

She shook his grip away from her and shot to her feet. "I don't know what you're talking about. No one is helping me... well, no one was. Someone opened a bank account for me recently, but that's it. And that only happened in the last month. I've been doing this shit for over a year now. With no help. *I* find my own sacrifices. *I* take care of that thing down there. *I* make sure it won't wake up, and no one, except Bam, has ever even offered any guidance."

"How is that possible?" Wulf said. "The Praestes have guided the guardians for centuries."

"Then how come I've never heard of them?" Freya demanded. "My aunt left a diary, and she never mentioned them, so I'm assuming she hadn't heard of them either."

"Holy fuck, you mean this seal is protected by just mortals?" Wulf's eyes were open so wide he looked as if he were about to hyperventilate. "When you got the bank account, did someone at least come to see you?"

"No, no one. I haven't met a single living person who has told me about the seal or even this house. I had to find out by myself."

Wulf closed his eyes and exhaled. He took a few seconds to compose himself before he looked at her. "What do you know about the seal?"

"Well, apparently not that much," Freya said testily. "Except that if I don't sacrifice someone every solstice and every equinox, a big monstrous man on an even bigger monstrous horse crawls out."

"You... you saw it?"

Freya nodded. "I found out the hard way." She took a deep breath. "It almost came out a little over a year ago. To stop it, I had to kill the father of my child." She looked down at him coldly. "So no, these Praestes guys you're talking about, they've never contacted me. Nor do they help me. At least, not that I'm aware of." She thought about the strange trial and the lack of police again, but she wasn't willing to give him that information. The possibility that there were people out there who should have helped her made her too angry to give them any form of credit.

"You can't guard a seal all alone," Wulf said.

"No, I can't. And I wasn't. I had Bam, but now..." She swallowed a sob.

"Hey, listen, you've still got me. I'll go figure out what happened, okay?" He got to his feet and stepped toward her, but she took a step back.

"Why should I trust you?" she bit back. "You came here, and you've done nothing but lie to me. You took advantage of my grief. You..." Tears welled up in her eyes. "And now you're pretending that you're on my side?"

"If you can't trust me, at least trust that we both want the same thing," he said, holding up his hands as if she were aiming a gun at him. "We both want that seal to stay closed."

"Do we?" she asked.

"Yes, I swear." He pointed at the TV. "You were right. What's happening now... it's related."

"What *is* happening, Wulf?" she buried her face in Emily's thin hair and sniffed in the comforting smell of baby shampoo.

"Those suicides, they're a result of the second seal being opened."

"The second..." Freya echoed the words with a hollow voice. "There are seven in total, and this is the seventh?"

"Yes. Each seal is located in a different part of the world. The second seal was placed in Japan. A forest called Aokigahara grew on top of it. It's known as the suicide forest."

"Charming," Freya said miserably. "Seven seals, and here I was thinking there were only four Horsemen."

"There are. The Horsemen are the most dangerous of the seals, but there are three more announcing the Apocalypse. If all were opened..."

"So, there are three more seals, aside from those that harbor the Horsemen? What lies underneath them? Is it like in the Bible?"

"The Bible isn't completely accurate, so don't get hung up on the text. There won't be any angels with trumpets, trust me on that, though I wouldn't be surprised if there is some form of sound or music. There are some actual truths to the texts, but if you knew the real history of the Bible, you would understand why the truth has been distorted. The texts were written generations after the stories actually took place, and have been translated and edited so many times you wouldn't recognize the original scripts and events. On top of all that, there has been some manipulation from the higher planes, if you know what I mean?"

She looked at him blankly.

Wulf sighed. "It does, however, have some good theories about what's under the seals. The Horsemen aren't the first four, though; they are the last. You're living on the final seal. When Death rides, the end of the world is upon us. Or, at least, the end of the world as we know it."

"That's helpful," Freya said glumly. "So, what do you believe the second seal is? Why are people killing themselves?"

"The souls of the martyrs cry out for vengeance," Wulf said. "The spirits of the unjustly dead are all part of the seal's magic, and it's driving some of the more susceptible living insane enough to kill themselves."

"A lot of people die unjustly," Freya said. Her mouth was cotton dry, and she struggled to swallow. "That's a lot of magic."

"Imagine the damage it's doing to the world right now." He pointed at the television again.

"Is this seal just going to make everyone kill themselves?" Freya hugged Emily a bit tighter.

"No, this is just a wave of madness. Only some are affected by it. The seal, it's changing the magic in this world, and a percentage of humanity is really susceptible to that. Places where the energy is strong will be highly affected. You'll get a high suicide rate there."

Freya glanced at the window. "Why aren't we affected here? Isn't this a place of power? I know Lucifer Falls is a great place for people to commit suicide. They even try it from this property at times, jump down from the highest point. It hasn't happened since I lived here, but there were rumours..."

"I'm honestly surprised there haven't been any mass suicides around this place. I would have thought this would be almost as attractive as Aokigahara itself." He rubbed his chin. "It could still happen."

"You're just the bearer of good news, aren't you?"

"I'm sorry," he said.

"So, New York is a strong magical place?" she asked.

"Yes, some big places are. You can almost feel it when you walk through their streets. They tend to be the type of cities that just feel 'different' from the rest of the country. New York, New Orleans, Berlin, Florence, Amsterdam, places like that."

Freya let out a sob. "Amsterdam?" She covered her mouth. "I have family there."

"Not everyone will be affected. You might want to give them a call and see if they're okay."

Freya wiped the tears from her face. "I'm going to put Emily down for her nap and then phone my parents. I need you to be gone when I come back."

"Freya, I don't think I should leave you alone," Wulf said.

"I really need you to go. Don't go far, because there are still a lot of questions I have for you, but right now, I need to sort my head out. I don't trust you anymore." Freya shot him a cold look. "And I can't forgive you for lying to me and using me. I need to figure out if I'm going to believe that you're here to help me, or if I believe you're a bad person. In order for me to do that, I need you to not be here."

He nodded. "I still think this is a bad idea, but I understand. I will be close, so if you need me, you can call me—"

"I'll—" All the lights went off, cutting her off mid-sentence and casting them in darkness. Her first instinct was to panic, but she took a deep breath and said, "Damn, must have blown a fuse."

A surge went through her core as if she had just touched a live feed of electricity. A familiar sensation rushed over her, the house waking from its half-slumber and reaching out for her with invisible tendrils. Freya gasped and instinctively touched her nose. There was blood...

No... oh god, no, not this...

Freya knew this; she had been in this position before. She couldn't see Emily's face in the dark, but she was relieved when she touched around the baby's nose and there was no moisture. *She's too young for the house to take.*

"Oh, dear lord," she said. "Wulf, did you do something to this house?"

"What? No! What would I have done?"

"I don't know if you know magic or anything, if you cast a spell?"

"No, I didn't cast anything."

"Well, someone did," Freya said. "I can't leave this house. It has a hold of me again."

"What do you mean?"

"Someone just tied my soul back to this damn manor. If I'm not mistaken, it probably took yours, too. Check if your nose is bleeding."

There was no response, but his silence told her more than she wanted to know.

"Jesus, Wulf. If you didn't cast the spell, then who did?"

CHAPTER TWENTY FOUR

In the early morning light, the village looked like a set out of a horror movie. Hundreds of bodies littered the streets, their broken shapes twisted in pools of blood. Wide eyes stared out of the torn open faces, and gaping wounds marred dead flesh. Household objects—scissors, knives, pens, screwdrivers, anything sharp—protruded from eyes, ears, throats and bellies. Tara walked between the deceased, her mind numb to the sight of the self-inflicted atrocities. They made the short time she'd spent wandering around helplessly with little food and drink in Aokigahara seem like child's play. She stopped briefly next to the body of a young girl who had scratched her face open with her own hands, leaving nothing but a mangled pulp of skin, which exposed the glint of bone underneath.

What would have gone through that girl's mind? she thought. *What went through Summer's? Or Lucas's? Or William's? Or any of them?*

The dead hadn't died long ago; the scene was fresh. The blood still looked wet, and there was a strange metallic smell in the air.

Tara couldn't wrap her mind around it. She didn't know how to react to this. It was as if her emotions had just been turned off. Koji responded differently. He cried the tears that she couldn't find in her soul. He vomited, as if he were taking on her pain, and Tara wondered what the fuck was wrong with her. Perhaps it was because she was tired after walking through the woods all night. Perhaps it was because the relief of finding the exit to Aokigahara hadn't quite worn off yet, or the shock of finding the first village a ghost town filled with dead inhabitants made her too numb. *Or maybe you're just a psychopath, and it's coming out now*, the dark little voice in her head whispered.

A movement made her jump, and Tara stared at a figure who sat hunched over one of the dead. It was a young woman—Tara couldn't really guess her age, which could have been anywhere between sixteen and thirty—with long, straight hair. The words of greeting died on Tara's lips when the woman looked up. An empty-eyed smile formed around bloodstained lips. That bright rust colour of drying blood stained her skin and clothes. The black eyes just stared at her, and Tara wished she had a gun. Whatever was in that expression, it chilled her to the bone. The corpse in front of the young woman was that of an old man. His shirt had been ripped open and his chest exposed. The woman gently touched the torso, her eyelids fluttered as if she were in a fit of ecstasy, then she ran one long fingernail across the naked skin. No blood spilled—the body was dead and the heart wasn't pumping—but when the woman bent over and licked the deep wound, lapping like a kitten, her tongue came away covered in deep red. She dug her fingers deeper into the skin, using both hands. The squelching sound turned Tara's stomach.

"Be careful," the voice of the old woman was suddenly very near. "That's not a normal person."

"You can see her?" Tara whispered with a hint of surprise.

"I can see everything from the other worlds. Clearer than you can, *ma cherie*." The old medium rested a hand on her shoulder. "That's no ordinary human being. I don't think I have ever seen anything quite like that."

"Wha... what do you see?" Tara's hands trembled.

"Despair... she seems to be made up of it." the woman said. "No wait, she's absorbing it, the despair around her, and it's forming her. *Mon Dieu*, I can see it clearly now. It's some sort of monster. It's here to eat the remnants of victims' emotions as well as their flesh."

The creature pulled at the chest of the corpse, cracking open the ribs with a sickening crunch. She dug her hands deep into the chest. She pulled out lungs and liver, then her hand came up cupped around a dark object; from a distance it looked like the rough shape of a large egg. The monster held it up to her face and then sank sharp teeth into it. Tara's knees buckled, but she couldn't look away. A foul odour invaded her nose, the ripe, organic stench of cow manure on a hot day, only stronger and more stomach turning.

"Did it just eat that guy's heart?" Koji asked, his voice thick with raw emotion and disgust.

"The heart and the mind are powerful things," the old woman said vaguely. Her bony fingers dug into Tara's soft shoulders.

They watched the creature tear away at the heart with a beastly delight. Its sharp teeth ripped through the muscular organ as if it were made of gelatin.

"We must stay away from it. I don't want it to turn on us." The old woman's voice was dark.

"What will we do if it does?" Koji asked.

"*Je ne sais pas*," the old woman said. "I don't know. I know about spirits, but this is not a mere lost soul. This goes beyond my realm of expertise."

"That's just fucking great. So... we're unarmed, we don't know what we're dealing with, but we're pretty sure it's bad ass and not human." Tara took a step back, pushing herself into the old woman. "Peachy fucking keen."

"What do we do?" Koji said.

"I don't fucking know, do I?" Tara snapped. "I'm amazed that I even believe this bullshit."

"It's not really a big leap of faith anymore, though, is it?" Koji said. "The village of the dead and that lady eating some old man's insides has pretty much turned me into a believer."

Tara almost laughed. Not a laugh of mirth, but one of sheer panic and blossoming insanity. She had to hold it together, not just for her sake, but for Koji and the old woman as well.

"Just back up," she said. "That thing is clearly content with all the fucking food lying around here."

"We can't just let her eat these people," Koji said. "Isn't that defiling a body, or something?"

Tara frowned. "Do we care? Those people are dead."

"My people believe that the spirits of the dead can be restless if they die in a horrible way, or if their bodies are defiled."

"Well, no offense, but fuck their spirits. They died horribly anyway... nothing I can change about that." Tara frowned. "I'm not risking my life for people who are already dead. I'll risk my life for you fuckers, but not for dead folk. Now back the fuck up. We're getting out of here. There's little chance we'll find survivors here, so I'm not even going to try. Let people with guns sort out that shit." A thought struck her. "And try to hold in feeling hopeless or anything. If these things are out for despair, like the old lady says, then the last thing we want to do is seem appetizing."

"There is sense in that," Koji said. "I'm finding it very difficult to control my emotions now, though." There were tears in his voice.

"Koji, we're going to be okay. We made it out of that fucking forest," Tara said in a slow tone, "and we're going to make it out of here. Just back the fuck up."

He did, taking the old lady with him. Tara kept her eye on the monstrous woman on the ground, who was staring at her with a morbid fascination. Tara would have preferred it to ignore them. It smiled at her again, but Tara refused to be afraid. She had seen a lot in her life—okay, maybe not people committing mass suicide, or women eating their hearts, but she had seen some fucked up shit nonetheless—

and she was determined not to let this make her weak. Not her.

Carefully, she took a step back, and the thing stopped eating and glared at her.

"Fuck you," Tara swore under her breath.

"Tara..." There was terror in Koji's voice and he sounded like he was about to lose it.

"Just keep going; we need to get out of here."

"Tara, you don't understand."

"Just go, Koji," she yelled, losing control of her own emotions. "Fuck..."

"There's more of them," Koji said.

Tara whipped her head around and saw two more people walking toward them—two men this time. When they moved, their bodies jerked involuntarily. Both had long, dark bloodstains running from their mouths to their chests, just like the woman. When she turned back to the figure on the ground, she saw that it had gotten up as well, and now moved slowly toward them. They were surrounded.

"What the fuck are these things?" Tara scanned the ground to see if she could find some sort of weapon. Anything to defend herself with. If she was going down, she would go down fighting.

I'm not going to lose this fight, she thought angrily. *I didn't make it out of that fucking forest to be eaten by some fucking cannibal, or monster or whatever. I'm going to get the fuck out of here and grab myself the biggest glass of tequila the world has ever seen.*

A door opened a few feet away from them, and Tara thought for a moment that more of these creatures would emerge, but to her relief, she saw the face of a bald Japanese man dressed in the robes of a monk. He said something to her, which she didn't understand. Briefly, she glanced at Koji, who just stared at the man with a blank gaze.

"What did he say?" She elbowed her friend hard enough to make his eyes focus again.

"He told us to follow him," Koji said with a tiny voice as he nervously pushed his glasses up his nose.

"Shit, Koji..." Tara pushed him forward to go follow the man. He almost lost his balance, but at least he was moving. She grabbed the old woman's hand and pulled her along, not caring for her slower pace.

"Let's go, lady. It isn't safe here."

The woman nodded and followed without a word. Tara stepped into the house, an ordinary home to one of these unfortunate dead, she had no doubt, and she vaguely thought how similar yet wildly different the Japanese houses were. The minimalistic decoration looked like something out of a US high society magazine, but it was the small table and the lack of chairs that made it look so alien. They moved through a few rooms, went out the back door, and straight into another house. The bald man was quick and very agile for a guy who wore at least three layers of robes and the strangest little wooden slippers with two blocks underneath. Tara turned Florifera around so she could guide the old lady in front of her, steering the bony shoulders with her hands. As far as she could see, there was nothing behind them, but it didn't make her feel any safer that she couldn't see the monsters. It made her feel hunted.

They must have gone through at least six different houses—Tara had lost count—before they reached a wide-open field. At the edge of the field was forest. The sight of the trees made Tara want to vomit.

"Where are we going?" she screamed at Koji, who was still following the bald man. "Koji..."

He half-turned to her. "We're following the monk." He

looked so lost and confused.

"Is he going back in that fucking forest?"

"I... I don't know. Is it even the same one?"

Tara stood still, clamping on to the old woman, who was trying to catch her breath by the sound of it. "I'm not going back into that fucking forest."

The woman's old hand found hers. "We need... to follow... that monk," she said between breaths. The medium inhaled deeply and straightened herself. "We can't stay here. I don't know what is happening, but it's bad. If we don't go, we'll die."

"But there's something wrong with that forest," Tara said between clenched teeth.

"I'm not keen about going back in the Jukai either," Koji admitted. "I'm not staying in this village, though."

"Isn't there an alternative?" Tara said. "Some other town or city?"

"What makes you think it will be different from this one?" The old woman shook her head. "I think we'll be in danger wherever we go. We need help. This man, this... monk, he might provide the protection that we need."

Tara let out a frustrated gasp. She looked back over her shoulder at the open door of the last house. There was no way she'd go back, but she didn't really want to go forward either. She could try to run, find a different route, but the old woman was right. There was no telling what she could find out there. Whatever happened in Aokigahara wasn't limited to that horrible forest; it had spread outside its boundaries, too, like a disease. The monk was like a safety net, and she needed to be guided through this bullshit.

"What happens if we go back and we aren't immune to that weird suicide shit?" Tara said. "What if we go back and the same happens to us as happened to all the others?"

"I... I don't know," Koji said. From the look in his eyes, Tara realized it was her choice. Whatever she said, they would do. The responsibility was crushing, and she wanted to be weak for a moment—follow instead of lead. She glanced past him and saw the monk had stopped running. He was walking toward them now, his face solemn.

"Ask him where he's taking us," Tara said to Koji, never taking her eyes off the monk.

Koji took a few steps toward the man and spoke to him. His body language was different, Tara noticed for the first time. He nodded his head a lot more when he spoke, while his posture was stiff and less casual. His shyness shone through, but that was something natural to him.

Koji nodded again and then ran back to Tara. "He's not taking us into the Jukai," he said, his voice filled with relief. "It's another piece of woods. The Jukai is that way." He pointed in a different direction. "There are more woodlands here, and the monk says theirs is protected."

Tara wasn't sure what to believe—the monk could be a serial killer, for all she knew—but staying here wasn't an option. Eventually, those things would find them, and she'd rather take her chances with a skinny guy in a dress. She nodded at Koji, put her hands on the old woman's shoulders again, and guided her forward. Their feet hit the soft ground as they ran, and it was comforting that even the soil seemed different than that in the Jukai.

The forest was like another world. It wasn't as dark, because the trees didn't grow as closely together and their tops let in the soft light of the morning sun, which took away the sense of menace that engulfed the suicide forest. There was a different vibe here, a protective one, though she wouldn't say it felt completely safe. Nothing would feel safe now, and perhaps ever again.

Their path was an easy one. The undergrowth wasn't as wild and overgrown as it was in the sea of trees, and though there was no clear trail, they weren't stumbling over roots and getting snagged on thorny bushes. A short walk brought them to a small wooden temple in between the trees. It was nothing like the temples they had seen during their travels through Japan, with their finely crafted pagodas and well-thought-out architecture. This place looked like it was built by men whose hearts were in the right place, even if they didn't know the craft that well.

The monk ran up the steps. There was no door, just a hole. Koji waited for Tara and the old woman to catch up. He grabbed one of the woman's arms, and together they led her up the steps. The monk took off his strange wooden slippers, and Koji immediately followed in taking his shoes off. Tara hesitated but bent down to do the same.

"You have to take off your shoes," she whispered to the old woman. "Do you need some help?"

The woman shook her head and kicked off her shoes with one fluid motion. Tara took them and placed them next to her own, at the side of the door. It felt oddly naked to enter a strange place on her bare feet, but she was afraid to offend anyone. Right now, she needed to keep all the friends she had.

Inside, they found a sparsely decorated room, so bare that Tara wondered if this was meant to be a place of worship or something else. Other than a strange design on the floor, painted in orange, there were no decorations. No statues, no effigies of Buddha, nothing. The design was two round circles, the smaller one perfectly centred in the large one, with a series of characters and symbols written between them. Tara assumed they were Japanese, but she couldn't be sure. The writing looked similar, yet different from what she'd seen during their travels. Thick wax candles had been placed around the circle and in each corner, lighting the room. On the floor huddled five monks, dressed identically to the man who had led them. They were on their knees, in the middle of the circular design, their heads pressed against the ground, and they were chanting very quietly.

The monk who had led them spoke, and Koji translated his words.

"You are safe here, but only for a little while. When it is safe, we will help you leave Japan." The monk looked youthful, but Tara found it difficult to guess how young he really was. He had no hair, not even eyebrows; everything had been shaven. The other monks were similarly devoid of hair.

"Who are you?"

"We are the servants of the guardian of the second seal," Koji translated. "Our master, who ruled over these forests, was murdered last night."

"I saw your master," the old woman said. "It was his blood that opened the seal. He was sacrificed."

Koji translated her words, and the monk responded.

"The sacrifice went far deeper than his life alone," the monk said, and there was a sadness in his brown eyes. "With the opening of the seal, a sickness has spread. Despair and anger will flood the world in ways that modern man is not prepared for. And it is only the beginning if the other seals are opened."

"So, it *is* about the seven seals in the Bible?" Tara asked. "Why the fuck are Buddhist monks protecting a biblical seal?"

"The seals aren't just biblical; they have little to do with religion itself. They're a fact," Koji translated. "Most of the secrets of the Apocalypse have been kept by the guardians, but millennia ago, some of those guardians believed it was important for humanity to have this knowledge, too. That's when parts of the Bible were written. Of course, the Bible comes from many sources, some of them not even human."

"Not human? This is all too fucking nuts. I—" She stopped as Koji grimaced, his eyes going wide. *Christ. How did I end up in charge?* She took a deep breath and gestured at the monk. "Ask him what those things were in town."

Koji spoke in soft but fast words, then turned to her. "He says they are the vultures of the other world... demons. There are always those who prey on the weakness of those who belong to this plane, who gain something from the defeat of others." The monk spoke to Koji in rapid tones. His body language betrayed a hint of agitation. "There are demons who want the Apocalypse to come to pass, and they are drawn to the opened seals. Perhaps they're here to make sure no one closes the seal again, or just to feast on the victims. He... he says he doesn't know." Koji touched the sides of his glasses with his fingertips. "He tells us we have to watch out. We're special, somehow; that's why we're alive. That means we have a responsibility."

Tara sucked in her breath and held the palms of her hands against her eyes. "How much do the monks know about this seal business?"

Koji patiently relayed her words to the monk, who answered with fast words and an intense look on his face.

"He says they only know about the seal they protect. There are six others, each with their own guardians. The seal they have been protecting was the second of the seven. He believes someone is trying to bring forth the Apocalypse, and if the seals are opened out of turn, they are very damaging, but they won't bring on the end of the world. Just random chaos. There are strict rules, and whoever is doing this is following those rules."

"The spirit of the girl that led me to the forest also spoke of the seals being opened," Florifera added. "She confirmed that the first seal was already open."

The monk touched Koji's arm, and he spoke again, this time in a low tone.

"He says they are aware that the first seal was opened, and that we must warn the other guardians..." Koji listened, nodded, and then added, "...but where once the guardians were united, they have separated over the centuries, and have lost sight of one another."

The monk lowered his head with a look of shame when he spoke, and Koji said a few words in return, then he turned back to Tara. "He wishes he could guide you to the other seals, but he does not know where they are. His knowledge is too limited. He says there should be people out there who do know, though."

The man touched Koji again, and he repeated a word a few times. It sounded like "Han-Sei."

"What does that mean?" Tara said.

"Something like 'half-made' or 'half-formed'... I honestly don't understand." Koji shook his head and shrugged.

"That's just freaking wonderful, isn't it?" Tara said. "That's mad vague. Tell him I just want to go home."

"He says that your home has changed."

"That's just fucking peachy," she snapped. Her fatigue was overwhelming. "I'm really fucking tired. We haven't slept all night, and with those freaky things out there—" she thought of the woman taking a bite out of the human heart "—I don't know if I'll ever sleep again. I can't fucking think straight."

"He says we're safe here. The monks are protecting this part of the land with their magic. We can sleep here tonight if we want."

"Sounds good to me," Tara said.

"Tomorrow, we'll leave and go back to the US."

"How?" Tara asked. "My plane tickets, my credit card, my money... everything is still in my suitcase, which is in our tent. There is no way in hell I'm going back for it, so I don't know how we're going to buy fucking plane tickets. Jesus. I don't even know what to do next."

"Can we worry about that in the morning?" Koji asked. "Can we just rest for a bit? I really can't deal with logistics now, okay? I'm so tired I feel like I'm going insane."

"It's not fatigue that makes me feel that way," Tara said, but she wholeheartedly agreed on the need for rest. "This place is as good as any, and at least we're surrounded by living people. We can't make plans if we're exhausted." She turned to the old woman. "You're all-knowing, or something... what do you think?"

The old, blind eyes stared at the circle of monks, a strange expression on the wrinkled face, and the woman said with a soft voice, "We are safe here, for now. But we can't overstay our welcome, or we will bring death to this place. Tomorrow, we will leave, and we will find a way to warn the others."

"Okay," Tara said. "Seems like we all agree." She looked at the monk. "Do you have beds, or do we just lay on the floor? Because, right now, I don't even think I care."

The monk led them to a small back room, which had several narrow futons on the wooden floor. Tara lay down on the nearest one.

"Fuck, these are uncomfortable." But as hard as the bed was, and as loud as her thoughts were, she fell asleep almost as soon as she hit the pillow.

Tara drifted into a world of frightening dreams.

CHAPTER TWENTY FIVE

Freya woke to footsteps and sat up in her bed, her heart pounding and her palms wet with perspiration. It wasn't just one pair of steps, but many. Perhaps it was the house that had woken her, seeing as the noises were too faint to break through sleep. For a moment, when she had just opened her eyes, still caught by the drowsiness of her dream, she wondered if they'd come from Wulf, but then she heard the other sounds of feet echoing through the halls. They were everywhere, not close yet, but close enough that she knew she didn't have much time before they reached her.

She had taken Emily back into her room last night, as much for the child's sake—Bam wasn't there to look after her anymore—as for her own. Part of her was tempted to stay in the panic room, but there was no clear reason to panic as yet—at least not in Freya's jaded perception of panic, which usually involved murderous ghosts—and the bed in there was rather uncomfortable. Plus, she didn't like being locked up. Having lost Bam gave her a strong need to keep things as "normal" as possible, if only to preserve her own sanity.

That was last night. She wished now she'd gone with her initial bloody instincts.

Old fears resurfaced, and she wondered if the house had anything to do with the mysterious walkers. It didn't seem to be warning her about them, but it didn't make her feel safe either.

Quietly, she made her way out of the bed, wrapping Emily in her blanket. The baby never even stirred when she lifted her up. She was so good about sleeping through the night now. There had been times when every little noise seemed to wake the girl, but lately...

The floor chilled Freya's bare feet as she crept out of her room. Carefully, she tiptoed to the bedroom she had assigned Wulf, and opened the door. He was sleeping. She could see him in the light of the moon, lying on his side with one arm draped along the edge of the bed. She leaned forward near his bed, holding Emily close to her chest.

"Wulf," she whispered as soft as she could, hoping to wake him. "Wulf."

He stirred, but his breathing didn't change. Desperation tickled her stomach, and she needed to take a deep breath not to panic. The footsteps were getting nearer.

"Wulf," she pleaded, a little louder now. "Please wake up."

His lashes fluttered, and he looked at her through heavy lidded eyes. They closed again, and Freya was about to shake him, when the eyes shot open so quickly it sent her back a step.

Wulf sat up. "What's going on?"

"There's someone in the house," Freya whispered. "Someones... It's more than one, I don't know how many."

She studied Emily's peaceful sleeping face and prayed the baby didn't wake up and alert the intruders. Wulf tilted his head back and sniffed the air. Slowly, he rose to his feet, as if his nose were guiding him.

"What are you doing?" Freya asked. "Have you gone mad?"

"I can hear something, but I can't smell it." Wulf touched the frame of his door and stood on his toes, sniffing along the edges. "This makes no sense."

"You're smelling them?" Freya wasn't sure what to make of this. "Are you awake, or is this some weird sleepwalking thing?"

"Be quiet for a moment." He stood very still. Then, with a minimum of movement, he opened the door. When the crack was big enough, he pushed himself through and disappeared. If Freya hadn't been holding Emily, she would have followed him, but she didn't want to risk taking the baby out there, and she didn't want to leave her alone either. At least there was a way out in this room. She couldn't run very far from Angel Manor, not with the curse back in place, but she could run, and that, for now, was enough. With a deep sigh, she sat on the bed, facing the door, and waited for Wulf to return.

***

Though he was only gone for minutes, he could have just as well left days ago. Freya sat on the bed, rocking back and forth, running through slivers of conversations that she'd had in the past few hours. The voice of her panicked mother on the phone had rattled her. They were both okay, but Amsterdam was a bad place to be right now. Then there was the conversation with Wulf, where he told her he wasn't who he said he was. The betrayal had hit her so hard, and yet he was the only one now who knew her secret, and despite it all, she was glad she could share this with someone.

She thought of the house, and tried, somehow, to reach out to it, but it wasn't reaching back. It was as if it were hiding from her—as if the spell had somehow changed their connection yet again. It worried her. The baby was asleep in her lap, her head supported by Freya's right arm, when Wulf came back into the room.

"Did you find anyone?"

"There are no living things in the house," he said carefully. "Aside from us."

"That doesn't bring me any comfort," Freya said. "I've seen what the dead can do. Especially in this place." She sucked in her lips and frowned. "Are there ghosts?"

"Not exactly, no. It's something... bad... though."

"What is it?"

"I believe that your house is filled with servitors." He sat next to her on the bed. "They seem harmless now, because they need to be near their master to perform any kind of task that's dangerous, but there was a reason why someone placed them here."

"What are servitors?" Freya asked.

"They're magical servants. Their power grows with the power of their master." Wulf rubbed his temples. "I don't like that they're here. The seals have some powerful magic of their own, if someone knows how to harvest that power..."

"Hold on, can we take a step back to explaining about these servitors?" Freya held up a free hand. "What exactly is in my house?"

"Dolls."

"Wait, the ones that I got in the mail?" Freya shifted her weight, and the t-shirt fell a bit further, exposing her entire shoulder now. He stared at her, and she pulled her shirt up self-consciously.

"You got porcelain dolls in the post?"

"Yeah, for Emily. Someone sent them, but we don't know who. I thought it was Bam's family at first, because the packages came from the US, but Bam didn't think so." Freya's words were like a raging waterfall. "Bam..." Something in her voice broke.

"What did you do with the dolls?"

"I thought they were creepy, so I locked them in my panic room."

"You have no idea how creepy these things are," Wulf admitted. "How did they arrive to you? One at a time? All at once? How many are there?"

"Eh, nine..." She pulled her legs onto the bed. "They all came in separate packages, though quite soon after each other. Then suddenly the packages just... stopped coming."

"Nine is not a good number for us." He squeezed the bridge of his nose between thumb and forefinger. "Whoever is sending them has decided there was a more efficient way of flooding your house with their doll army."

"That's a scary thought." Freya looked at her baby and ran a finger along the sleeping face. "What can dolls do, though?"

"When animated, they can do anything a human can do. I'm not quite sure how strong they are, but they can be dangerous. Especially in numbers." Wulf waited a bit before he went on. "Servitors are a part of blood magic, which is always dark, and requires the nastiest kind of sacrifice. You'll have heard of voodoo priests animating the dead and turning them into zombies, right?"

"Yes," Freya shivered.

"This is similar. The more there are, the stronger they become. They're like a hive that shares not only magic, but physical traits, too. It really depends on the power of the mage that created them. But the potential physical strength is not the worst part. What makes them truly terrifying is how much magic they can take in when they are placed on the right spot. Where one person can absorb the magic of an area and use it to their advantage, a controller of servitors—in this case our doll or puppet master—can absorb magic through all his servants. So, the more of them there are, the more magic he or she will gain for his spells."

"And Angel Manor is a hot spot for magic."

"It is. This place, but also Lucifer Falls... they all provide magic that can be accessed by mortals." He rubbed his chin. "*Strong* magic. You must have felt it. Why do you think the spells that are cast on this place are so extreme? Not many places can do this. The world only has so many magical 'hot spots,' as you called it."

"Oh, I've felt it," Freya said, thinking back to the fateful night of a particular equinox.

"It works the other way around, too. Not only do these servitors absorb magic, but they actually strengthen the magic that's been cast. The caster's power will be increased with each doll... or corpse, or whatever they're using. In fact, we should be happy these are inanimate objects instead of creatures that once were alive. The magic is so much stronger when the servitors still have a hint of life to them. That's the reason why some of these mages use animals, or undead humans. It's all the same principle, just a different outcome."

"Let me see if I can get this correct," Freya said. "There is someone who is taking over my house with dolls, because they want magic?"

"That's the simplified version, but... yes."

"At the same time, they're using these dolls to perform magic."

Wulf nodded. "That's correct."

"And the dolls are dangerous if their master or maker, or whatever, comes here?" Freya wrapped her arms around Emily, who stirred lightly. The baby let out a sigh, but didn't wake.

"Very. These kind of mages are usually not the most emotionally stable. There is a rumor that they were taught their skills by a dark entity that is referred to as 'the Lady,' but there is so little information about that, it could just be a myth. I don't know of any other teachers, and my knowledge is incomplete. What I do know is that in order to control their dolls, and make more, they need to make sacrifices. There is a reason why it's called 'blood magic.' It's cast with blood."

"Lovely."

"The servitors tend to be filled with blood-lust because of it. This means they are very aggressive." There was a silence for several seconds between them. The room seemed darker somehow, even though the lights were on.

"How do you know all this?" she said. "You haven't told me who you are yet."

"Please don't ask me, because I can't answer you," Wulf said. "I need you to believe me when I tell you that you're in danger."

"I'm always in danger," Freya said with a hint of bitterness.

"Emily's in danger, too." Wulf looked at her. "I could bring her to safety, get her away from this place."

"Wait, what?" Freya got to her feet, alarmed. "I don't even know who you are, and you're asking me to give you my baby? Are you mad?"

"She can't stay here with the dolls. Who knows what they'll do to her...?"

"Those dolls have been here for weeks... they haven't harmed her once. In fact, they seem to be warding off evil spirits." Wulf took a step toward her, and Freya took a step back. "Tell me that's not why you're trying to get rid of them, tell me that you're not the bad guy in this..."

"I'll never claim to be the good guy," Wulf said, "but I am trying to help you, damn it."

"I want to trust you, I really do." Freya relaxed a little. She felt silly and paranoid. "The dolls, they never sat well with me, but... I can't just give you Emily. Besides, where are you going to go? You're tied to this house, just the same as I am."

Wulf swallowed, and he couldn't look her in the eyes. "I'm not tied to this house."

Her eyebrows shot up. "You were there when the spell was cast. Didn't it affect you?"

"It can't affect me, Freya." He looked away, then back. "I don't have a soul."

"You don't have a fucking soul?" Freya shouted. Emily woke and instantly started wailing. "You don't have a fucking soul?" she repeated. "Who doesn't have a fucking soul?"

"Freya, I can't explain..."

"No, you can't. You come into my house with your lies, fuck me and then you tell me you don't have a fucking soul, but you want to take my child away from here. Sounds totally legit."

Emily's cries reached a new high pitch, and Freya yelled over them.

"Get out of my fucking house," she screamed. "Just get out, or I will fucking kill you and throw your bones in the basement with the rest of my victims."

"Freya..." Wulf pleaded.

"Do you want to fucking test me?" Her head was throbbing with the beginnings of a migraine. "I don't need you. I never needed you before and I don't fucking need you now. I don't need anyone, and no one is getting their hands on my goddamn child." She lurched toward him, stomping her foot on the ground as if she were chasing away an animal instead of a man.

"I'll go," he said, "but you know where to reach me. I understand that you're angry."

"You don't understand shit." Tears of anger and frustration were running down her face. "Get the fuck out."

He turned and walked away. Her screams echoed through the hall as she shouted profanities after him. Then she fell to her knees, her daughter still in her arms, and she sobbed for long minutes. When her tears were spilt, she got up to find the dolls he had been talking about. She couldn't find a single one in the house, and when she opened her panic room, all nine were there, exactly where she had left them.

"I don't trust you either," she muttered at the dolls. She grabbed the nearest one at the leg and smashed it against the wall. Once, twice, three times, but the porcelain didn't even crack. Sighing with frustration, she chucked the doll aside.

"I will deal with you later," she muttered at the dolls. "Fuck everyone."

CHAPTER TWENTY SIX

Marie-Claire couldn't sleep. Her whole body ached from the hike through the forest, and her mind refused to make peace with the horrors she had witnessed. The child who appointed herself as the Lamb had brought her here for a reason and had called her a beacon. The old medium wasn't sure she was ready for that kind of responsibility. Her knowledge wasn't complete, and she knew she couldn't guide anyone, not against whatever was happening.

There were too many questions she didn't have an answer to, and too many things weren't as they first appeared. The Lamb was a question. Who was the girl, really? Was she just a dead child, or was there more than that? It was important somehow.

Then there were those demons. She had heard of demonic existence before, but in her many years of dealing with the supernatural, she had never once dealt with an actual celestial being. There had been a possession once, but it turned out to be a very confused spirit. It had always made her wonder if demons weren't just a myth. But now...

Before Angel Manor, most of the dead she'd dealt with had been less of a danger to humanity. They could do some damage to a person's house or psyche, but the ones that could actually physically harm people were few and far between. Certainly not droves of murderous phantoms like those of that horrible house. Nothing had ever occurred like that.

Marie-Claire learned last year that the combination of magical places and spirits was a dangerous one. She had seen the dead take on physical shape, had been a witness to the murder and torment of the living. After Angel Manor, Marie-Claire believed the world had no more horrors in store for her.

She had been wrong.

She had stared into the demon's eyes and had seen the truth despite her blindness. Something within the depths of them had spoken to her, had explained things she didn't want to hear. There was a promise in those hollow eyes, that there was more to this world than humanity. The seal may not have brought these things forth, but it attracted them... made them more powerful. If allowed, they would bring Hell on Earth. Marie-Claire could feel their intentions. They didn't just want to eradicate the human race, they wanted to manipulate it, torture it, feed on its despair. Humanity would never be the same if the demons won this *war.*

Whatever she would have to do, Marie-Claire knew she had to keep the seals closed. She missed having Ruben by her side. At times like these, he would talk to her with his calm voice, and together they'd make sense of things.

The boy—Terrence—had told her that Ruben had gone peacefully. He hadn't been tortured to death, but had died of a heart attack. That, somehow, made things worse, made it even more avoidable. She should have known he had a bad heart, and she should have prevented him from the stress. It was nonsense, Marie-Claire knew, but emotions weren't always logical. Now, she felt as if she were at the dawn of a new battle—one that would potentially make her night at Angel Manor seem like child's play—and she wished she had some friendly faces by her side. She wanted a familiar hand to guide her through the human world while she saw deep into the heart of the spirit domain. But there was no one; she had pushed them all away. She was just a frightened old woman now, one who knew so many things, and yet knew so little.

Someone moved into the room. Marie-Claire heard the careful footsteps clearly. She doubted if any of the others were aware of them, but her ears were more sensitive. She held her breath and felt a presence near. It was human, or she would have been able to see it.

"You must come with me," a soft voice said. It wasn't speaking English, nor French... and yet she understood the words. She held out her hand, and a strong grip surrounded her digits. He pulled her to her feet, guiding her—with a gentleness that bordered on loving—through the room. They didn't go far, and the voice told her to sit down while her unknown guide helped her to the floor. There was a soft cushion for her to sit on, and the warmth, accompanied by crackling sounds, betrayed a fire nearby. The air smelled of faded incense, a woody, bitter scent.

"Who are you?" she said. "You have me at a disadvantage."

"You are as much of a mystery to me as I am to you, dear lady," the man said in his strange language. "I'm one of the protectors of this temple."

"Why do I understand you?" Marie-Claire asked. "We don't speak the same language."

"Because I want you to understand me." The man moved, making the floorboards creak under his weight. "This is one of the few magical places in this mortal world, dear lady," the man said. "I believe you were sent to us for a reason, and I think you know it, too."

"I do."

"We knew there was a threat that the seals would be opened ever since the first seal was broken over twenty years ago. It almost went unnoticed, but secrets like that cannot be kept."

"The first seal... do you know what it is?"

"Yes, the first seal heralds the birth of the Anti-Christ." The monk smelled lightly of sweat. "He is the one who will control the four Horsemen. It is he who will guide the Apocalypse."

A glimmer of hope blossomed in her heart. "So, if the Anti-Christ would choose to spare the world...?"

"None of us know what will actually happen. Most of our knowledge has been watered down with time. It was once deemed risky to write things down, so we told each other stories. But, as you can imagine, told tales are not the most reliable, and they change over the years. I apologize for any false information that I am about to give you. You must understand that some of the knowledge we hold is mere speculation. I am pretty confident that once the Horsemen ride across the earth, there will be some repercussion." The monk let out a deep breath. "Throughout our time, some of the Horsemen have ridden free. Not all at once, but there have been individual instances where the guardians had failed to... 'guard.'"

"How can they have ridden without the people knowing?"

"Sometimes their awakening was brief, not enough to create suspicion. The longest a Horseman rode the Earth was over sixty years. Its guardians were murdered, and it was left to spread disease in its wake."

"Sixty years?" Marie-Claire raised trembling fingers to her lips.

"Surely you have heard of the Black Plague? Millions of people died before it ended."

"That was the Horseman?"

"It was. And that was just one of the four, left unchecked. Imagine what would happen if all four of them rode."

Marie-Claire covered her face with the palm of her hand. Her ring finger ran across her eyebrow, stroking the coarse hairs. The thought of the world hit by something as devastating as the Black Plague... it was nauseating. She pictured children with black pustules in their faces, dying in their mothers' arms. It would be devastating.

"How did they contain the Horseman?"

"That information is a mystery to us, but it is believed the guardians of that seal have the knowledge written down somewhere."

"We will need that information."

"Indeed. Though, if whoever is doing this succeeds in opening the seals, we have a problem." There was sadness in the man's voice, and Marie-Claire wished she could see his face. The urge to raise her hands and touch his features, which was her way of seeing that which belonged in the mortal world, was strong. Instead, she folded her hands on her lap.

"A problem, you say," she said, squeezing her thumbs between her fingers. "But one we can solve?"

"The world is about balance. Every extreme has a counter. Humanity has a great gift, and that is the gift of choice. We have a certain power over fate, since we get to determine what path we take. We choose to protect the seals and keep humanity safe. If our choice is foiled by someone who chooses something different, we can decide to counteract. We are bound only by our sense of honor and logic."

"You're not answering my question," Marie-Claire pinched the bridge of her nose and inhaled a sharp breath. "If the seals are opened... if we can't prevent them from being broken... is all hope lost, or are these mysterious texts enough to help us save the world in time?"

"Hope is never lost. Only fools or the downtrodden give up on hope."

"What can we do if we are too late?"

The monk stood. She could feel the movement, hear the subtle noises, smell his salty body odour, which wasn't unpleasant, as he got to his feet. "There are rumours that, aside from the Anti-Christ, there is a way to restore all the seals at once. The Qumran Cave Scrolls are said to have a hidden message in them that will lead to human salvation."

"Qumran Cave..." Marie-Claire could almost see the scrolls in her mind's eye. "Why does that name sound vaguely familiar?"

"You have probably heard of them referred to as the Dead Sea Scrolls." The monk's soft footsteps made the floor groan. He was pacing, and the noise made Marie-Claire ill at ease.

"Yes," she confirmed with a nod.

There is one man who is the guardian of the guardians. It is said his life will last until the end of the earth, but I'm not sure if this is just a myth, or if this is fact."

"Perhaps it's not one man, but the task is given down from one generation to the next?" Marie-Claire felt weary, and fatigue was starting to take its toll on her. "Do you know how we can get in touch with him?"

"The man will be difficult to find. He is said to be a wanderer." The monk sat down again, and the fabric of his clothes swished as he leaned forward. "He goes by many names. Khidr might be one you know. Or... Cain."

"Another biblical figure?" Marie-Claire asked.

"His presence is found in many different religious texts."

"Is this the Cain who slew his brother Abel?" Marie-Claire asked.

"Perhaps. I do not know all the stories attributed to him. All I know is that he has wandered the earth for a long time, and he will supposedly do so for a long time still."

"How can I find him then? You must have some clue?"

"I have no answer to that. The only thing I can show you is the symbol of three. There are answers there, but I don't know more than that." With nimble fingers, the man drew a symbol in the air. Marie-Claire saw the magic light before her blind eyes, leaving a clear yellow mark.

She studied the symbol in her mind. A triangle, made of ovals that looked like flower petals, set in a circle. She had seen it before, often with her fingers, and knew it was to represent the maiden, the mother, and the crone. It was quite popular in Celtic jewellery It was funny how the young absorbed the true symbols of power into their fashion statements. They had no idea about what half of the things meant that they flaunted, otherwise they might not use them in such a flippant manner.

"You have nothing more than a symbol for me?" Marie-Claire asked. "I don't even know where to travel."

"The United Kingdom," the monk said. "That is where your path leads you."

Marie-Claire sighed. *"Pourquoi? Why?* Can't you be more specific?"

"I can't. I just see your path. Someone will find you there, and they will guide you on. We will retrieve your necessary belongings from Aokigahara in the next few days so that you can travel when the worst of the seal's effects on this area will have passed."

"The United Kingdom is a very big place... where will you have me go?"

"I do not know, but I truly believe that your path will become clear to you as you travel."

"You ask a lot from me, *monsieur,*" Marie-Claire said with a heavy heart. "I'm an old woman, and I don't have the knowledge you may require of me. All my expertise is set around the human souls that have departed but can't leave this world. You're asking me to search for mythical creatures." She clenched her fists, feeling the dull ache of her muscles. "I saw things in that village that I have never before encountered. These... demons, as you called them, what of them? Are they a danger to us? What must I do about them?"

The man coughed and said something in a language she could not understand. *He does not want me to hear, so I can't*, she thought. His voice gave her goosebumps.

"You saw them?" he asked. "Through your mind's eye?"

"Yes." Marie-Claire rubbed her arms as she recalled the hideous faces that had stared at her.

"But you have never seen demons before?"

"Never," Marie-Claire said. "I'm quite sure of it. I've seen monsters..." She remembered the look in the eyes of the naked nuns' spirits she'd guided to the light. There had been evil spirits, but those nuns... nothing had compared to them.

"This is odd, because the world is filled with demons that walk amongst the mortals." The monk's voice sounded as if he were drifting off in thought. "I wonder why you have not seen them until now. Was there something different about your actions?"

Marie-Claire tried to recollect all that had happened in the past twenty-four hours. "I was very close to the seal?" she said with uncertainty in her voice. "Perhaps..." Then she remembered something. "I... I was shown the world through the eyes of a spirit. That's something that has never happened to me before. This girl, this spirit, she was special. She called herself the Lamb. Do you know what that means?"

"It is said that the Lamb shall open the first seal, but other than that, it is a complete mystery."

The man let out a deep sigh. The sound of it spoke volumes to her; his mind was filled with as many questions as hers.

"When it came down to it, we failed at any form of actual guarding." The monk sighed. "In fact, it was the blood of the one we serve that opened the seal, so we aided it more than we prevented it."

"It could have been your task to begin with," Marie-Claire mused, hope blossoming within her. "Feasibly, it wasn't about keeping the seal closed, but witnessing its opening. This may be the very point where the choice comes in. We can choose to accept that it's open, or we can try to find a way to close it again. If there had been no guardians to the seal, there would be no knowledge of it. No knowledge means no choice."

He took a sharp breath, and she could sense him moving around. "Our job hadn't begun until the seal opened," he said with a slow voice. "We weren't guarding it before, we were merely holding knowledge. We were the watchers, and now... now we must guard... and we must heal."

"For one, you need to protect innocent people from those things out there." Marie-Claire grimaced as she pointed her finger in the direction she remembered the door to be. "You said you knew some magic to keep them at bay. If they are a threat now that the seal is opened, you need to help people and educate them. Whatever is happening, we can't keep secrets anymore. Ignorance is dangerous."

"What will you have us do?"

Marie-Claire rose to her feet. "For one, do not ask me. With your master gone, you are the guardians, and you have been assigned a task. Your knowledge on this matter is greater than mine, and yet you expect me to take this burden—*your* burden—on my shoulders. Speak to your people, speak to your superiors. Get someone to lead you again." She wrapped her vest tighter around her. "I don't quite know what my role in all this is, or why I was chosen to be a part of it. All I can think of is gathering knowledge of these seals. Perhaps this would lead us to someone who has the power to stop them from opening."

"It's very brave for you to join our cause." The monk

stepped closer to her, and for a moment, Marie-Claire thought she could hear his heartbeat. "Especially since you are a stranger to it."

"Well, I was led to this for a reason. Though I don't know how much fight I have left in me," she said. "Last year, I went through a terrible ordeal. Several people who I cared for were taken from me, and in a way, I lost myself that night. I fear that we're dealing with something even worse now."

"And yet... fate has picked you."

"Exactly. There is a reason why this 'Lamb' led me to witness the opening to the seal. It can't have been a coincidence." Marie-Claire shook her head. "In fact, I am sure it wasn't. I have always known in the depths of my heart. That is why I listened, and now I must take the consequences, *t'sais*?"

The man exhaled. "Perhaps Fate didn't pick you as much as you allowed it into your life," he said.

Marie-Claire nodded. "I have grown tired. It's time for me to rest. Tomorrow will be a long day."

"Allow me to escort you back to your room."

His hand was warm on her arm, and his touch was light as a feather. He led her back to her bed.

"Before I forget," Marie-Claire said, "there was a boy, in the woods... something had touched his mind, and he was a danger to us. We tied him up. Perhaps one of your men can find him, or at least report him to the authorities. I fear he might die if someone doesn't rescue him soon."

"I will send out one of my seekers immediately," the monk said.

"Thank you."

"Good night, dear lady," the monk said. "Rest well."

"Guard us while we sleep," Marie-Claire said, as she lowered herself to the bed. "May the world still stand when we wake."

CHAPTER TWENTY SEVEN

The porcelain eyes mocked her from the bone-white face. Freya strained her muscles and lifted the sledgehammer again. It felt unbalanced in her hands, as if she were about to lose control of it, and it might drag her off into some unknown abyss. Yet she managed to aim it at the doll again, and smashed it down with all her might. The floor next to the doll had shallow crumbling holes in it from the times she had missed, but this time she struck the doll full in the face.

It didn't so much as crack.

Freya let out a long, dry sob. She didn't cry. Not because she didn't want to, but she just couldn't. The frustration had turned into a big, painful ball of tension in her chest, and her own emotions constricted her. She had hit the doll several times, and by now she knew it wouldn't break, but she still brought the hammer back up and smashed it down again, roaring and cursing. It was all she could do to keep from feeling powerless.

Eventually, fatigue overtook her, and she put the hammer down. She kicked the doll, and it skittered across the marble floor with an audible swish. Freya leaned against the wall and lowered herself to a sitting position. Her eyes were on the doll, and she wondered what it would take to break it. *Magic, no doubt.*

She hated being stuck in the house on her own with these things. She hated it even more that they were in the same building as her child. The idea of getting Emily out of Angel Manor was starting to grow on her—Emily never had a nosebleed, and Freya was certain the baby was too young to be tied to this damn house—but she had no idea where to leave her. Perhaps her parents would take her, but the thought made her feel nauseous. She didn't want to be away from her baby, and she knew her parents had their own problems right now.

With a sigh filled with anger and frustration, she stood and snatched the damn doll from the floor. Quickly, and holding the doll away from her as if she were carrying a bomb, she made her way out of the house.

A soft drizzle was falling, turned frigid by the cold winds. Freya ran, the mud squishing underneath her feet, and she almost lost her balance when she came to a halt at the entrance to the mausoleum. Freya had been determined to not have the creepy toys in the house anymore. Wulf could still be telling the truth, and she wasn't taking any chances. All she could do was hope that the protection spells she had cast would hold up. The rain hadn't washed away any of the magic words she had scribbled all over the building in the strange waxy crayon. Her fingers brushed against the bricks of the building; a strong petrichor tickled her nostrils.

The grinding squeal of metal against stone sounded as she opened the door to the mausoleum. Shivering, she stepped inside. To her horror, she noticed the dolls had moved. Freya cringed, but didn't step back. There were more of them—twelve in total, thirteen with the one she had in her hand. She bent over to put the doll down when something caught her eye.

She froze.

A doll she hadn't seen before sat in front of the others. It was another porcelain thing, larger than the rest, but what was worse about it—worse even than it being here without her knowledge—was that it was dressed like a nun. A sickly acidic taste hit the back of Freya's throat, and her limbs trembled. To her, the toy was an ominous threat.

She dropped the doll in her hands and backed off, panic engulfing her like a black wave. Whoever sent them here, they knew what they were doing, and the protection spells weren't working against them.

She bolted from the mausoleum, anger rising to join her fear. "It's always something with this fucking place," she said through clenched teeth, pushing stray locks of hair in her eyes as the rain ran down her face. "I'm never going to be free of this shit."

She ran back to the manor. With angry force, she pulled open the door and slammed it behind her. She punched both her fists into a wall, then backed up until she couldn't go any further. She kicked back, then stomped on the floor like an angry child. Once, then twice, and then she kept stomping until she didn't have the energy to lift her legs again.

"I never asked for this," she shouted at the empty room. She balled her hands into fists; her fingernails dug into the flesh of her palms.

Invisible arms wrapped around her, with a sad gentleness. For a moment, Freya thought Bam had returned, but then she realised it wasn't her friend.

"What do you want from me?" she muttered. "Aren't I suffering enough?"

"I'm frightened, Guardian," the house whispered as it held her tight.

"You should be happy; I'm tied to you again. It's not like I can leave."

"The spell affects me, too," the house whispered. "Something is trying to change me, and it hurts."

"I don't know how to help you," Freya said, and she buried her face in her hands. "I don't even know how to help myself."

"There's more power in you than you know, Guardian. You are going to have to trust someone."

"Everyone lies to me, or leaves me... Who am I going to

trust?"

There was no answer; the spirit of the house had vanished.

"Typical."

CHAPTER TWENTY EIGHT

Tara woke several times during the night, her thoughts shrouded in a chaotic fog. She wondered where she was, and in a state of half-sleep, an overwhelming surge of panic took hold of her, only for her mind to drift back into fitful slumber moments later. Her mind couldn't find rest in this place, and the last few nights had been rough. The temple made her feel out of sorts. The monks had been nice enough, but she found it difficult to understand them, the few who spoke a little bit of English, and she was eager to leave.

It was still dark when the clutches of the sandman finally released her entirely, and she decided that sleep made her feel more tired than rested. The futon was uncomfortable, making her bones and muscles ache, so she sat up. She looked over to where Koji slept. His night wasn't going any better than hers by the look of the way he was tossing and turning.

Aokigahara seemed like a lifetime ago, though mere days had passed, and Tara felt as if she had aged ten years in that first night. What she had seen... she couldn't go back to her normal life after that. There were monsters out there, real ones, the kind that ate an old man's heart. The thought of it chilled her blood, but it also made her stronger and more determined. Not even monsters could bring her to her knees.

"Are you well, dear girl?" the soft accented voice of the medium whispered in the darkness. "Can't sleep?"

"No," Tara whispered. "I need to clear my head, because I'm restless as fuck."

"We're all struggling."

"It's like sleeping makes me even more exhausted, if that makes any sense?" Tara yawned.

"It does," the medium agreed. "I feel the same way. If you will be so kind as to help me, perhaps we can get some fresh air?"

"Yeah, that might be a good idea."

"We'll be able to talk without waking anyone. I say let Koji sleep for as long as he can."

"I can live with that," Tara said, and she stretched her body as she got up. Carefully, she helped the old woman to her feet, and they walked quietly through the silent temple, to the semi-circular hole that functioned as the entrance. The air was crisp and cold on her cheeks, but it reminded Tara she was alive. She leaned her back against the wall and took a deep breath.

"I wish I could get my fucking cellphone to work in this place," Tara said. "Not that I have a lot of people to phone or anything, but it would be nice to hear that everyone's okay, you know?"

"I understand. You should have better reception when we leave for the airport tomorrow," Marie-Claire said.

"I'm looking forward to leaving this place," Tara said. "The monks have been really nice, but..."

"I understand, I'm restless, too," Marie-Claire said. "I feel like I should be undertaking something rather than sitting here."

"Yeah," Tara sighed. "I don't think I've ever missed smoking as much as I do now." She rubbed her finger under her nose. "I quit about three years ago. I wasn't a heavy smoker, but still... it's something to grasp onto, you know. Amidst the madness."

"I'm afraid the madness we have encountered so far is only the beginning, *ma cherie*." The old woman stared into

222

the darkness with her blind eyes.

"Do you see anything right now?" Tara asked.

"Only darkness at the moment, but the earth is vibrating with... some form of energy." The medium pinched the bridge of her nose. "I feel anxious."

"You and me both," Tara admitted. It seemed like a lifetime had passed since then. There was a long silence between them before Tara spoke again. "Jesus, lady, I feel like you dragged me into this shit, and I don't understand a fucking thing that's going on. I know it's not fair to blame you, but you seem to have a clearer handle on what's happening."

"I'm facing the challenge of piecing everything together, too," the old woman said, "but I think I am starting to understand. We haven't had a serious talk since we arrived here, but I think it's time, don't you?"

Tara turned her head toward Marie-Claire. She looked so ethereal with her long, white hair, fragile figure and milk-white eyes—which were a stark contrast to her coffee-coloured skin. Like the spirit of an ageing wood nymph.

"You're right. Can you help me understand?" Tara asked, her voice a mix of the strength and fragility she felt. "You were talking about all this biblical stuff earlier, and I may not have been as open-minded as you asked me to be. I... I was just being stubborn. When I get upset..."

The old woman held up a slender hand. "You have a right to whichever way you decide to express yourself. We all have our initial reactions to things, and we must be forgiven if those reactions aren't the most elegant." A smile curled around the thin, wrinkled lips. "When I had my first encounter with the paranormal, I may or may not have reacted in a less than graceful way."

Tara snorted. "I don't think 'grace' would be my fucking thing if I saw a ghost."

"I can assure you that I am just as overwhelmed by all this as you are." Marie-Claire touched her own cheek; her white eyes had a distant look. "I have seen things... horrible things. Worse than I have witnessed this past night. A year ago, I got my first glimpse of how dangerous the world beyond the veil could be when the border between this reality and the next is crossed."

"What happened?" Tara asked, involuntarily hugging herself.

"I was asked to help cleanse what I thought was a haunted house," the old woman said. There was something in her voice that made the hairs stand up at the back of Tara's neck. "It turned out that the situation was more complicated than I thought. The spirits... they were not only malicious, but very deadly. Many people died that night, and perhaps in the days and nights preceding it."

"Shit," Tara said.

"That house, it's unlike anything I have ever experienced... and yet, when I was near the seal, I knew that whatever happened last year would pale in comparison." The old woman took a deep breath. "The power I felt, I can't liken it to anythi..." Her body language went rigid, and Marie-Claire gasped. "Perhaps I can..." She touched the wall, steadying herself. Tara grabbed the old woman by the waist, worried that she might faint.

"How did I miss this?" Marie-Claire said. "I *have* felt this power before, except that it was dormant, in Angel Manor. There must be a seal there..."

"You've seen one of those things before?"

"No, not seen, but I sensed great power in that house. I knew there was something there that was ancient and powerful, but I didn't realize quite *how* powerful."

Tara took a deep breath. "That's a good thing, though, right? You knowing where this thing is. That gives us a chance to stop it from opening..." The words sounded completely ludicrous to her as she spoke. "Who the fuck am I kidding; how are we going to stop anything? We need to tell someone. If there's people like these monks, I'm sure there are others who can do something more... erm, effective? We just need to tell an authority figure, or something. There should be one, right? Someone who can figure out how to reverse whatever was happening with that seal in the forest, before it kills everyone?"

"Calm down, child." Florifera spoke with a patient but stern voice. "You are right in saying we must seek out our allies, but you are wrong in assuming there is nothing you and I can do. There is a reason why fate has brought us here and has united us."

"I doubt that," Tara said. "I was just in the wrong place at the wrong fucking time."

"And yet I crossed your path, and here we are. Alive and in possession of some information that might save humanity. It sounds almost deliberate, *n'est pas*?"

"I don't think anyone would have deliberately picked me." Tara ran her hands through her hair and tugged at the ends. "I'm hardly a pillar of society; I've barely just scraped my act together. If you'd seen me two years ago... I was a wreck."

"And yet you were strong enough to keep your head cool in the face of demons," the old medium said. Her white eyes looked straight into Tara's as if she could see her.

"I've faced plenty of demons, lady," Tara said, "just never real ones."

"Just because demons aren't physical doesn't mean they're not real... or that they can't harm us. You are strong, and you are still here, my dear."

"I don't want you to think that I'm being a coward," Tara said. "I'll help you. I mean, fuck, I owe it to Summer. I owe it to all of them." She swallowed a hard lump in her throat, but she refused to allow herself to feel the emotional pain that was bubbling up to the surface. Instead, she turned her sadness to anger, which was the best coping mechanism she had. "If I ever find that fucker who is behind this, who is trying to break the seals... who is responsible for all this death..."

"It's not just one person," the old medium said. "The spirit spoke of thirteen, if my memory serves me well."

"Well, I'll fuck them all up, if I can," Tara said between clenched teeth. "You have to be a real twisted puppy to pull this kind of shit. You didn't see that town, but it was horrifying. Those people... they didn't deserve such a hopeless death."

"We rarely get the death we deserve." Florifera leaned against the wall. "Concepts like 'entitlement,' 'justice,' 'righteousness,' or 'fairness' are man-made. Life doesn't really work that way. It doesn't keep our feelings, or our efforts, in consideration."

"You're right. I hate it, but you are."

"I see."

Tara took a deep breath, letting the cold air fill her lungs. "By the way, what did happen to that Mark guy? Did they find him?"

"They did, though it took them a while," Marie-Claire answered. "The monks handed him to the local authorities. I don't know what happened to him after, but I'm sure he's safe."

"Good, he's a shit, but I don't think he could help it, you know?"

"I don't think he could either, *ma cherie*," the old woman said. "He is a very tragic young man, and I hope he will get the help he needs. I'm sure he has his demons to face. If Koji is right, and he hurt his sister..."

Tara shuddered, looking at the sky, which was showing

the first signs of turning from ink-black to grey. Everything around the temple was silent. There wasn't even a breeze playing with the leaves, or any animals making enough noise to be heard. It was as if they were at the edge of the world. "Mark feels so insignificant now, in a way. He was just the beginning of our problems. Right now, we need to come up with a good plan. You believe you know where one of the seals is, which is a start, but we need to find information and allies, as you said before. Maybe we should split up in our journey. You and Koji could go to the seal, and I can try to find some more information? I have some very savvy computer friends that could perhaps lend a hand tracking people down."

Marie-Claire Florifera straightened herself. "I think your idea is good," she said. "Though it worries me to send you out there by yourself, *cherie*."

"I've always been a loner," Tara said. "Don't worry about me."

"On our first night," the old medium began, her face tense with the memory, "I spoke to one of the monks of this temple. I told you I had, but I never really explained to you what he said. He confirmed what the spirit had told me about the seals. In his story, there were two things that I believe can help us. The first was that he mentioned the Dead Sea Scrolls and that they somehow have a message in them that could save us all. The second was that there may be a guardian of guardians."

"A guardian of guardians?"

"Yes. He would not only know the location of the seals, but also where the guardians can be found. If he exists, he will be very important to us."

"If he's the guardian of guardians, he should be aware of what is going on already," Tara said. "Wouldn't he be acting right now?"

"I would like to think so, too. If he is real, perhaps he is already acting. There is too little information about the man for me to give you straight answers. We can't put all our eggs in one basket, especially if that basket turns out to be a myth. The Dead Sea Scrolls are a more solid lead, but I wanted you to be aware of this anyway."

"Okay, but I can focus on both, because if he does exist, imagine what he can do for us."

"Or what we could do for him," Florifera said.

"Right..." Tara wrinkled her nose. "Though I'm still not too sure how much difference we can make."

"One person can do so much. Look at our history. That's the power of mankind. It takes one to stand up against darkness to spread the seed of light and hope. Think of Gandhi, Martin Luther King..."

"Hitler," Tara said with a frown.

"Well, yes, one person can bring a lot of darkness, too," the old woman agreed. "But let's assume we will bring light."

"We're leaving Japan tomorrow," Tara said. "We're sure that's what the monks said? Because my communication with them is troublesome at best."

The old woman nodded. "Yes, I'm sure."

"I'll be glad to get some other clothes," Tara muttered. "They only brought back my small bag, and I've been wearing the same two t-shirts for days now. Especially since I had to throw away my fucking favorite shirt, which was covered in... in blood." Throwing away the shirt hadn't been easy, as if she were betraying Summer by getting rid of it.

"Don't expect too much of the world out there."

"Yeah, you've mentioned that."

"We will need to plan our next actions," Marie-Claire

said, ignoring Tara's comment.

"You will go to that house, you and Koji, and see if you can speak to the guardian there. See if you can protect that place, somehow. All is not lost unless all the seals are open, right? I mean, any seal opening will still give us enough shit to deal with, but at least it won't be the end of the world."

"It's worth a try."

"Meanwhile, I'll fly to New York. I have friends there. It might take some convincing that I haven't gone fucking insane, but they can help me find out as much as I can about the subject. We have the Internet on our side in this one. Maybe we can even back trace that mythical man of yours. And if there are others—and there better be fucking others—on our side, I will find them, too."

"It sounds like a plan, *ma cherie*."

"Tell me as much as you know about him, so I have something to go on."

Marie-Claire nodded and repeated everything the monk had told her. When she was finished, Tara frowned and bit her lip.

"Cain and Abel? I remember them from church. My grandma will be so happy to hear she was right about the Bible, after all."

"The Bible is just an interpretation of facts. You shouldn't follow it, or any teachings, blindly."

"I don't intend to follow anyone or anything blindly."

"This is why I believe our paths crossed for a reason." The old woman smiled. "You are a smart and capable woman, Tara. And I am happy to consider you as an ally."

"You have a good man in Koji, too," Tara said, uncomfortable with the compliment.

"I couldn't agree more," Marie-Claire said. "I hope he

will agree to accompany me to Angel Manor."

"Knowing Koji, he will."

"I would understand if you all wanted to return to your families in this troubled time," the old medium said, somewhat defensively.

"Personally, I don't have a lot of family I would want to return to. My relationship with my mother is... complicated," Tara said. "The only family I have I've created for myself. But if I don't act, I'm putting them all in danger. Who knows what kind of fucked up shit the next seal hides? I can't sit by and do nothing. What happened to my friends in that forest... I never want something like that to happen again." She stretched her sore back. "No, lady... like it or not, we're coming with you."

CHAPTER TWENTY NINE

Freya froze at the sight of the doll.

What the fuck...?

It hadn't been there when she'd turned around to put the dishes away. Now it sat in the middle of the room, staring at her with those black, emotionless eyes.

All the dolls were locked up. She'd seen to that. So, either this thing had gotten out or someone—or something—had let it out. It hadn't been her. After her little incident with the sledgehammer, she had left the damn things alone.

Or... was this a new one? The damn things seemed to multiply.

Freya squinted her eyes and studied it. It looked vaguely familiar with the black ringlets and the navy-blue dress, but most of the stupid things looked similar.

At that moment, the doll turned her head. If it were any other situation, Freya would have found it comical, but now she was terrified, and her insides turned to stone. It was such a simple motion, but the sight of those cold, porcelain eyes made her knees weak. The plates slipped from her suddenly weak hands and hit the floor with a loud clatter. The sound pulled her back into reality enough to react. At that same moment, Emily let out a terrified cry. The doll blinked, which was the last time Freya looked at it before she turned and ran.

There was a strong sense of déjà vu as her feet hit the marble floor. Running through the corridors of Angel Manor felt familiar in ways she didn't want it to. Her thoughts were a jumbled mess as she made a sharp turn to the corridor that held the nursery, never slowing her pace.

The panic room. Take Emily to the panic room, she told herself over and over, the words a mantra that kept her from totally freaking out. She almost fell taking a corner, her stockinged feet slipping on the smooth marble. Cursing, she regained her balance and lunged for the door to the nursery, but she only managed to open it an inch before something on the other side pulled it shut.

Freya let out an involuntary yelp and tried the door again, but whatever was on the other side was stronger.

"Emily!" Freya screamed, as if it would make any difference. "Mommy's coming." Her fist slammed into her door, causing a hot pain to spread through her hand. "Open this fucking door, whoever you are!"

She pulled and jerked on the handle, but it wouldn't budge. Her heart was pounding so hard, and she was out of breath. "Calm down," she told herself. Panicking wouldn't help. She had to get into the room. Even if that meant going through the window.

Freya looked around for something heavy she could smash the window with. She could go outside through Oliver's old room, and...

"You have more power than you know," a familiar voice whispered. "The dolls aren't at their full power yet, and you and I are linked. My doors are yours. If you wish them to open, just make them."

"How?" Freya said, her voice filled with tears of frustration at the house's continued obfuscation. "Is there some magic word or something? Do I concentrate... how do I do this? No one taught me."

"Just will it."

Emily's high-pitched screaming came to an abrupt silence, and Freya's heart stopped for a moment.

"I will it, damn it, I will it," she screamed and slammed her body into the door. Behind it, something was pushing back, but an electric surge coursed through Freya's veins and it pulsed into the door as if it were an extension of her, blasting it open. Whatever was behind it got pushed away, and Freya stumbled inside. There were porcelain dolls everywhere. She didn't stop to count them, but there had to be more than a dozen. Two of them were in the crib, on top of her baby. Freya picked up the little wooden table that stood in the corner of the room. She wielded it like a shield as she barged at the dolls, swiping them aside. There was a strength in her that she never knew she possessed as she stormed across the room.

She plucked the doll on Emily's chest up and smashed it against the wall. The other, which sat toward the foot of the crib, she bashed with the table. With one fluid motion, she grabbed Emily with her free hand. The baby's face was red, going on purple, and for a horrifying moment Freya thought she wasn't breathing. But Emily gasped and screamed again, her voice hoarse this time. The dolls surrounded her, but they didn't attack, as if they were unsure of what to do next. Freya didn't give them time to plan; she swung the table back and forth, creating a path for herself. One of the toys pushed the nursery door shut, but Freya wanted it to open, and it swung back at the doll full force.

It gave her just enough time to run. As she crossed the threshold, the door slammed shut behind her. Freya hoped the house would keep it closed, but she knew she wouldn't have too much time. Emily was still wailing so violently Freya barely recognised her own daughter's voice. She didn't bother to hush or comfort her; Freya had only one objective, and that was to get to the panic room.

Run, Freya, they're coming, Angel Manor whispered. *They're not even hiding themselves from me anymore. He's on his way, and they're getting stronger because of him.*

She took a sharp right, almost tumbling into the panic room. Only when she closed the door and locked it with her code, did she feel she could breathe again. Stabbing pains in her side and chest made her double over, but she tried her best to keep it together. Emily's screams had lessened to soft whimpers. Panting, Freya picked up the phone. She tried to remember the number she wanted to call, cursing herself for not having her mobile on her. She knew the number, but she just couldn't think straight. After a moment of agonising, she remembered and dialled

"Freya." Wulf's voice sounded cautious. "I..."

"You were right, these dolls are fucking evil..." She could barely speak because she was so out of breath. Her chest was tight, but she went on, "They tried to hurt Emily. Oh my god, she was almost dead, and it would have been all my fault."

"Holy shit, Freya..."

"You need to come get her. I believe you. I need her to be safe, and even if I don't know you, I can't keep her here in this house. And I can't leave, so... you have to come get her."

"I'm coming right now."

She sobbed into the phone, "You have to promise me you'll keep her safe, Wulf. I need you to be a good guy. I need you to keep my baby safe."

"I promise," he whispered before the line went dead.

***

Freya had no idea how long she had been in the panic room, but when the knock came, she screamed, waking Emily—who had just dozed off—and making the baby cry again. With shaking hands, she pressed the button to the video intercom. Wulf's face came on the screen in a strange, distorted angle, as if she were looking at him in a fish tank.

"Oh, thank god you're here." She rested her head next to the intercom. "Are those things still out there?"

"I've looked through the house," Wulf said. "I can't spot a single one. That doesn't mean they're not here."

"I'm so scared," Freya said.

"You can let me in." He looked at the camera. In reply, she pressed the code, releasing the door from its lock. He stepped inside and placed his hands on her shoulders.

"Are you okay?"

"No," she said. "But I'm not injured, if you're asking that."

"That's at least something."

"How did you get in the house? Was the door open?"

"No, but I have my ways," he admitted. "Your panic room seems safe, though. I tried to get in, but I couldn't."

"That's a relief."

He took her chin and forced her to look at him—a movement that not long ago made her want to kiss him. "I'm so sorry for not being honest with you."

"You don't have a soul... that is pretty intense," she said.

"Not having a soul isn't as horrible as you think it is. Only mortals have souls."

"That's still pretty intense," she said. "You're implying that you're not mortal..."

He grimaced. "I wish I could explain everything to you, but it's a long story, and I'm not ready to share it yet."

"I need to trust you now, Wulf," Freya said. "Emily needs to leave this house right now, and I don't have anyone else to turn to. If I can't trust you..."

"I don't want to hurt you, or Emily."

She shook her head. "I can't be sure of that, can I? You

lied."

"Listen, I'm a very big, strong man," Wulf said. "If I wanted to hurt you, don't you think I would have done so when I had you alone in the house?"

"You have a good point there," Freya said as she picked up the baby.

"If I wanted to hurt Emily, all I would have to do is take her from you." Wulf touched the forehead of the sleeping child. "I won't do anything you don't want me to, I promise." He leaned in close, his face near hers. "I honestly care about you, Freya." He bent forward to kiss her, but she stepped back.

"No, you don't get to kiss me. Not now, not after everything... I haven't forgiven you yet." Freya lowered her eyes. "The only reason you're here is because I need you."

"Understood."

She looked up at him, fighting tears again. "You're not going to tell me where you're taking her, are you?"

"It would be safer if I didn't."

She nodded. Somehow, she had known, and she wanted it that way. "What's happening out there, Wulf?"

"Someone is opening all the seals."

"And they're coming for Angel Manor?"

"Yes, it will be the last one, but they're already working on it." Wulf caught a tear that escaped her eye with the tip of his finger. He held it up as if it were a precious stone. "I'm going to take Emily to safety, and then I'm going to figure out how to protect you."

"If they want the seal to open, all they have to do is make sure I can't make a sacrifice."

"I don't think it's that simple, or there would have been

attacks on your life already," Wulf said. "I've talked to... some contacts. It seems the guardians are being sacrificed. Whoever is behind this—and I suspect it's blood mages, because of the nature of the servitors—wants you alive for now."

Freya kissed the top of Emily's head and handed her to Wulf, her heart aching. "Yet another thing I am asked to sacrifice. I can't even be with my baby... When will this world stop demanding things from me?"

"I don't know," Wulf said.

"If I die, Emily is the next in line to protect this house," Freya said, her voice breaking. "Please make sure she gets trained properly for this. Don't let her come into this the way I did."

"You're not going to die, Freya," Wulf said, holding the baby to his chest. "Not on my watch."

"Just take care of her, okay?"

"I will guard her with my life."

When he left, she crumpled to the floor, curled in a fetal position. The tears ran down her face, while her heart was empty.

CHAPTER THIRTY

Shizuoka Airport was filled with anxious travelers. Desperate people hoping to be reunited with loved ones. An atmosphere of grim disbelief sat over the people there, as the big screens all around the airport showed the news reports of the thousands of suicides that were being committed all around the country, and even the world. The revelation of the increasing number of deaths put the survivors in a state of shock.

It had been pure luck that he and Marie-Claire Florifera had managed to get two tickets to Edinburgh, and Koji was grateful that they were leaving the overcrowded airport within the foreseeable future. Tara was less lucky. It turned out that New York was a popular place to travel to; she hadn't managed to get tickets to any of the main three airports, and was now trying to get a seat on any flight that would go to the East Coast. She had decided she could rent a car or maybe grab a taxi from there.

"I would still feel better if we all stuck together," Koji said as he wrapped his arms around Tara's shoulders. "When people split up in horror movies, it never ends well."

Tara, who had her head buried in his neck while they hugged, snorted. "Though reality is trying hard to prove otherwise, this is not a horror movie." She pulled herself free from his embrace. "And as much as I would like to stick together, if we split up, we can cover more ground. I'm much more useful if I get others to work with us."

"Why not just use the Internet? That way you can communicate with people and look stuff up, but still be with us."

"I will use the Internet, but I'm sure that there are texts

out there that need to be read that can't be found online. I'm going to visit libraries—probably across the world if I get the chance—and read actual old tomes, and shit. Besides, I need to look people in the fucking eye when I tell them I need their help to prevent the world from ending."

"With what's been going on, I doubt they will take much convincing." Koji nodded toward one of the screens, where a pale-faced Japanese reporter was speaking into a microphone with an expression of pure terror on his face. "I think people will be glad to get any type of explanation right now."

"You're probably right." Tara grabbed his hand and squeezed it. Her fingers were warm and strong. "Listen, I'm going to find other people who know about this, okay? We can't be the only ones who have discovered the seals, and if there are any leads to people who know more than we do, we're going to find them. We'll reach out to every crackpot that's out there, if necessary." Tara laughed.

"There will be many crackpots," Koji said. "Are you sure you have enough help?"

"Not by a long shot, but it's all we've got now, and maybe along the way we'll recruit more people who are willing to help. We need to bring people together and find a way to stop this."

Koji sighed. "Recruiting our own personal army..."

Tara let out a deep breath. "Sure does sound like that, doesn't it?" She shook her head. "It's pretty fucked up. A few days ago, we were just going to make a video about a suicide forest, and now..."

"Yeah, now look where we are."

She touched his cheek. "We need to make sure we keep in regular contact, okay? It's important for me to know what is happening on your end, and I really need to be able to tell someone what's happening on mine. We don't know what we're up against, but I feel that we stand stronger together—" she smiled "—even if we're not physically together."

"We'll get in touch with you as soon as we land."

A tall man with pockmarked skin walked past. He wore a long, dark grey coat and a fedora, and his eyes were hidden behind a pair of black aviator sunglasses. He turned his head to Koji and Tara and stared at them at length. Enough to make Koji highly uncomfortable. The man either smiled or sneered at him, he wasn't sure. One lip curled up to reveal sharp teeth. Koji wasn't sure if his eyes were deceiving him or if the teeth were filed into points. Before he could respond, the man disappeared into the crowd.

"Have you managed to contact the guardian to that manor yet?"

"No, we can't get through," Koji said, tearing his thoughts from the stranger with the weird teeth. "I can't reach my family, either."

"I went on Facebook, and they have that thing where people indicate that they're 'safe,' you know?" Tara said. "I posted a message, too, and some of my friends have already responded."

"My Mom and Dad aren't on Facebook," Koji said. "But it's a good tip. I'll do the same."

"You'll get through to them eventually," Tara said. "I mean, this thing can't last forever, you know."

The sadness in his heart bloomed when he pictured his mother and father. "I just hope they're okay."

"Me, too. Are you feeling bad for not going home?"

"No," he said. "There is nothing I can do for them at home, but if I go with Madame Florifera, maybe I can do something for them then, you know?"

"Yeah, that's how I feel, too," Tara said. "I need to make a difference."

"Yeah," he said, but he couldn't meet her eyes. He hoped they were making a difference.

"Hey, don't you two have a flight to catch?" Tara said, with forced optimism. Her eyes were wet with tears, and Koji swallowed his own emotions.

"Yeah, we really need to go," he muttered. "Are you sure you're going to be okay?"

"Of course. I'm a tough fucking cookie, remember?" She smiled and tugged at the shirt she'd bought on the way to the airport. On the chest was a picture of an Oreo flexing its muscles.

Marie-Claire Florifera touched his arm. "We really do have to go. Let's not risk missing our flight." She turned to Tara, her blind eyes staring past the young woman. "Good luck, *cherie*. I think what you are doing is very brave. And I hope your efforts will be fruitful."

"Good luck to you both. I hope that place treats you better than it did the last time you were there," Tara said. "I'm going back in to see if I can get my own plane ticket." She grabbed her jacket and turned her back to them.

***

The darkness was interspersed with glimpses of light for Marie-Claire. She could sense the people around her, smell their scents, and feel their anxiety. Not all of them belonged in the mortal world. A lot of people carried spirits with them, so this was no surprise to her. It didn't frighten her to see that so many people now had fading apparitions of loved ones standing next to them. It wasn't the spirits that made her catch her breath, but the... others. The dark things, darker even than the world through which she moved.

She accidentally brushed against someone in her haste. The touch of the man jolted through her whole body, as if an invisible anaconda wrapped itself around her soul and squeezed. An alien anger surged through her, and she felt defiled to the very core of her being. She needed to touch Koji's arm to stop herself from shaking. The boy had a calming influence, such an overwhelming sense of good coming from him, and she was grateful he had been put on her path. Marie-Claire wondered if she could maintain her sanity without him. He led her through the airport, fast and determined, steering her clear from the masses of people. After a while, he stopped, and he let go of her. Marie-Claire waited a few seconds, but she felt too exposed standing there all by herself.

"Koji," she whispered. He touched her arm, instantly calming her again.

"One moment, Marie-Claire," he said with a gentle tone. She could hear him speak to what sounded like a young woman. His words were fast and soft.

"I got you a seat," Koji said. "You must be exhausted." His hands were warm on her shoulders.

"Thank you, *mon chere*," Marie-Claire said, still trembling from her earlier encounter. "My feet are a bit tired."

"We have two stop-overs," Koji said as he guided her to the empty seat. "One in Shanghai and one in Frankfurt. I just hope the airports there will be less crowded."

"Don't count on it."

"No, you're probably—" He never finished his sentence, but Marie-Claire could hear the sharp intake of his breath.

"What is it?"

"This is the second time a very strange person has been staring at me," Koji said. "There's this guy... holy shit..."

Marie-Claire looked around the room, her blind eyes scanning the darkness. It didn't take long to realise what had frightened Koji. There was a group of... things, five of them glowing an evil black, while one had a light so strong it hurt her mind's eye to look at it.

"I count six of them," Marie-Claire said.

"Are they all demons?" Koji asked.

"I don't know," Marie-Claire said, "but I don't think so. The only thing I am pretty sure of is that they aren't human."

***

Koji had never been more miserable about his plane being delayed. The six strangers were still staring at them, which didn't ease his mind. He didn't want to leave the old lady alone, but his bladder was full enough to be a torment, and there was still no sign they would board anytime soon. The bathroom sign only a few feet from where they were sitting made his need even more urgent.

He glared at the strangers. The nearest one was a young man, tall and muscular, with black skin and a bright red mohawk. If the strangers had wanted to attack, surely they would have done so by now? Koji decided, as his bladder threatened to release its contents. There would be little risk leaving Marie-Claire out in public, right?

"I need the bathroom," he whispered. "Will you be okay here? With those... things?"

"Yes, go," the old lady said.

"Sure?"

"I can see them, remember? That gives me some advantage."

He nodded and stood, fighting the temptation to stick his hand between his legs like a little boy. He pushed open the door to the bathroom and made his way to the urinal, where with a blissful sigh he relieved himself. Eyes half-closed, he didn't notice the man who stood next to him at first.

"Why do you look like that?" a deep voice asked him in American English, and Koji almost pissed over his own feet. He turned to see the black man with the red mohawk taking a leak to his right.

"I... I beg your pardon?" Koji said.

"Why do you look like that?" the man repeated. He was frowning at him, and Koji realized the man had blue eyes. They looked strange and hollow in contrast with his dark skin.

"Look like what?" Koji asked.

"You have an inner light." The man shook up and down and tucked himself back in his ripped jeans. "You're human, right?" He buttoned his fly.

"Hu... human?" Koji stammered. "Yes."

"Humans are all the same. Except, you and the old lady ain't. Like, you've been marked."

"I... I..." Koji closed his zipper.

"Where did you come from?" the man asked, not allowing Koji to form a coherent thought.

"Just now?" Koji asked meekly.

"Yeah, where were you before this?" the man leaned forward, his tone harsh. "Did something happen to you?"

"We were in Aokigahara," Koji said, unable to help himself. He felt powerless against those blue eyes. The man flinched at the sound of the name.

"Ah," he simply said. "That explains it then. You better watch your back, human. I don't know what that mark means, but I'm sure that sooner or later someone or something is going to try to find out. And they might just try to get to the core of it, by getting to the core of you, if you know what I mean?" He gestured by running the nail of his thumb across his throat.

"Not, not really," Koji said, although he knew exactly what the stranger meant. The man just shook his head and walked out of the bathroom, leaving Koji feeling exposed. He wondered where Tara was. He worried about her; if he and Marie-Claire were marked, perhaps she was, too.

CHAPTER THIRTY ONE

"Pour me a Glenfiddich and make it a double." Wulf slammed a fifty-dollar note on the bar. The broad bartender with the long greasy blond hair leered at him and took the note between thumb and forefinger. He held it up and waved it slowly.

"Rough day?" he asked, curling his thick lips up enough to show the blunt edge of his teeth. "Are you sure you don't want me to pour you something... stronger?"

"Nice try, Andhrímnir, but you'll not feed me any of that shit you serve."

The man bristled, slamming a glass down in front of Wulf. "That *shit* is too good for the likes of you, under dweller. I've fed gods." He poured a liberal helping of the Glenfiddich. Wulf didn't like the man, but he couldn't fault his generosity.

"Don't you have a boar to kill?" he rumbled before he downed the single malt scotch in one gulp. The old god glowered at him, but said nothing, and just filled his glass again. There was a moment where the old grey eyes held his, then the large man turned around and served someone else.

"In a foul mood, are we?" said a soft voice. "I see your new life hasn't cured you of your hot temper." A woman sat on the bar-stool next to him, leaning in close. He could smell her, and she stunk of the old world. Of earth and honey. Of birth and of death. "I assume you would take the risk of being out in public to come see me and mine?"

He nodded and turned to her. The sight of her always struck him. She was a mixture of strength and softness, in the way of all women, which was the very thing that made her unique; she was a part of all of them. Her face was so fresh, and every inch was filled with an innocence he knew was a lie. All that was beautiful about youth was represented in her anthropomorphic personification. Her red hair—the colour of spun copper—was done up in a bun. A three-piece beige skirt suit clung tightly to her form in that sophisticated-but-sexy way. The outfit caused him to do a double take. It was so different from the white cotton maiden's dress she would wear if she were accompanied by her usual companions. It was strange seeing her as an individual, since she was so very much "one of three." There had been moments when she had invoked a feeling of wild lust within him, but now, as something stirred in his mind, he could feel the tugging of his captor, preventing Wulf being himself. Instead, he looked at the maiden with a stern calm.

"It's been a long time since I've seen you without your companions, Clotho."

With her fingertips, she brushed a lock from her cheek, which looked like it was made of red gold, and shot him a bright smile that was filled with the bloom of life. "I am never truly without my companions." There was a sparkle in her eyes. In front of her stood a Martini glass with a bright pink drink inside. He couldn't remember anyone putting it there.

"You're right. I have come to see you. I was hoping you'd find me here."

"Of course I would. You did call for me, after all. Besides, I've been taking a special interest in you lately."

He cocked his head. "Have you now?"

"Well, no... I've been taking a special interest in someone who you have taken a special interest in. Which is almost the same thing."

"You were at the house..."

"Did you sense me?" Her smile was almost coy.

"No, not exactly, but it just makes sense now." He rubbed his hand in his neck. "You already know why I'm here."

She took a sip from her Martini. "You want us to protect her baby."

He nodded.

Her eyelashes fluttered over her glass as she said—the rim still against her lips—in a breathy voice, "There will be a price."

He nodded again. "I'll pay it. Just keep the child safe."

She broke eye contact, drinking deep from the glass. After a long pause, she said, "A deal is struck."

***

Freya wiped the tears away, the salt stinging her eyes. With a heavy heart, she opened the door to the attic. Emily's departure had left a deep scar, as deep as Logan's death, but it also made her more determined. Her baby was safe now—she had to believe that—and it was her task to protect the world for Emily to grow up in, no matter how much she hated going up to the top floor of Angel Manor. She couldn't just sit still and not at least try to find some information. She and Bam had explored the attic over the past year, but the space was so vast they hadn't gotten through even a quarter of it. There had to be answers somewhere in this house, and the only two places she could think of to find them were the attic and the basement. The attic was the most logical choice of the two, because the basement didn't hold the same wealth of things to explore, save the seal itself. And perhaps a trapped spirit—if he was even still there.

She thought of Chuck, concentrating on his image.

No, he's gone, she thought. It was as clear as it was that Bam was no longer in Angel Manor. The house was empty except for her and Death, who stirred in his magical sleep;

the changes in the world had touched him as much as they had Freya. The rider still slept, but he was so near waking, his presence like an invisible noose tightening slowly around her neck.

Freya took a deep breath and stepped inside. The attic spread out over the whole of the mansion. There was a lot of clutter—furniture and other junk that had once been someone's treasure—so finding anything had always proved to be a challenge. The floorboards creaked under the heels of her Doc Martens. She tried to keep her heartbeat under control by adjusting her breathing. Her solitude made her even more wary. Without the distraction of Emily, being alone made her feel vulnerable.

Despite being practically interlinked with the house, the she hated the attic. She glanced at the old furniture and possessions from the previous owners, realising that these things weren't part of the house. They were a part of people long dead, and they didn't hold the same magical connection to her as the brick and mortar of the building did. That's why the attic never quite felt like home, because it didn't belong to her, and it held secrets that the house couldn't touch.

"Okay, Frey, focus." The sound of her own voice was a small comfort, but at least it was something. "What are you looking for?" Her eyes scanned the low-lit surroundings. "Something about the seven seals. Or maybe something about creepy dolls... or spells that can unbind me from the house... or..." The thoughts swirled through her head, and she inhaled again. "One thing at a time." She let out the air from her lungs. "Tomes... I haven't read them all yet. Let's start there." Her game plan was meager at best, but Freya decided that an educated woman was a better warrior, and with determined steps, she made her way to the west side of the attic, carefully avoiding the place where she had made love to Logan for the first time. On top of everything, she couldn't deal with that particular memory at the moment.

A noise—echoing from somewhere behind her—startled her, and as she turned, she walked into a large item covered in the same white tarp as most of the furniture. Freya clung on to the white fabric as she tried to maintain her balance, her eyes scanning the darkness to discover what had made the sound. She leaned on the covered furniture, causing the cover to slide to the side. Only when she was assured there was nothing up in the attic with her, did she look down at it. She pulled the rest of the tarp, uncovering a large wooden trunk standing on its side. The make and style appeared to be very old, but it was as clean as if someone had just polished it. The sides were topped by ornate gold bands. Heavy latches held the lid tightly closed. She stepped forward and jiggled the locks in the hope that she could open it. A tingling heat tickled her fingers when she touched the metal.

"How am I going to open this?" she muttered, inspecting the latches. She ran her hands to the side of the chest, hoping a key might be attached. There was nothing, not even on the ground near it. Freya pulled the covers off some furniture standing nearby, thinking perhaps there would be a cabinet or chest of drawers, or something that would bear a key. The trunk fascinated her, and she wanted to see what was inside—she had a gut feeling about it. If she had the right tools, she could probably get it open. She pulled the latches one more time, making sure it was really closed, and not just stuck with old age, and to her disappointment it was.

She took a step back and stared at it, remembering how the door had opened to her when she had willed it. Perhaps this particular trunk was a part of the house? It wouldn't hurt to at least try. She took a deep breath and focused her mind on the lock. It didn't budge. She tried it again, but the lock refused to open. With a sheepish sigh, she took another step back. There obviously wasn't a quick way to open this thing, so Freya made a mental note to come back later for it. It could wait, she told herself. It wasn't as if what lay in that trunk would make all the difference.

Stretching her back and neck, she took a moment to compose herself before she walked over to what she considered the attic's library.

It wasn't really a library, just a little corner that had two wide bookshelves—spanning most of the long wall—and over a dozen stacks of piled books. There were at least a hundred books for her to explore, and even though she and Bam had spent a fair amount of time here, they hadn't managed to read more than fifteen of the fat textbooks between the two of them. The texts had been dry and tedious at best, and totally incomprehensible in many instances.

A pile of pillows and seat cushions she had placed on the floor several months earlier still lay to the side. Some of the books they had been studying were open. Freya stepped toward the furthest of the two bookshelves—which she had yet to explore—and ran her finger across the spines of the books on the top shelf, scanning the titles. Most of them were grimoires dealing with the subject of magic.

"The Sixth and Seventh books of Moses, The Clavicule of Solomon, The Book of St Cyprian, The Book of Honorius, The Fourth Book of Occult Philosophy, The Magus..." She stopped at a tome called *The Book of Shadows*. From the faded cover, she could tell it wasn't a new book, and she wondered where she had heard the title before. With two fingers, she plucked it out from between its fellow books, and studied the cover. It didn't look familiar, but the title sounded like something she might have heard on a TV show, or something. When she opened it, she found it wasn't so much a tome as it was a journal filled with magic spells. The handwriting was atrocious, and Freya groaned at the sight of the floating letters with sharp edges, narrowly written together. It would take her some time to decipher what it said, but perhaps there would be some sort of aid for her in this. One of the previous owners could have written it, and perhaps they had bothered to discuss some of the secrets of the manor. Freya leafed through the pages, hoping that the handwriting would magically

improve somehow, but it didn't. Something caught her eye mid-flip, and she had to go back a few pages to find it. It was a drawing—a rather good one—of something that resembled an old-fashioned doll. The sight of the round angelic face scribbled with faded black ink chilled her blood. She squinted her eyes to decipher the scribbling underneath. The penmanship resembled chicken scratches more than it did letters, and Freya couldn't make head nor tail of it. There were a few words she thought she recognized like "to" and "from." The word that stood out most she was sure said "blood" and with a bit of creative guesswork she could make out "magic" next to it, but it was impossible for her to read what the whole description said. Freya swore and closed the book, but she put it on the pile she was making for books she would take downstairs to read further. There was something in that notebook, and she would find out what. Even if it killed her.

CHAPTER THIRTY TWO

The Internet connection on her phone was horrendous, and Tara struggled to keep her temper in check as she watched the websites load with agitating slowness. She refused to give up because she needed the distraction. There was only so much of her immediate reality that she could take. The airport was too crowded, and there were no seats available for her to sit on while she waited to see if she could make the next flight. Tara was flying standby, her only chance of getting a flight since everything was booked —and in many cases, overbooked. The nice, middle-aged lady behind the counter, with the bright red lips and purple cat-eye glasses, had assured her that she would have a greater chance getting on since she was a single traveller, but even with those advantages, Tara had spent her night in the overcrowded airport. The first forty minutes or so, she had kept her eyes peeled on the special announcement board that showed how many seats were still left on the next flight, but after a while, she decided to keep herself busy instead. Today, she had focused on Googling what she could find about the Dead Sea Scrolls. It wasn't an easy feat, with both Wi-Fi and 4G randomly appearing and disappearing.

"Miss Bell?" a female voice with a hint of a Japanese accent said. Tara looked up and recognized the middle-aged ground stewardess motioning at her. Tara got to her feet and followed the woman to the counter.

"I can't get you to New York," she said as her fingers typed away at a small keyboard with surprising agility, "but there are a few seats open to Amsterdam. You would have probably stopped over there anyway, had I been able to get you on a flight to New York. You have more chances of catching a plane at Schiphol." She pressed the glasses to the tip of her nose, in a very similar way that Koji did. "Would you like me to get you on the plane to Amsterdam?"

"Yes," Tara said. "At least that's closer to home than where I am now." The woman nodded in response, and her nimble fingers clicked at the keyboard.

"There will be two stop-overs, one in Okinawa and one in Taipei. Your luggage will be transported automatically."

"I... I only have hand luggage," Tara said, picturing her suitcase in the tent somewhere in Aokigahara. The monks had brought her the backpack that held her important belongings. Koji had been more fortunate; he had gotten some of his clothes back too. Tara had confiscated one of his t-shirts to wear.

The woman nodded but said nothing. Tara doubted she was the strangest case that lady had met today. Less than a minute later, the woman handed her a boarding pass and Tara, in return, handed her a pile of the unfamiliar money. The woman counted out how many yen she owed her and handed the rest back.

"What kind of currency do they have in Amsterdam?" Tara asked, her mind suddenly drawing a blank.

"Euros," the woman answered.

"Oh, right," Tara said sheepishly. "I knew that."

"You can exchange your money either at this airport, or in Amsterdam." The woman touched Tara's hand. "Don't worry, you will be fine."

"I hope so," Tara said, feeling anything but fine. "I really hope so."

The ground stewardess instructed her regarding which gate she had to use, and Tara thanked her. The airport was small, and it wasn't difficult to find where she had to be. All the seats were filled, and several people were sitting on the floor. There was a strangely hushed atmosphere for a place that was crowded with people. Even the children seemed to be more listless than usual, and little ones were curled up on the laps of their parents instead of running around and screaming. A lot of the travellers had their arms wrapped around each other, seeking silent comfort in the people they loved.

Tara found a spot near the window. Outside, the big jets sat waiting to be filled with the desperate passengers. With a sigh, she took out her phone again, and noticed she had a hint of a signal. When she got home, she'd probably have to get a job just to pay off her phone bill, but she really couldn't care about that right now. Not only did she need the distraction of the research, but she was curious about what she was dealing with. When the Wikipedia page finally loaded, she let out a sigh of relief.

*The **Dead Sea Scrolls**, in the narrow sense of **Qumran Caves Scrolls**, are a collection of some 981 different texts discovered between 1946/47 and 1956 in eleven caves in the immediate vicinity of the Hellenistic-period Jewish settlement at Khirbet Qumran in the eastern Judaean Desert, the modern West Bank.*

"Jesus," Tara swore, "nine hundred and eighty-one different texts? Those will be fun to read." She looked up, suddenly aware she was talking out loud, and she saw an adolescent Japanese boy gawk at her. He was leaning against his mother, a dainty woman in a business suit. The kid was young—Tara could never guess how old kids were, she didn't know about shit like that—but she guessed he was still in kindergarten, maybe he hadn't even started yet. The big brown eyes held hers, filled with a mixture of sadness and kindness, and a chill ran over Tara's spine. A line rose in her mind: "Blessed are the meek, for they shall inherit the earth." This child would indeed one day inherit the earth, but what earth would there be left to receive?

A single tear ran over the cheek of the little boy, and it startled Tara. He never took his eyes off her as he pointed at his mother. Her face was pale, with a bob cut that reached to her jawline, and dark circles were set under her eyes, as if she hadn't slept in days. The red painted lips were moving almost unnoticeably, and she was carefully mouthing unspoken words. There was something in the eyes that looked familiar, and Tara almost dropped her phone. The woman opened a large black purse and rummaged through it with a dreamy expression on her tired face.

"No, you don't," Tara said, and she got to her feet, pushing the phone in her back pocket. *You could be wrong, she might just be looking for a tissue*, the voice of hesitation ran in the back of her mind. But Tara wasn't risking it. She would rather attack a stranger for no reason than let this woman harm herself. Not on her watch. And this one she could take, she decided. *Please don't let her be a Kung Fu master... oh wait, that's Chinese... Karate Master?* Her thoughts were chaotic and filled with doubt.

The woman fished a silver-coloured pen from the contents of her purse. The sight of it made Tara run. The way the brown eyes studied the pen was enough to confirm any suspicion she had. She had seen Summer look at those scissors in exactly the same way. With a grandiose gesture, Tara raised her hand and slapped the pen from the woman's fingers. The woman didn't even look at her. Instead, her dreamy eyes just scanned the ground, searching for the pen.

Tara leapt forward and seized the woman's wrist. Around her, people were staring. A big white man with a brown beard, a bald head, and a hint of tattoos creeping up from his collar grabbed Tara by the shoulder.

"What are you doing?" he asked with a German accent. "Why are you bothering this woman?"

Tara turned to the man. "She's going to hurt herself. I have to stop her," she said, feeling tears well up in her eyes. The surge of emotions took her by surprise. The man let go of her and focused his attention to the woman who was on all fours looking for the pen.

"Scheiße," the man cursed, and he lunged toward the woman. "What the fuck is happening to people? I saw someone mutilate themselves with a freaking letter opener... it's pens now?" he said as he pulled the small Japanese lady to her feet. She was struggling to get loose, but the man held on tight. "What is wrong with you?" he said. "Your child is right there. Get a grip on yourself."

Two security officers ran in their direction, and the big German tried to explain that he was preventing the woman from harming herself. The guards only spoke a little English and Tara's heart sank. At that moment, the woman screamed and raked her short, manicured fingernails across her face, pulling at the skin. Red scratches appeared on her cheeks. The guards immediately lost interest in the German man and turned to the woman. She was thrashing and screaming now, as the guards held on to her arms. Tara couldn't understand what she was saying, but it stunned the Japanese bystanders. An old lady covered her ears, as if just hearing the words could hurt her in some way.

One of the officers called for help, while the other struggled to put the woman in handcuffs. It ended up taking three officers to escort the screaming passenger from the gate. A female officer picked up the little boy and held him in her arms as she followed her colleagues at some distance. The child never stopped staring at Tara with that solemn expression on his face. She wasn't sure if he was grateful or if he blamed her somehow.

An obese man with a friendly round face walked up to Tara and the German man. His gaze was following the screaming woman. "I don't know what the hell is happening to people," he said in a southern American drawl, "but whatever it is, I sure hope that our pilots are immune to it."

The words made Tara's blood run cold.

***

Marie-Claire saw the Lamb in her dream, or perhaps it was a vision; she wasn't sure. She couldn't remember if she had dozed off during the flight. Her surroundings were so very realistic, but held a hint of the surreal, as dreams often did. The soft wind stroked her cheeks and the scent of jasmine lay thick in the air, but at the same time, the land didn't look quite right, and the fact that she could even see it in the first place was a pretty big tip off. Marie-Claire focused on the child in front of her. The girl looked different now, but she recognised her. It was the essence that was the same. A random amused thought occurred to her, changing William Shakespeare's quote to suit her situation: *What's in a face?*

"Why are you here?" she asked the girl, not expecting an answer.

"Because you must see, even if you can't witness," the child said. She moved her lips, and seemed more natural this time, more human. "You must be one of the ones who have seen it all, and I will show you. I shall be your eyes where you have none."

Marie-Claire rested her hand on her chest, feeling the bones under her thin skin. Her heart was pounding under her fingertips. *Is it possible to feel this in a dream? Or am I simply imagining this?*

"My dear," she said, "I don't know if my heart can take more right now. I'm growing old."

"You must be strong, for you are a champion."

"C'EST N'IMPORTE QUOI," she said. *That's nonsense.* "I assure you, I'm a great many things, but I am not a champion." She looked over the girl's head and saw that they were at the edge of some sort of cliff. It looked familiar, but the land was different than it would look in reality, and she couldn't make sense of it. Marie-Claire Florifera had traveled to so many places in her life, and there had been a lot of cliffs she had stood on, but this one felt significant.

"Life doesn't always give you a choice on what your path

is, *petite*," the child said in the voice of her grandmother. She remembered the advice well.

"Life only gives you the choice if you're going to walk the path or not," Marie-Claire finished the old adage. "Who are you? Why have you sought me out?"

"The bloodline leads to you." The girl stared over the edge of the cliff, down to the valley below.

"The bloodline doesn't end with me." Her cheeks were hot, and she wondered if she was flushing. Her fingertips lightly caressed the spot right under her eyes.

"No, you continued your bloodline."

"Why seek me out?" Marie-Claire asked. "Why not find my son? He is still alive, isn't he?" She didn't know why she was so worried all of a sudden; she hadn't thought of him for months, maybe even years. She wasn't a good mother, never had been, and she had given the baby up without much remorse, knowing his life would be better where he was. Sometimes she would think of him, wondering what had become of him, but the thoughts were always fleeting. Marie-Claire wasn't born with a nurturing instinct.

"It all starts with you. This is your path, not his."

"I don't know how much longer I can walk this path," Marie-Claire said, tiredness dragging her down. "The burden on my shoulders may weigh too much."

The child looked at her with solemn eyes, and she nodded.

"Are you part of the bloodline, too?" Marie-Claire asked.

"I am. You come from a line of women. Yours was the first son. That's why you are special, why you have the gift. You broke the rules without even knowing it."

Marie-Claire blinked. "My son? Is he special?"

"Only in the way everyone is special. He holds no

purpose on your path, or on mine." She smiled. "I did not bring you here to talk to you about your boy. I came here to show you something." The girl pointed down the valley, and Marie-Claire saw.

"It's Lucifer Falls," she said, bringing her hand to her mouth. "I recognize it now." She turned to the manor behind her, the one that featured in many of her nightmares. It looked even bigger and darker in the dream than it had in real life. "Is this the seal? I thought it was in Angel Manor?"

"Not exactly," the child said. "You are right, the seal lies beneath Angel Manor. But this is a place that is linked to all seven seals."

A sound startled Marie-Claire and made her turn around to face Lucifer Falls again. From the depths of the black hole came the most frightening, and yet the loveliest, note she had ever heard in her life. It wasn't human, it was beyond that. The sound was nothing like anything she knew, and yet, she somehow pictured it as coming out of a glass trumpet. Or perhaps an instrument made entirely out of light. The note evoked a very visual response from her imagination. A second note followed the first, accompanied by a beam of light. Then a third note, and more light, this time in a subtle, different hue.

"This music... it's not meant for my ears," she muttered. Tears were falling down her cheeks.

"I'm allowing you to hear it as well as I'm letting you see," the Lamb said. The sound reached up to the heavens, piercing through whatever barrier held the two worlds apart, and Marie-Claire was sure it reached straight down to Hell as well. Every non-human in the world would hear the tune. And they would know. They would hear the harkening of... of whatever it was that made that sound. They would know the third seal was open.

***

Freya felt the change through the house. There was a sound, just on the edge of her perception. She couldn't hear it clearly, as if she just caught the last noise of an echo. There was another tremor, and something made the world seem worse for wear. If Angel Manor held the last seal, Freya was determined to keep it closed. The world wasn't ready to end yet. *She* wasn't ready for it to be over. She wanted to teach Emily how to walk, and she wanted to take her to school for the first time, read her books, take her to movies, see her go to prom... there was a future in her child, and she wanted to witness it. And if there was anything in that stupid *Book of Shadows*, she would find it after she deciphered the horrible chicken scratches.

After some contemplation, she had decided to leave the panic room. Wulf had checked the house, and the dolls weren't there. There was a whole prepper's food supply in her panic room—including such treasures as freeze-dried pasta and rice meals, tinned beans, fruits and veggies, cured meats and canned liquids—that would last her for months if it had to, but she figured she might as well get the fresh stuff out of her fridge while she could. And she really wanted to get Emily's blanket, which still held the baby's smell.

She had to get out of the panic room, anyway. Angel Manor still demanded a sacrifice. Her time was running out, and she didn't even have a victim yet, so she needed to get one within the next seventy-two hours. No time for caution now; she would face getting ill and just deal with the consequences later. Her plan of action was to set up a date and lure some guy back to the house on the evening of the solstice with the promise of sex, where she would kill him. She could use the dating profile she had, because she couldn't leave the house for too long. It wasn't ideal, but recent events had made her tardy about the whole sacrifice thing. Worst case scenario, if she couldn't find a date, she would call Wulf and ask him to help her find a victim.

Deep in thought, she opened the fridge door and grabbed the carton of milk. When she closed the door, she saw the figure of a little girl standing in front of her. Freya dropped the milk, but she didn't scream. The child looked... wrong. She was definitely human, not a doll, but she was dressed like one, and her lips were stitched closed.

"Jesus," Freya said in a gasp. The child just stood and stared at her.

Freya, the house cried out, *he's here. Run.*

"Fuck, you couldn't have told me this *before* I left the panic room?"

She turned and ran. Her exit toward the panic room was blocked off by another little girl. This one was a bit taller than the first, and her skin was a bluish black colour instead of a milky white. Freya considered knocking her over, but her courage gave out, and instead she made her way to her bedroom, the closest room in her path. She slammed the door shut behind her. Her plan was to go out the window, and then re-enter the house from the back, where she would be able to get into her panic room. A loud thump against the door made her scream. It came again, and in a reflex Freya jumped on her bed. There was another sound, one that was subtler, like the creaking of floorboards. The house flared in her mind, as if it were a child, calling out for her. Something was happening to it.

"Argh, why did I leave the freaking panic room?" Tears welled up in her eyes, and she turned to her window, wishing she had Oliver's room with the garden doors. She sized up the glass. The window couldn't open all the way, but if she forced it, she'd be able to squeeze herself through. There was no harm in trying.

Quickly, she ran across her bed, the mattress an unstable surface under her feet, and jumped off the other end. With trembling hands, she pulled on the window, but a static shock made her let go. Carefully, she reached for the window again, but stopped when she saw a black spot develop on the wood. Little veins shot out from the black centre, spreading quickly across the recently painted frame, like a plague. Freya took a step back, afraid to be near the black substance. She could feel Angel Manor cry in pain.

"I really fucking hate my life," she whispered.

CHAPTER THIRTY THREE

Out of all the supernatural creatures Marie-Claire had seen over the past ten days, the aura of the guy who sat across from her at Frankfurt Airport, where they waited for their plane to Scotland, not only shone the brightest, but he was the strangest. He wasn't just one entity, but seemed to be two at the same time. There was a strong, dog-shaped essence, but in the core of it there was a less distinguishable creature... something Marie-Claire couldn't quite make out; though it was difficult to see, she could sense it had as much power as the canine shape.

This wasn't like a simple possession. Humans could be hosts to demons or other celestial beings, and it wasn't the same as this. Whatever two beings were combined in that man, they were there in harmony. No fear gripped her as she watched him, only curiosity. Even when he took his hands from his face and stared at her. Something shifted in his being, and to her surprise, Marie-Claire could no longer see the two entities, but only one human-looking man. If she hadn't been blind, she would have been convinced he was human. Yet she could see him clear as day, and the image of the two entities had not yet been wiped from her mind.

The man, a beacon of light in her visual darkness, raised his chin a little and sniffed. The sounds indicated he was sniffing in her direction. Green eyes beheld her, and she wondered if she was looking at the dog or the creature that was within it. There was a curious expression on the man's face. It fascinated Marie-Claire seeing a face that was so human. She had only ever seen the faces of the dead, and they had lost a spark that this man still had.

A piercing scream, filled with a deep-rooted fear, yanked her from her thoughts. From the one scream blossomed another, and more and more voices chimed in until a wave of chaos spread down the line of gates.

Marie-Claire grabbed next to her, finding Koji's wrist, her eyes still fixed on the strange man, who had gotten to his feet and was staring in the direction of the screams. "*Mon chere*, what is happening?"

"I... I'm trying to figure that out. The lights... oh shit..." Koji grabbed her hands. "They're going out, one by one, from the end of the hall." He moved under her touch. "Both sides are going dark, and it's coming this way. There's people trying to run away from the blackness... oh my god!" Koji's voice was a strangled cry. "There's something in the dark, something terrible... it's dragging people back in." A warm arm wrapped around hers, pulling her to her feet. "We need to get out of here before it comes."

She tried to see, but her eyes couldn't pick up on anything substantial.

Someone who stank of sweat and fear bumped into them, hard. The pain of the impact nearly brought her to her knees, and if it weren't for Koji's firm grip, she would have lost her balance. Her young companion pulled her to him, shielding her with his body as they were hit by another bump and another.

"What is happening?" Marie-Claire tried to ask over the screams, but Koji didn't respond. She could feel his young body cradle her as much as he could, but it didn't stop her from being pushed into the chair in front of her. The edge of the seat hurt her shins as she clung onto the armrests to support herself. Impossibly strong hands grabbed her, bruising her arm, and yanked her away from Koji.

"Come with me," said a pleasant baritone voice. Marie-Claire looked up, straight into the face of the man who wasn't human.

"Do you mean me harm?" Marie-Claire asked, wondering if he could hear her voice as clearly as she had heard his.

"I'm not sure yet," the man answered. "But for now, I want to keep you safe."

"Why?" She was grateful of his protection, but at the same time, she had seen his essence and it made her pause.

"Your scent," he said, not explaining any further. His grip tightened. "Now come, the both of you, before they find you."

"Who is 'they'?" Koji asked, his voice almost drowned out by the ongoing tumult.

"The demons. They're responding to the opening of the third seal." The man looked at Marie-Claire with those strange green eyes. "You know about that, don't you?"

She nodded. "Who are you?" she asked.

"Call me Wulf," the man said. "From the smell of you, I believe we have a mutual friend."

***

Paranoia made the long flight to Amsterdam a particular slice of hell. Occasionally she would sleep, but Tara kept waking after just a few minutes, convinced that the pilots had decided it was their—and thus, her—time to go. Never had she been this afraid of flying.

"Do you need a drink or something?" the black man next to her asked with a thick English accent. He held up a little wine bottle that the stewardess had brought him only minutes ago. He was a young guy, probably not quite twenty yet, with a cleanly shaved head and a big, genuine smile. "You look like you're really enjoying this flying lark."

She snorted and shook her head. "I don't think alcohol is going to save me now," she muttered with a remorseful smile.

"Fear of flying?" he asked.

"Not usually, no," she answered, and immediately regretted it. He narrowed his eyes in curiosity.

"But now..." he said, leaving the question open.

"I don't want to be a fear monger," she said.

"Too late." A smile curled around his soft lips, and Tara realized that she really liked this stranger.

She lowered her voice. "It's just, with all the erratic suicides, I'm a bit worried about our pilots... you know?"

His smile faded. "Shit, now that you mention it..."

She held up her hands in an apologetic gesture. "See, I didn't mean to freak you out."

He laughed. "You don't think I thought of this?" He nodded toward the rest of the passengers, though his voice was as soft as hers had been. "Most of us have thought of it at least once, I'm sure. Can't let that drive you nuts, though. So far, I haven't seen anyone do anything suspicious, and we've been on this plane for—" he checked his watch "—over six hours. You wouldn't be any safer on the ground, either. Crazy bus driver could just go off the road. Or people can commit suicide and decide to take a bunch of others with them. Nowhere is safe."

"Wow, and I was worried *I* was going to freak *you* out," Tara said. "Thanks for that bleak perspective."

"Girl, this world is filled with crazy shit that you're not even aware of," the guy said. The twinkle had disappeared from his deep brown eyes. "There is so much to be afraid of that it can take over your life. That's no way to live."

"*You* have no idea about the crazy shit that's out there," Tara said. The vision of the Japanese woman eating the old man came back to her mind's eye.

"Oh, I don't?" said the guy, with a strong tone of

indignation. "Last year, I almost got killed by a house." His eyes were wide and round, and he folded his arms as he spoke. "And I'm not even going to start about the crazy naked ghost nuns...."

"A few days ago, I almost got eaten by what I think was a fucking demon. It was eating the fucking heart of a fucking dead guy, in a village where everyone had killed themselves."

"My brother came back from the dead."

They stared at each other for a second.

"That's pretty fucked up," Tara admitted.

"Demons eating hearts is pretty fucked up, too," the guy said. "I guess we've both seen some shit, huh?"

"What's your name?" Tara said, extending her hand.

"Terrence," he answered, as they shook.

"Tara. A house tried to kill you?" She raised her eyebrows.

"Yeah, it was a butcher. That fucking place murdered a lot of people I knew," Terrence said, almost in a whisper. "We didn't even know it was haunted when we went in. Though I guess the name Angel Manor should have tipped us off, right?"

"Angel Manor?" Tara said, as the blood drained from her face. "I know that name. We... we were just talking about that place. That's where Koji and Marie-Claire are headed."

"Marie-Claire?" Terrence asked. "Now that's a name that sounds familiar to me. Does she have a really dodgy last name? Something that sounds like flower, but then isn't?"

"Florifera?" Tara struggled with the pronunciation.

"Yeah," he pointed a long finger at her, "that was it.

She's a psychic, or something, right?"

"Yes," Tara said, her heart pounding with excitement.

"Blind lady?"

"That's the one."

"Small fucking world," Terrence said. "She was there when all hell broke loose over a year ago." He sat back, his eyebrows lifted in two arches. "Fuck, I can't believe you know her."

"I was just with her," Tara said, lowering her voice once more. "Before I got on this fucking plane. She saw the heart-eating demons, too."

"Did she?" His voice shot up an octave. "Jesus. That woman sure knows how to crash a fucking party, doesn't she?"

Tara laughed in wonder. "This is a weird fucking coincidence, though, isn't it? Us sitting next to each other on a plane from Japan?"

"I didn't even come from Japan, I just stopped off there. I'm headed back to London from Australia. After last year, I decided to live a little, you know? So, I spent the last five months backpacking through the whole country with one of my mates." He rubbed the bridge of his nose. "I was supposed to stay six months, but I wanted to go back home. John, my mate, he stayed behind. Met some girl, and he wasn't going to leave until they kicked him out, right? But me... I got all restless. So, I decided to bail. Great timing, too, because when I got to the airport, all fucking hell broke loose."

"The hell started in Japan, in Aokigahara... that's a forest. I... I was there. We were filming, and shit just got real fucking crazy." She bit her lip, pushing down the emotion that threatened to well up. "I lost a lot of friends."

"I'm sorry," he said, his dark eyes on hers. "I know how

269

that feels."

"This can't be a coincidence," Tara said. "Do you know how I found your friend? The medium?"

"No?"

"I found her wandering in the woods by herself at night." Tara scratched her brow. "I mean, how fucking weird is that?"

"By herself? At night?" Terrence shook his head. "She's blind, though."

"Exactly, and yet she was right there for me to just... pick up."

"That's bloody fucked up."

"Right?" Tara said. "And now you're here. Just sitting next to me on the plane. What if this really isn't a coincidence? What if some higher fucking power is bringing us together?"

"Eh," Terrence said. "What do you mean?"

"What if we're supposed to meet each other for some reason?" The idea excited her. "I mean, you survived something. That means you know more about this shit than most people do, right?"

"Bollocks, I don't know *shit*," Terrence said. "I know not to mess with fucking ghost nuns, and to stay away from creepy old buildings with stone angels. That's the extent of my knowledge."

"But you know ghosts are real," Tara said, "and you know they are dangerous. Marie-Claire talked about us meeting for a reason, and that we were special somehow, but I didn't fucking believe her. And yet here I am, finding myself in another fucking coincidence..."

"Wait, are you saying you and I meeting is some sort of destiny?"

She turned to him, feeling sheepish all of a sudden. "I don't know... maybe?"

"Because I'm not exactly sure what you are expecting of me right now." He raised one eyebrow at her.

"Expecting?" Tara thought about that implication. "I don't expect anything of you. I'm just saying, maybe there's a reason why people like us, who have seen similar things, end up speaking." She held up her hands. "I don't have some sort of sinister plan or anything. Don't worry. I'm on my own mission right now, and I barely know what I'm doing. But it's nice to know that there's others out there who know what I know, if that makes sense?"

He visibly relaxed. "Yeah, I guess it does." Terrence ran an elegant hand across his bald scalp. "It is weird that we both know Florifera, I'll give you that."

"Yeah."

"You said you were on your own mission," he prodded. "Dare I ask what that mission is?"

She frowned. "You're going to think I'm nuts."

"I saw naked ghost nuns."

"Fair enough," she laughed. "Marie-Claire has this theory that all this is happening because someone is opening the seven seals."

"Seven seals?"

"You know, like the ones in the Bible."

He responded with a blank stare.

"There are seven seals that lead up to the Apocalypse?"

He flinched. "That doesn't sound good."

"Definitely not fucking good," she said. "I wish I had paid better attention to Reverend Donohue when I was younger, because I barely know this crap myself. I'm a poor excuse for a Catholic."

"Who is opening these seals?" Terrence asked. "I mean, Apocalypse sounds pretty final. Who would want to end the fucking world?"

"That's what we don't know. We don't even know what all the seals are, or where they are... or, well, we don't know shit, really." Tara took a deep breath. Saying all this out loud made her anxious, and she realized how little they had to go on. "I do have one lead, though. Apparently, there are answers in the Dead Sea Scrolls. I've found some stuff on them online, but my Internet keeps crapping out. I may have even found some translations, but I don't know how accurate they are until I consult an expert."

"Who else is on this case?" Terrence asked. "I mean, there's you and Florifera, and you mentioned another person, but do you guys work for some sort of organization or something?"

Tara looked at him, battling a deeply awkward feeling as she answered, "No, we just met in those woods a few days ago. We met some monks that vaguely knew what was going on, but we're all pretty much flying blind here."

"Are you fucking kidding me?" Terrence exclaimed loudly enough for the person in front of them to half-turn and shoot him a questioning look. He lowered his voice again. "You're telling me we might be dealing with an actual Apocalypse here, and the people who are trying to stop it don't know what's going on?"

"Hey, I don't know if we're the only ones trying to stop it. I like to think that there are people in this world who will know what the fuck is going on and will try to intervene where they can. But this was thrown on our path, and fuck if I'm going to sit by and let it happen without at least putting up a fight."

"Good point," he said softly.

"There have to be others," Tara said again. The thought

of there not being other people who could help terrified her. "I just don't know where to find them, but I have some friends that are going to help me. They'll put out some leads on the Internet and see if anyone bites." She sighed. "We need all the help we can get."

"I know a few guys that are Internet savvy," Terrence said. "I'm sure I can convince them to lend a hand. This shit is important."

Hope blossomed in the darkness of her soul. "That would be awesome. I knew there was a reason why we met, Terrence."

"Fuck, you just recruited me for your crazy mission, didn't you?" Terrence said, and he laughed. "I walked right into this one."

"Yeah, I guess I did."

"Okay," he said, nodding, and he pulled out his phone, opening the little notepad app. "So, tell me everything you know. If I'm going to help you, I might as well know what I'm looking for." He looked up at her. "One thing, though... like hell if you think I'm ever going back to Angel Manor."

CHAPTER THIRTY FOUR

The black mark had taken over the entire outside wall. Freya sat in the middle of her bed, her knees pulled to her chin, and thanked whoever was listening that Emily was no longer in the house. At least she didn't have to worry about her kid anymore. She hoped the house would let her soul go if she died. The idea of being stuck here for eternity really bothered her.

Freya bit her knee in frustration, something she hadn't done since she was seven or eight years old and she thought she'd heard a monster in her closet. Tiny footsteps pattered outside her door. A child's voice giggled with a hint of menace. The innocent sound made her blood run cold. On the other side, the blackness pulsed and quivered as if a sickly dark heart of mould were emerging from the wall. The ebony tendrils had spread and now covered both the wall and the window glass, leaving the single yellow bulb of her lamp as Freya's only light. She anxiously checked for the hundredth time that the blackness hadn't spread. So far, the other walls, the floor, and the ceiling remained uncontaminated.

Something banged on her door again, and she jumped.

"Cut it out," Freya screamed at the door. "Leave me alone." The door gave her some sense of security, but she hoped the freaking things couldn't open locks.

"Miss Formynder?" The voice made her cry out in surprise. "I didn't mean to scare you."

Freya eyed the door in horror, but she was unable to speak. Her heart was pounding so fast it made her nauseous.

"Miss Freya Formynder?" the voice asked again. "My

name is Damien Radbury. I... I was sent to help you. Did the messenger give you my letter?" There was a short pause. "I see you got my dolls."

It was the doll man, and he was standing right outside her door. She didn't understand why he was talking to her in such a normal and calm manner, but she was planning to use this to her advantage, even if she didn't quite know *how* yet.

"Please tell me you are in there, Miss Formynder. I would never forgive myself if I were too late."

Freya shuffled off the bed, dragging the sheet with her as she moved, and made her way to the door. Her hand trembled as she touched the wood. Could it keep her safe from this guy? And if so, for how long? How long would she have to find a way out? She was trapped in this room.

"Too late for what?" she asked in a broken voice. *Keep him talking, Freya; keep him busy,* she thought to herself.

"I'm glad to hear you're still alive, Miss Formynder. I came as soon as I could in person, but as you should have read from my letter, I was still looking for the spell to help you with."

Freya looked around her room, searching for something that could function as a weapon. "I didn't get any letter from you. I just got those weird cards with the dolls." She tried to make her voice sound calm and collected, and not let him know she was moving around in there.

"I sent those, too, yes," the man sounded flustered. "I thought it would be more personal. The dolls are very important to me. I like to introduce them. I know it's silly, but..."

"I didn't get a letter," Freya repeated, pulling open a drawer and wishing she had bought a gun or hidden a knife or something. She had been prepared for ghosts, but not so much for men and their magic dolls.

"I... I did send a messenger with a letter explaining everything. He was to verbally guide you through some things. Did he not say anything?"

"Not a word," Freya said, hating this man more with each syllable he uttered.

"I hope nothing happened to him." There was a nervous cough. "I didn't want to send the dolls ahead, you see. I prefer to be with them. But, and I explained this in my letter, I felt that you needed the protection. The war has begun, Miss Formynder, and I'm afraid this house is very important to it. I... I don't know if you are aware of what you are guarding? But it's very dangerous."

Is this guy for real? she thought. *How stupid does this asshole think I am?*

Freya rubbed her neck with one hand, kneading the tense muscle that reached from her shoulder to her skull. "I know what's down here, mister... eh...." She opened her wardrobe and found the remnants of an old exercise trampoline she'd wanted to install before Emily was born. The legs—six of them—were made of metal, and they were collected into a bag. It wasn't the best weapon, but it was better than nothing.

"Radbury, Damien Radbury. I work for an organization called Praestes."

"I've heard that name before," Freya said, moving with the metal trampoline leg raised above her head. Subconsciously, her hand touched the door.

The man on the other side coughed. "Would you mind opening the door, so we can speak face to face? I swear to you that I won't hurt you. If I wanted to, I could open the door myself, but I prefer you to do it, because I don't want to frighten you anymore than I already have."

"Yeah, no, I don't think I can do that..."

"Why not?" The voice sounded so friendly.

"Because your fucking dolls tried to kill my baby," Freya said, her voice filled with venom now.

"Ah, that must have been a misunderstanding," the man said from the other side of the door. "I sent my dolls to protect your baby."

"Can we stop lying to each other now, Mister Radbury?" Freya said. "I'm so very tired."

"Very well, Miss Formynder. I hoped to have done this in a friendly way, but I guess you leave me no choice."

There was a silence that made the hairs stand up on the back of her neck. "Are you still there?" Freya called out. Something urged her to turn around, and she was just in time to see the black hole in the wall open up. One of those little girls with the stitched mouths crawled through it, on hands and knees. Freya didn't hesitate, and she lunged at the child with the metal rod. She beat the girl, but the child was stronger, and her tiny hand—the girl could be no older than four—held her wrist like a vice.

"That's not a way to treat your guests," the girl said, without moving her lips. She spoke in the voice of the man who had introduced himself as Damien. "I think I shall need to teach you some manners." With her free hand, the doll ripped out the stitches to her mouth, leaving bloodied gashes. "Look what you made me do to my precious doll," the girl complained in the man's voice. Then she opened her mouth wide, revealing dirty, black teeth, and she chomped down on Freya's forearm. It was painful, but the bite barely cut her skin. Just a bit, enough to let a drop of blood escape.

"Ah, blood," the man said. "That's all I need... one drop..." The doll's dark eyes rolled to the back of her head, and she whispered, *"Mihi crede, meis verbis persuadere."*

A wisp of grey smoke escaped from the painted lips and snaked toward her. Freya pulled back, but it was too late; the scent of orchids and sulphur tickled her nostrils, fogging her mind.

"What...?" The memory of the smoke was already fading, and with it went his strange words and her fear. Freya rubbed her eyes. She'd drifted off in the middle of a thought. God, she needed to sleep. Her tongue felt heavy as she tried to form a question.

"There's a good girl," the man's voice came from outside the door now. "Why don't you open it up for me?" He knocked on the outside. Heavy black spots blossomed in Freya's vision. A dizziness rang through her mind. The doll let her go, and she turned toward the door. She tried to form her own thoughts, but the honey-sweet voice of the man in her head was in control. With trembling hands, she opened the door.

She stared at the man on the other side. He was in his late thirties, maybe early forties, with thinning blond hair just starting to turn that salt and pepper shade. He wasn't a handsome man, but he had kind grey eyes, and a nervous smile. He was of medium height and build, and didn't look very threatening.

"See, isn't it better this way?" the man said, and he touched her cheek. "Now you don't have to be so afraid anymore."

"No," she said, as if she were answering from a dream world.

"I'm going to make everything better," Damien said softly. "You are going to believe everything I tell you now. You will forget about me trying to murder your baby, and you will think that I have come here to help you. Together, we are going to find a way to make Angel Manor self-sufficient again. You will believe that with the magic of my dolls, we can recreate a spell similar to the one that was in place before."

She looked at him through tear-filled eyes, hope blossoming in her chest. "You... you can do that? You can take this burden away from me?"

He grinned at her like a jackal grins at its prey. "Of course."

"I want that," she said, still groggy from the magic.

"Yes, though there is one downside to this..." He looked solemn. "We will need to find a lot of victims before the solstice. And you can help me, Freya. Together we will do great things." He pinched her cheek. "But we can't be squeamish now. This is a spell that can't be cast without spilling some blood."

CHAPTER THIRTY FIVE

Wulf recognised the darkness as it spread through Frankfurt Airport. It was a darkness the mortal world was not allowed to witness, and it broke every celestial rule there was. The world was going insane, and the opened seals were creating a chaos like there had never been before in his long existence.

He was sure he needed to protect the frail human woman with the pale blind eyes. Her scent told him she was important. She smelled like something ancient, but also like something he had detected before. There was a hint of Angel Manor on this female, but most of all, he could smell Freya. Her scent hadn't left his mind since the moment he had met her. Why a mortal woman would have such a deep effect on him, he didn't know, but she did. Not just on the human body he inhabited, nor just on his true self... it was the dog inside him that had bonded with her most of all. Without knowing it, this young human woman had cast her own spell, and he couldn't be more frustrated at her rejection of him.

So, when he smelled her on this woman, it fascinated him, and he had a strong urge to protect the old lady and her terrified companion.

"This way," Wulf said as he lifted the old woman off her feet and held her like a child to his chest. She wrapped her bony arms around his neck. He led them away from the fleeing crowds, who were seeking an exit as well, as they tried to stay away from the deadly darkness. Wulf led them straight to it, and he saw the hesitation of the Japanese-American boy. "Trust me," he added.

Wulf searched his mind for the spell that had saved his life many times before. It wasn't complicated, but the strong smell of human fear was distracting. He wasn't immune to the intoxicating effect of it. He stopped at a large, red vending machine that had a brand of cola printed on it in large white letters. The magic—once so natural to him, but now he had to borrow it from a place that was cold and dark—coursed through his veins.

"*Ad voluntatem meam*," he yelled at the vending machine.

"What did you say?" asked the boy.

Wulf pulled open the machine, revealing a cramped room no larger than a broom closet. "I said, 'Open Sesame.'" He winked at the kid, who looked miserable. "Get in."

The boy obeyed, and Wulf followed him, still carrying the old woman. The darkness snaked across the floor, shadows seeking their victims. He rushed to close the door, sealing it with his spell.

"*Ad voluntatem meam.*"

There was so little magic left in his system, and if he tried to use his true power, it would lead his enemies straight to him. Wulf wondered if, in light of recent events, he was still in danger, or if his foes would be too distracted with the end of the world.

There was a little light in the strange room, and through the glass of the vending machine, they watched the outside world slowly become engulfed in the shadow.

"What's happening?" asked the boy, tears glistening in his brown eyes.

"I'm afraid that this airport is being overrun by demons, who are probably feeding in preparation for the oncoming war."

"Demons?" The boy shuddered. "Why is everything going dark?"

"The darkness has two functions. First, it triggers a deep-rooted fear within humans. You instinctively don't like the darkness, which will trigger your amygdala to fire a chemical called glutamate into two other regions of your brain. What people don't know is that this chemical actually triggers reactions in both the mortal world and in the celestial world. It's the secretion of the glutamate that some demons use to fuel their powers. That's why they like to scare the shit out of you, because fear stimulates your amygdala."

"Oh," said the boy. "What's the second function?"

"It's more difficult for you to defend yourself in darkness." Wulf put the old woman down.

"That's comforting," said the boy.

"What's your name, kid?" Wulf asked.

"I'm Koji, and that's Marie-Claire Florifera," Koji said. "You say your name is Wolf?"

"It's Wulf, with a u," Wulf said.

"How, how did you do that with the vending machine, Wulf?" Koji asked.

"He used magic," Marie-Claire said, with a hoarse voice. "He used celestial magic because he is a demon." Her pale face was stern. "Or at least partially. I don't know what that other thing inside you is, but they're connected."

Wulf took a deep breath. "Right. And here's me thinking I covered my identities pretty well."

"Are you going to hurt us?" Koji asked.

Wulf looked at them and thought for a second. "No, but I would like to know what your connection is to Freya Formynder."

"I have met the girl once," the old woman said. "She lives in Angel Manor. We're on our way to that house now, because we believe that it holds one of the seals."

"It does," Wulf said. "The seventh, in fact. I know Miss Formynder quite well. Let's just say I believe Freya has a better chance of facing whatever is causing this shit storm with me by her side. Which is why I'm on my way to Skye, too."

"Lucky for us," Marie-Claire said. "I do believe this journey would have been rather fatal to us if we had not run into you."

"It's funny how fate can work, isn't it?" Wulf said. He inhaled the scent of the woman, and realized that it wasn't just a lingering residue of Freya he smelled; it was something stronger. This female was connected in a deeper sense than she was possibly aware of herself. The dog inside him stirred restlessly. "I believe we are going to have to make haste to get back to Lucifer Falls. Something seems to have accelerated the opening of the seals."

"Do you know who is opening them?" Marie-Claire asked.

"I don't know exactly who they are, but I believe they are a group of blood-mages. I hear rumors that either they are linked to this group of assassins that are called the Thirteen, or that they are, in fact, the Thirteen."

"You seem to know a lot about this," Marie-Claire said.

"Once upon a time, I was part of a brotherhood that had sworn to keep humanity safe," Wulf said. "But we were betrayed. It's a long story, too long to tell you now inside a safe room in a vending machine, but let's just say that our downfall wasn't the first step to this mess. The guardians of the seals have become too complacent over the centuries, and we believe they've been infiltrated by the enemy, making them weak and disorganized. I found out that there were no guardians to Angel Manor. Freya is running that hell house all by herself, and it's becoming increasingly dangerous."

"I don't know if it's even possible to get to Skye in this chaos," Koji said. He was visibly shaking. "I doubt any of the planes are going to fly."

"I'll get you on a plane," Wulf said. "It might not be the plane you expected to get on, but you'll get to Skye."

***

Koji would have gladly stayed behind in the strange little cubby hole behind the vending machine. It was safe there, and beyond the glass, there was nothing but darkness. They couldn't see what was happening in the creeping black void, but they could hear the screams. He imagined that this was how Marie-Claire Florifera experienced the world most of the time, and he wondered how confusing it was for her.

"We are going to have to brave the darkness at some point," the demon who called himself Wulf announced, and Koji nearly cried at the idea. The image of the Japanese village of the dead had not left his mind's eye just yet. It was as if the sight of the demon biting into the dead man's heart was burned on his retina.

"But what was the point of hiding here if we're just going out there?" Koji asked.

"We wanted to get away from the first wave of demons," Wulf said. "But mostly, we wanted to stay away from the panicked human masses. It's very difficult for me to navigate in this kind of chaos."

"And now most of those people out there are probably dead," Koji said. An empty feeling blossomed in his stomach.

"If you give it too much thought, you'll eventually go insane," Wulf said. "I'm afraid the world is changing from what you know, and if our enemies get their way, you will have to bear witness to a lot more death."

Koji frowned. "Is this your equivalent of 'get over

284

yourself'?" he asked, not bothering to mask the hint of bitterness he felt.

"It's the equivalent of whatever is going to get you through this without cracking up."

"It's a little surreal getting a pep-talk from a demon," Koji said, pushing his glasses up his nose. "Definitely a first for me."

"Don't mistake me for those things out there," Wulf said. "Not all demons are alike, and while I'm giving you these wonderful life lessons, let me warn you that not all angels are your friends. If you remember those things, you stand more of a chance of surviving."

The old medium put her hand on Koji's arm. Her blind eyes looked roughly in his direction, but the wrinkled face soothed him somehow.

"Mister Wulf," she said, her eyes still focused on Koji's cheek, "do you have a plan to get us out of here?"

"I do. My plan is to make it to the private jet terminal. From there, we can take a small plane."

"Can you fly an airplane?" Koji asked.

The demon looked at him, his eyebrows raised in obvious sarcasm. "I've been around for thousands of years... there are many things I can do."

"Right," Koji said. His nerves felt like brittle glass that was about to shatter.

Wulf picked up Marie-Claire as if she weighed nothing, holding her like a sleepy child. The old medium seemed quieter than usual, and her white eyes stared into the distance with a dreamy expression on her face. Koji wondered if she was really here with them, or if she saw things that were beyond his understanding. As afraid as he was, there was comfort in knowing he was taking action. Perhaps he wasn't the most effective ally to the survival of the human race, but he at least was an ally. If he had to die, then he'd die trying, and not be one of those poor people who never quite knew what hit them. With those thoughts, he followed the large blond demon into the darkness.

CHAPTER THIRTY SIX

I'm just one step away from being a naked, crazy murdering nun, Freya thought as she looked at the frightened children. Her brain was still filled with a strange grey fog, and she could not remember what had happened before Damien had come to rescue her. Everything was a blur, but Freya knew it was best not to think about it. If she just focused on the here and now... she would be okay.

There were four children, ranging from about three years old to six at the most, sitting in her kitchen, huddled together. She'd have to lock them up later, because they weren't allowed to escape. These... little... helpless... girls. Something in her head was trying to warn her, but the fog wouldn't allow the thought to come through.

They all reminded her of Emily. Where was Emily? She couldn't remember that either. But it was better not to think of such things. She had to focus on the four children in front of her. They were her new sacrifice. Her stomach turned, and of all the murders she had committed, she knew this would be the one that would stick with her most. More even than killing Logan. But that was the point, wasn't it? It wasn't just the children who needed to suffer... she did, too.

Freya tried to tell herself she wouldn't be doing the killing, the dolls would do the job—at least, that's how she had understood the plan—but that actually made things worse. When she killed, she took responsibility. Now she was keeping these poor girls captured, only to be murdered in a terrifying way. It was the same thing as killing them, only more cowardly. She was just an accomplice now. But Damien had assured her this was the right thing to do, and she believed him. She had to... even if she didn't want to.

"Do you girls want a cup of tea?" she said, a dreamy smile on her face.

The girls shook their heads, their large eyes filled with tears.

"I want my mum," said a little girl, no older than four, with skin the color of caramel. She was wearing a yellow sweater with the red Angry Bird on it. Her jeans were torn at the knees, and she was missing a shoe. Freya wondered where it had gone, but she pushed the image of the girl being violently dragged along from her mind. *It's best not to think of such things.*

All the girls had arrived sedated. Freya didn't ask where Damien had gotten them, or how. She couldn't judge him—he wouldn't allow her—and who was she to judge, anyway?

He had brought her one girl yesterday and the other three today. Damien had told her to keep them separated, but she couldn't do it. It was extremely stupid, she knew—because the voice in her head told her it was—but she kept them together. A last bit of defiance. She thought the girls might have some support in being with each other. It was only until he brought more girls; once that happened, they'd have to be separated. She couldn't run the risk of being overpowered.

"I want my mommy too," said the littlest girl. She was black and had an American accent. Freya wondered where he had picked her up. Damien had only been gone for two days, so she was probably a tourist. Or an expat. Or something. That surprised her. She'd expected him to choose orphans. She'd always picked victims no one cared about in order to avoid too much investigation from the police. Perhaps their parents wouldn't care. Damien knew what he was doing; she was sure he had done similar things before. Besides, he had told her he knew what he was doing. She had to believe him.

"Listen, girls. I'm sorry that you're here," Freya said, "but I need you all to be good right now, okay?"

"Are you going to hurt us?" asked the oldest girl with a soft Scottish accent, who was pale as milk and had red flaming hair.

"No, of course not," Freya lied, her heart dropping even deeper in her stomach. "You're just on a very important mission, girls. This house... it's important. And it needs special little girls to look after it. You four are very special." Freya sat on the chair across from them and folded her hands on the table. "You have magic in you. And with that magic, you can heal this house."

"I don't have magic in me," said the American girl. She wore her hair in little braids held by colorful beads. The girl had the prettiest hazel eyes that Freya had ever seen.

"You *do* have magic in you." Freya nodded and shot her another dreamy smile. "You just don't know it yet."

As if to emphasise Freya's words, the house trembled again. She looked at the frightened children and her path was clear to her once more. *Damien will make sure the seal doesn't open*, she told herself. Something inside her screamed, but it was hard to hear her real thoughts through the fog.

CHAPTER THIRTY SEVEN

She came to Marie-Claire amidst the chaos of the airport attacks. The little girl with the face that never quite looked the same. There was a calm in her that seemed to force all the drama and monsters into the background, as if she were the eye of the storm. The strong arms of the demon were wrapped around her legs and shoulders, but somehow his presence became as insignificant as everything surrounding her, and Marie-Claire felt as if she were walking instead of being carried. Every step the girl took in her direction was like a chord played on a piano, and the vibration resonated through the very core of Marie-Claire's being. All fear was forgotten, all sense of urgency and flight melted from her thoughts, as if there were nothing in the world but her and that little girl with whom she shared a bloodline.

"You must see. You must bear witness," the child said without speaking. Marie-Claire kneeled in front of her. The girl lifted her small hands, pressing her palms to Marie-Claire's eyes.

She opened her eyes, not in Frankfurt Airport, but outside a small church. It was a simple construction, mostly made of wood, and recently painted, the white in stark contrast to the green trees and grey sky behind it. In the front stood a large black sign with blocky white letters that read "Healer Weirs Baptist Church," and announced the times for Sunday school and worship.

"Is this where the fourth seal is?" Marie-Claire asked in a voice that barely sounded like her own. She feared the opening of this seal more than she did the last. This would be one of the Horsemen, and they terrified her more than anything. What they stood for...

The girl took her hand, and it felt familiar somehow. With a heavy heart, Marie-Claire followed up the four steps, toward the double white wooden door. The girl opened the doors without touching them. The inside of the church was dark, except for parts where the light from the big rectangular windows hit the floor, all pointing toward one spot in the centre of the interior.

A man... no, not a man... a dark figure, dressed in a cloak so black it looked like a deep shadow, stood in the centre of the light, holding an old woman by the hair. The woman was trembling. She wore a simple, white cotton nightdress with little pink rosebuds. Her dark grey and white hair was long and tangled around the figure's gloved hand. The figure forced her face up, and held a large, familiar-looking blade under her chin. Marie-Claire had seen it somewhere before.

"Audite me," the figure called out in a voice that could have been either male or female. "I make this sacrifice not to thee, sleeping rider, but to my order." With a subtle movement of the wrist, the figure cut through the woman's throat with the same unnatural ease as Marie-Claire had seen before, slicing through her windpipe. The woman's eyes fluttered open, and she gurgled as the blood burst forth from the wound. It came in a spray at first, but soon it turned to a gushing waterfall.

"This blood I spill forth on thy resting place is not for thee. I taunt thee with that which should be thine, and offer it to my order."

The floor rumbled, a sound Marie-Claire was convinced everyone on Earth, and perhaps beyond it, could hear.

"Wake, warrior. Wake and rise. The world is ripe for thine plucking." The figure dropped the body of the woman, letting her twitch and bleed out in the middle of the small church. Then the figure turned, and Marie-Claire gasped. She could see the face under the hood, and saw it was a woman. Not a human woman, though she almost looked human. The dark eyes betrayed her.

"Is it a demon?" she whispered at the girl.

"No, she is one of the Thirteen, which is far worse than any demon," the child answered.

"I see you, Guardian," said the woman in the black cloak, looking straight at Marie-Claire. "We will come for you and yours soon enough."

The words struck fear in Marie-Claire's heart. She turned to the child, who looked at her with a solemn expression.

"Can she see us?"

"She could always see you," the child answered. "That is why *you* had to see *her.*"

A shock went through the church, and when Marie-Claire looked up, the figure had disappeared. The ground cracked open where the body lay, as if it had been hit with an enormous force... something from the inside. Another blow, and the stone of the floor pushed upward, shoving the limp body to the side. Marie-Claire braced herself, but the shocks didn't affect her. She was like a ghost here—insubstantial.

A hole appeared in the centre, and from it a massive hoof appeared. A horse, larger than an elephant, rose from its prison, carrying an equally magnificent rider. The horse was the colour of dried blood, and the rider wore armour made of red metal and human bones. He shone in the bleak light, as if made of glowing embers. A helmet with a heavy visor hid his face. In his hand, he carried a huge flaming sword. Something in the air changed as the world reacted to the Horseman's presence. At the same time, something inside Marie-Claire changed as well. A new determination filled her, a determination to fight. Perhaps this lord of war could serve in their benefit... but most likely, he would be their doom.

***

They all felt the opening of the fourth seal. Human and non human alike. They all felt it, because when a Horseman rode, the hooves of his steed resonated through all the realities. The world seemed to stand still for a moment. Even those who were sleeping woke, feeling a terrible sense of dread. The opening of the seal did something to their minds. It made them angry, determined or afraid. Each had their personal reaction to the Horseman, but all reacted.

The war, which had raged between Heaven and Hell for aeons, had finally made its way to Earth. There was no escaping it now.

CHAPTER THIRTY EIGHT

"The solstice is at midnight," Damien announced. "This evening, we need to make the preparations and verify the spell is complete."

Freya nodded, feeling a simultaneous knot in her stomach and a sense of relief. They would kill the girls soon, and as much as that pained her, at least it would be over with, and maybe she would be able to think clearly again. The build up to the murders was always the worst part. But it would be the last time; if this worked out, she would never have to kill anyone ever again in her life. *Ever.*

She would just have to protect the house. That would be all. She could get her life back, and maybe even make it a happy one.

But first we will have to kill seven little girls, the voice of her conscience whispered through the fog.

"Is there anything you need from me?" Freya said, in an obedience that felt so alien to her.

"I'm afraid so." Damien's face was solemn. "I need your emotions, my dear, and your suffering. It will make the spell even greater."

Something glinted in his eyes, as if he had enjoyed the prospect.

"What do you need me to do?" she asked.

"I need you to bear witness, my dear." He rubbed his chin and looked at her intently with his watery eyes. "Your pain will add to the magic, and it will bind it to this house. You're connected to this place, and it feeds off you in ways you can't even imagine."

"Yes, I know," Freya said vaguely.

He laughed. A chill ran down Freya's spine. "No, my dear, you have no idea. You have only seen a glimpse of what this house can do to others, but not what *you* can do to this house. You are its guardian, and that makes you very important."

Freya gave him a weak smile. "What time do you want to perform the spell tonight?" "Midnight," he said. "It's a magical hour; that's when the solstice will begin."

***

Freya, the voice was more like an echo of a memory than a corporeal sound. She could barely hear it through the fog. *Freya...* It pierced through the spell, but only just.

"I know you," Freya said, trying to remember as she looked at the image of herself standing before her. The spirit barely looked like her anymore. The skin was so pale, and it was covered in some strange black material that she had seen before... if only she could remember.

He's hurting me, Freya, the house said in her mind, *and he's hurting you. We both need you to snap out of this.*

"Snap out of what?" Freya asked, battling with the misty thoughts in her mind that swirled into darkness. "Who is hurting you? No one is hurting me."

The master of dolls, he's manipulating you. He wants to change me, Freya, and if you don't stop him, he will... and he'll open the seal.

"He doesn't want to open the seal, he wants to keep it closed," Freya said. "He's helping me put the spell back up, so that I never have to kill anyone anymore."

You don't believe that, Freya.

She realised she didn't believe it, but he wouldn't let her think otherwise.

"It's true," Freya said. She squinted her eyes at the black stained figure. "You're the house," she said. "I know you. You're always trying to hurt me. You don't want me to succeed, you just want me to suffer. Everything I do... you demand sacrifices." She didn't feel the anger behind her words, because she didn't really believe them. But he wanted her to think the house was bad, and so she did.

Freya, you're our only hope. The spirit of the house stepped toward her. *He has weakened me, but perhaps I can do one thing—*

"I don't want you to," Freya began, but the spirit ignored her plight, and with unsettling speed, the image of herself collided with her, pushing itself into her very being. The spell that clouded her mind fought against the invader, but the spirit was strong, and Freya could feel the magic tendrils retract from her brain as the spirit claimed her dominancy.

"Holy shit," Freya whispered. Memories flooded back to her mind as if someone had left a tap open. "Thank you..."

Don't let him know that we've broken his spell. Freya quickened her step and made her way to her bedroom. Her thoughts were a jumble. Quickly, she entered and locked the door. She lay down on the bed and placed the pillow across her eyes. Something inside her told her she was being watched, and she hoped it was only the eyes of the house that were on her, but she wouldn't take the risk of doing something out of the ordinary now. He still had to believe that she was under his spell. If she hated him before he put her under his control, she loathed him even more now. The thought of having that man in her very thoughts made her feel dirty—violated somehow.

If it hadn't been for the house, she would still be in his power...

He had been right about her connection to the house, but he had been wrong about her not knowing. Each day, the house snaked around her soul a little more. Just because he had been clouding her mind, that didn't mean she hadn't felt it; she just hadn't been able to make sense of it. But now that she was free and everything had come back to her, she knew exactly how powerful her relationship was. Whatever was happening with those seals, it made Freya's bond with Angel Manor stronger, and she almost felt a part of the brick and mortar around her. She could sense the dormant angels who stood outside to hold guard over that which slept in the basement.

It, the Horseman, was turning in its slumber, waiting for the day it could wake.

She sat up and pinched her nose. The spell he was casting tonight obviously wasn't to protect the house, so what was he doing? How could she stop him?

The only thing she could think of was to bring the girls to safety. She couldn't get far, but bringing them into town to the local authorities would be enough. *Fuck the consequences*, she thought, realising full well that the girls could implicate her as an accomplice. She would cross that bridge when she came to it.

As soon as he left, she would gather the girls. The thought of not killing them was a relief, though she did wonder how she was going to make a sacrifice come this solstice. A thought came to her and made her blood run cold. She would sacrifice Damien, but his death would be a relief... would that be enough? It would have to be, because she had no one else to kill. She couldn't risk keeping any of the girls in the house. It was as if she were playing a game of Russian roulette, but she knew she had no choice but to pull the trigger.

Freya lay back down in the dark, waiting for her guest to leave.

***

She must have dozed off—which didn't surprise her, because shaking the spell from her mind had cost a lot of energy—but the house woke her with a start. It wasn't a voice, exactly, or a vision, something just... nudged her. She knew he was gone from the moment she opened her eyes, and she was instantly awake, which was rare for her. Her mind was sharp and determined. The feeling of being watched had lessened, but not completely gone away, and it made her wary. She would have to move fast, because she didn't want to risk Damien returning. If only she could leave this place. The idea of having to face the man and explain why she released the girls made her sick to her stomach. Perhaps he would be able to cast a spell on her again... it had been so easy the first time, easy enough to make her feel weak and fragile.

She hadn't quite planned out how she was going to kill him. The fact that he was a magic user worried her to no end. She had the house... but would it be enough to defeat this guy? If she tried to use the house against him, she had an awful suspicion that he would be able to use it to his advantage. He would not have come here without doing his research first. The only thing she could think of was lure him to where the seal was hidden. It was dark down there and had plenty of little hiding places for her to utilise She would need to surprise and overwhelm him... Perhaps the house would inspire her to something better, but for now she would have to stick to the plan she had, even if it wasn't a very solid one. It wasn't as if she had a lot of time to think things through. Her first priority was to lead the girls away from the property. He obviously needed them for something, and she wasn't about to let him have them.

She ran toward the rooms where the girls were locked up. As fast as she could, she unlocked the locks, jerking open the doors one by one.

"Come, girls," she said in a low voice. "It's time to go. Put on your shoes." Freya hurried them, helping the youngest to tie their shoelaces.

"Are you going to bring us to our mommy?" the girl she knew as Alice asked.

"Yes, sweetie, I am."

"What about the magic?" little three-year-old, Leah asked. "We were going to do magic."

"Well, we'll have to do magic some other time," Freya said, knotting a loop in the tennis shoe's laces. "We need to hurry now, before the man comes back."

"The man said he'd make us into dollies," Leah said, with a small voice. The words sent a tremor of realization through Freya. *That bastard... so that's what he was doing, he was going to make more dolls*. She thought of the creepy girl he had used to cast the spell on her. *That was a doll made out of a girl*. With a bitter grimace, she swallowed a gag reflex, trying to keep calm in front of the children.

"I don't want to be a dolly," Leah added.

"Then we better hurry, shouldn't we?" Freya asked, and she pulled the child to her feet. "Come, girls." And like a mother hen herding her chicks, Freya rushed the children outside.

Thick black strands covered parts of the door, but this time Freya was prepared, and she pushed them away. The material was icy-cold to her touch. The children hugged themselves as they stepped into the chilly air. It was raining, but that was no surprise because it rained so often. They ran across the courtyard, through the row of solemn stone angels. Freya motioned the girls to her car. She opened the door—first to the back seat, then the front—letting them crawl in. It was a tight squeeze, and some of the girls complained they had no seat belt Freya didn't care; they'd die tonight if she didn't take them away from the house. She drove carefully, since the rain made the road to the house slick and it was too close to the cliff overlooking Lucifer Falls for Freya to be reckless.

The atmosphere in the car was tense, and Freya felt relieved when she saw the huge gate that led to the house.

Her foot nudged the gas pedal just a little more, speeding the car slightly—feeling rushed to get the girls away from there. The gates were open, as they usually were, so it came as a surprise when the car crashed into an invisible barrier. For a second, Freya experienced a sense of being airborne, when the seat belt restrained her and pulled her back to the seat. A *whoosh* indicated that the collision was hard enough to deploy the airbags. The sound around her was deafening.

The white material of the airbag hit her so hard Freya thought for a brief moment something punched her in the face. Something hard grazed her temple, and a sharp pain shot up from her nose, spreading out through her head. She touched the offended area of her face, feeling for blood as an indicator whether anything was broken. There was no blood. Her mind was dazed, and it took her several seconds to remember that there were children in her car, and that some of them were not strapped in. She turned to the child next to her, and for a moment, she feared the little girl was dead, until she saw her chest move. The airbag had knocked her unconscious. Freya fumbled with her seat belt, which didn't come loose, and half-turned to the other children. Three of them were strapped in, but the other children were folded all over each other. Freya realised one of the girls, the youngest, had flown across the front seats and hit the window with full force. The glass was cracked, though not broken, and the battered body of the child lay limply across the dashboard. The eyes were open and stared blankly at the back seat. Her neck was placed in such an odd angle that Freya felt sick to her stomach looking at it. If she hadn't seen so much death, she would have broken down on the spot, but Freya had experience. She was a killer when she needed to be.

The image of the girl was still pressed on her retina when she turned to the other children. One girl crawled from underneath the seat, while another held up her arm, which was twisted in an unnatural way. The girl was screaming, but Freya raised her voice.

"Quiet, all of you. We have to get out of this car, and I need you to be brave." She kept her face harsh. "I know you're scared, and in pain, but things will get worse if you don't listen to me." She pressed the button on her seat belt again, and finally it let go. Releasing the belt was painful, and her chest ached from where the seat belt had jerked her back. Her whole body felt sore. With shaking hands, she pushed open the door and stumbled out. The rain hit her gently, licking at the scrapes on her skin.

"I thought you might try to run," a voice called out from beyond the fence. "There was something in your eyes. And I could feel that my connection to you was broken." Damien stepped out of the shadows of a cluster of trees. He was soaked, and looked like he had been outside for a while. There was a strange grin on his face. "I just wanted to test you... and I was right."

He walked up to the gate, touching what looked like open space. "Let's just say I took some precautions." There was a smile again. "Tell me, Freya, what was it that gave you the power to break my spell?"

"The house," Freya called back. "It doesn't like you."

A hint of chagrin crossed the wet face, and Freya disliked him even more than ever.

"The house will like me well enough when I'm done with it. When I make it submit to me."

"Good luck with that," Freya said, pulling at the back door. "You want the house? You're welcome to it." She wrinkled her nose and shook her head. The rain soaked her hair, running down her face. "Go ahead," she cried to the figure, "take the damn thing. I hope it'll do for you what it has done for everyone else. Just let the girls and me go."

"I'm afraid I can't do that, Freya." He stepped straight through the invisible barrier. There was something ominous about him, and Freya recognized the fear she felt all too well.

The girls were stumbling out of the car. The child in the front, Alice, was still struggling with her seat belt Freya wanted to run around the car and help her, but Damien was on his way. She knew she had to make a choice. Either help the other five little ones, or get caught and help no one.

Humanity makes sacrifices. The words spun in her head. She grabbed Leah, who was the smallest, and lifted her to her hip. "Girls, we have to run from the bad man." Then she took a sprint. The children ran behind her, screaming. The one girl with the broken arm—she couldn't remember her name since she had been the last one he had brought—was calling out that she was in pain. Freya ignored the child's pleas, hardening her heart.

"Keep running," she screamed. "We need to get back to the house." She looked at the looming building. It had always looked so freaking friendly, but the physical black net of magic that surrounded it now made it looked dark and dire. Angel Manor had always seemed welcoming in the past, and yet...

The angels outside stared down at them as they ran between. Freya wondered if they would protect her. Would they come to life as they had to push the Horseman back into his prison? Or would they just stand there and watch her die?

It surprised her how fast the girls could run. Only the girl with the broken arm lagged behind. When Freya turned to look back, she saw Damien was taking Alice from the car. He pushed her aside and leaned back in. She could hear him roar from where she stood, or perhaps she only imagined she could.

The door opened to her before she even touched the handle, and inwardly she thanked the house. She ushered the girls in, even the girl with the broken arm. It took her all her willpower not to drag the last child inside. Damien was taking his sweet time, and he was nowhere near the building. Freya slammed the door shut, locking it behind her. Her heart hammered against her chest, and she had to ignore her sore limbs. She took a second to catch her breath and reorganise her thoughts.

"Freya?" Leah tapped her on the shoulder. Her little voice sounded on the verge of tears. "I don't like the dollies." The other four girls pressed themselves against her legs and whimpered.

Freya's blood froze in her veins, and she needed to gather courage to turn around. Behind her, she saw about a dozen dolls. They stood and looked straight at her, with their chubby faces that were moulded in pouty not-quite smiles. The eyes, normally big and blue or brown, were now empty and pure white, which made them even creepier.

The smallest of the dolls, a petite thing with long blonde curls and a navy-blue dress, stepped forward.

"You broke one of my new dolls, you bitch," the doll said in Damien's voice. "I wanted that doll, and you broke her. You damaged another one, too. I'm not pleased with you."

"What did you expect, you crazy fucker?" Freya spat. "You're the one who put up the goddamned invisible wall."

"I wanted to make these girls into pretty dollies, like the others... but now you are forcing me another way, and I am very sad about that."

Freya snorted bitterly. "Like I give a shit about your feelings."

"You better let me in, before I get even more upset with you," the doll said. "You know I can get in eventually."

"Fuck you." Freya shook her head. "If it's up to me, you'll never set another foot in this house."

"You can try to lock me out, Freya." The doll held up her small hands with the tiny fingers. "But you forget that I'm already inside. My children are a part of me. There's nowhere to run, girl."

"And *you* forget that you're not the first one who's tried to kill me," Freya said, and kicked the doll with all the force she could muster. *They might be indestructible, and have strong little hands*, Freya thought, *but they're not heavy.* The doll flew across the room and bounced off one of the walls with a surprised cry.

"Run!" Freya waved at the girls to follow. "This way." She took a sharp turn and ran toward her panic room. Holding the girl, Leah, in her arms reminded her of holding Emily, and she clung on to the child as if her life depended on it.

One of the girls screamed, and Freya looked back. Two dolls had thrown themselves on the girl with the broken arm, and their hard fingers were clawing at the child's clothes and face. Freya turned back to kick the ghastly creatures away, but something stopped her in mid-stride. More dolls were rushing up, holding the child down, and one was forcing her mouth open. There was a sickly radiance to them, and Freya wasn't sure she wanted to touch them. Black veins appeared on the fresh white porcelain, and the white eyes glowed, while the perfect plump lips of one of the dolls opened and small black maggots squirmed around the opening. The doll leaned forward, releasing the creatures into the screaming girl's mouth. The girl on the ground started to spasm, and blood poured from her eyes.

"See what you're making me do?" the man's voice sounded from the porcelain lips. "There are better ways... less painful ones, where I can preserve the dolls longer. Now she'll just suffer and eventually die." The doll pointed at the little girl. She flopped around like a fish on land while the dolls all took a step back. The girl's skin cracked, as if she were made of porcelain and someone had just hit her with a hammer, not hard enough to break. Blood welled up from the gashes. Thick black maggots, twice their original size, pushed themselves from her skin tissue. Where they exited the body, the skin of the girl glowed and healed. Freya watched a maggot burrow its way back into the child's body, and she gagged. The little girls around her cried, snapping her back into reality.

"Don't look at it," she said sternly to the kids. "Keep running."

The girl with the broken arm suddenly stopped screaming. It was a blessing and a curse at the same time. *Three down, four to go... no... five*, Freya thought darkly.

***

Freya turned the corner and nearly dropped Leah trying to come to a stop. Another doll stood in the hall, but this was one of the other dolls—not made from porcelain, but entirely out of flesh.

Once upon a time, the grotesque thing had been a little girl, until someone had taken her life. The black thread that sewed her lips together seemed like a blessing this time— Freya couldn't shake the image of maggots. The big eyes, covered with the milky white film of death, stared at her. The child was dressed in a crisp, white dress, covered in ruffles and bows. Her waxy hair was styled into the same ringlets as that of the porcelain dolls. In her hand, the girl held a knife. There was no telling how strong this creature would be, but Freya suspected she couldn't kick her away as easily as she had the porcelain one.

A flash appeared before her eyes, and her head filled with alarm. *He's coming*, Angel Manor warned in her mind. Freya flinched as the crash came from the front room, and she could feel the presence of Damien in her house. Her name echoed through the building.

"Freya," Damien hollered. "There's nowhere you can run."

"Watch me," Freya said. She wished she had some sort of weapon, but even without one, she wasn't about to let this man get the better of her. The dead doll, who looked like a puppet with its strings cut, took a step toward her, and Freya noticed it was moving awkwardly. It couldn't be too fast. All she had to do was make sure that she was faster. A horrible thought came to her mind. *To survive, I just have to make sure I'm not the slowest one.*

Freya feigned in one direction, and the flesh doll took the bait.

"Go right," she yelled at the girls, and they all ran for their lives.

CHAPTER THIRTY NINE

"Not another one," Marie-Claire said, her voice almost pleading. "It's only been a matter of hours since the last seal opened. Why are they opening so fast?" She looked at the girl who stood before her. She couldn't see her surroundings, the airplane hidden from her vision, but she saw the child clear as day. Marie-Claire took a deep breath. She was so tired. Wulf had led them through the chaos of the airport. This time, the roles had been reversed. Koji had been blind, but Marie-Claire had seen. Once the girl had released her from her vision, Marie-Claire had witnessed the monstrosities that made their way from the depths of Hell to the mortal world. Everything had changed—the world would never be the same.

War has a hold on us, Marie-Claire thought bitterly. She didn't know exactly what strings Wulf had pulled, or if he had used magic, but he managed to get them on a small airplane. They were heading for Scotland, and that gave her a sense of peace, as if that was exactly where she needed to be. When she closed her eyes, she imagined the big stone angels outside the house calling to her. It was so stupid that she never realized what their secret was, that they were hiding one of the seals. She had felt it when she was there, but she hadn't understood it. Not then. Now she understood everything, and it terrified her. She feared what would happen if the other Horsemen were released from their prisons. What sort of world would they have left?

She understood all right, just as she understood why the child was here to visit her.

"You must bear witness." The child's tone was matter-of-fact, and the responsibility it brought added to the weight of age already sitting on Marie-Claire's shoulders. She knew she couldn't give up, not when there was so much at stake, but she just wished the burden didn't lie so heavily on her shoulders.

The child was merciless, and she pushed the palms of her hands to Marie-Claire's blind eyes. The vision tore at her senses, like none ever had before. Marie-Claire found herself on the border of two completely different worlds. On her right, she saw green grass and a lake that looked like it was made out of blue glass, with tall, snow-covered mountains in the background. On her left, the ground was a yellowish brown and cracked with the dry heat. The bodies of shrivelled cows scattered the ground. Hardly anything grew in the area.

"What is this place?" Marie-Claire said. "I don't under —" But then she understood. "This is not just one place, is it?" Her courage wavered. "I'm to bear witness to two seals opening at once?" Tears welled up in her eyes and threatened to spill down her cheeks.

The girl pointed in two different directions and repeated, "You must bear witness."

Marie-Claire looked from one side to the other, and saw two dark figures, each holding their victims, as she had seen before. On the one side, the figure held a thin black man with a gaunt face and sad eyes. His torso was bare, and the bulging stomach betrayed that he was malnourished. The other figure held a tall, pale young woman with a homely face and long black hair.

The shadowy assassins committed their sacrifice in such perfect unison that Marie-Claire could scarcely believe they were at different continents at the time. The one holding the skinny man cut so deep that his head almost came off his body. At least his death was faster than that of the young woman, who lay gasping and gurgling as she bled out over the uneven ground. From two sides came the familiar rumbling, twice as loud as before, and the earth cracked and shook as it burst open. Two horses crawled from their prisons.

On the right stood a pale horse as tall as the red horse had been, but its coat gleamed with a yellowish hue. On its back sat a rider, at least twice the size of a man, dressed in a long, black cloak with a yellow lining. He steered his horse into the clearing. Marie-Claire couldn't see his face, and she knew she didn't want to see it. The mere presence of it made her feel ill. *Pestilence*, Marie-Claire thought.

On the left side, a brown horse, as thin as the dead cows, stood firmly on its spindly legs. The rider was less magnificent than his brethren. He was as tall, but sat stooped over, thin hands clutching the reins. His cloak had been sewn out of burlap sacks, tattered and torn on all sides. From under his hood, a gaunt face peered at Marie-Claire. Skin like yellow parchment was pulled over an elongated skull. These were not the features of a living man; they belonged to something that should have been long dead. *Famine.*

Both riders spurred their horses on, and Marie-Claire was torn from her vision. She opened her blind eyes to the darkness of the air plane, and her hand sought that of the man next to her.

"Koji," she said, trying to catch her breath.

"Are you okay?" the familiar voice asked.

"I felt it, too," Wulf called from the cockpit in front of her, his voice solemn. "Did you see it?" he asked softly. She nodded and cried.

"Pestilence and Famine ride the earth, and I must bear witness," she said between sobs. A warm arm slid around her shoulders and held her tight. Marie-Claire allowed herself a few moments to let her emotions flow free, until she contained herself.

"Six down, one to go," she muttered. "I pray to anything that's listening that we'll make it in time to stop the last seal."

"I hope that we find a way to mend the seals," Wulf said.

"Even if we can prevent the last seal from opening, that will not stop the other riders from bringing destruction to the world."

"One step at a time," Marie-Claire sighed. "First, let's make sure the world doesn't end."

CHAPTER FORTY

"There's no point in hiding, Freya," Damien's voice sounded from the other side of her panic room door. She wondered how his voice carried so well through the thick wood. Freya was still reeling from the simultaneous opening of the seals. *How many was that now? Five? Six? Was she next already? They were opening so fast.*

The girls had felt it, too, but Freya had virtually seen it. As if she had been looking through the eyes of another, but the vision had been blurry. It had frightened her, and it reminded her of last year, when the final Horseman had almost ridden, and she had seen him on his larger-than-life horse. Damien's voice pulled her from her thoughts.

"You can stay in that room for a little while, but eventually you'll have to come out. I have the time."

"I won't be coming out this solstice," Freya said, wondering if he could hear her, too. From his laugh, she gathered he could.

"I can wait till the next one," he chuckled. "But can you? That seal will open without a sacrifice..."

He's lying, Freya thought. *He's desperate for me to come out.*

"I'm glad you're so patient," Freya called back. "Because we don't plan to come out for a while. You can deal with the Horseman when he comes from his resting place. I hope your spell is strong enough to control him." She wondered if he would call her bluff.

Something beat against the door, and the children cried out in fright. Freya hunched down near them. "Don't worry, he can't get in," she assured them—even though she wasn't at all convinced of the truth in her words. "I had this place sealed not only physically, but magically. I learned my lesson."

"I wouldn't make promises I can't keep, if I were you." There was rage in Damien's voice now. "I can get into that room. It's just a little... challenging. But your magic is nothing compared to mine. If it wasn't for this damn house, I would have broken your petty spell with a snap of my finger. I *will* have you and my lovely dolls with me tonight, and you will all be part of my rising to power. Not even this house can stop me. It will submit to me sooner or later."

Another crash against the door startled Freya, and she stepped back, holding the sobbing children in her arms.

CHAPTER FORTY ONE

Hurry...

Marie-Claire didn't know if it was a thought or a whisper that cut through the noises of the airport. From the sound of it, Inverness Airport was just as insane as the last one had been. Wulf hadn't dared take the risk of landing the plane on Skye itself. He had cursed not having a water plane to land them nearer to where they wanted to be. It frustrated the medium as well; she just wanted to stop travelling and reach her destination. It would still take them so many hours to reach Angel Manor, and time was running out.

Currently, the airports were filled with frightened people. She couldn't see them, but she struggled to block out their agitated voices and the strong scent of body odour Several times, they had to push themselves through a throng of people, all of whom wanted to be with their loved ones. The anger, frustration, and sadness that surrounded her were so strong they were almost palpable. Several fights broke out around them. The chaos made her feel more like an invalid than she had in the past few years.

She had to be strong now. It would be over soon, one way or the other...

The thought made her blood run cold, because she suddenly realised she was prepared to die. She always believed she should have died in Angel Manor, together with Ruben, and now she might soon get the chance to. Marie-Claire sucked in air through her teeth and wondered if she wanted to die now or if she wanted to live.

Live, she decided, *and not only because I feel I have a duty. I want to live because I want to love life again, and I will fight for that. But if I want something to fight for, I must hurry.*

She increased the tempo of her step, practically dragging along the man who held her hand. "We have to find a taxi or a train," she said, walking even faster.

"There's a train to Portree," said Koji. From the rustling sound, she assumed he had a map or a flyer in his hand. "From there, we can get a taxi." She turned to the demon. She could see through his cover once again, and the dog inside seemed brighter and stronger than before. Wherever they were going, they had stepped outside, because she could feel the cold air on her face and the intense scent of bodies and fear lessened. There were still a lot of people.

"How do we get to the train station?"

Wulf looked up, as if he were listening to something no one else could hear. "You will take a taxi. I plan to take a different route." He led them away from the people, and Marie-Claire's skin turned cold.

"You're leaving us?" Koji asked.

"Freya is in danger. I can feel it." The big man dragged her along as he spoke. "You might not get there in time, but I can..."

Marie-Claire heard a car door open, and a strong hand guided her inside a musty smelling taxi.

"The driver will take care of you," Wulf said. "I made sure of that."

"But what are you—" Koji said.

"I don't have time to explain now. We still have a long way to travel," Wulf answered. "Perhaps we shall meet again."

"Thank you for—" Marie-Claire said, but Koji's warm hand on her shoulder stopped her mid-sentence.

"He's gone."

"Then we are on our own."

***

It lay in a semi-dormant state, deep in his subconscious, but when Wulf prodded at it, the creature woke with a savage eagerness. The nickname for his monster was Black Dog, sometimes even Hell-hound, though the creature had nothing to do with Hell itself, and it only barely resembled a dog. It grew in his mind before it changed in his body. The change seemed to last a lifetime, but in reality was finished within seconds, the skin of his human shape bursting open, tearing away to reveal a black pelt underneath. The pain was incredible, and the part of him that was still human felt as if it might drive him insane. The dog part merely howled and let the pain feed its rage. He tore at the skin, wet with blood, meaty, with his growing canines. They pushed through his gums, forcing his human teeth out. He spat them to the ground. The most painful was the changing of his skull, the pressure on his brain beyond words, and he could feel his human part fading. The dog was taking over. The only image that remained in his mind, one that he could not shake, was that of Freya. He had to guard her, his instincts said; he would find her, and he would protect her from the evil. She was his, and he was hers.

For a moment the dog had been confused, because he had smelled her scent nearby, but then he realised it was another who was just close to the girl. He wanted to protect the other, too, but not as much as he wanted to protect the girl. He loved the girl, from the moment he had smelled her.

She was in danger. He could sense it with the core of his being.

CHAPTER FORTY TWO

"When next I make a panic room, I'll make it a bit bigger," Freya muttered as she turned around, careful not to knock the children out of the bed. It was big enough to hold two adults, snugly, but with five—even if four out of five were small kids—the mattress was bordering on tight. She had been growing increasingly uncomfortable over the past hours. Her body was still sore from the car accident, too, which didn't help. There wasn't much room to sit around, and the kids seemed to feel better when they were close to her. Freya didn't mind their presence either; they made her strong. If she had been by herself, she would have broken down. Having the girls around her reminded her of Emily. Her breasts ached again, something they hadn't done in days, a physical instinct to nurse her baby. She missed the little girl so much, and wondered—for the millionth time—where she was and if she would ever see her again.

Damien had left the door to the sanctuary alone for the past two hours, which had simultaneously created a sense of calm and a sense of foreboding. It was nice not to have him near. His voice set her on edge. At the same time, it was horrible that she didn't know what he was up to. She knew too little of magic, despite what she had tried to learn. Bam had been much better with that kind of stuff. She wondered if her friend had made it to that light, and if she was happy with what lay beyond it. Maybe she would find out herself.

Leah wrapped her chubby arms around Freya's neck, and the child's warm cheek rested on her forehead. The other girls all draped themselves around her like puppies on a mother dog. Freya sighed and closed her eyes.

She dozed, treading that world between sleep and

dream, where the thoughts were still semi-conscious. A girl appeared before her. Young, but Freya couldn't quite guess her age. Or her race, because although her skin was light, it didn't quite look white. Dark soulful eyes looked at her, and Freya recognised something in this child.

"Are you Emily?" she asked the girl, feeling silly as soon as the words left her mouth. The girl didn't answer, but she looked up toward the ceiling. Freya followed her gaze. Something made a sound up there, as if a heart were palpitating, but it was different. She had never heard anything like it before.

"What's up there?" she asked.

"Answers," the girl said. "*He* hasn't found them yet. You must find them first."

"Answers? There aren't any, I looked... I've done nothing but look."

"There are answers up there," the girl repeated. "I will show you."

"Okay," Freya said. She couldn't imagine what could be up there that would possibly help her with her murderous puppet master, but if she didn't try... what if he could break the protection spells cast on her panic room? This was not a time to sit still and wait, this was a time for risks.

Her eyes shot open when a sound, like nails on a chalkboard, and a strange sweet scent filled her head. The room trembled, and the girls clung onto her, whimpering.

He's getting in, Freya thought. There was a moment of indecision, and then Freya scrambled to her feet, pushing the girls away from her.

"Damien," she called out, but no one answered. Perhaps he wasn't near the door yet... this could be her only chance. Freya—almost mad with adrenaline and determination—grabbed the lock and opened the door. She didn't turn to the girls when she yelled, "Lock it behind me, and don't let anyone in, not even me."

There were screams of protest, but Freya stepped out, amidst at least a dozen dolls, and slammed the door shut. To her relief, she heard the locks click behind her. The dolls all turned their heads to her in unnatural angles, like a bad remake of *The Exorcist*. The sight of them made her regret her decision, and for a fraction of a second, Freya wished she was back in the panic room. But a fraction of a second was all she allowed herself, and then she ran, hoping and praying the dolls would be slower.

Damien had his dolls, and he knew a lot more than she did, but Freya knew she had something he wanted... and he had to want it for a reason.

She had the house.

***

The dog was near now. He had travelled on the human roads and the roads of the shadow world alike. More help was coming. He would be faster, but they would catch up quickly. The danger to the girl was growing by the second. She had protected herself with magic, but it wasn't strong enough. Not to withstand the powers he sensed. The demon inside him had felt it, too, and he was spurring him on, telling him to go faster. The dog liked it when the master agreed; he was stronger when they worked together.

The dog put his head down and pushed on.

***

"Fuck," Freya cursed when she reached the intersection between the two corridors and saw at least twenty doll heads turn her way. "How many of those fucking things are there?"

She couldn't remember there being that many dolls in the house. When did Damien bring them in? Not that it mattered now how they got here. If she wanted to get to the attic, she would have to make her way past them. There was no turning back; the dolls were gaining on her. A door swung open to the side of her, and Freya realised it was to one of the bigger rooms, which had two doors, one of which led to her destination.

"Thank you," she whispered to no one in particular, and skittered through the door, almost losing her balance. The door slammed shut behind her, and she could hear the small *thumps* as the dolls collided into the wood. Ahead of her, another door opened, so that she didn't have to slow down.

The hallway looked clear, except for a single doll. It wasn't a porcelain toy, but one of the dead little girls. To Freya's disgust, the girl was dressed up as an angel. It was almost appropriate, this little cherub in the house of angels, though the white feathered wings on her back and the pretty white dress, complete with petticoat, looked nothing like the solemn stone guardians that stood outside the manor. The doll's face looked like marble in the fluorescent light, and the dead eyes stared straight at her. Freya remembered that expression well. It was one of blood thirst. She had seen it before, over a year ago, in the eyes of the spirits that roamed these very hallways.

"You would have been perfect to torment dead people for eternity," Freya said to the doll. "If only I had a spell..." She thought of the looming solstice and realized her time was running out. She would need to sacrifice the insane puppet master before the Horseman woke. Again, Freya just hoped the sacrifice would be enough. There was no other option but to try. She could kill one of the girls—that would be a real sacrifice—but she wouldn't get the chance to do that with Damien around. She considered the girls her backup plan... if she lived to execute a backup plan.

The doll took a step forward, and Freya heard the other dolls moving into the corridor as well. If this thing could cast magic, too, it would be all over, but Freya wasn't ready to give up yet. She swallowed her fear away, grimacing as she ran toward the girl with her white eyes and many stitches. The doll had no weapons as far as she could see, and her mouth was still sewn shut, which suited Freya just fine.

Maybe they're only strong in numbers, Freya thought, and braced herself, ready to knock this child off her feet if she got in her way. She was wrong. When she neared the doll, a small arm whipped out with a speed that Freya hadn't yet encountered, and the hand wrapped around her wrist and pulled with a strength that would shame a grown man.

The pain was excruciating. White flashes appeared before Freya's eyes as the ground slipped away from her feet. In an insane moment, she believed that the doll had pulled off her arm. She landed on the ground with a thud that made her ears ring and her teeth vibrate. All sense was knocked out of her for a second, and when her fragmented thoughts reconnected to make sense again, she looked up at half a dozen porcelain faces. They smelled of lavender and something very sour, like vomit. Freya gagged, covering her mouth with her hand. She remembered the maggots and tried to sit up. Tiny hands pushed her back down. They were strong. Where they got the power from, God only knew, because it was physically impossible.

Freya kicked and squirmed, trying to get away. The porcelain hands were cold and sharp on her skin as they ripped at her clothes and limbs. One of the dolls showed the signs of the black veins that she had seen before, and Freya punched in its direction, pushing the doll away slightly. It wasn't enough, because another doll showed signs of turning. Freya kicked at it, but she couldn't focus on all the dolls at once, and their hands were so strong, pressing down on her, pinching and scratching her.

No, Freya thought, *I can't die like this. Not like this. Not after everything I survived. Not by fucking dolls*. She wasn't ready to give up, so she kept kicking and punching, but the dolls were so strong... so awfully strong.

CHAPTER FORTY THREE

Her hand touched her fragile chest. The old heart—still strong despite age and anxiety—fluttered against her rib cage, and she could feel its palpitations against her fingertips. Something was happening in the house. She knew it. Her mind tried to reach out to it, but it was too far away. She wondered in what state she would find Angel Manor... and if Freya was still alive. Over a year ago, she had shared a mind with the girl, which made her feel connected to her. Marie-Claire regretted leaving the girl to her own devices. She had been so weak. Her own fear of that house, and her sorrow over her losses, had made her a coward. The girl had her young gentleman, of course, but if that house hid a seal, then there had to be consequences for her, too. She wondered if Freya even knew what was going on with her house. She hadn't when she had called Marie-Claire. But a year meant a lot of change. The world hadn't ended before now, and though she wasn't sure what Freya had to do to keep the seal closed, she had a sneaky suspicion there had to be something. Each seal was different, she knew, but most of them wanted some sort of sacrifice. That's what the guardian had told her.

Angel Manor knows how to claim its sacrifices, Marie-Claire thought bitterly. *I'm sure before the night is over, it will have claimed more.*

***

Either more dolls had joined the pile-on or they were getting stronger. She could barely move now, and her struggling had little effect. One of the porcelain faces came closer to hers. There a strong scent of decay and lavender wafting from the toy. The mouth opened. Cold, porcelain hands pushed their way past her own battered lips, scraping against her teeth and forcing her mouth open. Freya let out a gagging cry as the fingers touched her tongue.

It was answered by a howl that sent the hairs on the back of her neck up straight. The doll that was on her chest, ready to spill its dark, crawling contents into her mouth, was suddenly ripped from her. A raw ache numbed Freya's mouth as the hand was jerked away from it. Snarling filled her head, and she smelled the musky scent of wet dog fur.

Weight lifted from her arms and legs as something flung the dolls from her with unnatural force. Dazed, but alert enough to move, Freya sat up, supporting herself on her hands. The dolls swarmed a huge, black dog. She had no idea where the hell it had come from, but Freya had never been more grateful for an animal as she was right now. The hound looked like a cross between a Labrador, a wolf and something demonic; the creature was roughly the size of a bear, or perhaps even bigger, and it was tossing the dolls around as if they were pieces of paper. With powerful jaws, it clenched around one of the porcelain creatures and bit down. Freya flinched, remembering how the dolls hadn't cracked under a sledgehammer, and how fire had done nothing to harm them. The dog, however, bit through the porcelain as if the doll were made of sugar.

The dog looked at her, ignoring the dolls that tried to climb up its legs. He stared at her with large green eyes, which looked kind and caring, the way a lapdog would look at its owner. Freya didn't want to leave the dog behind with those horrible things, but she knew this was her only opportunity to make it to the attic. Without a further thought, she jumped to her feet and ran.

If her body had been sore after the car crash, it felt positively violated now. Every part of her suffered from scrapes and bruises, and she could still feel all those tiny hands groping her. It didn't matter, her pain, her fear... she needed to get to those answers. She knew where they were, too. Something, or someone, was guiding her. It wasn't the house, it was something else this time.

Behind her, the dog yelped. One of the dolls must have found a way to hurt it. The sound went through Freya's soul. Wherever that dog had come from, he had saved her, and she was eternally grateful to it.

Her legs wobbled as she reached the stairs. She grabbed on to the railing, pulling herself up as much as she was running, holding on tight—afraid she would fall.

***

There was little light to illuminate the vast attic, but she made her way across the wooden floor without any problems, as if she remembered exactly where everything was. The only thing that frightened her for a moment was the porcelain doll that stared at her from the bassinet Her first instinct was to attack it, but she realised she had seen the doll here before. It wasn't one of Damien's, but it had belonged to some child of Angel Manor's own past. She would have been happier if she had disposed of the thing months ago.

"Freya," a faint but familiar voice called to her.

"Who's there?" Freya whispered in the dark, looking around to find the source of the voice.

"Freya, you have to allow me in your mind," the voice said. "As you have done before. I can't help you if you don't. I might not make it here in time."

"Madame Florifera?" Freya said, a surge of relief and familiarity rushing through her. *I'm not alone.* "Did you send the dog?"

"Is the dog with you?" the old woman asked.

"Yes."

"Freya, you need to allow me in your mind," Florifera urged again. "This is costing me too much energy. Let down your barrier."

A moment's hesitation crossed her mind. It could be a trick. Damien could be playing magic games with her, or perhaps something else. The voice didn't just sound familiar, though, it *felt* familiar, too. If she was going to make it through this, she couldn't do it without a few risks. Freya took a deep breath and dropped her defences, letting the old woman's spirit into her own, as she had done before. There was a sense of completion, now more than the first time, as if something had changed. As if she were part of a puzzle and she'd only now found the missing piece.

"I have a thousand things I want to tell you, *ma cherie*, and a thousand more apologies to make, but now is not the time," Florifera said. "You are looking for something?"

"Answers... this girl, she told me they were up here." Freya caught herself whispering in response, even though she just had to think of it, and Florifera would know.

Something moved from the corner of her eye, and Freya's adrenaline immediately started pumping. She thought the dolls had found her, but instead she saw the little girl from her dream standing there.

"Do you see her?" Florifera asked.

"I do. I've seen her before," Freya said. "She's the one who I was talking about."

"That girl is a spirit. She's been with you the whole time, but you couldn't see her until I was close enough. I guess you are looking through my eyes as much as I am looking through yours."

"Is she dead?"

"I think so, but I'm not certain. Perhaps she is just a symbol of something. I can't tell with this girl. She's important, though. You best follow her."

The girl was slowly walking toward a darker part of the attic. The darkness seemed to fade around the child, even though there was no light, and Freya could clearly see where they were going. She led her to a familiar-looking trunk, which stood on its side. It was the same trunk she had found earlier but hadn't been able to open.

"I don't have a key," she said. The ghostly girl looked at her, and with the touch of one small finger, the locks sprang open. Freya took a step back and allowed the lid to fall to the side.

Inside the trunk, she found two items: one was a golden necklace with a locket on the end, and the other was a silver ornate dagger. When she grabbed the dagger, it sang under her touch.

A strong emotion overwhelmed her. It wasn't her sadness, but Madame Florifera's.

"I... I know this blade," the old medium said. "My mother had one just like it. She got it from her mother, who got it from hers. A family heirloom, if you will. I don't know what happened to it."

"Could this be the same one?" Freya asked.

"It's identical," Florifera said, "but why would it be here?"

"It was a gift for a girl," the ghostly child said. "A handsome man fell in love with a woman, and he gave her the only thing, aside from his heart, that belonged to him. The blade was left behind when the woman escaped the home that she thought of as a prison."

"That handsome man... was my son?" Florifera asked through Freya's mouth. It was strange having someone else control her body, and Freya moved her hand, just to see if she still could.

"Yes. Your son married one of the potential guardians to this house. It was your mother who sent him the blade. She decided he would need it more than you did, seeing as he was the first son in the bloodline."

CHAPTER FORTY FOUR

The dog was still tearing at the dolls, but they were hurting him now. Their hands were stronger, hit harder, and their little nails cut through his thick pelt. They tried to use magic on him, but they weren't quite strong enough for him yet.

He crunched away porcelain limbs and heads, having destroyed at least two dozen by now, and their numbers were dwindling. It was a delicate treat when one of the dolls made of flesh threw herself at him. He ripped at their soft, succulent flesh, ripe and fresh, as if they had never died. With sharp teeth, he tore away at the stitches, revealing a magical filling of fragrant guts and dried herbs. He pressed his snout inside and licked and bit at the morsels, gobbling them up with delight.

But they were gaining power. The solstice was nearing; he could sense it. It had an effect on him, and he felt even stronger and more savage, but so did his foes. The one dressed as an angel frightened him for some reason. The master in his mind worried that their magic would become too strong if they didn't hurry.

The girl... he smelled her... she was coming back. Why did she return? The dog had wanted her to flee. His tail wagged in an automatic response to her proximity.

She had the other woman with her, the old one. He could smell her, but he couldn't see her.

The girl was running, swiping at any doll who got in her way with a knife. The dog shook the dolls from him and ran after her. She would need protection.

***

"It was very kind of you to come see me yourself," Damien said. He had his back turned toward her, but she could sense the smile in his voice.

"I don't have much time," Freya said, "and Angel Manor needs its sacrifice." She held up the knife. Florifera was with her, watching through her eyes, egging her on. Damien turned around now. His eyes were completely black.

"That's an impressive blade you have there," he said, cracking his neck, a twisted smile on his thin lips. "One of the thirty pieces of silver."

I have heard that expression before, Florifera whispered in her head. *Thirty pieces of silver... wasn't that in the Bible?*

"I don't know what that means," Freya said, "but this knife will be perfect for the job I need to do."

Damien's eyes went misty with thought. "Job, yes. We all have jobs to do, don't we?" He sighed. "I would have liked to have more blood sacrifices before I did this," he said. "The girls were meant for that. I will just have to do without." He took a step toward her.

From the back of the stone room, something growled. Damien looked up, and an expression of surprise crossed his face when a large, black dog slammed into him. The creature clamped its jaws around the thin man's neck, and bit down hard. Blood poured through its teeth, and the dog growled more muted now, while he shook his head. Damien was flung around like a rag-doll

"Don't kill him," Freya called out to the dog. The large creature froze.

"I need to do it," she panted, running toward them. "Otherwise, the sacrifice might not be enough."

The dog dropped the heavily injured man, but didn't step away. It looked ready to attack again. Freya rushed forward, hoping Damien wouldn't die before midnight. She could feel the hour draw near. The whole house was vibrating with the anticipation of the solstice. It was mere minutes away, maybe even fewer, but the twisted little puppet master would need to make it until then, or all would be lost after all.

She fell to her knees next to Damien. "Don't you die, you bastard," she whispered at him. "Not after all the shit you put me through."

Damien smiled at her. There was blood across his crooked teeth. "I won't die, Guardian," he said in a hoarse voice. The earth trembled, and the walls around them seemed to stretch.

"The house is waking up for the solstice," Damien said. "It's time."

Kill him, Freya. You need to be quick. I can sense something coming.

"Yes," agreed Freya, holding the knife high. "It's time." She put some force behind her thrust, aiming for the man's heart. She wouldn't even try to make him suffer, she just needed him dead now. A hand shot up, and Damien grabbed her wrist. He was stronger than she had given him credit for.

"You don't really think that your mutt is strong enough to kill me, do you?" Damien spoke, his voice no longer weak. The dog growled again, as if it knew the man on the ground was talking about him.

"Down, puppy," he said, and his free arm shot out. A bolt of black light blasted from the man's fingertips and hit the dog. The canine yelped as it was flung backward. The black light engulfed it, and it fell to the ground a few feet away. For a moment, Freya thought the dog was split in two, but then she realized it wasn't just the dog. A naked man lay right next to the canine form.

"What did you do?" she screamed.

"I simply split the two parts of its personality asunder." Damien sounded amused. "I haven't killed them yet. They might still be of use to me."

Allez, get away from him, Freya, Florifera screamed in her head. Damien held her gaze with those dark eyes.

"I have been preparing for this day for so long," he said, his grip around her wrist even stronger now. His neck healed before her eyes. Sour breath was hot on her face, and blood-flecked spittle touched her cheek. "Training, sacrificing." He leaned forward, his filthy mouth near her ear. "You're special, too, Freya. So special that killing you will make me so much stronger. You have no idea how fortunate I am that you are of this very specific bloodline." He chuckled. "Almost the last. Once I find that old bitch and your little baby, I will have killed all of you, and you will add to my puissance."

Freya's blood ran cold, and Florifera's fear was growing with her own.

"I have a knife, too, Freya," and with those words, he plunged a dark blade into the crevice between her neck and shoulder. It didn't even hurt; it was just very cold. Freya's mouth opened and closed but no sound came out.

"Audite me," Damien called out. "I make this sacrifice not to thee, sleeping rider, but to my order."

Freya's body twitched. She could feel her blood flow down her cold skin. It was so warm, and almost comforting. She thought of her daughter, of Logan and of Bam. Would she see them again beyond the light?

Freya, a voice urged her from far away. *Freya, I need you to listen to me.* The voice was faint, and the blackness bloomed in front of her vision like dark spots.

CHAPTER FORTY FIVE

The girl had been struck. Marie-Claire could feel her slipping away from her. She had taken the pain of the wound, but it hadn't been enough. The Lamb, the ghost child that had been guiding her, kneeled near the body of her dying granddaughter.

"This is where you have to make a choice," the child said. "You are the Champion who is the Martyr. You can choose to live and let your granddaughter die, or you can choose to give your life instead of hers."

Marie-Claire felt the fading thoughts of the girl. She saw images of her baby slipping by, and she realised she would give anything to know her granddaughter better than she did. To hold her baby and to be a part of her life. There would never be time for that.

"If you do decide, you won't be doing her any favors. The task of Champion is not an easy one."

"I am old, and I am tired. Part of me always knew that it was Angel Manor where I had to die," the old medium said. "I will gladly give my life for the girl's."

"You will give that which is yours to her, and she will give that which is hers to you."

The pain of the knife was overwhelming now, and Marie-Claire fully embraced the sentence of the dying girl.

"Freya," she called to the girl. "Freya, I need you to listen to me."

You have to take care of my baby, the girl thought. *Find her and protect her. Tell her, her mother loved her.*

"No, *petite*," Marie-Claire said forcefully. "You will have to do that yourself. I will take your place in death. This means you will be the Champion, Freya, and they will still try to kill you. As soon as you can get up, I need you to run. Get away from Angel Manor as far as you can. It's no longer your house, or your responsibility."

I can't leave. I'm cursed, the girl thought weakly.

"Not anymore. I will take your curse from you." Marie-Claire sensed her time was running out. "I have allies, Koji and Tara... I don't know their last names, but it's up to you to find them. They will help you. If you do, please say goodbye to them for me." A moment's hesitation touched the old woman's heart. She didn't know what was waiting for her beyond the veil of death. Especially not now.

"Remember what I said, girl, run as fast as you can."

Marie-Claire pulled outside of the girl's body, taking the wound, the death, the curse, and everything else with her. The house touched her, bonded with her, only to be yanked away with brutal force. Marie-Claire took many things from Freya, but she left behind that which made her the Champion of the New World.

***

"Holy shit, she's bleeding," Koji cried. The hot blood of the medium trickled down his hand and leg. He tried to push his coat against the gash in the old woman's neck, but the wound was too deep. The blind eyes opened, and the thin mouth gasped for air she couldn't inhale. Spasms rocked every inch of her body as the life drained from her white eyes.

"What is happening?" Koji asked, holding down the old woman. "When did you get injured?"

"Find... guardian... Freya..." her voice was barely beyond a death rattle. The old woman convulsed for the last time, and then she was still.

"No, no, you can't be dead." Tears welled up in his eyes.

"I don't know what to do now. I can't go on without you. How can you be dead?" He wrapped his arms around Marie-Claire. Her skin was still warm, and her blood flowed over his shirt—but he didn't care about that now. The loss of her hit him as heavy as it would losing a parent. He had barely known the woman, but she was so important, and without her he was lost. He wished he had a phone so he could call Tara, but he was truly all alone now. Should he even go toward that house without Marie-Claire? She had asked him to find the girl named Freya. Perhaps he would also find Wulf there. Koji didn't want to run away from this now. He didn't even know where to run to.

"Are we almost there?" he asked the driver.

The man just nodded. Koji realised he hadn't looked back once, not even when the old woman was dying.

***

"How are you still alive?" Damien cried. "I sacrificed you." He held up the blade that was still covered in her blood. Freya scrambled to her feet.

"It wasn't me you sacrificed," she said, anger pulsing through her like a hurricane.

"I will make you suffer," he screamed in a high-pitched hysterical voice. "I sacrificed the guardian to the Horseman. You can't just change the rules."

Freya managed to smile at him, despite her anxiety. "Apparently I can."

She wanted to add another snide remark, but the giant stone slab began to crumble. Without a word, she looked around for the heirloom silver dagger. It was lying only a few feet away, near the fallen dog and the naked man. Freya rushed toward the spot, and when she bent to pick it up, she recognised the naked man as Wulf. He opened his eyes when she was near.

"Oh my god," Freya gasped, "I thought I would never

332

see you again."

"Can't get rid of me that quickly," he said with a smile.

She looked at the knife, horrified, wondering if she would have to repeat the sacrifice she had made over a year ago. Freya tried to sense the house, to determine what it wanted, but she couldn't. Whatever bond they had, it was now severed. Florifera's words came back to her. The old woman had taken more than her curse from her; she had taken her task as guardian. And she had left something in return.

There is nothing I can do to stop what is happening right now, she thought. *And if I kill Wulf, I may kill my only ally.*

The sound of giant hooves hitting the stone made their joyous reunion short-lived. Freya turned to the familiar sight of the horse crawling from its tomb, the dark rider on its back.

"It worked..." Damien had his hands in the air, outstretched as if he were about to embrace the Horseman. "I can feel it. The sacrifice I made worked. It was a guardian I killed, after all. Angel Manor is now mine."

Freya remembered that she had to run. She needed to get away.

A wet nose poked her in the side, and Freya saw the huge dog stand unsteadily. It shook its body, as if it were trying to dry off, and regained its strength.

"You survived," she said, feeling the tears well up in her eyes.

"Get on the dog," Wulf screamed, and he ran toward her, lifting her before she had time to respond. "We need to get away from Death."

Freya wanted to look back at the Horseman, but Wulf jumped on the dog behind her and blocked her line of sight.

Everything around them became a blur as they fled from the house.

Angel Manor was warping around them. Stone and wood were shaping into different forms, and the building seemed to grow. Pieces of debris fell, and the large, black dog managed to narrowly escape a beam that clattered to the ground. Freya closed her eyes and clung onto the dog.

She knew this was the last time she would look at Angel Manor as it had once been. Her duty here was done, and the life she had lived was over.

***

The earth was not so much trembling as it was splitting around them. The taxi driver had stopped the car. Whatever was happening, it had taken him out of the trance that Wulf had put him in and established a new one. He stared at the building over his steering wheel.

"Jesus," the driver said as he opened the door and stepped out to get a better look. He gasped as the house grew, like one of the beanstalks from that fairy tale It reached higher and higher.

"It's turning into a tower," Koji said, climbing out of the car. "And it's feeding from Lucifer Falls. Can you feel it?"

"I feel something," the driver said. He was shaking.

"We're too late," Koji said. "Death rides the earth. Can you see him?"

They couldn't, not really, but they could feel him. There was a faint hint of a phantom rider in the distance. "So many will die."

***

Tara held on to Terrence in the middle of Schiphol Airport. Everyone around them was quiet. Loved ones were holding onto each other, as if they instinctively knew the world was broken and they might not have the pleasure of each other's company for much longer.

"They were too late," Tara whispered. "Fucking hell, I was so sure we'd be on time. That we would win this, somehow, because we're the good guys... you know?" She pushed her face into Terrence's neck. He was a stranger to her, but she needed to feel as if she wasn't alone.

"Is this the end of the world?" Terrence asked. "Will we just all die now?"

"I don't know," Tara said, breathing in the scent of his warm neck. "But I don't intend to go quietly."

EPILOGUE

She didn't know how long they had been riding, but it felt like years. In reality, she knew it couldn't have been more than hours, maybe a day at most. The dog seemed tireless.

She had slept a little, but her stomach was growling. If she didn't eat or drink soon, she'd be ill.

Wulf moved in and out of consciousness. He was still very weak. The spell Damien had cast had hurt him. She had gathered that he had been one with the dog, and as separate entities, they both were weaker.

"Where are we going, Wulf?" she asked him when he seemed more lucid.

"To a safe place," he said vaguely, through cracked lips.

"Is there such a thing in the Apocalypse?" Freya asked. "It's the end of the world, after all."

"You're wrong. That's not what the Apocalypse is. It's a reset. It's up to us to see what it resets to." He rubbed his neck. Wulf was still naked, yet he didn't appear to be cold, even though the weather was stormy and chilled. In fact, it was his body that kept her warm.

"There are several safe places in this world, Freya. From there, we need to make a plan."

"Is Emily in one of those safe places?" Freya asked.

"She's in the safest of all," Wulf said. "I had to protect her."

"Thank you," she said. "I can't go get her yet, can I?"

"It wouldn't be wise... not just yet." He squeezed her shoulder. Freya looked at the sky. It was tinted with a strange red color, and in the distance, fire rained down.

"This is the world now," she said, not quite believing it. "This is what we tried so hard to prevent. What I killed innocent people for. What little girls died for." She thought of the four girls she left in her panic room. Of little Leah with her chubby arms and round cheeks. She didn't even know what had happened to them. "It was all for nothing."

"That's the way to look at it," Wulf said sarcastically.

"What do you want me to do?"

"Fight, Freya. The battle is not over yet. Florifera gave you an important role. Nothing you have ever done has been for nothing."

She nodded. If anyone could handle this insanity, it would have to be her. After all she went through, she was still alive. What better practice was there than that?

"We will build our own army, Freya," Wulf said, holding her tighter.

"I'm glad you found me, Wulf. I don't want to do this alone again. It's just too tough."

"I'm fairly certain that what we do next will involve a lot of people, Freya," Wulf answered. "No more secrets. We're going to teach people everything we know. And we'll show those fuckers what it's like to mess with us."

We could take back the world, Freya thought as she leaned her head on Wulf's chest. *We'll make this new world a better place too. The Horsemen will be buried so deep, this time, that the world will never again feel their effects.* Her eyes fell shut, and with thoughts of the new world, Freya dozed off into blissful dreams that would help her face the morning to come.

***

The spirit watched the fire rain from the sky.

"Is this what I came back for?" she asked. "To watch the world end?"

"Where there is an end, there is a beginning," the man said, resting his hands on her shoulders. She turned to him and noticed that behind him a shadow of a gigantic pair of wings marked the wall. "Humanity is a phoenix," the man smiled, his face handsome. "From the ashes, it will rise."

"And you want me to help it?" she asked.

"Yes, Bam... that's exactly what I want from you. You will be their ally."

"I was taught that you were here to destroy humanity and collect their souls," Bam said, wrinkling her nose. "Why are you trying to save it?"

"Because, dear heart, it is God's word that demands humanity to survive... and I am God's most loyal servant."

"I thought you were his enemy."

The man smiled. "Don't believe everything you read..."

THE END

THANK YOU FOR READING

Thank you for taking the time to read this book. We sincerely hope that you enjoyed the story and appreciate your letting us try to entertain you. We realise that your time is valuable, and without the continuing support of people such as yourself, we would not be able to do what we do.

As a thank you, we would like to offer you a free ebook from our range, in return for you signing up to our mailing list. We will never share your details with anyone and will only contact you to let you know about new releases.

You can sign up on our website

http://www.horrifictales.co.uk

If you enjoyed this book, then please consider leaving a short review on Amazon, Goodreads or anywhere else that you, as a reader, visit to learn about new books. One of the most important parts about how well a book sells is how many positive reviews it has, so if you can spare a little more of your valuable time to share the experience with others, even if its just a line or two, then we would really appreciate it.

Thanks, and see you next time!

THE HORRIFIC TALES PUBLISHING TEAM

ABOUT THE AUTHOR

Chantal Noordeloos lives in the Netherlands, where she spends her time with her wacky, supportive husband, and outrageously cunning daughter, who is growing up to be a supervillain. When she is not busy exploring interesting new realities, or arguing with characters (aka writing), she likes to dabble in drawing.

In 1999 she graduated from the Norwich School of Art and Design, where she focused mostly on
creative writing.

There are many genres that Chantal likes to explore in her writing, but her 'go to' genre will always be horror. "It helps being scared of everything; that gives me plenty of in-spiration," she says, and storytelling is the element of writ-ing that she enjoys most. "Writing should be an escape from everyday life, and I like to provide people with new places to escape to, and new people to meet."

ALSO FROM HORRIFIC TALES PUBLISHING

High Moor by Graeme Reynolds

High Moor 2: Moonstruck by Graeme Reynolds

High Moor 3: Blood Moon by Graeme Reynolds

Of A Feather by Ken Goldman

Whisper by Michael Bray

Echoes by Michael Bray

Voices by Michael Bray

Angel Manor by Chantal Noordeloos

Bottled Abyss by Benjamin Kane Ethridge

Lucky's Girl by William Holloway

The Immortal Body by William Holloway

Wasteland Gods by Jonathan Woodrow

Dead Shift by John Llewellyn Probert

The Grieving Stones by Gary McMahon

The Rot by Paul Kane

Deadside Revolution by Terry Grimwood

Song of the Death God by William Holloway

High Cross by Paul Melhuish

Rage of Cthulhu by Gary Fry

The House of Frozen Screams by Thana Niveau

The Cold by Rich Hawkins

http://www.horrifictales.co.uk